SAVE YOUR FRIENDS!

HYEWON KYUNG

 GREENWILLOW BOOKS, an Imprint of HarperCollinsPublishers

For Giyun, Giseong

Save Your Friends!
Copyright © 2019 by Hyewon Kyung
All rights reserved. Manufactured in China. For information address
HarperCollins Children's Books, a division of HarperCollins Publishers,
195 Broadway, New York, NY 10007.
www.harpercollinschildrens.com

The art was digitally composited in Adobe Photoshop™.
The text type is Shag Lounge.

Library of Congress Cataloging-in-Publication Data
Names: Kyung, Hyewon, author, illustrator.
Title: Save your friends / written and illustrated by Hyewon Kyung.
Description: First edition. | New York, NY : Greenwillow Books, an imprint
   of HarperCollins Publishers, [2019] | Summary: A variety of friendly fish
   and other sea creatures enlist the reader's help in escaping a shark.
Identifiers: LCCN 2018037901 | ISBN 9780062683151 (hardcover)
Subjects: | CYAC: Fishes—Fiction. | Marine animals—Fiction.
Classification: LCC PZ7.1.K99 Sav 2019 | DDC [E]—dc23 LC record available
   at https://lccn.loc.gov/2018037901

19 20 21 22 23 SCP 10 9 8 7 6 5 4 3 2 1
First Edition
Greenwillow Books

spoke. Each night he told her a new chapter, and so many nights had gone by, so many chapters had been told, that they referred to it as *chapters* rather than *story*, because stories had endings and theirs had none. According to her father, the green-bodied aliens had destroyed their planet in an interstellar civil war and had migrated to the moon to begin again. Each night, as civilisation collapsed around them, he told her of a new one being built on the lunar surface. She hoped her father was there, among them, up on the moon.

Sonja strode through the door, reeking of cigarette smoke, her eyelids puffy and her fingers jittering. 'You're here,' Sonja said, surprised.

'Yes,' Havaa agreed. 'I'm here. This is the waiting room.'

Sonja glanced down to the floor, to the chairs, puzzling over this and then nodding. 'You're right. This is the waiting room,' she said, and sat in the folding chair beside Havaa.

'How was your day?' Havaa asked.

Sonja shrugged, sparked her cigarette lighter, and stared vacantly towards the wall. 'It was an OK day. You?'

'It was OK.'

Sonja sighed, closed her eyes, and sparked her lighter in a slow, senseless rhythm.

'Are the Feds going to take me too?' To ask the question was to acknowledge that it could happen, and in Havaa's experience, any horror that could happen eventually did. Better to armour yourself with the unreal. Better to turn inward, hide in the dark waters among the sea anemones, down deep where the sharks can't see you.

Sonja's hand found hers between the chairs.

'Will the Feds take me to my father?' she asked, while knowing the question had no answer she wanted to hear. Her father was her door to the world; he was the singular opening through which she saw, heard and felt. Without him she didn't know what she saw, or what she heard, or what she felt; all she felt was him gone.

'Let's go to bed,' Sonja said. Still holding Havaa's hand, she stood. 'We close our eyes and there they are, right where we left them, in their own waiting room, waiting for us.'

Chapter 7

FOR EIGHTEEN DAYS NATASHA SLEPT AS IF HER lidded dreamland were her true home, to which she was repatriated for fifteen hours a day. So what, then, could Sonja do? Natasha was here, safe, alive, and real enough to begin resenting. In the flat white light of morning she entered her sister's bedroom, a cup of hot tea in her hand, and inspected her sister's body as she might a corpse, or a comatose patient, or someone whom she had, once, long ago, envied. Her gaze crawled the curves of Natasha's hips, the odd angle of elbows she could unhinge and bend at will, the bitten rims of fingernails, her legs, still long, still lithe, and the little brown hairs on her forearms, which, when they had first appeared in puberty, Sonja had used as evidence to convince Natasha she was turning into a boy. Natasha's skin said what she wouldn't. The scars of habitual heroin use webbed her toes. A buckshot of cigarette burns stippled her left shoulder. If Sonja found these scars on a patient in the hospital, she wouldn't feel pity, but in Natasha's bedroom, she felt it all over. For eighteen days she went to wake Natasha and turned back, afraid of the dreams her sister would rise from, leaving no alarm louder than a cup of tea cooling on the bedside table.

But Natasha wasn't right. On the eighteenth evening, standing at the cutting board, chopping two onions and a potato, Sonja broached the subject. 'I think you should talk to a psychiatrist or someone.'

From the look her sister gave her, she might have announced they'd be eating the cutting board for dinner.

'I just think it would be good for you to talk with someone. About what happened in Italy. About what it's like being home,' Sonja said.

'Talking doesn't do anything.'

'It might do one or two things.' Sonja punctuated her sentence with a chop.

'All the words in the world won't put those onion halves back together.'

'The human mind is a little more complex than a yellow onion.'

Natasha held back her hair as she lit a cigarette from the hotplate her father had, twelve years earlier, purchased second-hand from a woman who would never find a flame that cooked an egg quite as well. 'Some of us would be lucky to have something as large as a yellow onion between our ears.'

Sonja could see her sister backing away from her, from the subject, from whatever had happened in Italy. 'Think of the mind as a muscle or bone instead,' she said, looking down to address the more respectful audience of cubed potatoes. 'Emotional and mental trauma doesn't heal itself any more than a broken bone left unset.'

Natasha nodded to the cutting board. 'You talk those potatoes and onions into jumping in that frying pan and I'll talk to a psychiatrist.'

Despite its monumental aggravation, Natasha's resistance

was a good sign, wasn't it? The obstinacy was a pillar running alongside her spine that would support her when not lodged firmly in Sonja's hindquarters. And while she might yearn for a little civility to grease the rusty gears of their relationship, she gladly endured the back talk and eye-rolls to know that Natasha hadn't lost the ability to drive her fucking crazy. Her sister was a snarky chain-smoking hermit crab that emerged from her shell in the safety of Sonja's presence. When Natasha believed she was alone – those days when Sonja slammed the front door and stayed to spy on her – she searched for thicker shells. It was awful, watching Natasha through the keyhole as she divided her room into smaller increments of shelter. She moved the desk, bed and chest of drawers like a child arranging the furniture into a make-believe castle, even encircling the structure with a moat of water glasses. On the keyhole's far side, Sonja prayed it would keep the dragons at bay; her heart, as if drawn on a piece of paper in her chest, crumpled every time. When she returned in the evening, the fortress was disassembled and the pieces of furniture had returned to their white rectangles of wall space. She never mentioned what she'd seen, holding it as a reminder to be gentle and patient as she prepared dinner. She whispered sweet nothings to the potatoes and onions, but the little fuckers were as stubborn as her sister, the great big fucker.

Natasha relented when Sonja pointed out that compared with her inexhaustible exhortations, a chat with a psychiatrist would be as pleasant as a summer picnic. She admitted to having spoken to a psychiatrist at the women's shelter in Rome – the one that had provided the six-month supply of ribavirin, which Sonja found in the bathroom, which was generally used to treat hepatitis, which Natasha refused to admit she had, which Sonja thought was total bullshit.

'She spoke Russian in this ridiculous Italian accent,' Natasha said. 'I was always afraid she'd start singing an opera.'

'I never make promises to my patients, but I promise that whoever I find won't speak a word of Italian.'

And she tried. She combed through her contacts only to find that every psychiatrist in the city was dead, exiled or missing. The ranks of the hospital staff didn't contain a single mental-health professional. She fumed one afternoon in the hospital car park, wanting to punch the clouds from the sky but instead venting on a closer object, the bonnet of an '83 Volga so decrepit she felt the sickening thrill of beating a wounded animal to reiterate its pain. How had she got to this point? She was fluent in four languages and yet her fists against the rusted bonnet were the fullest articulation of her defeat. In the months before the repatriation her heart had hardened around her sister's absence, letting her love Natasha in memory as she could never love her in reality. The fact was that her exile had prompted Natasha's. The fact was that she had left Chechnya first. The fact was that she had escaped the war Natasha had endured alone. It only made sense that her sister would attempt the same transaction with the only currency she possessed: her body. But now she was home and needed medical care Sonja couldn't provide. Being a bad sister was one thing; being a bad doctor was the more serious sin. Deshi found her out in the car park, beating the rust off the Volga bonnet. Her tears turned brown when she wiped them with her knuckles. 'Do you want to talk about it?' Deshi asked. 'Go to hell,' she replied.

At dinner Natasha took the news with typical smugness. 'It's just as well,' she said. 'Head doctors are a decadence unsuited to a country like ours. They are the bidets of the medical profession.'

'You could talk to me,' Sonja offered with enough snarl in her voice to ensure that Natasha would demur. Which she did. In seven years and three weeks, when Natasha disappeared for a second time, Sonja would orbit that moment, circling every angle without ever touching down: what if she had tried harder, been kinder, gentler?

As the street noise filled the gap in the conversation, Sonja gave up. If the world was determined to drown her, she'd stop swimming. She lengthened her hours at work, then lengthened her commute. At the bazaar, vendors sold everything that could be lifted and carted away: emergency rations, grain sacks, spools of uncut cloth, raw wool, floorboards, industrial kitchen appliances, abandoned Red Army munitions, traffic lights and oil-refining machinery. She wandered past racks of used shoes that had clocked more kilometres than the average Federal fighter jet, past blocks with more craters than her sister's left shoulder blade, past exoskeletal scaffolding, workmen hoisting wheelbarrows of masonry, all the way to Hospital No. 6.

And as eighteen days turned to twenty, forty, sixty, the trauma ward became the capital of the reconstructed republic. Each day patients arrived with heart attacks and kidney stones, the lesser emergencies of peacetime. When a man limped in with a football injury she kissed his cheek; that man and his wife would create the plaque honouring the hospital staff of the war years, which was to be set into the pavement eleven years later to little official fanfare. The war was over; no one knew it was only the first. Still, the scarcity of medical supplies remained a constant problem.

She contacted the brother of a man with a moustache made of dead spider legs whose life she'd saved when a landmine had lodged eight ball bearings, four screws and three ten-kopek coins in his left leg. The brother met her in the back seat of a Mercedes that drove in tight circles on a tennis court-sized slab of asphalt just outside his Volchansk garage, the only unbroken stretch of road worthy of such a fine Western motor car. He pinched a Marlboro filter between his manicured fingernails. She didn't need to look past his first knuckle to verify his access to the smuggling routes snaking through the southern mountains.

'You saved Alu's life,' the brother said, setting the cigarette between his delicate lips, moisturised nightly with aloe balm. 'For that I owe you a favour. A small one, because of my six brothers, I like Alu the least.'

She handed him a list limited to easily procurable medical supplies: absorbent compress dressings, adhesive bandages, antiseptic ointment, breathing barriers, latex gloves, gauze rolls, thermometers, scissors, scalpels, aspirin, antibiotics, surgical saw blades and painkillers. 'It's basic stuff. Any medical distributor will have it. You can find most of it in an average first-aid kit. I just need a lot of it.'

'Alu spoke highly of you,' the brother lamented. 'I should have known you would be a bore. Anything else?'

'I thought I only had one favour?'

'Let me tell you a story,' the brother said, holding his cigarette like a conductor's baton. 'When I was a child I had a pet turtle, whom I named after Alu because they shared a certain – how can I put it? – bestial idiocy. Once I went to Grozny with my father and five of my brothers for the funeral of my father's uncle, and we left so quickly I hadn't the time to provide food for Alu the Turtle. My brother, Alu the Idiot, had a fever and stayed home with my mother. In a moment so taxing on that little intellect that steam surely shot from his ears, Alu the Idiot remembered to feed my turtle. He caught grubs and crickets, likely tasting them before he gave them to my beloved crustacean. Since then

Alu the Idiot has grown into a Gibraltar-sized haemorrhoid, but when he was a child he used the one good idea this life has allotted him to feed my turtle, and because of it, you get a second favour.'

'Turtles aren't crustaceans,' she said.

'Excuse me, half crustacean.'

'They're full-blooded reptiles.'

The brother gaped at her. 'You should hear yourself. You sound ridiculous.'

'A turtle is one hundred per cent reptile,' she said. 'I imagine even Alu knows that.'

'Don't insult me. Everyone knows a turtle is crustacean on its mother's side.'

'Explain that to me,' she said, shifting in the seat as the car spun in circles.

'A lizard fucks a crab and nine months later a turtle pops out. It's called evolution.'

'I hope your biology teacher was sent to the gulag,' she said. She caught the driver's eyes in the rear-view mirror. The driver had grown up in a mountain hamlet where more people believed in trolls than in cars. The first war had catapulted him from the back of a mule to the inside of a Mercedes, and he would look back at that war as the one stroke of good fortune in a life otherwise riddled with disappointments.

'I can't believe you're allowed to operate on people with such an incomplete understanding of nature,' the brother said.

'Any other animals come about this way?'

The brother pursed his lips. 'A whale.'

'Let me guess. A fish fucks a hippo?'

'Close, an elephant,' the brother said, laughing.

'Of course,' Sonja said. 'How could I forget about the herds of elephants roaming the open ocean.'

'I would never dishonour my mother, but someone less noble might suggest that Alu is half monkey. So shall I include Darwin as your second favour?'

She wrote several titles on the list and passed it back.

'My God,' he said. 'You're worse than I could have ever imagined. No wonder you and Alu got on famously. *Modes of Modern Psychological Enquiry. Post-Traumatic Stress Disorder: Causes, Symptoms and Treatment. From Victim to Survivor: Overcoming Rape.* This is what you want? I was thinking cocaine and a prostitute or something.'

'Do I look like someone in need of a prostitute?'

The brother was all grins. 'I've never met someone in greater need,' he said.

'Can you get them or not?'

'We'll see. Guns, drugs, uranium, whores, hostages, no problem. But I've never been asked to find books or medical supplies. These will be a challenge.'

The Mercedes drove in dizzying circles. She wanted out of this spinning, nauseating contraption. What was wrong with Alu, anyway? Compared to this ridiculous man, who spoke as if he lived in a genie's lamp, Alu was a model citizen. But what could she do? Those who have the bullets also have the bandages.

'Can you get them or not?'

'Don't insult me,' he said. 'I can steal the spots off a snow leopard.'

'Then thank you.'

'That's it? Nothing else? Once you leave this car you'll never see me again.'

Could she ask for it? Transport to Georgia? A plane ticket from Tbilisi to London? A visa stamp in the passport she still carried with her, in the money belt around her waist, each time she left her house?

'Yes,' she said. The air hummed. The yellow clouds watched indifferently. 'I'll have one of your cigarettes.'

She took that cigarette and smoked it while walking to the bazaar, where several days later, on a trip in search of fabrics, she stumbled upon an industrial ice machine at the stand of a Wahhabi arms dealer. It was a great grey piece of machinery with a plastic interior the colour of potato broth and fretwork ventilation at its back end. The steel lid held her unfocused reflection within the logo of the Soviet Intourist Hotel. Three half-brothers, now sixteen, eleven and eight, had been conceived on that steel lid, none yet aware of the others' existence. A merchant with nicotine-stained fingernails, wire-rimmed glasses and the long beard of a Wahhabi described the machine. 'Gorbachev, Brezhnev and the Bee Gees all had their drinks cooled with the ice produced by this magnificent machine. It is a celebrity among ice machines, envied and admired among its kind. All around Chechnya ice-cube trays have photographs of the Intourist Hotel ice machine pinned on their freezer walls, and they are all told that if they work hard, and believe wholeheartedly in the ideology of ice, they may some day rise to its ranks. And you might say, "But Mullah Abdul, I don't *need* an industrial ice machine that can provide twenty cubic metres of ice an hour, when required." To that I counter, what about clean water? You see, pure flawless H_2O freezes at precisely zero degrees, the temperature at which the carefully calibrated thermometer of this magnificent colossus is set. Water containing minerals and sediments and bacteria and parasites freezes at slightly lower temperatures, and thus remains liquid and flows out the drainage. The frozen water left behind is as pure as the virgins in Paradise, with whom I hope to soon be acquainted, should God see me fit.'

Sonja nodded, not unimpressed. On the card tables beside

the freezer lay guns of all sizes and calibre, brass belts of ammunition, septic pipes fashioned into home-made Stinger RPG launchers, landmines and VHS recordings of *Baywatch*.

'What are you looking for?' the merchant continued. 'Fragmentation grenades? Hollow bullets? If you give me a few days, I could find a C-4 vest that would fit you nicely.' She remembered him as the chemistry professor who had slapped her behind three times in as many months, and expected her – a first-year university student then – to thank him for saving her from the invisible bee that lived in his office. He'd been a different man back then, arriving at class each morning with freshly shaved cheeks and a stale-smelling corduroy jacket, but she recognised his delicate bee-swatting hands, now curled around the butt of a rifle. 'Perhaps it would be better if I spoke to your husband,' he said. 'I'd like to have a word with him about how he allows you to dress.'

'Fuck off, you disgusting little man,' Sonja said, in English.

'She speaks in tongues, too,' the merchant muttered to himself. 'Another sign of the end times. Listen to me, woman. This is serious business. If you dress with your hair and your face uncovered for the devil himself to see, the Russians will come back, make no mistake, and you women will be responsible.'

Had he not had the contents of a small armoury in arm's reach, she might have kicked him squarely in his now-pious balls. Instead she shook her head and turned towards the fabric stand.

She returned home with sheets of green and purple cloth, and unfolded them across the floor of her bedroom. As a teenager, she had declined her mother's offer to teach her to tailor her own clothes; even at that age, such a domestic skill had insulted her ambitions. Now, eyes downcast, glaring as though a pair of trousers might materialise from the cloth by force of her concentration, she felt like Sonja the Idiot. Only one idea came to her. She took her measurements with a ruler and drew them on the cloth and cut outlines of her legs with nail scissors. For the next half-hour, she stitched together the two cut-outs with the same stitch she used to close wounds. When finished, she examined her creation. The stitching held tight when she pulled the seams, and her pinkie just fitted through the holes of the button flies. She envisioned pockets, perhaps even belt loops. If this worked, she might design a jacket and a blouse. Perhaps she could even begin a clothing line – *haute couture du guerre-zone*, all proceeds to support the hospital – and export hand-made fashions to the boutique-lined avenues of London, where she had been privy to the conscience-balming Western consumption of Third World charity art and cheeseburgers.

It wasn't until she tried on the trousers that she realised her error. She had traced the exact measurements of her legs without allowing any extra wiggle room, and so she struggled with the trousers, falling onto the mattress and raising her feet towards the ceiling in the vain hope that gravity might pity her. An exhausting effort. It had been years since she had floundered this much without at least the prospect of an orgasm. When she finally pulled the trousers past her hips, she found Natasha's hundred-watt smirk in the doorway. 'How long have you been watching?' she demanded.

'Not nearly long enough.'

'You're always fucking asleep! You're always asleep when I'm making dinner or sweeping the floor or finding car batteries or crying or doing anything mature and useful, but then you always somehow wake up to witness me making a fool of myself. Do you have clairvoyance? If you do, you can see what I'm thinking; and if not, I'm thinking of a very rude gesture.'

'Try to stand up,' Natasha suggested, far too cheerfully. Sonja would rather have amputated her legs with the nail scissors than further humiliate herself, but what could she do? Refuse? Admit failure? No. She placed her palms on the edge of the bed. She pushed forward. Arms flailing, legs inflexible, she would have let the prurient chemistry professor slap invisible bees from her behind all afternoon for a pair of trousers that fitted. At the apex of her ascent, when she saw Natasha, her eyes burst into coals, because was it really too much to be thanked? To be appreciated? To be assured that all the scones in England were worth less than all the potatoes and onions with one's own sister? *Yes, apparently that is too much to ask,* Sonja told herself, *or at least too much to ask from you, my potato-eating friend, you who believe you are the only person in the world to understand loss, and even that you're unwilling to share with me.*

But her glare broke with her balance. The wooden planks of her trouser legs pitched her forward and, arms flapping, she reached for Natasha. There was no one else to help her.

And Natasha caught her. The impact shimmied down Sonja's spine, loosening the tension coiled between each vertebra. How had they descended so far? How had they become so embittered that Natasha preventing her from falling on her face felt like an act of tremendous sisterly love? Tears squeezed through Sonja's closed eyes. A plug was pulled from the centre of the floor through which the tension drained.

'Those are the ugliest trousers I've ever seen,' Natasha said, still holding her. It was the first time they had hugged since she returned. Two and a quarter years would pass before it happened again. 'They look painted on.'

'I can't feel my toes,' Sonja cried. 'I don't think my blood is circulating past my knees.'

'You should use them as tourniquets at the hospital.'

'I don't want to be here, Natasha. I'm so fucking unhappy. I want to be back in London.'

'It's OK. They're only trousers. Here's what we do.' Clasping the waistline, Natasha halved them in one clean flourish. Sonja pulled the ends over her heels and stretched her sore thighs. She picked up the sheet of fabric stencilled with the silhouette of her legs, and tilted her head to see Natasha through the cut-out.

'I think this is my knee.'

'It is a lovely knee.'

'What should I do with it?'

'I don't think you've ever asked my opinion before.'

'I won't make a habit of it.'

'You could.'

'Tell me what to do.'

Natasha looked to the fabric. 'I could use a new pair of trousers, too.'

Sonja smiled and gave Natasha the nail scissors.

Despite their moment of reconciliation, they soon returned to a policy of polite avoidance. When, after work, Sonja wanted less complex company, she visited Laina next door. Laina never looked particularly pleased to see Sonja, but she never looked particularly pleased about anything these days, and Sonja didn't take it personally. The old woman received daily visitations from ghosts, angels, prophets and monsters, and some evenings, Sonja wondered if she herself was, to this old woman, a trivial hallucination.

'I saw an ice machine at the bazaar the other day,' she said. Laina didn't look up from the scarf she was knitting, afraid to raise her eyes with so many visions crowding the air. 'It once cooled the glasses of the Bee Gees, or so said the freezer merchant. Never turn your back to him, Laina. There is no bee.'

'You can tell by the way I use my walk, I'm a woman's man,' Laina said, without lifting her eyes from the needle tips.

'You know that song?'

'Of course. People used to recite it in the war. I didn't know it was a song. For the longest time I thought it was from the Qur'an.'

Sonja smiled, glad she could still be surprised. 'I never knew the Bee Gees were so profound.'

'I saw six chariots in the sky today. I would have rather seen an ice machine.'

For the next hour Laina described abounding supernatural phenomena. The angel Gabriel had fluttered into a rooster-less henhouse in Zebir-Yurt, and the next morning a farmer found eight immaculately conceived eggs. A boy in Grozny defeated his grandfather, a chess master third class, ranked one thousand six hundred and eighty-fourth in the world, after a game lasting thirty-nine sleepless days and nights that left the grandfather so bewildered, proud and exhausted he promptly died. A band of corpse-devils rose from the earth at the Dagestan border to hijack three Red Cross cargo trucks, leaving the drivers tied up and blindfolded and magically suspended three metres in the air.

'Stalin has been resurrected,' Laina said.

'I know,' Sonja replied. 'He's the prime minster of Russia.'

On her way to work a week later, when the black Mercedes found her, she was sure she'd wandered into one of Laina's deliriums. The Mercedes braked sharply, drawing a curtain of dust along the street. The tyres – before so dainty they could only drive in circles on a tennis court – were replaced with those of an armoured jeep, raising the body of the car by a half-metre. Swedish number plates, she noted, were still attached. The window descended and those gorgeous fingernails beckoned her.

'I thought we wouldn't see each other again,' she said, pulling the door closed.

'And I keeping saying I'll never see Alu again and he keeps on being my brother. You intrigue me. You lived in London for several years, if my information is correct, which it always is. Had you stayed, you would be eligible for citizenship now. Even I can't get my name into one of those beautiful maroon passports. And yet you returned.'

'I have family here,' she said uneasily.

'I hide the toilet paper when my family visits so they won't stay too long.'

'Could you get me back to London?'

'You could ask. But then who would I have to talk to? No one with your intelligence would return from London, which means you are either one of those idiot savants, light on the savant, or something entirely different. The only people who return are people like me, people who know how much money can be made.'

Through the window, the city limits gave way to brown fields tilled by tank treads. They were on the road to Grozny. 'I'm not here to make money.'

'That's why you are so intriguing.'

They reached the Grozny garage two hours later. Two dour-faced men met them at the door holding Kalashnikovs, one still three weeks from killing the other in an argument that would begin over driving directions, and Sonja feverishly hoped that the smuggler's love for Alu the Turtle still surpassed his loathing for Alu the Unluckiest Younger Brother in History. Three trucks sat at the end of the concrete tarmac. The brother led her to the first truck, whose shot-off lock clung by a half-broken, glimmering grip. He lifted the door and shone a torch into the trailer. A Red Cross first-aid kit sat in the circle of yellowed light. The circle spread to illuminate torn cardboard boxes and hundreds, no, thousands of first-aid kits. 'These were stolen,' she said.

'Of course they were, and not without some headache, I'll have you know. But as you said, nearly all of what you asked for can be found in a first-aid kit.'

'What happened to the drivers?'

'Why do you care?'

She could feel him testing her, ready to blunt the slightest edge of moral outrage with a lecture on relativism in war, or maybe with another example of his contempt for Alu. She unsnapped the first-aid kit and surveyed the contents. Four absorbent compress dressings, eight adhesive bandages, a tube of antiseptic ointment, a breathing barrier, two latex gloves, a gauze roll, a thermometer, a packet of aspirin and a pair of scissors. She closed the lid, refastened the clips, had nothing but gratitude to give him. For all she cared, the drivers could be tied up and beaten, since she now had the ointment to disinfect their cuts, the gauze to bandage their wounds, even scissors to cut through whatever magical threads held them three metres off the ground.

'What about the morphine?'

'I nearly forgot.' He pulled a black nylon duffel bag from the front seat, set it on the bumper and unzipped it. A plastic-wrapped brick of white powder lay at the bottom. 'Morphine is too expensive,' he said, handing it to her.

'What is it?'

'Heroin.'

The word alone weighed ten kilograms. This powder had been boiled and squirted between Natasha's toes twice a day for eight months. My God. And for the first time in how many days, she breathed the relief of knowing Natasha was safe at home, barricaded behind a water-glass moat, safe from the fangs of dragons. 'Is it unadulterated?'

'Not enough sugar in there to sweeten a cup of tea.'

'I asked for morphine.'

'And even had you done me the favour of lobotomising Alu while he was under your care, I wouldn't get you morphine. Heroin is much cheaper.'

'I want something else, then.'

'So do I. There are only a few departments open in your hospital, yes? If you rent me some unused space, we can continue this arrangement.'

'For what?'

'My wares.'

'No guns, drugs or people.'

'Of course not,' he said. 'I keep them at home. No, mainly national treasures looted from city museums that can be sold abroad.'

'Fine. I want an ice machine. The hospital has been without one for several months. A bearded man at the bazaar is selling a nice one from the Intourist Hotel. Feel free to be rough with him. And where are the books I asked for?'

'You've chosen the wrong profession,' he said, enjoying her stubbornness. 'You're a natural swindler. You'd run me out of business. I've had difficulty finding them, but they should come in shortly. A third cousin in the West is asking for them from Amazon.'

'What's that?'

'I haven't any idea. This kid can make your books appear from the ether. He'll run me out of business, too.' He shook his head. 'The whole world is conspiring to run me out of business.'

'And another thing.'

'Now you're really beginning to annoy me. If you keep it up, I'll have to bring my brother with me next time.'

'I want new clothes.'

And he laughed and laughed and laughed.

Two weeks later Sonja returned from the hospital wearing a maroon cashmere sweater, tan leather boots and a pair of one-size-too-tight jeans displaying curves that the chemistry professor would have found a whole hive nesting on, had his eyes still worked. The weight of the psychology textbooks strained the rucksack straps against her shoulders. Her left hand, wrapped around a glass of ice, was numb.

In the hall she stopped at Laina's door, wanting to leave the ice for her neighbour. The murmur of voices inside stopped her. She crouched to the keyhole. Were Laina's hallucinations speaking back to her?

'There were twelve chariots in the sky today? That's two more than yesterday.' Natasha's voice basked beneath a sun that never shone when she addressed Sonja. It was good to hear Natasha care, even if it wasn't for her.

'Twelve,' Laina said. 'I think they're up to something.'

'Like what?'

'Who knows? Trying to steal the moon to sell at the bazaar. Protecting the skies from Federal planes. Maybe trying to figure out how to get their horses down from the clouds.'

Natasha's voice softened. 'In the winter of the war, before I went to Italy, when the bombing was at its worst, I was afraid the apartment block would be hit. So I lived in City Park. I remember the City Park Prophet once said everything that isn't darkness or death is a vision. I remember he said we are all God's hallucinations.'

'I remember once, on my birthday, when I was a child, I came into the kitchen and saw a huge wooden box on the table,' Laina said. 'I was so happy. I couldn't imagine what wonderful present lay inside such a big wooden box.'

'What was it?'

'A coffin. My aunt was inside.'

Sonja bit her knuckle. When they were children they had pretended to have a third sister, a black-haired girl named Lidiya. Like Alu, the ghost sister was never around, and in her absence they had teased, chided, scorned, blamed and hated Lidiya so they could love each other more simply.

'I'm afraid to leave the apartment,' Natasha was saying. 'I'm afraid of the city. There's just so much open air now. I'm afraid of nearly everyone. I don't know why. Everyone scares me but you. Even Sonja can be scary. Sometimes, if I let myself think about Italy, my body shuts down. It's like I'm not in charge anymore, my brain turns off, and I have to lock myself in my room and barricade myself with furniture. I feel so stupid. I'm such an idiot.'

'Do you see the chariots?'

'No, not yet. I see a wallet, though.'

'A wallet?'

'Yes, there was this man, and when he was dressing his wallet fell out of his trousers and he had a picture of his children in one of those plastic credit-card flaps. That was the day when I gave up.'

'It's good to talk about these things. It will keep the chariots and wallets of the world honest. They will know we see them, and are not afraid to sound like madwomen.'

'Yes, I like talking with you.'

'We're staying alive.'

Sonja stood and walked to the flat, afraid of what she might hear next. At the kitchen table she examined the glass of ice. Each cube was rounded by room temperature, dissolving in its own remains, and belatedly she understood that this was how a loved one disappeared. Despite the shock of walking into an empty flat, the absence isn't immediate, more a fade from the present tense you shared, a melting into the past, not an erasure but a conversion in form, from presence to memory, from solid to liquid, and the person you once touched now runs over your skin, now in sheets down your back, and you may bathe, may sink, may drown in the memory, but your fingers cannot hold it. She raised the glass to her lips. The water was clean.

Chapter 8

FIVE HOURS AFTER HIS FIRST SUCCESSFUL amputation, Akhmed's hands stopped shaking. The frost-caked road glared up at him, the more menacing since he'd seen, up close, what it could do. He had sawed straight through that poor man's leg. He hadn't been able to grip the saw until Sonja's fingers had wrapped around his. Until hers had pushed his hand forward. The man he had imagined himself to be had died the moment she set the blade against the bone and pushed his hand forward. He was one more instrument for her manipulation. Her face had hardened with a marble-like resolve unmoved by both his and the other man's suffering. As if she hadn't known that leg belonged to someone. As if she hadn't known the hand she held did as well. Pushing the blade forward, she had observed him as if he were the patient. And he had been. As the saw teeth caught on the bone, she had performed a second surgery, one less bloody but no less brutal, excising from his heart the impulse to run, to cower, to let the man bleed to death rather than face the horror of saving him. The amputation had left both patients lighter.

Watching for the slightest rise in the road, he still felt more like that young man than he did that doctor. He was nothing like Sonja. She was the strangest Russian he'd ever met, a riddle wrapped inside a mystery inside a set of unattractive but very white scrubs. What parts had she discarded for the sake of her sanity? What had she cut from herself? Had he stared into her pupils he would have emerged, bewildered and blinking, on the far side of the earth. Was he awed by her? Absolutely. Did he respect her? Unequivocally. Want to be anything like her? No, never, not at all. If he never again saw the beige corridors of Hospital No. 6 he would call himself lucky. But he had to go back in the morning; he had an agreement. A woman so casually capable of cutting off a leg was capable of throwing out an orphan girl.

Two hundred metres away, at a crook in the road, a diffuse fan of headlights turned into view. He ran. Birch trunks divided the beam into pale yellow blocks as he sheltered behind a half-rotted log, sucking on snow to mask his breath. Once the headlights passed he glimpsed the red of Ramzan's pickup heading towards the city. He bit his knuckle, unable to recall its Latin name. Ramzan couldn't know. He couldn't. When the tail lights shrank to a distant scarlet flush he returned to the road, massaging the soreness between his thumb and index finger. In that busy afternoon his palm had had two more opportunities to callus.

A half-kilometre from the village the flicker of a campfire jumped through the underbrush. With the pickup truck halfway over the horizon, curiosity rather than fear led Akhmed back into the forest. He crept with the faith that the flames spoke louder than the frost beneath his boots. There, in the clearing, a man made of shadow passed pamphlets to that shivering brightness. The dogs, lounging beside the fire, heard him before the man.

'It's Akhmed,' he called over the dogs' growl. Never had he understood the obligation Khassan felt for those filthy, diseased animals. His son made him a pariah, but the dogs weren't helping. Another handful of pages fluttered into the fire. 'What are you doing?' he asked.

Khassan was studying the sheet of paper in his hand, where in the fifth sentence of the second paragraph, in the gap of a missing comma, he found the sorrow of his life. The sentence described the upbringing of a minor eighteenth-century tribal leader, and it would be the last time human eyes would read the name of the tribal leader's mother. 'A punctuation error,' he said, with the tremble of more ominous inaccuracy. 'I've read through that paragraph hundreds of times and never caught it.'

'Don't do this,' Akhmed said. He could have reached out, caught it and kicked snow on the fire, but the page with the punctuation error was already smoke, and the name of a mother who died two hundred and twenty-three years earlier was already lost. He emptied his lungs but his sigh wasn't finished; it went on emptying him. One spring day, when Akhmed was a child, Khassan had led him to a logging field a half-morning's walk from the village. Men with roaring orange saws had leaned into beech trunks and the trunks had spumed clouds of sawdust and groaned as the green treetops toppled. He was eight years old and the stumps were shorter than he was. 'Hundred years to get that tall,' Khassan had said, and turned for home.

'I was thinking of someone I lost many years ago,' Khassan said. 'She called me a coward once. It wasn't what she said, but the way she said it. As if her judgement just passed through me. As if I were a cloud.'

The fire had thawed the overhanging branches. Droplets sliding down the slender fingers turned to steam before landing in it. Nothing Akhmed could say would put this man back together. 'You were a good husband,' he said. 'Your wife loved you.'

Khassan looked confused, as though he hadn't been thinking of his wife at all, and reached to the ground for another stack of pages. 'My wife didn't, but thank you,' he said, nodding to the fire. 'Forty-four thousand three hundred and thirty-eight pages. It took five hours to count. Over twenty trips to carry them. No wonder these pups are so tired.' He knelt and patted the bald dog's stomach with an awful affection. 'Each page averages three hundred and fifty words. That's fifteen million words I've written.'

'There are more words.' The firelight twitched across their faces. It was all he could say.

'There are more writers.'

'You can't do this.' He spoke from a fear that closed his stomach into a fist, helpless like a child, his emotions a magnification of what he detected in the elder. If Khassan lost hope, where would Akhmed find it?

'You wouldn't understand, Akhmed, but you might, if you reach my age. I was thinking of the stories my mother used to tell me about princes and warriors who went to great measures to ensure their names would endure, and were punished by Allah for their pride. I want to be forgotten. There is something miraculous in the way the years wash away your evidence, first you, then your friends and family, then the descendants who remember your face, until you aren't even a memory, you're only carbon, no greater than your atoms, and time will divide them as well.'

'What are you saying?' Akhmed asked, though he didn't want Khassan to say any more.

'I'm saying that I want to disappear.'

Once, while hunting in these woods, Akhmed came upon

a doe flopping on the ground and struggling to breathe. A distended pink wound spread her hind legs, and her snout held a long line of anguished groans, and to end her suffering he aimed for her neck. But before he pulled the trigger, the sac-wrapped end of a fawn split open the wound. His jaw slackened. He set the rifle among the leaves, hid his forefinger behind his back, ashamed of what it had nearly caused, and watched one life begin where another had nearly ended. And now, with the final sheets curling on the coals, fear rose to wonder as he witnessed a moment of equal profundity. Not once for as far back as he could recall had Khassan ever admitted to a shortcoming, a mistake, not even a lapse as trivial as a missing comma. Tonight he confessed total failure.

The returning headlights stretched their shadows across the clearing too soon to have gone all the way to the hospital. As the beam of light swung towards them, he saw, briefly, paw prints in the ashes of fifteen million words.

Held aloft by distant tacks of starlight, the night was a blackout curtain concealing Ramzan's truck until it was too late for Akhmed to turn back. Ramzan climbed from the cabin, lit a cigarette, and stared at what had been Dokka's house as Akhmed approached.

'Have you seen my father?' His face dipped into the orange orb with each inhalation. If he had the flat face of an ogre, or the many heads of a hydra, Akhmed might understand. If he had the cleft tongue of a devil, or the snake-hair of a Medusa, or the matted hair of a wolf-monster, Akhmed might understand. But Ramzan had two eyes, a nose and a mouth, pairs of arms and legs and ears, hair greasy but not slimy and certainly not slithering, and Akhmed did not understand. They had been born in the same village, had gone to the same school, had their knuckles purpled by the same metre stick, kicked the same football down the same dirt patch where in summer the grass grew thick enough to block a penalty kick.

'What do you really want?' Akhmed asked, too tired to be intimidated.

Ramzan frowned, his cheeks the white of pounded metal. 'Just to talk,' he said. 'It's been a long time since I've spoken to anyone. Two weeks. I keep a notebook and sometimes I write things down, and you can fake a conversation that way, for a little while, but—'

'I don't want to talk to you,' Akhmed interrupted.

'The last person I talked to was Dokka. Two weeks ago. I came by to ask if he wanted more firewood. And now look what happened. Our poor friend. What did he get himself into?'

'Nothing. He couldn't kill a loaf of bread with a butter knife.'

'And I'm told the girl, Havaa, even she was disappeared. But not by the security forces, praise Allah. No, she was taken by someone else. Someone else took her, but I don't know who. I think I have my finger near him. Or her. He could be a she. But I think he is a he. A him. A—'

'Where was she?' Akhmed asked, as calmly as he could manage.

'The security forces didn't find her. She wasn't there. She wasn't anywhere.' Ramzan paused only to breathe. 'Not in the living room or bedrooms or under the floorboards or in the cupboards, nowhere, nowhere, nowhere.'

'Why do they even care?' he asked, hoping Ramzan, who sold information, might give a small piece for free. 'What could they possibly want with a child?'

'No one is off-limits because there are no limits. The *why* and *what* aren't for us to consider. Those are questions for philosophers and imams and not for people like us, whoever we are.' His lips glowed in amber light. 'The *who* and the *where* are all we must know and all we must answer.'

'I don't see the why and what of a child.'

'There you go, Akhmed. Asking the wrong question. She's wanted. That's it. It doesn't matter why. All that matters is where she is and with whom.'

'If I see her I'll tell her you'd like a word.'

'You're being smug, smug, smug.' Ramzan's lanky arm wrapped around Akhmed's shoulder and the sweet, decadent scent of deodorant wafted from his underarm. The first time Akhmed became fully aware of his own odour had been on his wedding night, when, pressed against her in bed, awkward and struggling and generally doing it all wrong, he noticed Ula tilt her head to the open window.

'Dokka is gone,' Ramzan said, close enough for his breath to warm Akhmed's neck. 'He's gone. It makes me sad. He's gone. I wish he were here so I could ask him what to do. So I could say hello. I could talk to him. He always listened to me. He always spoke to me. He always answered when I asked a question.'

All too aware of that, Akhmed said nothing. It hadn't always been like this. For years he, Ramzan and Dokka had been friends. Every other Sunday they had gathered at Dokka's house to play chess, feast lavishly, and for just a few hours overthrow the fear and deprivation that had replaced the old order. In another life Ramzan's weaknesses would have manifested no tragedy greater than a cheated chess victory. Ramzan was the youngest of the three, so poor a chess player that Dokka had given him private lessons. He had learned well: made a board of the village, a pawn of the master.

'So tell me, where have you been all day?' Ramzan asked, his voice flat and solid, the voice of the anvil rather than of the metal flattened to it. 'Tell me where you've been, who you've seen.'

'Nowhere, no one.'

'Come on, Akhmed. We both know that you will tell me. You are a clever man, you have a sick wife to consider, you know what will happen if you don't. Let's try it again. Akhmed, my dear friend, where were you today?'

Akhmed said nothing.

'Shy today, aren't we? Well, let's start small. Tell me something you've done today, hmm?'

'Praying.'

'That's good. You should pray. I pray ten times a day. Five times for me and five for my father. I'm taking care of him, don't worry about that,' Ramzan said. His lips were banks unable to seal the stream gushing between them. 'Prayer is important. Prayer is very important. Especially now that we are living in the end time. You know that, don't you? The final Caliph will appear and the prophet Jesus will descend and he will slaughter the pigs and break the crosses. We don't have much time left, I don't think. That's why I pray ten times a day. I should probably pray fifteen or twenty times. My father needs it. You believe in the last days, don't you?'

'I believe in final judgements,' Akhmed replied. 'I believe we will each be called to account for our lives.'

'When I was a child, my father bought me an eight-track tape player. Most of the tapes he bought me from the university library were violin concertos and operas and symphonies. Can you imagine anything more boring for a ten-year-old? But it was a wonderful present. I loved it. I enjoyed messing around with the speeds and knobs more than I enjoyed listening to it. If I slowed the speed of the tape, the whine of the violins sank to lower, more ominous pitches. It makes me think of Al-Haaqqa. Are you familiar with verse thirteen? *When the trumpet will sound one blast, the earth with the mountains will be uprooted and broken, that is the day when the inevitable event will come to pass, the heavens will fracture and fall, the angels will be on all sides, raising the Throne of the Lord that day, above them.* And I used to think that the trumpet blast would come sudden and all-consuming. A true blast. An atom bomb. A pinprick in the balloon that is the world. But maybe not. Maybe not. Maybe the trumpet blast has been slowed like an eight-track tape, sounding on the lower frequencies, and maybe the trumpeter's breath lasts for many years, calling us not in unison, but each at a time.'

'You forgot Al-Haaqqa's next line,' Akhmed said. A swollen bead of sweat slid down Ramzan's forehead, following a thin ridge of scar tissue. When Akhmed was in his first year of medical school, he returned one November weekend for the Festival of the Sacrifice. Ramzan, still a teenager then, attempted a midnight liberation of the goat pledged for slaughter, partly because he believed the barbaric custom antithetical to Soviet rationality, but mainly because he wanted to see his pyjama-clad father chase it through the night. In the ensuing struggle – Khassan, no fool, lay waiting – the goat, unable to distinguish its liberator from its executioner, grazed Ramzan's temple with a sharp kick. He became Akhmed's first patient. As Akhmed stitched a seam in his skin, the usually sullen teenager kept asking for Latin words. Ramzan spoke the words as if to spell them, holding the vowels like grapes between his rounded lips. And Akhmed couldn't have imagined that the teenager reverentially intoning *fellatio*, believing it the name of a Roman god, would grow into a man who spoke Chechen as a dead language, selling its words as he had sold firearms and explosives, without knowing their real worth, without regard for who they might kill.

'The next line in Al-Haaqqa?' Ramzan asked uncertainly.

'*On that day you will be revealed and nothing of you can be hidden.*'

Ula smiled sleepily and rolled onto her side when Akhmed entered the room. He drew little eights on her forearm with his thumb until Ramzan's voice, addressing no one, faded with the splatter of gravel. In the kitchen he pulled a stool to the wood oven. He wanted to perch over the open oven door and bathe in the flicker until the ghost of this exhausting day disappeared into the chimney pipe. Havaa was safe. She was safe and he would have amputated his own legs for Dokka to know that. Thinking of Dokka and Havaa, he began sobbing. He'd forgotten the swell of pride, how it could overwhelm when least expected, how it could grow back – and how good it was to know there were parts of him a surgical saw couldn't remove. The flames dissolved in his eyes and through them an ache sounded: laughter. He couldn't explain it. His face couldn't express the thing in his chest. He was the most incompetent doctor in Chechnya, the single least distinguished physician to ever graduate Volchansk State University Medical School, and he had saved Havaa's life. He wiped his eyes on his sleeves, wanting to stay there, perched before the fire, but he had to feed his wife.

'How was your day?' he asked, after Ula swallowed her first bite.

'It was so busy,' she murmured.

'Yours too?'

'I spoke to your father.'

138

His father, a botanist and collector of pressed flowers, had passed ten years earlier. She had never met him. 'He must have come a long way to see you.'

'He did. He looked terrible.'

'And what did you talk about?'

'Your mother,' she said, as if it were nothing. He set the bowl on the floor and lay beside her with his arms folded so their noses and kneecaps nearly touched. Her forehead felt as though she'd spent the day in the sun. Maybe it was summer in the exile his father had returned from, and maybe he'd brought a bit for Ula. She didn't turn to the window when she inhaled; he kissed her nose for it.

'What did he have to say about my mother?'

She closed her eyes for so long he assumed she'd fallen asleep. 'I saw a birthmark,' she finally whispered. 'An oval on her stomach.'

Soon she slept. He finished the bowl of rice, disappointed by how little she had eaten, and rinsed it in the pail that had become the kitchen sink. After he stitched shut his pockets – to prevent checkpoint soldiers from planting contraband on him the next day – he brushed his teeth with baking soda and climbed into bed. He wiggled his toes. They felt wonderful there, at the ends of his feet. A question surfaced as he swam to meet Ula in sleep. By morning it would be forgotten, drawn back into dreams, but for a moment it sat there left by the tide. The oval-shaped birthmark on his mother's stomach. He had never told Ula, yet she knew.

Chapter 9

THIS IS ABOUT YOUR FATHER. I REMEMBER HE wrote tracts of pure classification, every idea an -ism, every person an -ist, and when I once criticised him for this reductive habit, he said, 'We know the meaning of nothing but the words we use to describe it.' I remember he wanted to teach you to read and write but didn't know whether to teach you the Cyrillic alphabet (which would be used if the Russians won) or the Latin alphabet (which would be used if the rebels won), and so he taught you the Arabic alphabet instead, and said he would have taught you to read and speak in Japanese if he knew it. I can't write Arabic. I hope you can read this. I hope there are still people speaking Chechen when you read this. These are stray memories, plucked from the air. But if I closed my eyes and forced myself to find your father, to truly find him, I would find him at his chessboard. In his forty years he lost only three matches. One was to you on your sixth birthday.

I would find him peeling a plum. You haven't forgotten, have you, how he peeled the skin with a paring knife? A dozen revolutions and the skin came off in a thin, unbroken coil, a metre-long helix. He transformed the skin of that squat little fruit, smaller than your fist, into a measureable length. Then he held the blade to the naked flesh and rotated the plum vertically. One half fell from the other, the cut so clean not even a filament clung to the seed. Pale pink beads dripped to the plate. If Sharik was with me, the dog would contemplate his hands eagerly. But when your father finally let them fall within reach of Sharik's tongue, he tasted the disappointment of dry skin. Your father wasn't a graceful man, but he could cut a plum like a jeweller.

He pretended to prefer the skin, and always gave you the flesh. You devoured the slices because you had to wash your hands before touching the chess pieces. It was a beautiful set, hand-carved, purchased by your great-grandfather, before the Revolution, when a postal clerk could afford such intimate craftsmanship. He taught you to play chess, and on your sixth birthday, he let you win. Your father did many things in his forty years. Yet if pressed to recall his finest moment, I would choose to see him in the living room, with you, by the chess set, peeling a plum.

The Third Day

Chapter 10

THEY APPEARED FOUR YEARS BEFORE HER father was taken, one or two at first, eyes glazed as if they'd never before seen a house, then more. They came stooped and waxen, downcast and wary, from Grozny, Shali, Urus-Martan, one long exhalation towards the mountains. Some carried the most necessary provisions: boots, woollen socks, more woollen socks, bribe money. Those who had lost everything, even their reason, carried the most ridiculous things: a man who lost his parents and children in the same Uragan rocket blast carried the key to the flat they perished in; a thrice-widowed woman carried the framed portrait of a face no one had seen alive for over a hundred years, and no images of her husbands; a retired bureaucrat carried a twelve-hundred-page regulatory binder, convinced that these rules were for ever inviolable. Others carried nothing at all. They kept coming and their clothes kept getting bigger on them. Havaa had just learned the Arabic alphabet, and she found the letter shapes in their figures. An eye raised to the mountains was ﺍ, forehead sweat formed a stammer of ه, each jawline was as sharp as ﺩ, the smoke dotting an old man's bark-loaded pipe was the point above ﮐ, and strung together they were an unpunctuated sentence the road wrote.

Her father seated the first one or two at the kitchen table and put enough food in front of them that they nearly refused to leave. Word spread through the refugee lines, and soon the number exceeded her parents' modest means. One day she came home from the forest to find her bedroom furniture scattered across the yard, her father and Akhmed modelling new beds on hers, the air pungent with sawdust, the sun glimmering off their bare backs. Two days later her bedroom was converted into a three-bunk hostel. The refugees – that's what they were, she could say the name in Chechen and write it in Arabic – paid for the night's sleep, two meals and washing line however they could. The shame that tightened Dokka's ventricles each time he asked for payment soon weakened to a slight, ignorable twitch. The first and thousandth refugees came from different peoples: the former deserving of his compassion and hospitality, the latter of nothing. Let them sleep outside for as long as their grandmother's jewellery will warm them. Let them eat their rubles. But since so few had jewellery or rubles, and since Dokka was incapable of turning away those truly in need, his parameters for payment expanded to include nearly anything. The tokens and trinkets went to Havaa, who collected them as souvenirs, and so rather than toys or homework she played with and learned from the plastic figurine of a ballerina in pirouette, the field guide to Caucasian flora, and whatever else her father and guest agreed was worth a rickety bunk bed on a winter's night. Now she slept on a mattress on the floor of her parents' room. Many nights she woke to find herself in their bed, her body heat held between theirs, distinguishing each in the darkness by the size of their fingers.

Others came on the weekends, strangers better dressed and rested, to see Akhmed. If they had heard rumours of the paedophile's ghost, they left their children outside when they entered the abandoned house, arms heavy with donations of linen bandages, fishing-line sutures, dry plaster, and slings of old magazines and bandannas. In the waiting room they sat straight-backed and motionless, afraid of breathing too hard, of squeaking the sensitive folding chairs and thus breaking the solemnity the proceedings demanded. Akhmed called them, one family at a time, as if they were his patients. And he wished they were, because they treated him with greater respect than his real patients, and he could do more for them. The family, as it entered Akhmed's office, likely knew he was the worst doctor in Chechnya. Sitting at the folding chairs before his desk, likely they knew he had followed the wrong calling. Likely they knew the worst doctor in Chechnya was its most talented portraitist.

The father might break the silence with a wet cough, and, praying that Akhmed not ask to examine his chest, describe the shape of his son's nose. Flat and wide, he might say, as if knocked in the face with a frying pan as a child. No, no, no, the mother might deny before Akhmed's pencil reached the paper. It is a normal nose, a shapely nose, a beautiful nose, and he was never hit with a frying pan, or a soup pot, or even a kettle; a ladle, yes, of course, that is to be expected because a mother's kitchen is her sanctum and she must maintain order. Then in might jump a cousin, a sister, an aggrieved daughter who too clearly remembered the slap of a ladle on her outstretched palm. The conversation might never recover if Akhmed didn't raise his finger to quieten them; he had heard these arguments before, had seen grief warp the fabric of memory such that a mother refused to recognise her son when described by the father, and the father, usually compliant to his wife's requests, truly believed his son's nose was so crushed he could only breathe through his mouth. He asked them to close their eyes, and hoped their mouths would follow suit. He asked them to concentrate.

Hunched over the steel-legged desk, a cup of lukewarm black tea within reach, Akhmed might think back to childhood, to the sketches of snake skeletons, knee tendons and blood veins his father mistook for an interest in science. He might think back to medical school, when he skipped a year of pathology to attend art classes. By that point a career change was beyond consideration; he was a bottle, thrown to the sea, into which the villagers had folded their wishes, and though he was willing to give up on himself, he wasn't willing to let down those who believed he could carry them over the water. Yet he drew still lifes when he should have drawn diagrams, studied models when he should have studied corpses. When he graduated from medical school in the bottom tenth he didn't know the disgrace weighing on him like a hundred rubles in five-kopek coins would one day be converted to less cumbersome denominations, when families, like this one, came, knowing he was too incompetent a doctor to save their son's life, but so skilled and well trained an artist he might bring their son back.

Each half-minute he would slide the paper across the desk and search their faces for the pause of recognition. Yes, those are his ears, just like that. No, my wife is right, his nose isn't so wide, and she never hit him with a frying pan. Mistakes would disappear beneath the corners of a pink eraser. That's him, they say. He is ours.

Some portraits found their way to kiosks where they stared out at the passing refugees, searching for their reflection in the line. Others rested in more intimate spaces: set in a glass frame over an empty bed, or folded in a wallet with nothing else in it, or locked in a chest drawer beside the birth certificate documenting the exact hour, date and place that life had entered the world. The missing remained missing and the portraits couldn't change that. But when Akhmed slid the finished portrait across the desk and the family saw the shape of that beloved nose, the air would flee the room, replaced by the miracle of recognition as mother, father, sister, brother, aunt and cousin found in that nose the son, brother, nephew and cousin that had been, would have been, could have been, and they might race after that possibility like cartoon characters dashing off a cliff, held by the certainty of the road until they looked down — and *plummeted* is the word used by the youngest brother who, at the age of sixteen, is tired of being the youngest and hopes his older brother will return for many reasons, not least so he will marry and have a child and the youngest brother will no longer be youngest; that youngest brother, the one who has nothing to say about the nose because he remembers his older brother's nose and doesn't need the nose to mean what his parents need it to mean, is the one who six months later would be disappeared in the back of a truck, as his older brother was, who would know the Landfill through his blindfold and gag by the rich scent of clay, as his older brother had known, whose fingers would be wound with the electrical wires that had welded to his older brother's bones, who would stand above a mass grave his brother had dug and would fall in it as his older brother had, though taking six more minutes and four more bullets to die, who would be buried an arm's length of dirt above his brother and whose bones would find over time those of his older brother, and so, at that indeterminate point in the future, answer his mother's prayer that her boys find each other, wherever they go; that younger brother would have a smile on his face and the silliest thought in his skull a minute before the first bullet would break it, thinking of how that day six months earlier, when they all went to have his older brother's portrait made, he should have had *his* made, too, because now his parents would have to make another trip, and he hoped they would, hoped they would because even if he knew his older brother's nose, he hadn't been prepared to see it, and seeing that nose, there, on the page, the density of loss it engendered, the unbelievable ache of loving and not having surrounded him, strong enough to toss him, as his brother had, into the summer lake, but there was nothing but air, and he'd believed that *plummet* was as close as they would ever come again, and with the first gunshot one brother fell within arm's reach of the other, and with the fifth shot the blindfold dissolved and the light it blocked became forever, and on the kitchen wall of his parents' house his portrait hangs within arm's reach of his older brother's, and his mother spends whole afternoons staring at them, praying that they find each other, wherever they go.

Every other Sunday Akhmed and Ramzan came to play chess with her father. Ramzan arrived first, knocking with his forehead, his arms hugging a stew pot; sometimes he brought self-awarded gratuities from the shipments he transported to and from the mountains, pickled trout or plum jelly, cured lamb, candied nuts. Then came Akhmed, entering without knocking, grabbing Havaa and hoisting her over his shoulder and threatening to marry her to a toad. In the living room Havaa would serve them tea, and rather than a chore it felt like her own modest contribution to the afternoon. In her eyes, the three men formed a family to whom she wasn't a daughter but a very young sister. This changed when Khassan joined them, once every few months, as the invisible structure built between them failed to support the weight of another man. In his presence the lustre of Ramzan's laugh dulled and resentment built beneath his quiet face. Akhmed and Khassan monopolised the conversation and Ramzan observed, searching for an opening, but when one came he never knew what to say.

While the men ate she and her mother remained in the kitchen. The custom seemed so unfair, and she didn't understand why her mother, usually as stubborn as a sleepy ox, submitted to it. Her father allowed her to join them when they finished, provided she didn't bite her nails, and the ottoman provided the perfect perch from which to watch the chess game. It was a beautiful set of lacquered beech bordered with mother-of-pearl. The board had to have been carved from magical wood, since for all the time she spent in the forest she'd never come across so shiny a tree. The little figures, demarcated by colour and bound by rules, made warfare a clean and orderly enterprise. The bulbous heads of pawns and imams, rubbed bald by the touch of too many fingers, were her favourite; months later she would wonder why the rebels and Feds, most in their teens and twenties, still had so much hair. Her father was so skilled that Ramzan and Akhmed played in a team against him. The two consulted and conspired before making their next move, and her father would read a book while they decided, so confident in his mastery he didn't care if Ramzan cheated. Once he told her that a true chess player thinks with his fingers, and she would remember this, thirteen months later, when he lost his. When his turn came he probed the air indecisively; then, as if each digit independently reached the same conclusion, they came together on the wooden scalp of the imam who slayed Boris Yeltsin, like any good jihadist.

Her father only lost to them twice. The first was in 2001, the Sunday after a company of wounded rebels spent one night of an eighteen-month retreat in Eldár. They came from the hospital in Volchansk, a fact that Akhmed might have exploited when he later took in the girl, had he remembered. When they hobbled into the village square, arms in slings, eyes purpled by exhaustion, the assembled villagers thought the rebels had fled the hospital too soon. One was in a wheelchair. How had the Feds failed to catch them? Their green headbands proclaimed *Allahu Akhbar* in a golden Arabic script. The villagers, Havaa among them, approached the rebels with cautious curiosity. Many, Havaa among them, had never seen a rebel in the flesh. They were a land over the horizon; sons and brothers would go *to the rebels* and never be seen again. Several mothers spoke to them directly, asking after their sons, but most, Havaa among them, watched silently. A shudder passed through the entire assembly when the short field commander planted the green flag of national independence in the square. With this act the rebels — so weak a few children with gardening tools could have overpowered them — had officially seized the village, and thus damned it to a Russian liberation.

They demanded medical attention and were taken to Akhmed's clinic by a dozen villagers who introduced the rebels and disappeared, grateful for the clinic for the first time. Only after checking the linen cupboard for a potential Federal ambush were they willing to disarm. On the other side of the village, Havaa saw none of it. She sat with her mother, in the safety of the kitchen. Had she seen the short, squat field commander, she might have thought he looked like a half-emptied grain sack in fatigues. He addressed Akhmed courteously, reiterating the importance of communal sacrifice in the campaign to defeat the godless Russian scourge. Akhmed held his hands together but one couldn't stop the other's tremble. He warned the field commander that he wasn't a very good doctor, that a paedophile's ghost was said to haunt the clinic, and that he would much rather draw his portrait. In a deep, even voice as he unbuttoned his shirt, the field commander informed Akhmed that if he didn't become the best doctor in Chechnya within the next five minutes, he'd soon haunt the clinic as well. A surgical thread Akhmed had never encountered held the field commander's chest together.

'What is this?' Akhmed asked.

'Dental floss,' the field commander said. Given the lichenous growth on the field commander's incisors, Akhmed assumed the floss hadn't seen much prior action.

'Dental-floss stitches. I've never seen such fine work. Who put them in?'

'A doctor at the Volchansk hospital. She was both a woman and an ethnic Russian. Can you believe it?'

The self-doubt that had unfolded from the envelope with every hospital rejection letter again stole Akhmed's breath. 'No,' he said, dispirited. In three and a quarter years, when Sonja was to offer him a job, Akhmed would finally find that breath.

On the other side of the village Havaa was studying the pale blue flowers on her mother's skirt, annoyed she couldn't find them in the Caucasian flora guide. Why invent flowers when so many real ones would be honoured to find their faces on a skirt? Her mother had spent the afternoon in the back garden and now chopped carrots, beets and thyme lay on the worktop. Havaa, standing on a step stool and stirring the broth, found an unfamiliar gratitude for the smallness of her life. Everywhere beyond these four walls smelled of smoke and petrol, but here, no calamity was greater than an egg falling to the floor. Later that afternoon the door would quietly close and her father would enter. He would speak with that deliberate, deceptive tone he used when reading her a story whose ending he already knew. She would ask if the army men would be staying with them and he would say, no, they're not refugees, and leave it at that. She wouldn't know that her father and Ramzan had spent nearly an hour conversing with the field commander. She wouldn't know that the field commander, impressed by Ramzan's experience as a trader in the mountains, had put him in touch with a sheikh who was looking for a capable man, a man like Ramzan, to deliver arms to the rebel encampments. All she would know was that the following Sunday, a day before the Feds arrived, her father lost Boris Yeltsin to a rook.

Three mornings after the rebels tottered from the village, Havaa woke to her parents' hushed panic. Her father hoisted her in his arms before she could change out of her night-clothes. The impact of each footstep jolted through her, and as he ran into the forest, she watched the village shrink over his shoulder.

'What is it?' she asked.

'We are being liberated,' her mother panted from beside her.

A rotten log shielded them from all but the *zachistka*'s sound. When a ten-second spray of gunfire flooded the sky, Havaa couldn't have imagined it was directed at eight villagers deemed too dangerous to be transported to the Landfill. Lying on the mossy topsoil for hours, she thought of her father's defeat the previous afternoon. She knew that Russian soldiers could destroy a village, but she hadn't known her father could lose a chess match. He lay next to her, twitching at the slightest shift in the wind, his fingers white around the handle of the kitchen knife. The rising smoke was so thick dusk came at three o'clock. Her father peered over the log with a pair of binoculars. He passed her the binoculars, the two-night payment of an ornithologist, who was now homesick, studying birds in Ecuador. As she spied Feds through the gaps between tree trunks, her father explained the difference between *kontraktniki* and ordinary draft soldiers.

'The draft soldiers in blue uniforms are scared teenagers. They are what we might call the victims of absurdism,' he said, not one to miss an opportunity to lecture a captive audience. 'They would surrender if you waved a soup spoon at them. Most can't find Chechnya on a map and don't care if Putin, Maskhadov or Father Christmas presides over the republic; most arrived by train in passenger carriages but most will return as Cargo 200, sealed within zinc-lined coffins in the freights. But the *kontraktniki*, the ones you see wearing sleeveless black T-shirts to show off their tattoos, they are nihilists, immoralists or misanthropists, take your pick. They were released from prison provided they serve a certain number of years in Chechnya. They *want* to be here because this is the only place they can express their true nature, and, if I weren't hiding behind a log, I suppose I might even admire them because they are committed to the dialectics of their philosophy, no matter how horrid.'

At that moment, a blond-haired conscript had pulled Khassan from the line of men that were to be taken to the Landfill. He hid Khassan in a tin-roofed shed and gave him his grandparents' name and address. 'You must survive,' the blond-haired conscript said. 'You must survive and tell my grandparents. Tell them their grandson is not like the other solidiers. Tell them that they raised him well, that he's trying so hard to stay the boy they brought up.' Khassan would write a letter to the conscript's grandparents, but without access to a functional postal system, it would remain in his drawer for seventeen months, until the autumn morning when a Russian woman knocked on his door, asking if he had seen her son. It wasn't uncommon to see the mothers of missing Russian soldiers searching the Chechen highlands for their sons. Khassan wouldn't be able to help her, but he would ask her to post his letter from Russia. He wouldn't know that in Novosibirsk the grandparents of the blond-haired conscript would receive his letter eight days after they received word of their grandson's death and would read it as a eulogy at his funeral.

By evening the village still lay under an awning of smoke. Twenty-three had died. Fourteen from gunfire, three from collapsed houses, two from mortar fire, and one from suicide: a ninety-year-old man who had survived two world wars, three heart attacks and, most debilitating of all, the shame of his firstborn son, a boy who could have been anything but chose to be a puppeteer. The Feds forced three into a cellar and lobbed in a live grenade before shutting the door. Another eighteen were taken to the Landfill, which meant forty-one villagers disappeared that day, to return only by the grace of Akhmed's pencil. Shortly after Havaa followed her parents home, Akhmed appeared in the door frame and knelt to knock on the kicked-in door. He needed Havaa's fingers. In his clinic the wounded lay on every surface flat enough to hold a body. The butt of a Kalashnikov had for ever shut a woman's left eye. The arm of a man who would go on to summit Elbrus bent as if it had three elbow joints. Akhmed's hand, flaccid on her shoulder, guided Havaa through the waiting room. His office was an operating theatre. Mountainous tarpaulin topography spread across his desk, streams flowing into lakes of blood. A lamp sat on the floor, its light pinning the silhouette of Akhmed's head to the ceiling where it would blankly observe the scene. He spoke as if accountable to her, explaining that this wasn't a hospital and he wasn't a surgeon, that he could draw lovely sketches of the wounded but couldn't save their lives, that the doctors at Hospital No. 6 were unquestionably superior and had the *zachistka* cordon not blocked all traffic to the city, he would carry each to the hospital on his back to avoid the responsibility of their care.

Two neighbours helped him carry a limp body to the desk. He cleaned the wound with water, but he had run out of iodine solution and had to use a half-bottle of *spirt* for sterilisation. He made a home-made haemostat by wrapping clean bandages around the head of some pliers and clinching the handles with a rubber band.

Akim was thirteen, the first wisps of a moustache filled in with soot. Red dishrags were wrapped around his thigh, and between half-opened lids, his eyes found Havaa's.

'My fingers are too big,' Akhmed repeated as he tightened a leather belt around Akim's thigh. The adults in her life all acted like children, and rather than compounding her fear, this forced her to be calm. Piece by piece she broke down the room, chopping the ceiling from the walls and the walls from the floor, amputating her shadow from her feet, until the one floorboard holding her was all that remained. Akhmed explained that Havaa had to help him ligate an artery with thread from a frayed skirt. A few months earlier her mother had taught her to sew and he knew that for her father's birthday she had mended the toes of all his socks.

'OK,' she said, though she didn't want to help Akhmed, though she wanted to hide in the forest, where birch branches were the only limbs that ever broke. But she did it for Akhmed, rather than for the boy, who once had found her talking to a pine cone and had teased her so badly she had wished him dead.

She couldn't sleep that night. In the quiet of her parents' bedroom she could still hear his screams. Everything was different now. She couldn't say how or when, whether it had happened when her father had carried her to the woods, or when her fingers had sunk into the hot ooze of Akim's open thigh, but everything was different. On either side her parents lay awake, and when she squeezed the flaps of their pyjama tops, as she had always done for reassurance when she had a bad dream, her mother squeezed back.

No one wanted to risk moving the unexploded shells that lay scattered across the village, so the next morning Havaa's parents, among other villagers, prised toilet bowls from the rubble of collapsed houses and dragging them upside down and two by two gently set them over the unexploded shells. Havaa would never forget the sight. So many dozens of upside-down toilet bowls crowded the street that cars wouldn't pass for weeks, and in that time, she would occasionally hear the overdue explosions, the shrapnel ringing within the ceramic, but those bowls, the one decent legacy of the Soviet Union, never broke.

In the afternoon, she and her parents went to the clinic. Akhmed wouldn't meet their eyes when they entered his office. The blood-hardened tarpaulin lay on the floor, and in its red desert Havaa remembered streams. Akhmed slouched forward, his head propped against the desk by his pencil.

'I can't remember their faces,' he muttered.

'Whose?' her father asked.

'I promised I would draw them, but I can't remember any more.'

'You should sleep,' her father said, and beside him, her mother gazed at Akhmed with an expression of concern Havaa would only later recall.

When Akhmed woke, he kept his promise. He mounted blank pages on plywood boards, and over the next ten days drew forty-one metre-tall portraits. He used ink and charcoal, the cinders of burnt houses; there was a word for it, when artists used parts of the subject to recreate the subject, an -ism only Dokka would know. The portraits were larger and more detailed than anything he'd ever drawn. Eyelashes five pen strokes thick. Pupils the size of plum pits. When finished, he brushed the portraits with weatherproof finish and left them to dry overnight. By morning they shone like the lacquer of Dokka's chessboard. One at a time, he carried them to the street. Some he mounted within the doorless frames of abandoned public buildings; others he fixed into the walls of private homes, or hung over broken windows, or strung from empty planters, or raised to the top of flagpoles, or nailed to lamp posts, tree trunks or fences. One covered the hole punched into a wall by a mortar round. Another he staked upright in the cemetery, a tombstone for a man whose family couldn't afford one. They appeared with no commemoration louder than Akhmed's solitary hammer rap. Sometimes weeks or months would pass before the bereaved stumbled across the face of their disappeared, and when they did they might approach in awe, or pat their breast pocket for a cigarette, or laugh as if just understanding a joke, or ignore it entirely, having grown used to hallucinating their loved ones on walls, tombstones and clouds.

Havaa experienced the sensation only once. After the *zachistka* she spent all her daylight hours in the woods. The village shrank to slender stripes as she receded into the trunks, meandering back and forth, building barricades of loose sticks, helping little insects find fresh leaves, all while measuring distance by the diminishing volume of her mother's call. One afternoon she looked over her shoulder and froze.

A head, swollen and decapitated, hung from a tree behind her. A giant's head, she thought, and then, two steps closer, she recognised it. Akim had survived the night but died the next morning. Akhmed said that those hours were a gift she'd given Akim, that time became more important the closer to death one was, so an extra few hours to make peace with the world were worth more than years, though how he could have made peace while screaming, she didn't know. She stood close enough that her breath, chilled by the winter air, reached his lacquered lips. Akim once had found her talking to a pine cone and had watched, fingers barring his mouth, until snickers erupted from his nostrils. She had hated him then and still did. But standing before the portrait she felt something wrap around that hatred as a flame wraps around a candlewick, and soon there was nothing but a burnt taste in her mouth, his solemn face staring back at her, and the awful fact that it would never laugh again. Only then did she wonder how Akhmed had known to place the portrait where only she would find it. For a few more minutes, she stared at the portrait, and said goodbye.

When she woke the following Sunday, a single question pulsated in the cold morning air. What if there was no chess match today? The biweekly matches were the last heartbeats of the society in which she so badly wanted citizenship. She lay in bed until the sun had climbed into the first pane. When her mother, Esiila, asked her to help in the kitchen, she refused to answer, and poured a stream of indecipherable half-words onto her pillow. The girl always surprised her mother. During the *zachistka* she had hidden in the woods as quiet as the stones at her feet and twice as tough, calmer and more sensible than Dokka, who had gone on and on, lecturing them, knowing they were trapped. And now, the girl who hadn't cried once since the rebels arrived in town was bawling over morning chores. Believing the girl's endurance had at last reached its limits, Esiila quietly closed the door.

Havaa only left the bedroom when she heard the soft tapping of her father setting chessmen on the board. Later that afternoon, when her father lost Boris Yeltsin, again to Akhmed and Ramzan's rook, Havaa didn't care.

Quiet and cautious, the months moved like men slipping into mosque after *salat*. Villagers slid into the refugee lines without telling anyone and the taste of concrete dust hung in the air for a full season. Once a month, Ramzan's red pickup pulled up and her father sank into the cracked leather passenger seat, and she would watch through the window as the tail lights shrank. When he returned a week later, his whole body would smell like an armpit and he would pause at the threshold, eyes narrowed, rebuilding his family in his mind before pushing the door open and telling them how much he had missed them. Though Havaa never discovered where her father and Ramzan went, or what they did, she knew from her mother's voice that they were probably doing something more dangerous than flipping blini in the frying pan with their bare fingers.

The kitchen window was left open even in winter to ventilate the oven air and, in the mornings, her father's indigestion. She paused at it on the day before her father was to leave. Her parents' voices ran together like ribbons of smoke. Her father said it would ensure their survival, and her mother called him an idiot for thinking anything involving guns or Ramzan was safe, and Havaa dashed back to the woods, where songbirds spoke to one another in more pleasant tones. Ramzan's truck arrived before dawn. At the door, Havaa placed a pebble in her father's palm. 'If you roll it in a hundred circles you get a wish,' she said. He slipped it into his shirt pocket, and leaned forward, and his lips were two slats of sunlight on her forehead. The warmth glowed pleasantly, and after he turned to her mother, she pressed her fingers to her skin to hold it there.

Ula had taken ill in spring 2002, one year after the *zachistka*, and so when for the first three nights of her father's final trip Akhmed filled Dokka's seat at the table, it seemed only natural that he should come alone, as he had on other occasions when her father was in the mountains. It was January 2003. Havaa hadn't seen Ula in eight and a half months. On the first evening, as Havaa set plates on the table, Akhmed followed behind her and picked them back up, muttering, 'These won't do.' He left for his house and returned a few minutes later with a shorter, narrower stack of dishware. Between the knives and forks Akhmed's saucers looked like shrunken heads attached to enormous metal ears. Her mother frowned at the reconfigured table setting; men, she knew, would take everything from a woman, even her plates.

'To trick our stomachs,' Akhmed told Havaa, loud enough for her mother to hear in the kitchen. 'Tonight we dine like aristocrats on an elegant meal of modest portions. But I find nothing sadder than a small amount of food lost on a large amount of plate. But this,' he said, holding a saucer in his palm, 'is just the right size. If we trick our brains into thinking our dinner fills an entire plate, we might trick them into thinking our stomachs are full.' On the kitchen window Havaa thought she caught a smile in her mother's reflection.

The tension that had seemed staked to the floorboards the previous night fluttered out the open kitchen window as her mother and Akhmed conversed. They reminisced about Dokka's arrival in the village. He had presumed the village had its own newspaper, a presumption some took as evidence of insanity. He had brought more boxes of books with him than there was floor space in his rented room, and rather than discard the precious tomes, he had turned them into furniture. He slept on a mattress raised on book boxes, and sat at a desk made of an old door laid across pillars of science manuals. It didn't help his standing among those already questioning his sanity.

Dokka had grown up and been educated in Grozny, and Akhmed, just graduated in the bottom tenth of his class with no job prospects and the noose of the village's expectations tightening around his neck, did his best to transform Dokka into a local celebrity, partly because he had never befriended a man from Grozny, but mainly so Dokka could replace him on the tongues of gossiping widows. An arborist by training, Dokka was assigned to a three-year position researching the potential environmental benefits of clear-cutting, the professional equivalent of Siberian exile. When the Soviet Union collapsed and the timber industry disappeared — along with Dokka's funding — he remained to take advantage of this rare opportunity to research new-growth forest. By then he had moved into a home large enough to accommodate both books and furniture, and the villagers, most anyway, didn't run to the other side of the road when passing him. Though Esiila's father belonged to the camp still questioning Dokka's mental health, Khassan fully endorsed the young arborist, and Dokka was willing to marry Esiila for such a small dowry, the father would have been judged insane himself for refusing.

Havaa watched the conversation as she would a chess match, each side testing the other, searching for weaknesses to exploit. Now and then her mother glanced at her and the reflection of candlelight revealed an unfamiliar intensity in her eyes.

'Has Ula shown any signs of improvement?' her mother asked.

'No. She hasn't left the bed for over eight months now.'

'Are you any closer to a diagnosis?'

Again, Akhmed shook his head. 'Her vitals are fine. Whatever she has exceeds my ability to detect, let alone treat. I make sure she rolls over every couple hours to prevent bedsores. What else can I do?'

'You don't think there is anything wrong with her, do you?' The question was a queen driven eight squares forward.

'I think the human mind isn't built to sustain trauma after trauma.'

'Perhaps she needs to learn to care for herself. Perhaps your care is her paralysis.'

Havaa focused on her fingernails. She wanted to speak but didn't, wanted to flee but couldn't.

'I've considered leaving her for a few days, seeing if her body might jump-start her mind. It seems too cruel.'

'Both of our spouses have disappeared into themselves. Cruelty may be the line to draw them back.'

The conversation then veered back down the unmined road to the past, but when they each reached for the water jug, her mother's fingers brushed his, and they all blushed.

Akhmed stayed with them the following day and night, and the one after that, spending most of the daylight hours planted in front of the living-room window, staring across the street to his house. At night, when he thought Havaa was asleep, she heard him sneak into her parents' room. It wasn't until just after the *fajr* on the third morning that he finally left. He didn't return. Esiila stood at the window, where he had, and she could see him across the street watching from his living-room window, and they stood there with a bridge running between their eyes. Something awful had happened, but Havaa couldn't put a name to it. She and her mother didn't speak for the rest of that day or the next, as if Akhmed had been the substance through which they communicated, and without him they were alone with what they knew. The longer they went without speaking it, the heavier that first word became. On the day her father was to return, her mother hummed while she swept, scouring the silence with the dust from the rooms. Daylight dissolved into marbled twilight and Havaa fell asleep waiting for her father to appear.

They steeped in that silence for eight more days and nights before the uneven crush of gravel broke it. The door edged open and her father's full weight collapsed against her mother's chest. She would remember the yellow-grey of her father's cheeks, how she'd seen that colour frozen in deer urine but never on a human face. 'Help me,' he whispered. Only then, when he tottered forward, did she see the dark red rags rubber-banded to his wrists. Akhmed must have seen from his house because he ran in with his doctor's satchel before she could scream.

Akhmed would later explain that the bolt cutter had severed each finger so cleanly no skin remained to stitch over the bone. He would later explain that though ten strips of gaffer tape closed the wounds for the journey from the Landfill, infection was a greater threat than blood loss, and so he had no choice but to cauterise, no choice but to put out each finger like a cigar stub on the side of a heated butcher's blade. But when he ran in he couldn't explain what he was doing any more than could a man asked to put out a forest fire with only the water he could carry in his mouth. He asked her mother to start the stove and asked Havaa to go to her room. She hesitated. In the *zachistka*, she'd helped him when his fingers were too large and fumbling. Why wouldn't he let her do the same for her father? The thunderclap of her name, this time shouted by her mother, and she ran.

The clatter of kitchen utensils passed through her closed bedroom door. Akhmed shouted for the butcher's blade, and for more petrol, and with an intake of air the bar beneath the door brightened.

For three days her father slouched on the divan. Each night her mother unwound the gauze to polish the dark stumps with ointment. After a minute or two she cut a new strip of gauze, taped it around the shiny nub, and sighed, knowing she had nine more.

Late afternoon on the fourth day he stood. He paused at the coat stand, studying the buttons, and decided it was too warm for a coat. Havaa opened the door for him and he set his hand on the back of her neck and the heat of five missing fingers held her shoulder. They walked like that to Khassan's house. Ramzan opened the door. They both looked to Ramzan's fingers. Not even a nail was missing, and Ramzan blushed, and shoved his hands in his pockets.

'How ...' Ramzan began to ask, but didn't finish. 'You look better.'

'I need a gun,' her father said.

'What? No, Dokka.'

'I need to know that my family can protect itself.'

'Dokka, they let us go from the Landfill. Do you know

166

what they'll do to you if they have even the idea that you are involved with guns again?'

'What, Ramzan?' her father asked, raising his hands. 'What will they do to me?'

Ramzan looked down. 'Fine,' he said, after a moment. 'Come in.'

They walked past Khassan's desk to Ramzan's room. Ramzan pulled up the rigged floorboard and retrieved a Russian-made Makarov pistol from a cache beneath the floor. 'Why did you bring the girl?' he asked.

'To pull the trigger,' her father said, looking down at her. 'She's six years old. It's about time she learned how to handle guns.'

Ramzan took her outside, showed her how to load and unload the bullets, to set and release the safety. He told her to aim at the feral dogs clustered at the tree line, but she chose a tree trunk instead.

'It's a semi-automatic,' Ramzan explained, 'so you don't need to cock the hammer. Don't hold it out, that's for American movie stars. You want to keep it just in front of you, your elbow against your chest, like you're carrying a water jug. This won't have the kickback of a high-calibre gun, but it isn't designed for children, so you'll feel it. Where do you think you should aim? The head? Never on the first shot. Too small a target. Aim for the chest, right in the centre, that's the kill shot.'

When she returned to the front of the house, her father sat back on the steps, eyes closed, basking in the sun with a faint smile on his lips. She put the gun in his jacket pocket. He still hadn't said what had happened to his fingers. As they walked home, she was worried he might, but his feet ground into the glinting gravel, and hers did too, and they conversed only in footsteps.

Two women and a man waited for them at the front door. The man's hair looked painted and polished on his head; in another life he'd had a good job, a good flat and a good wife, but now his lustrous head of hair was the only good thing he had left. 'Is there space for us?' one of the women asked.

Her father looked at his shoe as if just stepping in dog shit. With a sickle-moon smile he shook his head, but they all knew it wasn't in response to the question. Havaa would never know her father had spent the past three days paralysed by the realisation that his fingers would never again save Boris Yeltsin, or rake April soil, or flip the pages of a book, or wrap around his penis in the outhouse, where for the space of an inhalation he felt content.

'Yes,' he said. The three refugees beamed with a gratitude that would fill him even longer than a final trip to the outhouse. 'We have several beds.'

Chapter 11

SONJA DIDN'T SEE HIM WHEN SHE CROSSED THE car park, didn't know him when she unlocked the doors, didn't hear him when he greeted her good morning, when he climbed into the truck after her, when she released the brake, gunned the engine and followed the grey road to Grozny. Twelve hours earlier he had nearly fainted at the sight of her palm calluses. But why think about this when the snow melted into muddy veins, when the blue of a peaceful sky radiated from all the metal of the jeep, when Havaa was safe and he was alive and Grozny waited like a great lake at the end of this river of asphalt?

To conserve petrol, Sonja accelerated for several seconds, then freewheeled out of gear. Too much oil in the ground, never enough in the tank, he thought; it could be the national motto. They progressed haltingly, the truck leaping forward and then rolling to a near standstill. He felt carsick, but knew better than to ask her to drive more evenly. Fifteen silent minutes passed before he flipped on the radio and gave the dial a quarter-turn. A crush of warm static filled the cabin.

'There's no working radio tower in the country. It's all static,' she said, without looking to him.

'I know. But 102.3 plays the best. Not too tinny. Full and robust. If a cello were to perform static, it would sound like this.'

She shook her head and turned the dial. 'I prefer 93.9,' she said. She still hadn't looked at him.

'It's too thin and monotone. There's no variation. It just sounds like static.'

'And that's why I like it,' she said. 'It sounds like static is supposed to sound.'

He reeled the dial to the far end. '106.7,' he said. 'Just listen.' Snatches of foreign transmissions laced the white noise. Syllables surfaced like glowing bubbles from the harsh swirl. Voices in a storm. She turned the dial back to 93.9 and they listened to static-sounding static. Fog fell over the fields. A bus was parked in a meadow. Paint chips pointed down a gravel road to the rusted remains of a tractor factory. Dormant smokestacks. Nowhere was a fire less likely to be found than inside a factory furnace.

'Do you worry about landmines?' he asked.

'Not really. There's a steel plate mounted beneath the driver's seat.'

'Does it happen to cover the passenger's seat, too?'

She *had* to smile, but before she shook her head and said he could amputate his own legs now, her gaze hardened around a figure a hundred metres down the road. An elderly woman with the posture of a parenthesis. A twine-strapped bundle of blue tarpaulin hung from her shoulders. A lavender dress hem fluttered at her ankles.

'Don't you know this road isn't safe on foot?' Sonja asked through the open window. 'Do you need a lift?'

The woman shrugged the blue tarpaulin, and watching

her Akhmed wanted to reach out, to wipe the damp grooves of her forehead and tell her that he too had suffered Sonja's questions.

'Only a fool would sit in a truck,' she said, pace unchanged.

'But we are doctors,' Akhmed said, emphasising *we*.

She glanced at him and back to the road. 'And you're sitting in a truck.'

Thirty minutes of empty fields passed without remark before Akhmed and Sonja reached the first checkpoint. An OMON lieutenant approached, followed by two scrawny privates who mimed his movements down to the way he chewed his bottom lip between his sentences; and contemplating these slight, unconscious facsimiles, Akhmed wondered if fear so consumed the young men that they would fuck, fart and die on their superior's schedule. Sonja passed the lieutenant their documents: two ID cards, one expired medical licence, and three letters penned by Federal colonels, which persuaded the lieutenant more compellingly than their legitimate documents. A hundred metres past the checkpoint she reached across his lap and slid the letters into the glovebox. She still hadn't looked at him. He grabbed her wrist before she could shut it and pulled out more than two dozen envelopes. The letters varied in formality, from official endorsements typewritten on Defence Ministry stationery to a few approving words scrawled on the back of a rebel field map. The signatories formed an index of the top brass on both sides of the war: General of the Federal Army Valentin Vladimirovich Korabelnikov, Special Battalion Vostok Commander Sulim Yamadayev, Commander of the Northern Caucasus Military District Alexander Ivanovich Baranov, the deceased mujahideen leader Ibn Al-Khattab, separatist field commanders Ruslan Gelayev and Shamil Basayev, even a deputy from Putin's office, both rebels and

Feds cohabiting peacefully by the thin partition of letter envelopes.

'Be careful with those,' she said, pulling her hand away.

'Why do you have these?' he asked, as the first of long-overdue misgivings unsettled him.

'For unhindered travel. They take care of bureaucratic formalities.'

'I wish you'd told me before I'd sewn shut my pockets.'

She smiled.

'Have you actually met these people?'

'Of course not. Most are from the man we're going to see. He says he can steal the spots off a snow leopard.'

'A criminal?'

She shook her head and glared at him with complete disdain.

'Is common decency too much to ask?'

'Excuse me?' she said, but he knew she couldn't claim affront. Common decency was the one thing he had that she didn't, and he held on to it as a rare, improbable triumph.

'You said every doctor and nurse to ever work for you has left but Deshi. Do you think that might have something to do with the way you treat people?'

'I think you'd better have brought your boots, because you're walking home.'

He spoke in a measured tone as her knuckles whitened on the wheel. 'You think I'm an idiot. An embarrassment to your profession. You are probably right. But that doesn't mean I'm wrong.'

'I think you need to be quiet, Akhmed.'

'Why?' He didn't dare turn to her.

'Because two days ago, I thought I was adding a competent doctor to my staff. Instead I'm babysitting a child who speaks in riddles and a man who couldn't identify his own foot if he tripped over it.'

'That doesn't give you the right to treat me dismissively. I'm trying to help you.'

'Actually that gives me every right to treat you dismissively. It gives me every right to dismiss you and the girl and fuck off back to London where even eighteen-year-old biology students know better than to give an unresponsive patient a questionnaire.'

'The Feds are looking for Havaa,' he said. 'You're this prodigy surgeon, right? Leaving London to come back and save lives? You are saving hers, Sonja. Each day. And you don't even have to cut off her legs.'

'How do you even know they want her? Why would they care about some child?'

'An informer was waiting at my house yesterday.'

'I don't want to hear about it.'

'I'm sorry,' he said. 'I'll be quiet.'

'What could you possibly be sorry for?'

'I'm sorry for you. Something in you is broken.'

'Another razor-sharp diagnosis, Dr Akhmed.'

'No, it isn't that.'

'I've amputated one thousand six hundred and forty-three legs. You've done three, and you think you have the right to diagnose me?'

'I'm not diagnosing you.'

'Then what the fuck are you doing?' She turned fully from the road and he saw her pupils, as wide as kopek coins, for the first time that morning. He shook his head at the windscreen. Brown fields were everywhere.

And Grozny appeared, grey on the horizon as the road devolved to a basin of broken masonry and trampled apartment blocks. Cigarette kiosks slouched on the pavement. Akhmed wished he had taken paper and a pencil with him to capture his first trip to the city. Sonja brought the jeep to a crawl as they tipped into a crater. The street rose and disappeared somewhere above them, the whole world of dark wet earth, the tyres spinning and reaching the lip. No scent drifted through the open window but the engine burn. No sewage or raw waste. Nothing. A flattened desk basked in the sun, knobs prised out. The flicker of an oil-drum fire three streets down came as a small, welcome signal of human habitation. Behind the flame a man turned a rotisserie fashioned from clothes hangers and a gardening stake on which was impaled a pink fist of flesh. Two pigeon claws revolved over the fire. Behind the fire, wooden gangplanks connected pyramids of rubble. Some lay over craters, others were suspended two or three storeys high, bridging alleyways. This is Grozny? He should have visited sooner.

'It's like scaffolding,' he said, the first words in many kilometres.

'Built by the street kids that live in the ruins,' she said, and in a tone of apology added, 'You were smart to bring her in.'

No faces peered from the yawning walls. The thought of his dreary, soul-crushingly backward village sent an unfamiliar flare of pride up his chest.

'How do they survive?' he asked, glancing at a building with more plank bridges than floors. An ingenious strategy; these young engineers were clearly ethnic Chechen. Collapsed floors would take construction crews years to lift and rebuild, but plank bridges could be reassembled in minutes.

'They sell the rubble back to the Russians. Construction has begun on defence and petroleum ministry buildings. They buy back the bricks at two rubles each.'

'More than I would have thought.'

'Bricks purchased at dawn are cemented by noon, so the kids have to chisel off any remaining mortar. You see those white rubber casings in the rubble?'

'Like snake skins.'

'It's electrical wire insulation. They strip and sell the copper wire. Just about any metal is worth its weight. Most of these kids can't read or write, but they've created metal-based currencies.'

'Scrap metal and disappearances,' Akhmed said, flat and without irony. 'Our national industries.'

The warehouse stretched wider than a football pitch with half its windows stained tar-black and the other half blown out, and when Sonja nodded to it he knew something was wrong. They passed a toppled chemical drum, its top peeled back like a bean-tin lid; a glowing blue sludge, too thick to evaporate, pooled at the bottom. A guard blocked the warehouse drive. His bloodstained bandoliers intersected at the sternum, the only red cross Akhmed would see that day. A dull glint, less recognition than knowing, appeared in the guard's face when he saw Sonja. 'Only a fool would sit in a truck,' the woman had said; if only Akhmed had met her a day earlier. The vice tightening in his chest had been there since the morning, since Sonja had refused to acknowledge him. She parked the truck, went to find the snow leopard thief, and he was alone, brought by a woman who didn't trust him to a warehouse large enough to hold his village, a place where he shouldn't have been, in a city unworthy of even an imaginary plane ticket. Three Mercedes sedans sat at the centre of the warehouse floor, Scandinavian number plates hanging from shiny screws. The walls were Western department stores: racks of leather and fur coats, fridges and dishwashers with warranties dangling from plastic ribbons, cardboard boxes stacked two storeys high. A folding chair sat open on the floor, pliers and gaffer tape on the seat. A tap turned on in Akhmed's mouth.

'It was the most remarkable thing I've seen in years. I couldn't think. I was stunned. Do I bow? I didn't know what to do.' The thin, excited voice belonged to the thin, excited man entering the warehouse beside Sonja. 'I never thought I would meet someone from China.'

The two strolled with a familiarity – she touching his shoulder, he timing his footsteps to hers – that left Akhmed uncertain and unaccountably envious. The wide arc they walked around him drew a line of tension across the room. 'What was he doing here? A journalist?' Sonja asked, avoiding his eye.

'An oil man. He wants to buy a refinery.'

'You're selling refineries now?'

'Just the machinery,' the man said simply. He wore a beige summer suit and a white dress shirt unbuttoned to exhibit a triangle of voluminous chest hair. His loafers reflected the pale light. A man dressed like this would be stripped, tied up and beaten within one city block, but he didn't seem like the type of man that went anywhere alone. 'Is this our friend?' the man asked, and nodded to the folding chair, pliers and gaffer tape. 'Have a seat, please.'

Akhmed pivoted sharply, but the guard was behind him, the gun barrel levelled to his chest. A tourniquet gripped the corridor between his brain and body, and directions came to his limbs in halting dribbles that wouldn't save him. That morning Ula had been asleep when he left. He hadn't said goodbye to her.

'You haven't been honest, Akhmed,' Sonja said. The way

she studied him he knew his skull was just another bone she could amputate.

'I'm sorry,' he gushed. 'I lied about being in the top tenth of my graduating class. I was in the bottom tenth. In the fourth percentile.'

No relief in her smile. 'Do you think that's what this is about?' she asked.

What else could it be? The only lie he had told was that he was a good doctor.

'You knew my surname and patronymic, Akhmed.' She had said his name twice now. The third time would be the last. 'No one knows those. But you did.'

'She wouldn't even tell me,' the man offered. 'Not that I had difficulty finding out, but still, she's rather cautious, don't you think?'

'You have to explain yourself,' she said, and she paused for a breath. 'Or I'll leave you here. I can't risk having an informer on my staff.'

Had the gun barrel not pressed against his spine, he would have laughed. He would have treated the set-up as another one of Sonja's tests. Treated the whole thing like the misunderstanding it was, because how could she mistake him for the man he had saved Havaa from? Havaa. The thought of her removing the insulation from electrical wires reconnected his nerves. He couldn't swallow. In the mouthful of warm saliva a pearl formed; an irritant hardened into white gleaming fury at the possibility that the war would end his life as indifferently as it had a hundred thousand others, that he was no more privileged. He didn't want to die before an audience of stolen fridges. He had kissed Ula's forehead in the early morning and felt the flutter of her lashes on his chin but when he raised his face she had already gone back in the gentle wash of wherever it was she went when she wasn't with him. He hadn't said goodbye.

'I saw your work before I ever met you,' he explained. 'The rebels, they came to my village a few years ago, and the field commander had a chest held together by the most magnificent dental-floss stitches. I was so impressed. The commander said it was the work of a Russian woman and I assumed they had kidnapped a Russian medic. But then, later on, I met a refugee from Volchansk who used to work at the hospital. She had stayed with Dokka when he was running a hostel for refugees.'

'What was her name?' Sonja asked, eyes as fixed as constellations. She stood close enough for him to hear her teeth grind. There was so much of her, right here, in his face, and he would have stepped back, had a gun not pushed him forward.

'I mentioned the dental floss and the Russian woman doctor. It was only in passing. I wanted to know if the hospital was hiring. And she looked up and said, "Sofia Andreyevna Rabina. Sonja." I tried to ask her more, but she didn't want to talk about you. Your name was the only one I had when Dokka disappeared. I thought a doctor good enough to stitch a man with dental floss would be good enough to take in Havaa.'

'What was her name?' she demanded. He was afraid to answer, afraid even to exhale; the hope wrapped within the question was so small and flickering a breath could extinguish it.

'Was it Natasha? Was her name Natasha?'

Chapter 12

TALL, SWAN-LIKE AND FOUR YEARS HER SISTER'S junior, Natasha stood in the spotlight of her family's affection. In his daybreak voice, cold from seven hours without the heat of a cigarette, her father would offer her good morning first, even if she entered the kitchen two paces behind Sonja. Her mother treated her with the pride and envy of a woman who had fallen in love with sixteen boys in secondary school, none of whom reciprocated her affection. 'My Natasha,' she would say, running her fingers through the girl's long brown hair with a possessiveness suggesting the strands were an extension of her own. Natasha's eyes were brown spattered with glimmers of emerald and uncut diamond. Hazel, technically. Her mother stared in quiet awe of this more artful rearrangement of her genetic code, and slipped into a contentedness that usually appeared only after the red wine had fallen below the bottle label. Natasha's elevated station in the family left in her only the slightest scratches of arrogance. Better than anyone, she knew she had done nothing to deserve the beauty she was blessed with. Their parents' plain features, replicated predictably in Sonja, had reacted violently in Natasha to create something as surprising as a dove hatching from a pigeon egg.

Within the variations of beige composing the corridors of State Secondary School No. 28, the spotlight of attention expanded. As an ethnic Russian she belonged to the national minority that ran the republic. Her ethnic status propelled her into the elite echelons of adolescent popularity, where a personality cult had arisen around her, fuelled by the adoration of obsequious underclassmen. In Moscow, Gorbachev's reforms barrelled the Soviet Union towards the precipice, but in a far-flung city in a further-flung republic, the old rules still applied. Ethnic Russians controlled all major positions of power, from head waiters to heads of government, and the two-hundred-year history of imperial order reiterated itself within State Secondary School No. 28. With magnanimity, Natasha accepted her rank. She wasn't nearly as vicious as the girls who, in florid Cyrillic on the inner flap of their homework planners, graded boys on a twelve-point scale. Nor did she hold herself above the roiling sea of refectory gossip by pushing others under. Years earlier, when she was still young enough to need a goodnight kiss, her father would plant his chapped lips on her cheek and, in a whisper of sweet tobacco, say, 'Sweet dreams, my sweet tsarina.' Even after she outgrew goodnight kisses, she liked to imagine herself as the long-lost grandchild of Grand Duchess Anastasia Nikolaevna, and acted in a manner befitting a wise and humble monarch.

It was this – her ethnicity as a Russian, the stalwart minority defending the borders of Western civilisation from the barbaric Muhammadans – that let her slip through her adolescent years with freedoms her Chechen classmates didn't enjoy. She could harbour lascivious thoughts of Ivan

Yakov — a man her sister would revive three times in the second war — who was far more handsome than any literature teacher had a right to be. She could shave her legs without worrying if a prudish deity would smite those parallel beams of smooth skin. Overnight, it seemed, electrical lines were laid in her veins as she realised that the awkward, self-conscious boys around her were growing into men. The complications of puberty weren't further complicated by culture or religion. Only when comparing herself to her classmates, many of whom were subject to arranged marriages, did she come to understand that in Chechnya gravity pressed upon women with heavier hands. Her Russianness exempted her from its grip, and so yes, often she floated.

Though Russian, she'd never been north of the Chechen border. Her parents had been born in 1930s Moscow and had grown up in communal flats four streets away from each other. They took the same buses, attended the same primary school, spoke an accent flavoured by the same fog, ate eggs laid by the same chickens, watched the same setting sun impale itself on the bronze spire of the Central Pavilion of the All-Russia Exhibition Centre. They each lost relatives to Stalin's purges. NKVD agents wearing uniforms the blue of a cloudless summer sky would stride into the apartment block past midnight, and the next morning residents would strain their tea without mentioning the scream-pierced night. Her parents blamed Stalin personally for the purges, and Natasha's state-approved history textbook confirmed that Stalin, and only Stalin, bore responsibility. But the terrible past of night-time disappearances was locked within the pages of that history book; she never imagined she would one day disappear as easily as her forefathers.

In 1946 news spread of the deportation of Chechens and the need for ethnic Russians to resettle the empty republic. Her father was fourteen when he last drank a glass of rusty Moscow tap water. Her mother, eight. Trains carried them over the war-sickened land. They arrived in Grozny and stayed two weeks in a draughty university auditorium, sleeping on benches before receiving a residency assignment to Volchansk. They journeyed to the city by the same bus, two days apart. Natasha's mother and father each felt so lonely in this silent country. They didn't believe they would ever find someone who had seen what they had seen, felt what they had felt. Twenty-one years after the end of the Great Patriotic War, they waited beside each other in a bread line. Their small talk surged to revelation. Neither could believe they had shared the same primary school, tap water and sunset from adjacent apartment blocks. Neither imagined they would some day share two daughters: one beautiful, the other brilliant.

Though she was the elder, Sonja was always thought of as Natasha's sister, the object rather than subject of any sentence the two shared. She walked alone down the school corridors, head sternly bent towards the stack of books in her arms. To Natasha she was the п-letter volume of the Large Soviet Encyclopedia: wide and filled with knowledge no normal person would ever need. On weekend nights, when Natasha returned from the cinema or discotheque, she would find a thin bar of light glowing beneath the door of her sister's room, and if she put her ear against the closed door, she would hear the whisper of a page turned every forty-five seconds. She believed Sonja to be a genius in the classical mould: a single great streak of lightning in an otherwise muddled sky. In all likelihood, Sonja had more academic journal subscriptions than friends. She could explain advanced calculus to her fifth-form algebra teacher but couldn't tell a joke to a boy at lunch. Even in the summer months, she had the complexion of someone who spent too much time in a cellar.

Everyone knew Sonja was destined for great things, but no one knew what to do with her until then. Even in academia, her natural habitat, she was an exotic species. Though her Russianness gave her certain dispensations, the idea that a young woman of any ethnicity could so excel in the hard sciences was a far-fetched fantasy. Their parents encouraged her at a distance. Neither understood the molecular formulae, electromagnetic fields or anatomical minutiae that so captivated her, and so their support came by way of well-intentioned, inadequate generalities. Even after Sonja graduated secondary school at the top of her class and matriculated to the city university biology department, their parents found more to love in Natasha. Sonja's gifts were too complex to be understood, and therefore less desirable. Natasha was beautiful and charming. They didn't need MDs to know how to be proud of her.

Sometimes, while struggling to earn average marks, Natasha thought herself the only person in Volchansk who understood and envied Sonja for the wonder she was. Her existence was so narrow, her energies so focused, she lived like a nail driving through the surface of daily routines and disappointments. When, in May 1989, Natasha needed to receive a three on her final chemistry exam to graduate from secondary school, she forced herself to ask Sonja for help. They sat at the kitchen table. Sonja opened the textbook and frowned at the landscape of unhighlighted text. She didn't comment, didn't put her sister down in any way, but simply said, 'Let's start at page one.' Natasha would always remember that.

She passed the exam, but she wasn't admitted to a single university in Chechnya – probably because she didn't apply. She wasn't stupid, not even academically – she received top marks in history class, and at that point knew more English than Sonja – but after nineteen years living next to the searchlight of her sister's intellect, Natasha felt ready to point her own little torch in a different direction. Instead of a university acceptance letter, she received a secretarial position at the Volchansk office of Grozneft, the Chechen branch of the Soviet Oil and Gas Ministry, working for a leering, bloated man who assured her that fifteen typed words per minute was more than sufficient. Natasha kept the nails of her index fingers filed a half-centimetre shorter than the others, and from eight in the morning to five at night she punched out reports on a black-ribboned typewriter. She worked in an office painted the colour of cloud cover, but even in the ministry's sombre shades, she felt all the exhilaration and uncertainty of the restructuring world. The Berlin Wall collapsed and soon the Soviet Union began to follow. Autonomous republics fell like pebbles from a crushed boulder. Anaesthetically dull oil reports suddenly pulsed with significance. Chechen fields produced a relatively modest thirteen million barrels per year, but most of the region's oil ran through the republic's refineries. Ninety per cent of Soviet aviation fuel was refined in Chechnya, along with much of the automotive-grade petroleum. With short-sightedness typical of a country whose first step in building an economy was to kill all the economists, the USSR had built its energy production infrastructure on the far side of Russia's borders. When Azerbaijan declared independence, Moscow lost its oil-drilling-equipment assembly. When Kazakhstan and Turkmenistan left, they took extensive oil and natural-gas reserves. The sunken treasure of the Caspian could have lit Moscow for a thousand years, and that too was lost. In the urgent memos crossing her desk, Natasha read estimates of the Caucasus' total recoverable reserves that varied between twenty-five and a hundred billion barrels, the majority of which resided in the newly independent states, and the only available pipeline to convey Caspian oil from Baku to European markets ran straight through Chechnya. Then, a miracle. She began to enjoy her work. She read records of pipeline efficiency, the crude production rates, reducing the aggregate data into easily digested summaries, and, like an oracle that envisions but cannot intervene, she saw the prosperity of an independent Chechnya.

The ministry offices were housed in a six-storey building bordering City Park, and each evening, on her way home, she passed a homeless man whose wispy beard reached his belt line. The man, a resident of the park, was known to most of Volchansk as the City Park Prophet. She gave him a few rubles each evening, and asked, half in jest, that he remember her poor tired feet in his prayers. The City Park Prophet's eyes would lower in gratitude, and he would promise to remember her when the end came.

She spent her Fridays at a nightclub called Nightclub, situated in what had been an aviation assembly plant. The floor spread across the eight-storey hangar, wide enough to contain the gyrations of half of Chechnya. Nightclub never had reached, and never would reach, capacity. After downing drinks at the bar, Natasha and her friends shimmied their way to the centre of the hangar. There, red velvet ropes created a ten-square-metre dance floor where the young, well-dressed and secular could press against each other, shrieking and shaking in epileptic spasms of floodlight, freedom found in the ruins of empire. Natasha lost all elegance when dancing. Her heels hindered movement, but she couldn't take them off – no matter how often it was swept, loose bolts and rust-resistant rivets appeared on the floor, gently throbbing with the bass – so she listed. The majority of her dance moves consisted of attempts to stay upright. And one Friday night, in March 1991, with her hair, heels and three-shot tilt no different from the previous dozen Fridays, she wobbled into Sulim's arms.

His 1990 black BMW convertible had been stolen in Belgium and driven across all of a European winter to reach him. He had three missing teeth – and one so black it was clearly on the way out – because for all his money, he still couldn't afford a decent dentist. He had the habit of raising his voice at the ends of his sentences, turning declarations into questions, as though when he whispered her name he wasn't really sure to whom he was talking. He had a bed the size of Natasha's bedroom, two Soviet pistols, his great-great-grandfather's *kinzhal* still brown with the blood of imperial infantrymen, a short beard that never grew, eleven toes, and a long white curve of scar tissue on his pelvis that, in the seven months they saw each other, Natasha learned to desire and despise in equal measure. He had a cousin in the upper air of the *obshchina*, the Chechen mob. The cousin, educated at the London School of Economics, a man whose occupation reduced his life expectancy to that of a gulag labourer, had taught Sulim to open new markets with a crowbar. Their first month together was perhaps the happiest of Natasha's life. The following six perhaps the most miserable.

The cancer in her mother's liver metastasised and she spent the last ten weeks of her life in the chlorinated air of Hospital No. 6. Through Sonja's connections, her father was allowed to spend the nights on the floor beside her bed, cocooned in his olive Red Army sleeping bag. Natasha gave

Sulim a key to the flat. She fitted her fingers in the furrows between his ribs, thought of them as rungs. The whole world was falling, but here was someone strong enough to hold on to. The two men with whom she'd been intimate previously had treated her like a slight, fragile thing, as if trying to fuck a Grecian urn. Sulim held her as if unafraid of crushing her kidneys. In her shoulders, he left perfect moulds of his imperfect teeth that would turn red in the morning. He asked her to scratch him and her longer nails drew a tiger's coat on his back. Her body by itself seemed a beautiful but useless instrument. Sulim's grip on her wrists, his canines gnawing at her clavicle, this pressure in her chest, this flushed flesh.

But Sulim never stayed until morning. At 2 a.m., he began to yawn. He stood and ran his fingers across his stomach, pinching the skin. He had more money hidden in his mattress than the entire apartment block had in the bank, yet he had the waistline of a pauper. His navel had stretched to the shape of an almond. The waxen light of the corner lamp wrapped around his chest as he turned. His spine curved into a thin ridge when he reached for his socks, and she counted the rises of vertebrae. He wore wide-collared Hawaiian shirts. He fumbled with the spare button, slightly too big for his trousers' buttonhole. At times it felt like trying to build a meaningful relationship with a tooth fairy. He came at night, leaving behind presents, but always left by two. By the second month, he was leaving at one thirty. Then one. He shrugged when she demanded to know why he hadn't introduced her to his family, why he didn't dance with her at Nightclub, why he dressed her as a mistress rather than a partner. 'Because that's what you are,' he said, and walked out the door.

The state police arrested him in November 1991 for fraud.

An informer had linked him to the notorious *vosdushniki* – 'air men', they were called, for their ability to draw billions of rubles from the air. Using falsified promissory notes, they authenticated bank transfers from an invented company in Chechnya to an invented company in Moscow. Enough paperwork went through for the *obshchina* men to withdraw the forged transfer in cash from Moscow banks. A bribe from Sulim's cousin released him from custody within two days, but the government still had enough thump in its baton to force him into hiding. He arrived at Natasha's flat at five in the afternoon. The living-room curtains were drawn open and the smog-filtered sunset bathed his cheeks in ochre. She had never before seen him in natural light. In his left hand he held a blue nylon duffel bag. He explained the situation, drained of the swagger that had so entranced and infuriated her. He couldn't stay with family or friends, no one with whom he had a known relationship. He would stay here with her. She'd never seen him so in need. For the first time in their relationship, she realised that she had more power than him, and this was all she needed to let him go. He kept glancing to his feet. She would miss his eleventh toe. 'I'm sorry,' she said. 'You need to leave.'

Her mother passed a few weeks later. Natasha was at work, her sister at medical school, her father at the dessert counter in the hospital cafeteria. No one was there to see what the dying woman saw, in her final moments, when her uncle, the man who had disappeared when she was no more than twelve centimetres of fetal tissue in her mother's belly, emerged from the yellow wallpaper and led her the rest of the way. Ten days after the funeral, Natasha's father took a lorry job in Turkmenistan. On the morning he left, he wore a red sweater with golden diamonds woven across the chest. He had never filled it out, as her mother had predicted he

188

would when she had given it to him five Christmases earlier. He would be wearing that sweater two and a half years later, just north of the border, when a stolen cement mixing truck would slam into his lorry cabin, cutting short his life, his final haul and his five-week odyssey to return home to his girls.

Natasha went to work but couldn't pay attention to the reports she copied, collated and conveyed. She lost her job soon after the declaration of national independence, when all essential oil ministry personnel were transferred to Moscow, her bloated boss included. She drifted, a kelp rope on the tide that washed away her country, family and future. She made dinner one night, Sonja the next. Having graduated from university at the top of her class, Sonja was now in her third year of medical school. She studied while they ate, paying more attention to diseases of the digestive system than to her dinner. Natasha tried to construct conversation with scraps of the day: *Did you see the car accident on Lenin Square? What classes did you have today?* But Sonja didn't believe in small talk and answered in monosyllables, a fact Natasha would remember when, sitting at the same table four and three-quarter years later, Sonja tried to convince her of its therapeutic qualities.

In the six months she lived without Sulim, without her mother or father, only one dinner was shot through with enough excitement to make her forget the awful cooking. Just before they were to eat, Sonja returned from the mailbox with a brown Manila envelope riddled with international postage, and flung her arms around Natasha, panting and screaming joyous gibberish, with more life in her face than Natasha had thought possible. 'London,' Sonja finally said, and the word would remain with Natasha, its six letters stretching to accommodate every conceivable hope. 'I've been given a full fellowship to finish medical school in London.'

Natasha tried to smile, tried to pretend her tears were of joy rather than dread, but when Sonja threw her arms around her, when they embraced, Natasha held her sister tightly, so scared of letting her go.

Though Natasha had learned to sleep through the screech of tyres, the curses, the celebratory gunfire, the explosions, the cries, the laughing, the whole hell of the street below, she stayed awake that night and watched speeding tail lights stretch into crimson bars across the asphalt. The young men leaning on the bonnets of European cars were gangsters and mercenaries and gamblers. They made dangerous bets with safe foreign currencies, laying on the dash the annual wages men of their education would earn in a lawful society. Some nights they tried to jump the decapitated Lenin statue in the square. That night was a simple drag race. Four cars looped through the city centre along a course marked by waste-bin fires. Reports of aerial bombing in Grozny had filtered in, leaving the city flushed and agitated. In the morning, she would take the bus to Grozny to meet Lidiya Nikitova, a shuttle trader who flew through Tbilisi to Hamburg once a week and returned with suitcases packed with Western electronics and clothing. Natasha would fill two duffel bags with clothes, but also Walkmen, Game Boys, satellite phones, portable televisions and the increasingly popular noise-cancelling headphones to sell in the city bazaar. The Feds blocked the border, the airport looked like another shuttered factory along the Baku-Rostov motorway, yet the bazaar was flush with Japanese electronics, Burmese silk, Belgian chocolate, Brazilian spirits, Indian spices and American currency. Only three cars came past on the next lap. She breathed against the glass of her bedroom window, summoning from the fog a smiling, finger-drawn face. It was November 1994. She hadn't seen her sister in more than two and a half years. She hadn't seen her father in more than three. She wondered if it would snow.

News came third-, fourth-, fifth-hand. Fact was indistinguishable from hearsay, so all was believed and all was disbelieved and all were right. *Grab as much sovereignty as you can swallow,* Yeltsin had urged, and Chechnya had opened its mouth. The president was still named Dzhokhar Dudayev, and he still had a fountain pen-drawn moustache. He was the first Chechen to make general rank in the Red Army and ten years earlier he had served in Afghanistan, where Russian bombs had fallen on Muslim civilians for neither the first nor final time. In bed Natasha listened to his radio address, his voice a lullaby compared to the screech of car tyres. The fantastical marked his presidency. The government needed money, and so, after minting its own currency, Estonia sent its entire reserve of Soviet rubles to Grozny rather than to Moscow. The government needed an army, and, the previous year, when the Feds had abandoned their Chechen bases, they had left behind stockpiles of heavy artillery, ammunition, guns, armoured jeeps, and more tanks than there were licensed Chechen tank drivers. She set the radio beside her pillow. The drag race had finished. She lowered the volume and rolled towards the black mesh speaker, imagining the voice of revolution to be the whispers of a friend talking her to sleep.

The rumours proved true; in Grozny, bombs fell. On the weekly trips to the capital, she paid attention to the crowds. The density of pavement debris ensured they only lifted their eyes at the murmur of planes. The traffic lights went out and policemen, still wearing the blue uniforms of Soviet road police, directed traffic with the tips of their cigarettes.

She stood in a clogged avenue and scanned the skies. Only once did she see them fly over. Five planes in tight formation. She craned her neck while all down the avenue commuters left their car doors open as they fled. Five parallel lines of exhaust striped the empty sky. Kilometres above, men who didn't know her name wanted to kill her. A man in a bright purple suit grabbed her shoulder, shaking her, and asking if she was deaf or stupid or both. Following him down the line of abandoned vehicles, she pushed the driver doors closed, and in this simple act restored order to the world. He took her to the basement of a party supply store. They sat on sacks of inflatable plastic balloons. The man kicked over a box and whoopee cushions, Slinkies and glasses with fake noses toppled out. 'I can't believe I'm going to die somewhere so stupid,' the man said, and began weeping. She asked how he knew this place. The man held on to his purple lapels. 'This suit,' he said, 'I'm returning this stupid suit.' He was thirteen years into what would be a forty-eight-year career as a clown; he had an IQ of 167.

When the bombing stopped, she left the sobbing purple-suited man and went to Lidiya Nikitova's apartment. She found Lidiya packing a suitcase on the unmade bed. Natasha expected to find it filled with Prada handbags, Gucci blouses, Ferragamo neckties, but instead found coarse woollen sweaters, baggy sweatpants, grey socks, a photo album. For ten minutes Lidiya shook her head in despair. Natasha worried the poor woman's head would fall off. 'Chechens have family,' Lidiya said, as she pulled out a pair of boots buried beneath a mound of toeless shoes. 'They have their *teips* and their ancestral homes in the highlands to flee to. The barbarians. It's nearly the millennium and they still live in clans. Even now, in the middle of all this, they don't believe orphans or vagrants can ever exist because the *teip* will provide. The barbarians. What do we ethnic Russians have? No *teip*. Our countrymen are dropping bombs on us. No, back north for me. I've never been to Petersburg, but my cousin says it's much more civilised.' After Lidiya Nikitova left, Natasha spent an hour browsing her apartment. She took a pair of high-heeled leather boots, cashmere sweaters and silk evening gowns. She wouldn't have an opportunity to wear them, but beautiful things were so rare it seemed wrong to leave them behind.

Time no longer marched forward. The giant clocks hanging from office buildings began to confuse the minutes for the hours. They displayed June dates in November, August weather forecasts in December. Dudayev changed the national clock in an independence declaration from the imperium of Moscow time. His supporters set their watches an hour back, everyone else remained in the standard zone, and no one knew what time it was. At first, Natasha ate at pre-planned points in her day to maintain the illusion of structured time, then only when she was hungry, then only when she had food. The phone lines trembled with static. The debilitated independence government promised at least five hours of daily electricity, but the five hours usually came in the middle of the night. The crumbling infrastructure turned time back further than any presidential mandate. When had you last lived a day with the starting bell of your alarm clock? With breakfast *djepelgesh*? With news from Moscow and New York and Beijing beamed on the back of television waves? With the heat of that first cigarette in your throat and the Route 7 bus turning the corner, unfailingly three minutes behind schedule, just like you? With truant children hitting construction crews with snowballs, and the steam curling from the Main Department Store corner, filling your skirt, a convection tingling your thighs?

With morning drunks, lining the pavements of City Park, switching from alcohol to mouthwash? With a mid-morning coffee break, sipping Nescafé that has probably a dozen actual beans per kilo, huddling within the yellow fluorescent wash of a toilet stall, the only place you can be alone? With lunch? With a pause taken from work for the length of an afternoon cigarette? With the soft pinging of five thirty street lamps, coming to life as you pass, and the City Park Prophet waiting for you, his beard tucked into his trousers, his hand outstretched and humble, and you with ten rubles to press into his palm? With a home to come home to? With electricity in the wiring as you flick the lights, and heat humming from the radiators, and water in the tap, showerhead and toilet cistern, and voices saying *hello* and *how was your day* and *shut the fucking door it's freezing out there*, and you hearing them in your ears rather than your head, they who know your name? With a meal that is actually that, a meal, with family, both of which sustain in ways you will only understand in their absence? With soapsuds coating your forearms, the bubbles blinking out against your fingertips and rinsing away as you pass the plate for your sister to dry? With evening television, your parents on the divan, and you've never seen them hold hands, but they kick off their slippers, and on the floor their little toes touch? With your father's snores turning the hall into an echo chamber you walk through to reach the bathroom, warm enough you don't think of wrapping yourself in a blanket when you get out of bed? With toothpaste? With your sister's pencil scratches coming through the shadow-thin plaster walls, the mumble of rote memorisation, her nightly prayers to a god you neither know nor comprehend? With your belief that no matter how badly you fuck up, you will always belong to these people, and that they will never let you disappear?

She went to Sonja's bookshelf. Extra brackets supported the heavy textbooks, and her index finger brushed past the spines of books too heavy to hold in one hand. How had civilisation survived long enough to accumulate the knowledge contained in these books? The slimmer volumes stood on the upper shelf, a yellowed Red Army field manual the most useful of the bunch. Scanning the shelf, she recalled how Sonja always read the last page of a book first, how her sister had to know what would happen, where the story led, to see if it was worth the effort. She didn't open the torrid romance novels at the end of the shelf. The worn bindings had an intimacy absent from the rest. She imagined Sonja lying in bed, reading melodrama with an ache in her chest she couldn't quantify or explicate, and thus couldn't understand. Instead, she took a slender volume entitled *Origins of Chechen Civilisation: Prehistory to the Fall of the Mongol Empire* by Khassan Geshilov.

She read by the slow burn of candlelight. Folklore said God had scattered ethnicities across the earth with a salt shaker; the shaker had slipped from His fingers when He reached the Caucasus, and a few grains of every nation had landed in its valleys. Other origin theories: the Chechens had descended from Scythian hordes, from the daughters of Genghis Khan, from a penal colony established by Alexander the Great, from a lost Roman legion. After finishing the first chapter, she flipped to the dust jacket. According to the three-sentence biography, Khassan Geshilov taught at Volchansk State University and lived in Eldár. This book was the first of a proposed multi-volume history of the Chechen lands. In his photo he had clear brown eyes, a thick moustache silvered with grey hair, and a smile suggesting he was thinking of a flaky pastry or a woman's smooth calves rather than ancient hordes. Until the candle died, she read of ancient invasions: the Scythians in 850 BC, the Greeks two centuries later, the Romans in the first century BC, the Baltic Goths in AD 240, the Asian Huns in AD 370, the Avars, Khazars, Circassians, Mongols and finally, ultimately, the Russians.

Without electricity or gas, the kitchen became a twilight mausoleum of dead appliances. One day, Natasha had an idea. Wearing latex gloves she found in Sonja's room, she scrubbed the innards of the oven and fridge with steel wool and bleach. She cut a broomstick to the width of the fridge compartment, jammed it in below the thermostat control, and pulled out the plastic shelves. In her bedroom, she gathered clothes from the floor in sweeping armfuls and deposited them before the fridge and the oven. Ever since she had begun working for the shuttle trader, her wardrobe exceeded her cupboard space. She hung silk evening dresses and cashmere sweaters on the broomstick bar, set folded jeans and blouses on the oven rack. When finished, she opened the doors to her new cupboard and chest of drawers and felt pleased with her ingenuity. This is how you will survive, she told herself. You will turn the holes in your life into storage space.

Smoke turned the days into twelve-hour twilights. In the afternoons, when the chance of aerial bombing was the greatest, she wandered through the suburbs. She thought of her sister often. In their weekly conversations, Sonja described her boyfriend, Brendan, a Slavic Studies PhD candidate from Scotland, whose Russian was worse than Sonja's English. She described the international dormitory, which housed students from thirty-four different countries, none of whom tried to kill each other. She described pubs and monuments, black taxis that looked like bowler hats on wheels, a massive obelisk supporting the statue of a tiny man in Trafalgar

Square, Buckingham Palace guards who wouldn't shoot her even if she openly mocked them, supermarkets with entire aisles devoted to breakfast cereal and salespeople who actually seemed pleased by the presence of customers. That first year, for the first time, the sisters had become friends. We are all the other has, Natasha had thought, but she knew Sonja had so much more. Sonja promised to find a way to bring her to London, promised to plead her case with the university, the Home Office, the goddamn Queen, but nothing came of it, and Natasha wanted to flee but couldn't, didn't know how to, had heard horror stories of what happened to lone women refugees, and so their conversations grew shorter as civil society disintegrated. Teenagers with stolen firearms replaced policemen on the streets. Hand grenades cost less than jars of Nescafé at the bazaar. She didn't want to hear about the scones, and decided Sonja didn't want to feel guilty for eating them.

Days passed without speaking, then weeks. The telephone lines went weak from electrical shortages, but the central telecommunications exchange hadn't been hit. Natasha left the phone off the hook for days and the soft throb of the dialing tone became the voice of stability in her solitude. When she wanted to speak to her sister, she went to the bookshelf instead. She read *Origins of Chechen Civilisation* twice in one month, focusing on the last pages of each chapter, where the ancient invasions ended. After she wrung from Khassan Geshilov's words all the consolation she could, she returned the book to the top shelf, beside the romance novels, and kneeling on the floor, tugged at the largest reference book. A massive thing, a dining-room table's worth of pulped wood. *The Medical Dictionary of the Union of Soviet Physicians.* She rested the book on her thighs and its weight soon put her legs to sleep. The four thousand eight hundred and eighty-four translucent pages held the most arcane and useless information. The names of buried blood vessels in Latin, Russian and the official languages of the fourteen Soviet republics. The weight ranges of internal organs: 117 to 170 grams per kidney, 1.4 to 1.6 kilograms for a liver, 250 to 350 grams for a heart. She flipped through the book and found answers to questions no sane person would ever ask. The definition of a foot. The average length of a femur. Nothing for *insanity by grief*, or *insanity by loneliness*, or *insanity by reading reference books*. What inoculation could the eight-point font provide for the whisper of Sukhois in the sky? Based on the average life expectancy of a Soviet woman, she could expect to live for another forty-eight years, but the Soviet Union had died, and she hadn't, and the appendices couldn't explain this discrepancy in data, when the subject outlasted its experiment. Only one entry supplied an adequate definition, and she circled it with red ink, and referred to it nightly. *Life: a constellation of vital phenomena — organisation, irritability, movement, growth, reproduction, adaptation.*

If she stood on the stool in the south-western kitchen corner and pointed the radio antenna due south, she could occasionally pick up Russian-language news broadcasts from Nazran or Tbilisi. From there, she gleaned what information she could from the outside world. Porous enough to allow luxury cars, American cigarettes and Russian firearms, the borders remained too dense for objective journalism. A Georgian accent raised the newscaster's Russian by half an octave and from that lilting, disembodied tenor she learned that Yeltsin had an eight per cent approval rating and an election eighteen months away. The Communist Party of the Russian Federation, the primary opposition party, denounced him for losing the vast territories of the former

Soviet Union. She understood precisely that this wounded pride would lead to punishment, would lead a crippled country to start a war to prove itself more powerful. On 9 December 1994, Yeltsin issued a statement ordering the Federal army to execute the disarmament of *all illegal armed units* in Chechnya, or, as they were known locally, *the government*. On 10 December 1994, he went to a hospital for a nose operation. On 11 December 1994, upon hearing reports that the first of the forty thousand troops amassed at the northern border had crossed the Terek River, she realised that the war had only just begun.

On the evening of 11 December 1994, when Natasha returned the receiver to its cradle, and the ringer burst into a tinny tremble, she let it ring for twenty seconds before lifting the receiver to her ear. 'Hello,' she said. 'Finally, finally, finally,' Sonja cried. 'I've been calling you for days, weeks, all afternoon.'

Chapter 13

'I DON'T KNOW,' AKHMED SAID SOFTLY. HE watched her with such compassion it seemed he had forgotten the gun against his back. 'I didn't ask,' he said.

'You didn't ask? How could you not ask? How could you not ask her name?'

'Hundreds of refugees stayed at Dokka's house. I stopped asking their names.'

'Where was she going? Didn't she say? She must have said something. Some hint or reference or mention. She must have said something. She must have. How could you not ask? How could you?'

'I didn't think I'd be asked to remember.'

Her entire reflection fitted in his widened eyes. Had Natasha's reflection once fitted in his pupils? Drawn by light? Disappeared by a blink? 'What did she look like?' she asked.

Akhmed could have filled a dozen lungs with that sigh. 'Dark-haired and malnourished,' he said.

The description would fit half the world. 'Her eyes, what colour?'

'Brown.'

'But brown with shards of green and emerald? More hazel than brown?'

'Maybe. I can't remember.'

'And her face?'

'She reminded me of Zakharov's portrait of the niece of Nicolas I.'

'Nicolas I? What are you talking about? I need to know what happened. Where is she?' She felt nauseous. She had to know but he would not tell her. What had happened to her sister? When she died, this one need, so near to eternal it could be her soul, would survive her. 'I need to know, I need to know,' she repeated. 'She was beautiful, wasn't she?'

'As beautiful as the Nicolas's niece, yes,' Akhmed said. 'She was probably heading for the refugee camps. They all were. Probably Ingushetia. Maybe the Sputnik or the Karabulak camp?'

He spoke, it seemed, as if he had been speaking to her for years, as if she was expected to follow the arcs of his cadence, landing on the full stop before he reached it. She was afraid to look down. 'She was wearing traditional maternity clothes,' he was saying. 'And a green headdress.'

'Where is she?'

Her hands tightened on his shoulders. She didn't remember putting them there. The loose handcuffs of his fingers raised them and held them and slowly placed them by her sides. She would remember this; with a gun to his back he was gentle. 'I don't know,' he said.

Far away Alu's brother nodded and the guard stepped back. 'Our friend may be a terrible doctor,' Alu's brother said, 'but I don't think he's informing.'

They walked to the supply crates shoulder-to-shoulder to avoid seeing each other. Akhmed helped her load the cardboard boxes into the truck and later she would remember him mopping his forehead with a grey handkerchief, asking if she needed help with a box of surgical saw blades, his poise as unsettling as any ruin she had seen that day.

As children Sonja and Natasha played hide-and-seek in the dust-thick catacombs of the apartment cellar. Light streamed through the high windows in long diagonals. On the floor each semicircle was a pool of lava, and light-caught dust motes were the remains of children who had stumbled into those incandescent rays. Natasha would drape a filthy curtain over Sonja and Sonja would count to fifty and the beat between each number would shrink as she neared that moment when she shouted 'Fifty!' and sprang from the curtain and into that other-worldly place. Natasha was slender enough to hide behind a broomstick, but Sonja always found her. She always did.

'Who is she?' Akhmed asked as the warehouse shrank in the rear-view. Ten minutes earlier she had told him they would stop at a pay phone and had said nothing else until she was behind the wheel and facing the mud-streaked windscreen.

'My sister,' she said.

'I'm sorry,' he said.

Nothing could have made her feel worse.

'I'm the one who should be apologising,' she said to the gravel.

'Why does he help you?'

'Just after the first war I fixed up his brother Alu.'

'And he still supplies the hospital?'

She nodded.

'He must cherish his brother.'

She smiled. Poor, berated Alu, whose name was beaten more than a donkey's arse. Six months after they first met she had learned his brother's name was Ruslan, but she would always think of him as Alu's brother. She knew he had amassed a small fortune smuggling arms, heroin and luxury goods for warlords, and had used that small fortune to rebuild his ancestral village after the first war. She knew his pet turtle was still alive, still named Alu, and housed now in the largest terrarium in the northern Caucasus. When his ancestral village was destroyed again in the second war, she knew he had paid passage to Georgia for his parents, brothers, aunts, uncles, cousins, in-laws, thirty-seven in total, even the oft-cursed Alu, plus the neighbours on either side of every uncle, cousin and in-law, one hundred and seventy-four in total, where they lived in the Tbilisi apartment block he had purchased for the occasion, neighbour by neighbour, his ancestral village saved for a second and final time. She knew all this of him and more, but still didn't know why he didn't like Alu. 'You may be right,' she said, finally. 'I think he just might cherish Alu above all.'

The ruins opened onto what was once a central square filled with importunate street vendors, veiled mothers and squirming toddlers. Pigeons missing eyes and wings hobbled on the granite stone like portents of a war still years away. There had been the statue of a Chechen, an Ingush and a Russian poised in comradely unity, officially called 'The Brotherhood of the People', but known locally as 'The Three Idiots'. Someone had dumped a few goldfish into the fountain and they had multiplied until the water thickened to a squirming orange mass. Rockets had demolished the five-storey buildings that had floated on arcades of equilateral arches, the tree-lined pedestrian paths, the wooden benches dedicated to Party bosses, the fountain where in winter children ice-skated over the suspended carcasses of two thousand goldfish. The ruins had been bulldozed to an uneven field of rock. She parked the car. Akhmed frowned. 'I don't see any telephones,' he said.

'We'll stop on our way back,' she said. They climbed out. 'You said you've always wanted to go to Grozny, so I wanted to show you the central square.' She didn't look at him. It was the nearest to reconciliation she was able to go.

He smiled, nodded, held his hands behind his back. She exhaled. 'Is that what this is?' he asked.

She shielded her eyes with a salute to the afternoon sun. 'Right there, where the ground is blackened, just to the left of that cloud, that's where the Presidential Palace stood.' Rotating in a slow circle, her index finger pressed the past into the empty panorama. The market selling Levi's two decades before any licensed clothing shop. The music college, where some years earlier a prodigy had learned to play the viola by listening to the two-hundred-year history of chamber music lilting through those open windows. She reconstructed the square for Akhmed – her voice raised every edifice from the dust, replanted every linden tree – because that was easier than apology.

'Thank you. I've always wanted to see Grozny.'

They passed through two more checkpoints before reaching a clean, freshly paved street. The anomaly of unmarked asphalt never failed to surprise her. A grey stone building filled most of the block. The sheet-glass windows, intact and absent of fractures, proclaimed the building's significance more eloquently than the Petroleum Ministry sign hanging over the entrance. Armed soldiers stood at ten-metre intervals along the perimeters, as tall and broad as door frames.

'I'm not going in there,' Akhmed said, arms folded, refusing to leave the truck.

'Don't worry. All the letters in the glovebox wouldn't get

us in. We're going over there,' she said, pointing down the block to what had been a shopping centre. 'The Petroleum Ministry has working international lines. Some clever entrepreneur tapped the outbound line and set up some phones in the basement.'

The shopping centre was a cave of broken shopfronts, empty shelves and stalagmitic glass. Even the plastic flowers had been looted from the planters. She led the way by her cigarette lighter.

'In London this would be an escalator,' Sonja said as they descended a staircase.

'What's an escalator?'

'It's a moving staircase.'

'Like a children's ride?'

'No, it's not a ride. It's just a staircase that moves. That's all.'

'Then this is a broken escalator.' In three years that staircase would become the first escalator in Chechnya. On weekends families from as far away as Lake Kezanoiam would bring their children to play on it.

She descended on the right side; even in a choice as arbitrary as which side to walk on she strove for order. At a brown door at the end of the basement corridor she knocked to the beat of an Umar Dimayev song. The deaf boy opened the door, and the blind man, his father, stood just behind him. Two spoonfuls were missing from his face.

'It's Sonja,' she said. The blind man reached for his son, who tugged his left index finger in confirmation, then, looking at Akhmed, tugged the blind man's right middle finger.

'Yes, I've brought a friend. His name is Akhmed.'

The blind man nodded to his son and reached for Akhmed's face. The first time the blind man had touched

Sonja's cheeks she had known by his fingers that he would have made a great surgeon. 'Don't make a face,' she said, as the blind man parted Akhmed's beard. 'You don't want to be remembered as a sourpuss.'

Light bulbs dangled from a brown electrical cord held by rusty staples to the ceiling. Somewhere a generator was humming. Card tables with dial telephones sat evenly across the room. The whispers of five callers overlapped. She gave the deaf boy three hundred rubles and stepped over the plaited wires to her telephone.

'City University Slavic Department,' said the voice on the other end once she dialled.

'Good morning, Janice. It is Sonja. May I speak to Brendan?' Wrapped in the formality of proper English, her request sounded insincere to her.

'Hang on a mo, Sonja. He just left his office, but I'll see if I can't fetch him.'

In the static hold she saw his chest, pale as a tadpole; she could have stood him before a bright light and seen his organs. Eights years on and he would have filled out, perhaps a paunch to accompany his promotion to Assistant Department Director, perhaps even a tanning salon gift token. When she backed out of the engagement he had spent three days on hold with the airlines and paid for part of the ticket when the cheapest, most circuitous route exceeded her savings. Going through her medicine cabinet, he had made a list of her favourite toiletries and purchased a half-dozen of every tube, bottle and canister for her to take home. She said she would come back. He said she would come back. The morning she left he wheeled the Samsonite, another parting gift, to the kerb outside the international student dormitory, and sat beside her in the taxi, a cool perspiration on his palm, the city gliding past. When she said, half jokingly, as they reached the Heathrow turn-off, that he must be glad to be rid of her, because why else had he made it so easy for her to go, he buried his face in the crook of her shoulder and twelve hours later, in a lavatory twenty-five thousand feet over Ukrainian wheat fields, she found a streak of his hardened mucus and for a moment mistook it for her first grey hair.

'Sonja?' Janice said. 'Brendan's left for a meeting. Can I take a message?'

They hadn't spoken since the previous month. He had contacts at Memorial and the Red Cross and if Natasha's name were to be typed into a computer he would know of it. Usually the moments before the call went through were honed with the hope that this month, this time, he would have an answer. But today was different. Today she just wanted him to know she was still alive. 'Just tell him I called.'

'And you spell your name with a *j*, yeah?'

She had asked him about it once, on their third or fourth coffee after classes. She wanted to know why Raskolnikov's love was transliterated as Sonia or Sonya but never Sonja. 'Because that's how you spell it in English,' Brendan had said. 'Only Swedes spell it with a *j*.' 'Swedes are foreigners, too,' she said, and held that *j* as the one letter in her name that was hers.

'Oh, and Sonja?' Janice said. 'Is there a number where he can call you back?'

'How do the Swedes spell Natasha?' she had asked, but Brendan didn't know.

Chapter 14

THE WINTER BRENDAN AND SONJA FELL IN LOVE, all of Volchansk became homeless; even those like Natasha, whose homes hadn't been hit, found the cold easier to sleep through than the fear of falling rubble. She spent the winter in City Park, a twelve-square-block refuge of brown grass and barren trees, designed, it was said, by the dim-witted fourth cousin of Boris Iofan, where the tallest man-made edifice was a corroded jungle gym. The homeless, insane and alcoholic reigned in this world. Trained and experienced in the art of surviving a winter outdoors, the city pariahs were inundated by professors and lawyers and accountants whose degrees were worth the five seconds of warmth they could fuel. Natasha and her cohort took direction from the City Park Prophet. The great bib of gnarled hair, now reaching mid-thigh, shook indignantly when he reminded them of his prophecy. No one had listened when he predicted the fast-coming day when the sky would split open and God would fall upon the indecencies of man. Natasha remembered passing the madman each evening as she returned from the oil ministry, and he remembered the coins she had given him. 'I told you I would remember you,' he said when she first moved into the park; soon she realised that all of the City Park Prophet's flock had been daily alms-givers the Prophet now felt obligated to protect. He taught them to camouflage their tents and to scavenge for pine cones buried in the frost; to hunt feral dogs with cudgels and bait pigeon traps with the viscera; to pray five times a day and perform the proper ablutions, and Natasha, who had never stepped in a church, let alone a mosque, praised Allah because she knew better than to challenge a man who spent his life preparing for the apocalypse. In fourteen years those accountants and lawyers would collectively purchase for the City Park Prophet a studio apartment in a newly rebuilt apartment block. They would search for Natasha, hoping she would contribute to the considerable down payment or at least be there when they led the Prophet into his new home, but the combined brainpower of six lawyers, three accountants and eight PhDs couldn't solve the mystery of the former secretary's whereabouts.

By spring, when the Feds took the city, the bombing ceased and the siege settled into occupation. The City Park refugees dispersed to ancestral villages and *auls* scattered throughout the highlands, where they could count on the hospitality of distant family and clan. But Natasha had no family left. Her apartment block still stood, now the tallest building on the street. The windows had blown out but the bathroom mirror was still intact. She hadn't seen herself in months. Her options dwindled to subsistence and scavenging. Her reflection said she wouldn't last long in a city of drunken, vengeful, sex-starved soldiers. But avenues of escape still existed for women who could make themselves attractive without the benefit of running water.

Against the ringing of her last two kopeks of common

sense, she found Sulim. He lived in the open now, in business with both Feds and rebels, and occasionally with the smuggler Sonja would later know as Alu's brother. They met in a bar that served nothing. No door, no alcohol, no employees, no windows, but the regulars still returned each afternoon. Their lips were blue from drinking windscreen wiper fluid.

In comparison to them, Sulim looked well. His eyes, unclouded by exhaustion, scanned her approvingly. The Parkinson's that would turn him into a quivering jelly mould in eleven years was already fermenting in his midbrain, but his hands didn't shake when he went to light his cigarette. War served him well. From mountain hideaways Dudayev's economic and police chiefs issued statements praising an economy and a police force that no longer existed, and in the vacuum of legitimate authority, organised crime provided the only meaningful order. He offered her a cigarette.

'You want to get out,' he said. 'Who doesn't?'

'I can do well in the West.'

'Anyone can do well when they aren't dodging bullets.' He scanned the ghost drinkers; those with the bluest lips had gone blind, and they reached out, touching the faces of their drinking partners. Sulim reached into his jacket pocket and pulled out a vodka bottle. 'I don't know how they got it in their heads that we smuggle it in barrels of windscreen wiper fluid.'

'I'll work off the debt.'

'Will you?' he asked.

'You know how hard I worked at Grozneft. I'm productive.'

'Are you?' he asked.

'Please.' He took a small sip from the bottle, savouring it as he watched her. He hadn't forgotten how she had denied him at her door, his skin sallow in the daylight. He crossed his legs, leaned back, waiting for her to beg. 'I know there are trafficking routes,' she said. 'I know you can get me out. Please, Sulim.'

'Under the Soviets, women who disappeared had to reappear on the other side of the world to make money. Now women can turn a profit simply by vanishing. Reappearance has too high an overhead. Chechen families will pay a higher ransom for the body of their daughter than they will for her alive. I've looked at the numbers.'

She stood to leave.

'But you aren't Chechen,' he continued. 'You have no family to pay for your corpse. You have no afterlife for which your body must be prepared. You can have another cigarette.'

He lit it for her with a bent match. She had kissed those knuckles. She had loved them.

'Will you help me or not?'

He was holding her index finger and he nodded it up and down. Crippled by tremors, unable to control his limbs, an embarrassment to his family, he would spend his final years in a windowless room with a television set for companionship. 'You didn't really think I would deny you? Where do you want to go?'

'London.'

'Then in London you will be an au pair. Do you know what that is? It's a French word. It means you will watch the children while the parents are at work.'

'So I will be a grandmother?'

'Yes, something like that.'

'I'm not my sister but I'm not a fool.'

'There may be other things. Dancing, entertaining. Being, what's the word, enticing.'

It meant prostitution. Waitressing, nannying, those were

for pretty girls from poor countries, not pretty girls from war countries. Some repatriated women called it slavery, but even if it was true, so what? Paid sex with London civilians couldn't be worse than forced sex with Russian soldiers. And in London, Sonja would find her other work. Sulim watched her from across the table. His lips twisted into a slight smile, a challenge. Did he think she was afraid of him? Did he think he could possibly scare her?

'London,' she said. 'Make me an au pair. Make me reappear.'

A young man with a soft, round face transported Natasha and five other women to the Dagestan border. They sat on crates in the near-darkness of a Federal supply van. The wind pulled against the olive canvas awning, and occasionally a sliver of sunlight slipped through and was gone. She wanted to ask their names, where they were from, if they, too, were au pairs. Conversation seemed possible a moment after the round-faced man, looking like their younger brother, hoisted them into the truck bed. But the air clotted with doubt too thick for any words to pass.

Some hours later the van shuddered to a standstill and the round-faced man unlatched the back. Natasha shielded her eyes against the bright burn of noon and the light warmed her hands. A smock of dark evergreens wrapped around the nearest mountain. The round-faced man led them a hundred metres down a gravel path to a jeep flying the flag of national independence. Wooden benches replaced the back seats. They crowded in.

The jeep carried them up ravines of dried creek beds, along an unending jawline of pale stone. Conifer cones hung from drooped branches. The landscape appeared on the precipice of collapse. In the glens below, trickles of silvery light wound through empty pastures, glittering ribbons tied off at the horizon. It wasn't fair. She hated the outdoors. A sex worker was one thing, but a weekend hiker? The sun silhouetted wide circling wings. A pigeon, she first thought, grown to fit the monstrous proportions of this habitat.

The round-faced man parked the jeep when the incline became too steep. When she stood straight her hair hung off her shoulders, held back by the invisible hands of gravity. Sick, dizzied, she wanted a patch of asphalt she might sit on and feel whole. *Pretty Woman* wasn't anything like this. The round-faced man began climbing the rock-ridden slope and called for them. No, no, no, she wanted to say, the carabiner in my bag is only a key chain. But what could she do? The top was closer than the bottom. No threat or command, just his finger beckoning, and following it, she left Chechnya.

Dagestan was three unbearable hours of hiking, then another hour by jeep. The nod of the border guard's chin stubble was the only official record of their crossing into Georgia. Time was measured by toilet stops until they reached the water. The Black Sea was blue. They boarded a fishing trawler and the wind swept the scent of salt through her hair. Holiday homes stood like dominoes on the coast, the white dots of lit windows numbering into the hundreds. When the sun fell below the waterline the sea at last went black. She lay on the driest bit of deck she could find, used her duffel bag as a pillow, and fell asleep as the boat rocked on the water.

In Odessa they were divided. Three went with the round-faced man and as they disappeared into a Yugo something small and sharp panged through her; she didn't know their names. She and two others followed the man who had purchased their passports into the back of a delivery van.

The door slammed shut. When it opened they were in Serbia. They stayed with eleven other women in a stone cellar. Manacles looted from the Sarajevo archaeology museum lay coiled on the floor, the implicit threat more constricting than the rusted cuffs. A tin pail tilted in the far corner; when one approached it, the rest turned away. Slurred voices seeped through the damp wooden ceiling. An argument over whether fire hydrants were a good idea. She touched the cheeks, forehead and lips she had once gazed at in the mirror, proudly. Now she wanted scar tissue, missing limbs, cheeks buckshot with acne, teeth pointing every which way.

'What is this?' she asked.

No one spoke.

'Does anyone know where we are?' she asked again.

The girl sitting next to her, who couldn't have been more than fourteen, was the only one who answered. 'The Breaking Grounds.'

Chapter 15

'SHE NEVER TALKED ABOUT HOW IT HAPPENED,'
Sonja said, thirty minutes outside Grozny's outer suburbs,
ten since she had begun telling him. 'How she got to Italy.
If they took her on a plane or in a car or what. She never
even told me who took her there, when she left, how she
survived the first war. Nothing. She probably just didn't want
to think about it, but I always thought it was her way of
punishing me for leaving her.' Akhmed had set the radio to
102.3. She barely knew him and that was the only reason
she told him; he was, himself, static. She couldn't explain
her confession any more than the calm that followed.

'War is unnatural,' Akhmed said. 'It causes people to act
unnaturally.'

'Even you?'

'Of course,' he said. 'I was never this charming.' He
stretched his hands in front of him; brown fields wedged
between his fingers. 'In the first war Dokka began classifying
everything. He was an arborist by training, so he was used
to dividing plants into species and genera and family, and
one day he began doing that with everything else. With

people. Everyone was a pacifist or an imperialist or a fascist or a classicist or any other number of -ists, and anyone who criticised his system was an anarchist.'

'Havaa speaks in more -isms than a philosophy PhD.'

'Yes, she really does take after him. She began making up her own and I remember hearing them discuss moustachism and shearistry and they were so excited. I had no idea what any of it meant. It was like a language they created to speak to each other more fully.' He paused. He was breathing heavily. The flush of his cheeks had seeped to his neck. 'I don't know why I'm telling you this.'

'She plans to be a sea anemonist.'

He laughed. 'I bet. We were friends for years, Dokka and I and Ramzan. Every other Sunday we played chess, Havaa watching. Ramzan was the one who was waiting for me yesterday. The informer. We played chess every other Sunday for over a decade.'

'What happened?'

'Ramzan began running guns for the rebels. He would invite Dokka on his expeditions, pay him well. I never understood why. He didn't need Dokka's help to drive a jeep into the mountains. The same way you thought Natasha was punishing you by her silence, I always thought Ramzan was punishing me with those trips. He never invited me along even though I needed the money as much as Dokka. We were friends, Ramzan and I, but I always felt Ramzan resented me for something I had done. Now I think it's more complicated than that. He was detained in the Landfill in '95, and I think he resents me because I know what happened to him there.

'I was jealous of Dokka. Of his trips to the mountains with Ramzan. Of the money he made. Of his wife. Mine has been bed-bound and senile for nearly three years while

216

his had more vitality, more urgency in her little finger than most men have between their legs. I was jealous of his daughter. We tried for years but . . .' His voice trailed away. Beyond him a single smokestack rose a hundred metres into the sky, no building in sight. 'Dokka was my closest friend and yet I wanted his family, his opportunities, his life. He and Ramzan would go to the mountains for a week or two and I would eat dinner with Esiila and Havaa. I would spend the whole day and night there. On his final trip, in January 2003, I slept in his bed for three nights. Of course I couldn't have known that he and Ramzan had been detained and sent to the Landfill. I couldn't have known that his fingers were snipped off with wire cutters while I was at his house, sleeping with his wife, eating with his daughter, because I thought his life was perfect. Whatever we were to each other was lost then. I'm not sure if Esiila told him or not, but he knew. Never said anything but he knew. I would go over and talk to the refugees staying at his house when I wanted to talk to him. He didn't say a word to me last year when I spoke to the woman who told me your name. If I saw Dokka again, I wouldn't apologise or try to make it right. That isn't what I would say.'

'What would you say?'

Akhmed smiled, shook his head. 'I don't know.'

The shadow of a fresh crater darkened the road. At the bottom an arm reached upward. The rest of the body lay there and there and there. Lavender tatters, caught in an updraught, twisted in a wide ocean of sky. 'We offered her a lift,' Sonja said, meaning *I told her so*, meaning *this isn't my fault.*

Snow sprayed from the tyres, cresting in the rear-view. What would she do if the war ended? Of all the possibilities and permutations she had played out in her mind, peace was never among them. What would she do? The war that turned lieutenants into colonels, and unemployed men into jihadists, also turned house officers into chief surgeons.

'Tolstoy was here two hundred years ago,' Akhmed said. 'There was a war then. He wrote a novel about it.'

'I don't care for fiction.'

'*Hadji Murád* it's called,' he said. 'I'll bring it for you tomorrow.'

'Why aren't you angry at me?' she asked. The question had been burning in her all afternoon.

Akhmed folded his hands, but said nothing.

'I had you interrogated at gunpoint. If you were deceiving me I would have had you shot.'

'If I were deceiving you, I would have been another man.'

'You're a decent man,' she said, and smiled. 'A terrible physician, but a decent man.'

'I know. I shouldn't spend so much time with you. You'll turn me into a first-rate surgeon and boor.'

'I think it's the other way round,' she said. A gauze of afternoon cloud cover had wrapped around the sky and she looked up and into it. 'I'm overcome by the inexplicable desire to speak to you with common courtesy.'

'I doubt that very much.'

'I'm sorry I called you an idiot.'

'You only implied it. Do you want to make it up to me?'

'Not really,' she said.

'Then tell me who Ronald McDonald is.'

'Very soon I'll have to apologise for calling you an idiot again.'

'Imply,' he reminded.

'No, this time I'll likely come out and say it.'

'I already know he isn't the American president.'

'I think you'll be disappointed.'

'I almost always am.'

'He's a clown.'

'A clown?'

'A clown who sells hamburgers.'

'Does he cook the hamburgers?'

'Does it matter?'

'I may be an idiot,' he said gravely, 'but I would never eat a hamburger cooked by a clown. Anyway, you were telling me about your sister. When she returned from Italy.'

Chapter 16

IN THE WEEKS AFTER SHE RETURNED, NATASHA travelled no further than the three metres of grey carpet to Laina's flat. She drank weak tea, interpreted hallucinations, and returned, that fourth metre sealed behind an invisible wall of terror. Sonja watched distantly, wanting to take Natasha's hand and pull her down the hallway like a petulant child. Laina's flat − where, three weeks earlier, she had crouched at the door, a glass of ice melting in her grip, and heard Natasha's voice inside − seemed like the first step on recovery's staircase. But that step had stretched into a landing, then a floor, and Natasha couldn't have disappeared, not then.

Sonja, more talented as physician than as sister, withheld her diagnosis as long as she could. Then one Tuesday, Sonja returned from the hospital with feet swollen and shoulders heavy, too tired, really, to begin tending to her most difficult patient of the day. Natasha sat on the divan, a stack of books propped on the cushion beside her. *Origins of Chechen Civilisation, The Third Soviet Guide to Ornithology, Life and Fate.* A yellowed tome covered her lap. *The Medical Dictionary of the Union of Soviet Physicians.*

'I can define any words you don't understand,' Sonja offered, and immediately regretted it. Not the right tone to take. 'Looking up anything particular?'

Natasha shrugged, of course.

'I hope you didn't read that all day.' She turned to the bare wall. Her open mouth, pointed at Natasha, invariably projected condescension. 'Surely there are more exciting books on the shelves.'

'I don't want to be excited,' Natasha said flatly. 'I want boredom. I want to be lobotomised by boredom.'

'Listen, Natashechka, something is wrong,' she said, and hated her lack of specificity. Something? Wrong? How could a surgeon diagnose with such imprecision? 'Have you heard of post-traumatic stress disorder?'

Natasha nodded without looking up from the page.

'What is it, then?'

Golden lamplight outlined the text as she flipped the pages. 'It is a psychological reaction that occurs after experiencing a highly stressing event outside the range of normal human experience, which is usually characterised by depression, anxiety, flashbacks, recurrent nightmares and avoidance of reminders of the event.'

Natasha hadn't spoken a complex sentence in months, and even recited, the clause-heavy bluster made her sound alive again. 'Sound familiar?' Sonja asked.

'The Italian head doctors went through this already. I don't want your help.'

Help was the last thing Sonja knew how to give her sister. 'Can you remember the last time you went outside?' she asked. Natasha could have lit a cigarette off the end of that glare. 'I'll tell you when. When you were repatriated. You haven't set a toe outside this apartment block since you returned to it.'

'You weren't there,' Natasha said, shrugging. 'So you don't get to tell me what to do.'

For months she'd withheld, stopped herself, thought better, bitten her tongue to shreds. 'I'm right here. Now. Here I am.' She spread her arms, not to embrace her sister, but to show how wide she was, how much of her was here. 'Do you know why? Do you have any idea?'

Natasha didn't move. She couldn't unlock the cellar door, not for Sonja, not for anyone. What had happened down there was still happening inside her, and she wouldn't let anyone, least of all her sister, into what she was still trying, still failing to escape from.

'Because of you. Because I was afraid you were here alone. Everything was so good in London. I was happy there. But I came back for you and that entitles me to your respect. You can hate me and think I'm a self-righteous bitch, but you will treat me with respect, because I came back here for you.'

Again, that fucking shrug! Sonja couldn't imagine, then, with exasperation surging inside her, that one calm morning, eight and a half years away, after her sister had disappeared for a second time, she would wake on a hospital bed with her shoulders as stiff as her collarbones, and shrugging once, twice, failing to relax them, she would remember Natasha's shrugs, how fluid, how easy, and that would be the first definitive, the first known, that wherever Natasha was she would be shrugging.

'Do you want me to feel sorry that you left your nice life in London? Are you the victim here, is that what you're saying? Maybe you should talk to a psychiatrist about it, Sonechka. No, you made a mistake returning here for me,' Natasha stated, as simply as if still reading from the dictionary. 'Just as I made a mistake leaving here for you.'

A window might have opened; a breeze might have slid

across the walls, clearing the air, because Sonja smiled, and said, 'We're sisters. In that way, at least, we're sisters.' She took a clean breath, now that they had each said what they had to say. 'I bought you a souvenir,' she said, surprising even herself. 'In London.'

Exhibiting great restraint, Natasha didn't shrug. 'What sort of souvenir?'

'I'm not telling you. I'm keeping it for myself.'

'It's not a souvenir if you keep it.'

'Of course it is. It's a gift to myself. I deserve it.'

'Why didn't you give it to me?' Natasha had sat up and cocked her head to Sonja.

'Because,' Sonja said, picking up the dictionary and fanning the pages with her thumb, 'you're always on my nerves.'

'All the time?'

'Stampeding on my nerves.'

'I wouldn't want it even if you were giving it to me,' Natasha said.

'Good, because I'm not.'

'I bet it's a book about intestines.'

'You know I'd keep that for myself,' Sonja said. 'I'll give it to you right now.'

'Why?'

'How many intestines books does a woman need? I'll trade it to you for a promise,' Sonja said. Natasha had taken up the clarinet when she was twelve, and Sonja, sixteen at the time, already sitting in on university classes, had heard every squeak, every warble, every pinched sharp through their shared, shadow-thin wall. She had paid Natasha, by the hour, not to practise. That same glint of easy opportunity returned to Natasha's eyes.

'What promise?' she asked.

'Promise that you'll come to the hospital with me tomorrow.'

'And?'

'And nothing. Just that. If you think you're well enough.'

'What, you think I'm not?'

'No, no. I'm not saying that.'

'I know what you're trying to do,' Natasha said. 'Fine. I promise.'

Sonja went to her room and returned a minute later. 'Close your eyes,' she said, and handed her a sturdy oblong object wrapped in a plastic shopping bag.

'What is this? A doll?' Natasha asked, pulling it from the bag. 'I'm a grown woman.'

'It's not a doll. It's a nutcracker of a Buckingham Palace guard.'

'Who are they?'

'They stand outside the Queen's palace. They're not allowed to laugh. They just stand there. They're not very good at guarding, when you think about it. They just stand there. You could dress up a lamp post and get as good a guard.'

'Yes,' Natasha agreed, cranking the nutcracker's mouth up and down. 'A bad guard and worse souvenir. What should I call him?'

Sonja bit her lip. 'What about Alu?'

'Alu the lousy, boring, worthless souvenir.'

'Yes,' Sonja said. 'That is the perfect name for him.'

'I'm a little disappointed. You spent five years in London and all I get is a doll?'

'The real gift was my absence.'

Finally, a smile.

The next morning the hospital was quiet. The few patients Maali couldn't scare off with promises of an amputation cure-all waited for her: a sprained ankle, a case of the common cold, nothing urgent. She took Natasha through the ghost wards of deserted laboratories and examination rooms. Pigeons roosted in split IV bags. A manhole cover, leading nowhere, lay in radiology. The rooms would look unchanged eight and three-quarter years later when Sonja led Akhmed through. The powdered heroin, provided by Alu's brother, would still slouch against the canteen cupboard wall, but when she led him past she would do so without worry, without wondering if his veins, like her sister's, might tingle from proximity.

'This was once among the foremost oncology departments in the USSR,' she said, as they shuffled into a room relieved of its doorknobs and light fixtures. 'Party officials came from as far as Vladivostok for treatment.'

They paused at a hulking MRI machine which the former hospital director had sacrificed his pension, his marriage and all the black in his hair to procure. 'It's a shame we can't use this, but a single scan would kill the generator.' A metre from her foot the bronze rim of a shell casing was silhouetted in dust. 'Besides,' she added, 'there's so much embedded metal in here the magnetic field would turn the room into a shooting gallery.'

The tour ended on the fourth-floor maternity ward, where a woman who had given birth the previous night smiled at everyone in placid exhaustion. Her child had emerged with a collapsed lung but the doctor on call had acted quickly and the child had lived. The mother held the infant to her breast. Its little lips bent the nipple. She beamed as they approached.

'God is great. She will live,' the mother said in a slow cadence to make it clear that the two statements were logically dependent. She glanced up at Natasha, mistaking her white sweatshirt for scrubs. 'I'm so glad you're here.'

'I'm no one,' Natasha said.

'Nonsense,' the mother said. 'You save lives.'

Natasha crossed her arms, and Sonja couldn't see it, couldn't know it, but right then, when Natasha dipped her head, looked to her palm, to the floor, to Sonja and back, she believed that their body temperatures rose by some fractional degree, that this they shared. The baby finished suckling and tilted its square little face upward.

'Do you want to hold her?' the mother asked.

'No,' Natasha said, ratcheting her frown.

'Nonsense,' the mother said. 'You want to hold her.'

'I need to go, but you stay here. There is a case of the common cold in need of my attention,' Sonja whispered as Natasha took the infant in her arms.

That morning, in the cavernous wards, Natasha's brain finally hushed. When the newborn sniffed strangely at her chest, she stared into its eyes and saw a world only two days old. Those two and a half kilograms righted her, turned her vantage to a future kinder than experience had taught her to expect. The next morning she woke when Sonja woke, left when Sonja left, and the next morning and the next.

Deshi and Maali, her superiors, were nurses and twins. Deshi, on the eleventh of her twelve loves, reminded her of Sonja, and she preferred Maali, the younger by eighteen minutes, who treated illness and injury as the practical jokes of a God wheezing with laughter, and suggested amputation for every cough, chest cold, ulcer and eye infection that had the misfortune of seeking her counsel. In the maternity ward, Natasha cleaned towels, bed sheets, the linoleum floor, plastic tubes and hoses, bottles, baby bottoms and bedpans. Her fingertips reddened in the bleach, and in this good hurt and those clean bottles, she found herself warmed by the small suggestions of her agency. In her day's rare pauses, she restored the view to the boarded windows. It began with a few right angles pencilled on the plywood. She hadn't known what she was drawing until it took shape. Two squares, one atop the other. In the pencil's descent a stray line became a downpipe, the pulsing overhead fluorescence became a blue afternoon sun, and a small curl of wood-grain became a secretary's brown hair blown back by a desk fan. Drawing by division on the plywood, she parcelled the building into floors, floors into windows, windows into panes. Familiar, but it still floated a centimetre off her memory; she placed a Soviet flag over the arched entrance, placed pigeons on the flagpole, placed a strong westerly breeze so the flag caught every squirt of pigeon shit. Pencil lead smudged on the thick of her palm as she dredged the building from its ruins. When finished she wrote its name in block Cyrillic above the awning. The Volchansk State Bureau of Vehicular Licensing and Registration. Of course it looked familiar; it had once stood on the other side of the window.

Over weeks and months, as spare minutes became hours and the hours days, she added linden and poplar trees, rusted street lamps, drooping electrical lines, shingled roofs, a skyline of television antennae, clothes lines curved by wet laundry, smoke ribbons unwinding from exhaust pipes, the pavements and cigarette kiosks and everything she could remember. She added no fire hydrants.

Behind her back, and later to her face, Deshi and Maali opined.

'A dreadful thing,' Deshi said when she thought Natasha had gone to the car park for a cigarette.

'Completely inaccurate,' Maali concurred. The nurse understood what it was like to be the younger sister, if only by eighteen minutes, and her criticism hurt Natasha the most. 'The perspective is skewed. It isn't possible to see so much of City Park from this window.'

'Perhaps we shouldn't be so hard,' Deshi said. 'She's never actually seen the view from this room.'

'That's the problem, isn't it? She's drawing something she's never seen.'

'She isn't even Chechen.'

'Her greatest shortcoming.'

'She deserves pity rather than scorn.'

'We retired three years ago,' Deshi lamented. 'What are we even doing here?'

The unlit cigarette somersaulted from her fingers as she pushed open the door, dashed between her critics, and closed the curtain over the boarded windows. She had felt more humiliated before, but never by people whom she trusted. She grabbed her lighter from the worktop and pushed past the nurses, but Maali's grasp, surprisingly firm on her wrist, held her.

'Let me guess,' Natasha said. 'The only way to fix the mural is to amputate the hand that drew it.'

Maali smiled. 'It's not quite so serious.'

'Really?' She felt strangely honoured that Maali didn't want to chop off her hand.

'It's just that there was never a bus stop at the intersection of Lenin Prospect and City Bureaucrat Street. I know because I stared at that corner for thirty years.'

'We'll help you,' Deshi added, and under the combined guidance of eyes that had spent some sixty years in front of the maternity ward windows, she erased and redrew, swept up the eraser lint, erased and redrew again. Deshi and Maali argued over every signpost and street lamp, every tree in City Park, every shopfront, kiosk and traffic light; they had stared from different windows onto different cities, and in trying to bring back both, she created her own. She shaded the buildings with ash and coal, sliced advertisements from unread magazines still stacked in the waiting room and pasted slivers of colour across the plywood. The blue waves of a Black Sea resort became sky. Mint gum became linden leaves. Some afternoons the nurses would become lost in the mural, pointing to the distant corners and alleyways like faded pictures in a photo album. The finely detailed ventilation grate that had once suspended a thousand-ruble note in its draught, where Deshi plucked three months' rent from the air. The above-ground gas pipes from which their mother had hung laundry and their father a hammock. Or the school-playground tarmac, where Maali's son had played soldiers years before the war took him. In sixteen years, when glass replaced the plywood boards, Natasha's murals would find their way to Sonja's cupboard where they would remain a private treasure for some sixty-three years, until Maali's great-great-grandson, an art historian, put them on display in the city art museum.

She was studying her city when the nurses arrived on the morning she was to perform her third solo delivery. 'It's going to get busy,' Maali said, with no small amount of glee. With her rain jacket, windcheater, and overcoat hung on different pegs, the coat stand suggested a fully staffed ward. 'We heard landmines on the way in.'

Deshi wagged her head. 'You enjoy this job too much, sister. I worry your head has broken.'

'It's too bad you can't amputate a head.'

'You can. It's called a decapitation.'

Maali noted it excitedly on her clipboard.

'We're all working trauma today,' Deshi said.

'What if there are deliveries?' Natasha asked.

'Then you'll do them, Natashechka. It doesn't take much to deliver a child. The mother does most of the work.'

The first casualties arrived a half-hour later; red heat radiated from their skin. Natasha disinfected the ropy ends of a calf when Deshi came calling. 'We have a delivery. Go.'

The patient lay gowned and supine on the maternity ward bed. Her face throbbed against the white sheets, as flushed and anguished as those four floors below. Two men stood beside her, each holding one hand. She recognised the cleft in the older man's chin, but now wasn't the time for pause, for reflection; now was the time to act. She stood between the woman's pale open legs, trying not to look down.

'The contractions are three minutes apart,' the younger man volunteered. He spoke with the halting formality of an outsider.

It was all she needed in order to remember what to do. 'Lasting how long?'

He didn't know. Sweat grew heavy on the woman's forehead and trickled towards her temples. After washing her hands to her wrists, rubbing sanitiser to her elbows, she snapped on a fresh pair of gloves. Another contraction came; they all heard it.

'Do you feel like you have to shit?' she whispered into the woman's ear, afraid of embarrassing her in front of her husband.

The woman nodded.

'What did you ask?' the younger man asked. 'Is she OK?'

'The child is in the birth canal, putting pressure on the rectum, that's all.' These people knew nothing of her, and she drew enough confidence from what they did not know to keep her voice level. They didn't know that her name was Natasha; that she had performed only two solo deliveries, one and three weeks earlier; that six months earlier, as she detoxed in a Rome psych ward, God had pulled her through a needle's eye so narrow that this thread in front of them was all that remained.

She told the woman to lift her pale little legs, place her feet in the stirrups, and the woman did. She pulled the woman's dress into a crumpled hoop around her stomach. They thought she knew what she was doing and she made their faith hers.

'My chest hurts,' the woman said.

'You need to breathe.'

'My eyes hurt,' the woman said.

'You need to blink.'

She set two pillows on the floor, beneath the woman's open legs, just in case. The vice of the woman's grip crushed the older man's fingers to squirming scarlet tendrils. 'I've seen you before,' Natasha said, but was swallowed within the woman's wail. 'Push,' Natasha said. 'Push.'

A mat of damp hair ringed by pubic curls began to crown.

'Gently,' she said, extending her hands as the mat of hair became a head. 'Take deep breaths. Slow breaths. Imagine you are inflating a balloon. Your breaths are slow and deep. Blow through your mouth at the most painful point of each contraction. Try to whistle.'

She steadied her hands beneath the crowning skull. Instinct told her to palm the back of the child's head so its first sensation was of warmth and comfort, but she kept a finger's width between the child's skin and her own. Maali had warned her never to touch a child's head before seeing its face; doing so could cause the child to inhale amniotic fluid. But it wasn't the child who gasped, it was Natasha as she watched the damp forehead emerge. The birth canal sheathed every slip of skin as the mother slid her child into life. Its little eyes didn't move. Far away, the mother emptied her lungs in an unshaped melody. They all inhaled her whistle.

'The head has come out,' Natasha announced, trying her hardest, for the sake of professional decorum, to stifle the smile widening across her face. The mother pushed and the room hushed, dampened, narrowed by her exertion. The shoulders stuck. With the most tender turn of her gloved hands, Natasha rotated the child's head so its lids looked into the fleshy pale of the mother's thigh. The right shoulder slid through. She lifted the child's head and when the mother's next whistle pushed out the left shoulder, the rest glided into her hands like an afterthought.

She lifted the umbilical cord over the child's face, and the warm wet weight of the head pressed to her palm. She angled the child towards the floor. 'A girl,' she said. The child opened its eyes and a sharp chill ran through her to know that hers were the first hands to hold the girl.

'She doesn't look right,' the father said.

Natasha rubbed the girl's back through a towel, then tilted her head to open the airway. She stroked the girl's nose, dried the girl's mouth, suctioned residue through a plastic syringe, tickled her feet, but still the girl hadn't cried. Should she run downstairs for help? Could she perform CPR on a newborn? She pushed her fingers into the child's soft, soggy soles, and begged them to kick back. At the ends of her feet the protruding toes seemed in error, so curled and delicate they might sink back into the doughy flesh. These are the feet of a human being you brought into the world. She will not die.

She didn't. Lips drawn to the pink edges of her toothless gums. A sharp gulp.

'She's breathing.'

'I can hear,' the father said. The girl wailed. 'She breathes like her mother.'

She placed the girl on the mother's bare skin. The mother stared through a frame of damp hair and recognised her daughter; they were both breathing. Pink liquid trickled from the girl's mouth, striping the incline of her mother's still swollen stomach. With a fresh towel Natasha wrapped the two together.

'You should start nursing as soon as you feel able,' Natasha said. She didn't need to borrow their confidence. It was hers. 'It will help the placenta come out and stop the bleeding.'

The mother nodded weakly, happily. Her voice was unfamiliar when she spoke. Natasha had only heard it in screams. 'This is my daughter?'

'Yes,' Natasha said, finally allowing herself a smile. 'She's yours.'

The older man approached as she washed her hands under the sputtering tap. There was much yet to clean, but first, her hands. He thanked her.

'The mother did most of the work,' she said. In his wrinkles she recognised his face as she might a photograph crumpled and flattened. 'I've seen you before.'

'Have you been to Eldár?'

In a truck, with five other women. 'In passing.'

'What about the city university? I taught there. Or the Café Standard? I enjoyed their bebop nights. Do you like bebop?'

'I don't like trumpets.'

'But what if a trumpet is playing the music you like?'

She thought of loose screws trembling on the Nightclub dance floor. 'The music I like can't be played on a trumpet,' she said.

'If it can't be played on a trumpet, it's not music.'

'My name is Natasha, ' she said, smiling.

'Khassan Geshilov.'

Repeating the name aloud, she saw the black-and-white dust jacket photo. 'I've read your book.'

He gave a bashful laugh. 'You're the one?'

'It ended before the Russians arrived. A stupid decision, if you ask me.'

'If only you had been my editor! *Origins of Chechen Civilisation*,' he said fondly, as if he had also forgotten the title. He turned to the boarded windows. 'This is the whole city, isn't it?'

'As much as can be seen from the window.'

He strolled the ash-shaded streets and verdant leaves, reading the city so he might later remember. He lingered at an intersection between City Park and the university library, hesitated, then pressed his finger into the street. 'The love of my life was nearly killed by a bus here. She had been following me, and I only found out then, with the screech of bus tyres.'

'You have stalkers? No wonder you didn't have time to write about the Russians.'

'That's a story for another day.' He glanced back to the newborn. 'Let's introduce ourselves.'

The father and the historian embraced, all gratitude and congratulations silently locked between their arms. The father lifted the girl from the mother. His long fingers held her.

'What will you call her?' Natasha asked.

'Havaa,' the father said. 'Havaa.'

Chapter 17

HAVAA'S FATHER NEVER AGAIN PLAYED CHESS after returning from the final trip to the mountains with Ramzan in January 2003. He spent his days caught like a coin between the divan cushions. Sweat seeped into his shirt collar, leaving a rim the colour of crushed mustard seed. His fingers had, well, *healed* wasn't the right word. The stumps had hardened into pink lumps rising from the webs of his palms. He struggled to button his shirt, open the door, eat, tie his shoes, and Havaa, insistent and unrelenting, became his hands.

The heat of the following summer weighed so much it would take an extra autumn to fully lift. Her mother kept her waistline hidden beneath wide skirts and aprons, refusing to wear maternity clothes. She still slept in her parents' bedroom on a mattress so thin she felt the pattern of nail heads in the floor. Refugees still arrived, still overdressed and bewildered, and her father still took them in.

That summer the leaves drooped in the heat. Decay baked at her feet and in it crawled little insects that made homes in her boot prints. She hiked as if the forest were a fragile thing, careful to sidestep saplings so slender they bowed with the breeze. Her father told her that Soviet timber interests had controlled the forest before the wars, but she couldn't find a tree stump on her side of the forest, and rust-chewed saw belts, buried like relics of a prior civilisation, were the only evidence of past industry.

Flocks of migrating birds clutched shaded branches. Lizards hid in dewy deer tracks. Once, she saw a wolf slaloming between the birch trunks; its pink tongue lolled from its open mouth and the sunlight glimmered on its fangs. When the wolf spotted her, half hidden behind a hornbeam, its ears snapped skyward. It found her eyes amid the leaves and studied them, questioningly, and she stared back, unnerved but not quite afraid, until they came to an understanding, and the wolf continued its saunter through the long, lovely shadows. Despite her sprinting pulse, she had only pity for the wolf, sweltering, as it was, under that heavy silver coat.

She visited Akim often that summer. His portrait survived the February frosts and March thaws, but even the varnish, smeared like sunblock across his cheeks, couldn't save him from the summer heat. His face slumped and faded. How the summer aged him. In life he had preferred the cold and dreamed of visiting the North Pole. In eighteen years his oldest brother, a geologist, would bury what remained of Akim's portrait in Arctic snow, not quite at the North Pole, but close enough to make a compass needle spin in circles.

The sight of Akim's half-erased face left Havaa crestfallen, but an hour's trek from the village, she found the solution guarding a fallow field. The scarecrow wore a burlap sack and sun-bleached blue trousers, its straw-stuffed waist wider than that of any villager. A faceless cloth crammed with dead leaves sat where the head should be. Crows perched on its brim and mice nested in the sags of its shirtsleeves. Her parents warned her against venturing into the fields, but the chance to extend Akim's life, once again, outweighed her fear. Each step planted with cautious deliberation, she reached the scarecrow. A wooden post, rooted in the soil, impaled the limp straw body. She kicked the post, then excavated its base. The dirt scratched her knees and she scratched the dirt back. The scarecrow tilted with the post, arms and legs hanging back like a refugee collapsing into bed. Mice scurried from the sleeves when they at last brushed the ground. The whole glaring sky focused on her as she tied a rag around the splintered post end, gripped and pulled. The scarecrow's head nodded as it fell along the furrows. His arms stretched across the dry soil as if searching for mines.

It took three afternoons before she joined the straw body to Akim's head. When the sun set on the first evening, she left the scarecrow to sleep in the driest part of a roadside ditch. The next evening she hid him in the shadow of a fallen tree. Finally, she had the wilted torso leaning against the tree, and taking gardening shears by their blue rubber handles, she decapitated the faceless cloth head with a few rusty snaps. She dug a small hole, slid the post in, and the scarecrow stood. Browned straw jutted from the scarecrow's neck, bearding Akim, but another few clips shaved him. Though the scarecrow looked better, it was still no more than a lax, lifeless body propped up beneath a fading portrait, requiring resuscitation. She snipped her hair with the gardening shears and pasted the clippings on Akim's crown. She pricked her finger with a sewing needle and rubbed her warm blood onto Akim's cheeks. Re-enacting Akhmed's movements, she thumped on the scarecrow's chest, as he had thumped on the boy's chest, and when the breath of life erupted – her own – she stood back and wiped the sweat-sting from her eyes. The air was clean, her hands brown with dirt. Pride surged through her, raw and immense; she had believed happiness to be an absence – of fear, of pain, of grief – but here it roared in her as powerful as any sadness. She looked at her fingers and loved them. They had carried the scarecrow for three kilometres of field, road and forest without setting off a single mine. They had saved Akim for a second time.

As the summer burned on she would lie on her back and describe to Akim the shapes of clouds spotted through breaks in the trees. She would lie on her stomach and report the gross and fascinating news from the insect world. She would complain about her mother and father, how the Landfill had changed them both and how the dry evening air combusted without refugees to douse the tension. Silence, she had learned, was safer than questions. Even as her mother's belly grew, Havaa kept her questions and comments for Akim, who, in death, treated her more graciously than he ever had in life.

Havaa was sitting beside Akim when she heard her mother's screams, first mistaking them for the breeze through thicket, but the air lay thick and still, and wind couldn't call for help. She ran home. Her mother lay on the floor beneath a blood-soaked apron. Her father and Akhmed knelt beside her. 'She's haemorrhaging,' Akhmed was saying. 'I don't know what to do. We need to get her to the hospital.' She waited with her father while Akhmed hurtled towards Ramzan's for his truck. In a shuddering voice her father kept asking the pale-faced woman – who looked like her mother and wore her mother's apron but couldn't be her mother – for forgiveness. If she had been dying every minute of every day, they might have been a happy family. The blood consumed every centimetre of apron cloth and Havaa was afraid the wound would become hers if she came too close. Her mother stirred, looked to her father, and wrapped her five fingers over his none. She opened her mouth, but he shook his head, told her to save her breath, and Havaa would always remember how he had shushed what might have been her goodbye so that she could breathe.

The splatter of gravel outside and Akhmed ran in, now in the living room, now kneeling on the floor, now lifting the head of the woman who would not be, could not be, but was her mother. Her father tried to help but he couldn't even lift the hair from her eyes. They left Havaa at the house with instructions shouted from the open passenger window and swallowed by the road before she could ask for clarification. The road distended, becoming a cloud the truck fell into. She asked Allah to save her mother, and, as her prayer vanished in dust, wondered if she should ask again in Arabic.

Back in the house she went to her parents' bedroom and opened the top chest drawer. She plodded over the cool circles of coins, rummaged through silk handkerchiefs and leather wristbands. She found it at the back of the drawer. It was wrapped in a cotton bandanna, next to the jewellery her mother tried on when she thought she was alone. Even through the bandanna her fingers remembered the grip. The knot was simple, loose, gone with a tug. The silvery finish shone as if in those months of darkness it had reserved its reflection for this. She held it as Ramzan had taught her. Close to her chest. As if carrying a water jug. What lay at the other end of the barrel didn't matter. She couldn't see past the trigger. The whole world was howling and if it kept on, if it didn't stop, she would let the barrel reply.

She would remember the cool metal warming in her

hands, how she gripped it like a banister. Later she would learn that Akhmed had shouted instructions as he drove; her father performed them as well as his hands allowed. She would never understand why Akhmed hadn't thought to bring her when he needed a second set of fingers. In the panicked departure no one remembered her mother's ID card. The sergeant at the checkpoint nodded often, sympathetically, and then explained there was simply no way he could allow her through without proper identification. There are few rules in war, he went on, but those that do exist must be upheld, because if so simple a rule as this is broken, then couldn't the more complex, convoluted, one might even say absurd rules of the Geneva Convention break with even greater ease? Her father raised his hands in response, but the sergeant, a man who had grown up in a mining town above the Arctic circle, and found the Chechen climate so fine he had renewed his contract three times, had seen worse. Her mother died and the argument went on for several more minutes before anyone noticed.

The gun was buried in the back of the drawer before her father returned. The look on his face told her what had happened and that hurt burrowed deeper than anything she'd ever felt, deep enough to change from the thing she felt to the thing she was. Love, she learned, could reduce its recipient to an essential thing, as important as food or shelter, whose presence is not only longed for but needed. But even on those days when she ran to Akim in the woods, her pain wasn't complicated by guilt. She hadn't caused or contributed to her mother's death. She couldn't have saved her.

That was the difference in how she mourned each parent. One and a half years since her mother had died and she grieved for her cleanly because she wasn't at fault. But when the security forces had come for her father three nights earlier, she could have taken that pistol and aimed it at the first face appearing in the kicked-in door. She could have fired all twelve rounds, let the magazine drop, ducked and reloaded, just as Ramzan had taught her.

But she didn't. Instead she'd followed her father's hoarse command and run through the back door and into the safety of the woods with her pre-packed just-in-case suitcase. The shadows of the Feds moved across the windowpanes. The bookcase tipped and the book covers opened like wings over an underbelly of white feathers, dirty with ink. In the living room the men gathered with their faces to the floor. From behind the mouldering log, she couldn't make out what the men were laughing at, and because she couldn't see she could still believe it wasn't her father. She sucked snow, breathed through her mouth, her breath invisible in the cold. Their shoulders strained with an unseen weight. They vanished, reappearing in the next window, and she crept to the edge of the clearing until she could see the parked truck. The gaffer tape stretching over her father's mouth wrinkled. When she saw that they had even taped his hands together, she would have fired three shots right then, if she had had the pistol. But there was no gun. The silver Makarov was not in the chest drawer. It hadn't been there for some time.

Chapter 18

THE SILVER MAKAROV PISTOL WAS ALL RAMZAN thought about for the two weeks preceding Dokka's disappearance, in which he failed to produce a single bowel movement. Each morning, venturing into the cold in nothing but a robe and lambskin boots, he turned the corner of the house, passed icicles filling the gutter's missing segments, passed the frostbitten fingers of fallen birch limbs, and waded down the sharp incline to the scattered pine cones that had amassed into an ankle-deep mound at the outhouse door. Inside, he sat with his elbows burrowed into his knees, a full-bodied clench that left him red-faced and winded. Snow flurries fell through the roof's missing half, landing on the back of his neck, and melted into sweat. His scrotum was an empty coin purse flattened between his legs. He was unable to father even a soft dollop of excrement. As the stagnant days stacked one atop the next, he altered his diet, already limited to what his father hadn't thrown to the dogs. He stopped eating his favourite meal of cured beef spiced with paprika, chillies and coriander, the one sumptuous dinner his father allowed him each week. He left the butter off his bread and by daylight ate only the apples his father once favoured. He yearned for vegetables. Vegetables! Raw and leafy, flavourless and coarse, yes, cucumbers and turnips and beets. Haunted by what he knew to be feminine cravings, he was unmanned for a second time, but not even the intimacy of his shame could repel his yearning for cabbage and sprouts, for roughage sweeping through his system like the bristles of an enraged broom. Even if he broke down, debasing himself by requesting greens in his biweekly provisions from the state security forces, he would receive only a few yellow heads of frozen lettuce, which his father would, no doubt, feed to the yapping beasts in the yard. But he felt increasingly certain that it was neither the surplus of cured meats, nor the dearth of vegetables in his diet, but rather the conversation with the Cossack colonel that had fossilised his lower intestines. He considered prayer, but asking for spiritual laxative was surely sacrilege. Inspired by the long, leaky shits he'd taken as an eighteen-year-old Red Army private, he performed post-*fajr* calisthenics. He vomited twice from the exercise, but still failed to coax even a pale, watery squirt. The weather, at least, provided solace. If ever there was a season for constipation it was winter. Beneath the wooden toilet box, the cesspool had frozen into scentless stone. Surely that was preferable to the faecal fever baking beneath the wooden seat in summer. He sat. He pushed. Struggling against his body, he came to the dismaying conclusion that his viscera had betrayed him. Even when his rear end felt tied closed with drawstrings, he checked himself. But each time he examined the rough square of military-issue toilet paper, it was white. Even after he spoke to the colonel for a second time, two weeks after their initial conversation, and gave up Dokka, no relief arrived. And three days after Dokka disappeared, when Ramzan closed the satellite phone and ended, the last of the three conversations he would have with the Cossack colonel, he considered what his father had suggested that morning about Akhmed. Could it really be true? No, it couldn't be, not really, and he couldn't believe it, couldn't allow it, because it was no more than a ploy to trick his conscience into mercy. But would his father break his two-year vow of silence to tell a lie? Not that it mattered now. Ramzan had given the Cossack colonel Akhmed's name. The plea spoken from his father's prideful lips earlier that day had quickly betrayed itself, degenerating from appeal to denunciation, and yes, he would take away the one person in the village his father loved if only to teach his father what it was to be alone. Wherever Akhmed was, wherever he had hidden the girl, he was no more than a ghost still ignorant of his death.

It was the Cossack colonel, Ramzan came to believe, who had tied the knot in his intestines. His deep timbre could constipate the Volga. The smoke of three daily packs blew through his sentences. He spoke with a velvety menace as he asked Ramzan if the sun was shining over the village, and the collision of the colonel's tone and the childlike question gave Ramzan the impression that to the man on the other end of the line death was an unremarkable hazard of his trade. The sun was shining, beaming even, yet Ramzan felt compelled to lie, to say the cloud cover sat as thick as spoiled milk, as though enough small lies would absolve him of the larger truths divulged. But he didn't lie. He said yes. The sun shone. The colonel grunted in approval, then read from the military meteorological report for the village. Static breathed through the transmission. Ramzan lifted the antenna towards the sky like a lightning rod pulling the full force of the colonel's voice from the heavens. When reception returned, the colonel asked about the silver Makarov pistol.

But when Ramzan left his house in early December 2004, two weeks before Dokka was disappeared, he still had forty-five minutes before hearing the Cossack colonel's voice for the first time. A blue nylon duffel bag the size and slump of a dead cat dangled from his wrist; inside swung the satellite phone. He opened the back door and, stepping into the wind, crossed the field. The sun filled the frozen slant of the outhouse half roof, but the privy hadn't yet consumed his hope and dread, as it soon would, and he passed without looking back, walking as snow hardened into the deep treads of his leather boots, following the narrow corridor of bed sheets left stiff on the clothes line, over the brittle yellow grass, over his grandparents' plot, to the uneven edge of the field and into the forest.

Snow had thickened the ground. The quiet of his house followed him into the woods. Two hundred metres in, raising his head in a long scream, he tore a hole in the silence through which he could walk more freely. His father, he hoped, would mistake it for the wounded bawl of his pack. Before the wars, the winter had been warmer. A meteorologist might beg to differ, but weather prediction was an act of infidel witchcraft that could not be trusted.

For the duration of the three-kilometre hike, he scanned the snow but found no tracks wider than a rabbit's foot. The conditions that allowed the forest to flourish had devastated its wildlife. The village economy depended upon logging, and when the enterprise and its administration vanished with the Soviet flag, the villagers were left without the means or infrastructure to extract any real money from the forest. So they hunted. Aided by the wartime influx of munitions, they hunted deer, wild boar, brown bears and wolves like men who believed they would always be hungry and the forest would always be full.

The cell of subsistence hunting eventually metastasised into the gun-running operation that would take Dokka's fingers and transform Ramzan into a man who hiked three kilometres in December to make a phone call. His first taste of trading came when he worked for a small crafts concern that bloomed under the relaxed regulations of perestroika. He scavenged the mountains for the stone sculptures of shaman artisans. The hamlets he found were no more than high-altitude islands in a sea of mining waste, and he exchanged petrol, medical supplies and tinned food for the carved stone. The artisans always chose to bargain through a *shura* of elders, upon whom time had acted like a substance that repeatedly dissolved and refroze their faces, and Ramzan, in his early twenties, felt like a foreigner among these aged creatures, and nearly always gave much more than the carvings were worth. To his mind, the stone sculptures of goat hooves, a child's hands and a mutilated deer weren't worth the last spittly sip of a shared vodka bottle. He took the sculptures to an industrial park outside of Grozny, where they were examined, priced, crated and shipped to distant countries where wealthy cosmopolitans would pay vast sums to display the hoof of a Chechen goat.

In 1999, years since Ramzan had ventured into the mountains for sculptures, he traded cured meat for shotgun shells in a neighbouring village. A welder there made home-made ammunition. New buckshot was prohibitively priced on the black market, so the ingenious man packed the casings with ball bearings cannibalised from trolley wheels. They exchanged words before ammunition and meat, and soon realised that each had worked in the industrial park. The welder explained that immediately following the birth of his first son he had begun working as a nightwatchman at the industrial park so he could, at the very least, get a good night's sleep. They talked about how, in 1991, the crafts concern had stopped purchasing authentic mountain sculptures and begun mass-producing them in Grozny with the help of a professor at the Fine Arts College and the serf-labour of his undergraduate sculpture class. The recollection was a tunnel through which trust travelled. They shared nothing in common but the memory of the industrial park, and it was enough. Ramzan took the welder fresher cuts of meat, and in exchange the welder gave Ramzan a Kalashnikov. Ramzan returned to the welder several days later with the hind legs of a brown bear bleeding in his truck bed.

And one day the welder vanished to join the independence fighters. For the next year, Ramzan struggled to survive. The task, already a great challenge, was compounded by his diabetic father. In a country where clean water was scarce, insulin should have proved impossible. But Ramzan found a way.

In a small, unassuming collective farm, known locally as the Miracle Fields, Ramzan worked as a petrol farmer for the insurgents, or the Feds, or more likely both. The pipeline running through the untended pear orchard conveyed oil from local wells to a regional refinery, but the pipe was riddled with so many bullet holes that the refinery had long since ceased operations. The reek of rotting, unpicked pears filled the air as Ramzan dug pits, called barns, alongside the pipe. Dark fountains of oil filled the barns, which fed into a system of irrigation channels that, in earlier times, had been used to water the pear trees. Perhaps as much as half of the oil seeped into the soil, into the groundwater below, but the oil spouted from the pipe in such abundance that no one ever thought to seal the barns with concrete or plastic. Twice a day, a tanker truck arrived to siphon the oil through a long rubber hose and distribute it to covert factories, where the crude oil was refined into a highly sulphuric diesel with eighty-year-obsolete machinery looted from the National Museum of Oil Production. The women who bottled the diesel in glass jars and sold it on street corners were the nearest entity to a working petrol station for several hundred kilometres. Sometimes the moonshine diesel worked, and sometimes it caused the cars to explode, but it always filled the coffers of the insurgents, or the Feds, or more likely both. Ramzan, for his part, was well paid, and he used his earnings to buy insulin and syringes on the black market. Due to regular territorial disputes along the pipeline, the work was more dangerous than the war itself, and Ramzan was sustained not by love for his father but by the fear of failing him.

In 2001, when a band of wounded rebels briefly occupied the village, Ramzan recognised the welder among their ranks. They embraced as brothers, as though bonded in a crucible more dramatic than an industrial park. The welder introduced him to the field commander, a man with very bad teeth and dental-floss stitches in his chest. Impressed by Ramzan's familiarity with the mountains and eager to set up supply routes for the coming winter, the field commander referred Ramzan to a Saudi sheikh who had come to Chechnya to support the holy warriors in their *ghazawat* against the infidel oppressor.

The sheikh wasn't the first foreign Wahhabi Ramzan had seen break sharia law, but he was the first to break it in the name of Internet poker. 'The Qur'an specifically says, '*He who plays with dice is like the one who handles the flesh and blood of swine*,' but makes no mention of playing cards,' the sheikh explained at their initial meeting, conducted between bets in the midst of the quarter-final round of one of his tournaments. The sheikh had perhaps the only working computer in Volchansk, and connected to the Internet – a technology that surely allowed far too much freedom to be pious – via a portable satellite dish. The sheikh, a short, brimming, gourd-like man, smiled at the computer screen. 'I play in the morning,' he said, 'when it is still late night in Western Europe and America, and the judgement of the other players is clouded by whisky. All my winnings, of course, go entirely to jihad.'

No fundamentalist undercurrent ran through the national culture before the first war. Sufism had always been the predominant Muslim sect, and Wahhabism was a foreign, wartime import. A few times a year, Arab Wahhabis came through the village in search of recruits. They promised rations, shelter, an eternity in Paradise and, until that day of glorious martyrdom, a monthly salary of two hundred and fifty US dollars. Few young men followed the mono-chromatic Wahhabi faith, but many were quite willing to be radicalised for a monthly salary that eclipsed what they would otherwise earn in a year. The war of independence so quickly conflated with jihad because no one cared about the self-determination of a small landlocked republic. Arab states would gladly fund a war of religion, but not one of nationalism. And in this way it didn't matter who won the war between the Feds and fundamentalists: the notion of a democratic and fully sovereign Chechnya would be crushed regardless. Martyrdom was the easiest way to make a living, but death didn't appeal to Ramzan, and he was pleased when the sheikh, gleeful after winning the ten-thousand-dollar tournament, crossed his spindly legs and offered a different proposal.

The real war was one of supply, explained the sheikh,

who had been trained as a tax lawyer before giving his life to Allah, and would return to tax law in five and a half years, when Allah failed to warn him, for the final time, of his opponent's full house. The *dzhigits* had to be restocked and rearmed, the sheikh said, and failing to do so was more destructive to morale than a barrage of mortar rounds. At times, the sheikh continued, when the fighters were encamped in mountain caves, without the firepower to defeat a pack of wolves much less the Federal army, the jihad subsisted purely as a prayer in the hearts of its devout adherents. By this point, it was difficult to pretend that a few thousand men hiding in the mountains could overcome one of the world's largest armies. Yet they had to pretend. The illusion of victory in the minds of the newly converted was, in itself, victory. And morale was essential in maintaining this ancillary conquest for Chechen souls. If the foot soldiers died in bomb blasts, they would blame the Russians. If they died of hunger, they would blame the Wahhabis. Trustworthy transportation was needed more than all the prayers of the Arab world, yet was so difficult to obtain, for the sheikh was a foreigner and didn't know the land. Ramzan did. In the end, he was easily coaxed. The sheikh gave him an envelope with ten pale green twenty-dollar bills and Ramzan pinched the money with his fingertips. For some reason, he'd always imagined American notes would be thicker.

While his neighbours slogged further into the forest in search of game, Ramzan drove to Volchansk, Shali, even Grozny. The weapons he would deliver to rebel encampments all came from Russian munitions factories. Some he purchased in bulk from a crooked Federal captain who would order his company to attention when Ramzan arrived, and would then walk down the line with an open parachute bag as Ramzan read aloud from the sheikh's handwritten list of needed munitions; in reports to his superiors, the captain would refer to such incidents as rebel ambushes in which his soldiers had no choice but to surrender. Others came through the smuggling routes that ran through the border regions like veins through marble. One day, when discussing supply routes, the sheikh showed him a map of the entire republic, pasted together from a dozen low-resolution pages printed from the Internet. 'What's wrong?' the sheikh asked when Ramzan goggled at the misaligned segments held by peeling tape. It was the first time he had seen a map of his own country. The Soviets had banned maps of the entire republic for fear that such a symbol would serve to foment national solidarity, or, at the very least, make long-haul truckers a little too complacent. In the frenzied smuggling following the Soviet collapse, no one, to Ramzan's knowledge, had ever thought to sneak a map across the border. And here was one, right in front of him. His country looked like a rectangle drawn by a man suffering from delirium tremens. He hadn't known that. It did make him feel patriotic. 'This is a beautiful map,' Ramzan answered, at last. The sheikh let him keep it.

Over the sixteen months he worked for the sheikh, Ramzan transported semi-automatics, machine-gun belts, Makarov pistols, aluminium pails of loose bullets divided by calibre, telescopic sniper rifles, hand grenades, clothes-hanger trip lines, brown paper-wrapped blocks of Semtex, stopwatches, coils of multicoloured rubber-coated wires, black-and-white photographs of Russian military bases, maps redrawn to include roadblocks and checkpoints and ruins, jars of thick dark grease, red plastic jugs of petrol, batteries, butane lighter fluid, compasses, bandannas, powdered soap, iodine tablets, cigarettes, sacks of rice, spotted potatoes, plum jam, dried apricots, condensed milk, lentils, ground pepper, communiqués, translucently thin ricepaper, pens, envelopes, letters from family members, pay, prayer rugs, paperback Qur'ans and steel septic pipes used to launch home-made rockets, which he also transported. Compensation was subject to the exigencies of combat. Sometimes it came in envelopes: US, Russian, British or EU currency. Other times as a cut of the delivered goods: a pair of dull leather military boots, a basket of fresh corn, a boar's hide, a sheepskin overcoat, a silver Makarov pistol. When he felt like a criminal, he reminded himself that a land without law is a land without crime.

Combat enlarged the resupply journeys beyond the simple calculations of time and distance. Covering a hundred kilometres could take weeks to prepare for and days to execute. He packed his truck to capacity and used only a frayed blue blanket to conceal its contents. It didn't matter if the Feds caught him with a butter knife or an atomic bomb. A gunshot would announce the same sentence. He drove towards ridges that sawed further into the sky as he approached. Danger resided beneath, on and above the main roads – landmines, patrols and helicopters – and so he instead followed the trails of shepherds, flattening the tall grasses. Plains grew to foothills and foothills to mountains. He ascended switchbacks so sharp they required three-point turns. Both sideview mirrors snapped off. The rock scraped the paint from the door. Now and then he'd glance down to the gullies of indefinable green funnelling towards slivers of water that marked the depth and decline of the land. Cloud cover dwarfed distant cities and villages. Invader and invaded held on to their fistfuls of earth, but in the end, the earth outlived the hands that held it.

He drove until the mountains no longer let him. Then came the shortest and most arduous distances. He loaded the supplies on a plywood frame and strapped the frame to his shoulders with strips of canvas and bungee cord. If properly balanced he could carry forty kilograms up the mountain. The rebels would not assist him, believing such labour beneath men of their pious patriotism, and he carried the forty kilograms up boulders and bluffs while the drop of the valley glared up at him. Every ten minutes he checked the compass and mountain line. He tied a bell to his wrist so the lookouts would hear his approach before their scopes saw him. They materialised in camo fatigues faded to the same moss-spotted tan of the stone. Beards hung from their sun-darkened faces and the martyrs greeted him with imperious gratitude. Depending on where the rebels were camped and where the road ended, he would invite Dokka, never Akhmed, to join him.

There.

The hoofprints of an elk.

He squatted to the ground, stopped by a set of prints that marked the snow like a long ellipsis leading nowhere. The tracks hadn't yet frozen and the elk was likely within a few hundred metres. To come upon an elk again. To admire rather than shoot. He stood and checked his watch. The sunlight turned the silver hands golden. Twenty minutes before he was due to check in. Staring down the trail of prints, he tried to follow its line through the birches and pines. Somewhere in that distance of frost and shadow, movement disrupted the stillness and the disturbance had carved a distance within him. He continued. The call couldn't come late. Not even the sighting of an elk would excuse it.

The trees opened to the most recently clear-cut swathe of forest. Already the saplings had grown taller than him. They loomed over the short, frost-buried stumps of their antecedents. His footprints wove among them, larger and more apparent than the elk's, halting at the deep-treaded tyres of a dilapidated logging truck. The loggers had abandoned the truck when they fled, and in the intervening decade its yellow paint had faded, chipped and been recoloured in a maroon coating of rust. The tyre treads were so deeply cut he used them as rungs to climb to the cabin. Spiderweb fractures spread across the windscreen, but the glass still held the snow. Seated in the driver's seat, he unzipped the duffel bag and assembled the phone. The satellite consisted of three metal rectangles coated in hard resin, which, when set up and positioned at a fifteen-degree angle on the cabin roof, looked like a cooking sheet basking in the sun. He connected two black rubber wires to the satellite. One led to a battery pack, which he left sitting beside the satellite on the roof, and the other ran through the cracked window and attached to the receiver. The pea-green keypad lit up. Three minutes remained before his call was due. Though wrapped in shame and remorse, these phone calls constituted the best moments of his month; for nearly two years, the military men on the other end had been the only people interested in speaking to him. He measured the cold by the length of his breath, which grew and vanished, like a tusk that kept dissolving from his face. The entire forest's quiet was concentrated in the cabin.

Later he would store the memory of this moment with that of his mother's rolling pin, how just the sight of it emerging from the kitchen cabinet would make him salivate. He would treasure it as he treasured the ball of yellow yarn, still attached to the amputated sleeve of a sweater she had been knitting for him when she died. He would weave those three minutes into the fabric of his mother's memory, because she had loved him, and believed him a kind and generous child, and died before she could see the half-man he had become. For nearly two years he had worked as an informer for the state security forces. He had given up neighbours who had wished him a happy birthday every year of his life. And still he believed himself the victim as much as the perpetrator of his crimes.

At eleven o'clock he punched the nine-digit number into the keypad. An adjutant answered, and in the cramped cold of the cabin his voice trilled like a clarinet. The adjutant passed the phone to the colonel, whose voice – if he were being honest – had no effect on his bowels until it spoke of the silver Makarov pistol.

Nearly two years earlier, in January 2003, he drove into the mountains for what would be the final time. The morning of his departure, he woke early and performed his ablutions and prayers on the trapezoid of dawn light that lay like a prayer rug on the floor. The winter sun kept the same hours the Soviet post office once did, and he prepared to leave without even the light of a kerosene lamp. Nine years had passed since the house he shared with his father had received reliable electricity, and darkness no longer felt like an absence, but rather a thickening in the air, a viscosity that slowed his movement and called upon his spatial memory. His long underwear had stretched in the knees and as he pulled the elastic band to his hip, he mourned the fact that he could obtain a crate of Special Forces sniper rifles more easily than a decent pair of thermal underwear. Before leaving his room, he reached into a wicker basket of unwashed clothes. The wool socks and grey vests parted and compressed as he pushed through them, but at the bottom, the Makarov pistol kept its shape.

In the kitchen, steam surged from the kettle spout.

Ramzan opened the stove door and cupped his hands in the orange heat. Pages rustled in the living room. His father knew he would leave for the mountains today. A fan of mustard light fell from the living-room doorway, and after preparing a cup of tea, Ramzan walked towards it. The light rose from the floor to his feet and up his legs, outlining the droops in his long underwear and then jaundicing his hands, wrists, forearms, elbows. 'You are leaving soon,' his father said with a foreknowledge that made a statement of the question. His father sat at his desk in the pool of lamplight. Ramzan took a seat on the brown ottoman; the backside had paled from years facing the morning sun.

'What are you reading?' Ramzan asked.

His father gave an abashed smile, as if caught eating *manti* from the pot with his fingers, and tilted the cardboard cover towards the light. It was a conspiracy story about an inept American spy who infiltrated the Kremlin and was discovered by a commissar whose proletariat spirit and exceptional good fortune compensated for his lack of deductive reasoning. His father only read these potboilers when Ramzan was in the mountains. For a man whose life revolved around academic texts, the shift to pulp fiction announced his paternal worry with the volume of a megaphone.

'You've read it before?'

'Twice.'

'Who wins? The Americans or the Russians?'

'Both,' his father said, glancing to the frost-filled windowpane.

'Then who loses?'

'Everyone else.'

'I should be back in a week.'

His father nodded, and looked down to his book. Two

years would pass before he had another conversation with his father.

'I'll see you soon,' Ramzan said. His father marked his place with a pencil, stood, and wrapped his arms around Ramzan's shoulders. His father's breath warmed his cheek like a small, surviving cloud of summer humidity. On the desk, beneath the novel, the typewritten carcass of his manuscript bled red ink. 'If you were writing your book instead of reading others, you might be finished by now.'

'Perhaps,' replied his father. Their embrace didn't break off so much as dissipate, an exhalation releasing whatever tenderness was briefly held between them. His father's hug was an act of precaution rather than love, so that if Ramzan did not return from the mountains, his father would have the consolation of knowing his final gesture towards his son had been one of kindness rather than disappointment.

In his bedroom he pulled up two rigged floorboards and felt through the shadows for the frayed tail of rope. Coiling the rope around his wrist, he drew the wooden pallet across the concrete foundation. A duffel bag with his most treasured possessions sat on the pallet. In it were three fragmentation grenades, a Kalashnikov and eight full magazines, a hunting knife, an old membership card to the village *banya*, two hundred thousand rubles divided in eight shrink-wrapped stacks, and a small sandalwood box containing a single yellow sweater sleeve still attached to the yarn ball.

He slid a stack of notes into the upper right pocket of his old Red Army jacket – a jacket that appeared to be composed entirely of pockets – and slid his arms into sleeves that felt like the largest of the pockets. He looked like a fisherman. He pulled the silver Makarov from the wicker basket, wrapped it in a vest and set it in the duffel bag, to keep for himself. The side arm was one of the twenty he was supposed to transport to the mountains that day, a small gratuity he had awarded himself. In three weeks, he would teach Havaa to shoot it.

Outside, the rising sun flashed on the frost as he stomped towards his truck, carrying his backpack and the kettle. He opened the bonnet and, after letting the kettle cool in the snow, filled the radiator. Antifreeze was an unaffordable luxury, so each evening he drained the radiator and each morning refilled it, and he did this until spring. The weapons and supplies – the nineteen other Makarov pistols among them – were already packed in back. It was a risk leaving the weapons outside overnight, but less of a risk than bringing them in. The temperature difference could easily fracture the rifle operating rods. His father stood in the door frame, his frown the largest wrinkle on his face.

In two minutes his home was indistinguishable from the other snow-capped dwellings scattered in the rear-view. He honked twice when he reached Dokka's. Through the living-room window, an argument between Dokka and his wife halted with the second horn blast. Havaa stood in the doorway, watching Dokka forlornly as he slung a knapsack over his shoulder and clomped through the snow to the passenger's side.

'Difficult morning?' Ramzan asked.

Dokka smiled. 'I'm married. What morning isn't?'

No vehicles had passed since the last snowfall and without tyre tracks to follow he couldn't be sure where the road was. As long as he didn't run into a tree, he thought, he was going the right way. Slouched in the passenger seat, Dokka pushed a pebble in small circles around his palm.

On the road, the snow rose from ten to twenty centimetres as they drove south. Ramzan kept at forty kilometres an hour for so long the two digits seemed skewered on the speedometer needle. They stopped to eat lunch and relieve themselves beside a thicket of pines, whose snowy boughs provided camouflage for the red truck.

'The snow is like my wife's mother,' Dokka said, kicking it over the tyre tracks. 'She will name every place we've been.'

'Have a cigarette.'

'You haven't hunted this year. You've forgotten that a buck is easiest to track in fresh snow.'

Ramzan hoisted himself on the warm engine bonnet. What accounted for Dokka's sudden anxiety? Yes, they would likely be shot if discovered by the Feds or state security forces, but that could happen as easily in Eldár or Volchansk, in their homes or in the street, while they slept, or while they played chess, a fate so likely to befall a Chechen man it seemed silly to worry about it too much.

Before them stretched a white field that had, for eight years now, grown nothing but weeds and dust. The snow erased all measure of distance and the field expanded past the horizon, wide enough to extinguish the sun.

'You won't be able to do this much longer either,' Dokka said. 'The war is over. Grozny has fallen. These skirmishes are final breaths.'

'You're an optimist, Dokka.'

Night fell and they drove through terraced valleys until they reached a hamlet built of the same pale stone that crowned the slopes. Centuries earlier, the hamlet had been home to several thousand; but in 1956, when the Chechens returned from Kazakh exile, Soviet authorities prohibited them from returning to their ancestral homes, and this hamlet of pristine ruins was one among hundreds scattered throughout the highlands. It seemed so unnatural to Ramzan to see a village decimated not by bombs and bullets but by time and neglect. The thirty-nine residents who gathered around the truck shared the blood of common great-great-grandparents. The men wore lambskin hats and tall leather boots, the older women wore grey and black headscarves and long plain dresses, and the younger women wore blue and pink hijabs folded to the width of a hunting blade. The children stood just outside the splay of headlight, afraid it might burn them.

They were met by the tall, arboreal elder, known for eating snow to numb his stomach ulcer. After washing in a tin basin, they dined at his home. Slabs of white stone sealed with clay-lime mortar formed the walls. Weathered petroglyphs adorned each stone: spokes of light jutting from plum-sized suns. In the main room they ate on the mats they would later sleep on. They chewed differently here. Their bowls full, their bites unrationed. No need of words when the tongue could converse with mutton.

Unaccustomed to such portions, Ramzan and Dokka finished last. As soon as they set down their bowls, the women filed in through the back door. The women waited for the men to leave before taking their places on the lamb-skin blankets. Ramzan, the last out, heard whispers and suppressed laughter as the door closed behind him and very much wished he could have remained behind. The men followed a deer trail past the ice-glazed remnants of a stone tower. In earlier centuries, it had been a fortress, watchtower, signal light and anchor to the long-since-scattered *teip*. Past the tower they reached a clearing. A series of elevated planks formed a flat, dry, tyre-shaped platform in the centre of the clearing. Its axle was a ring of stone containing the ashes of a bonfire. The men carried logs from a lean-to deeply entrenched in the hillside. Within minutes the fire reached above Ramzan's head, so bright he could count the rings of the logs yet unconsumed. It had been years since he had last participated in a *zikr*.

Ramzan and Dokka removed their boots and joined the others in a circle around the fire. The elder began the *zikr* with prayer. A steady call, the voice of a man, he thought, in a country bereft of men. *La ilaha illallah, la ilaha illallah.* The elder repeated the cry, and its slow rhythm sliced the words into syllables that stood alone as if locutions of a higher language. Voices on either side joined in harmonies that buoyed the elder's call. Then clapping, not to keep the rhythm, but to propel it. The silver of the moon and the orange of the flames entwined on the elder's tilted face. *There is no god but Allah.* The men swayed from side to side as the pace increased. Swaying grew to stomping, and sawdust rose from the shaking platform, and the men shed their outer garments. Against the burn of bonfire, the men combusted. The flailing arms of overcoats, the falling hands of woollen gloves, but the cries were not the cries of a landmine or shelling, and the pain of the elder's call was the merciful ache of longing. *There is no god. But Allah. No god. But Allah.*

Ramzan clapped and he stomped and he shouted as sweat slicked his face. Without warning, a man three down from Ramzan let out a long wail, and though Ramzan couldn't tie one word from the string of utterances twisting from the man's throat, he understood precisely what the man meant. The man's eyes were closed, and the uncommon serenity of his features suggested he had seen all that could be seen. The elder's voice dropped an octave and in unison the men's stamping became a dance. They marched joyously, anticlockwise, sliding the left foot across the platform and dropping hard on the heel of the right. In unison they spun. Three hundred and sixty degrees flattened to an indivisible plane. The pressure had built in his chest and he tried to contain it with reminders that he was no longer Sufi, that these weren't his people, that human sorrow was the prophecy of an empty heaven, but it built, and built, like the memory of a long-extinguished orgasm, and the pressure closed the space between his cells, and he was released. No melody ran through his wail. His voice was hoarse and broken and he raised it. The other men took no note above the tremble of palms and planks, but Ramzan's next breath brought peace.

The following morning Ramzan woke with a sore throat. After breakfasting on nuts, dried fruit and goat's milk, the elder led Ramzan and Dokka to their truck. In exchange for the hospitality, he gave the elder ten kilos of rice and a litre of butane. The elder refused any offer of munitions besides buckshot, and despite his protestations, Ramzan pressed the issue. He couldn't recall when he had last felt so moved to ensure the safety of a stranger. But the stiffness of the elder's frown made it known that he would never be persuaded of a hand grenade's safety. Driving away, Ramzan struggled to focus on the road. The lives lived behind him were so small and anonymous they had escaped the notice of state socialism, of the first and second war. The previous night, for the first time in a long time, he had felt whole, and his eyes returned to the rear-view, where his dignity was held within a few square centimetres of glass.

They drove another five hours, through mountain passes so narrow the side mirrors would have snapped off, had they not already, and back down to valleys; five hours of listening to Dokka praise his wife's resourcefulness and her gardening and her talent for creating sumptuous dishes with only a third of the requisite ingredients, five hours of compliments so lavish and exaggerated that Dokka could only mean them as insults, for why else sing the praises of marriage to a man who could never marry, why else recite the wonders of companionship if not to wound Ramzan, who, for those five long hours, felt so deficient he would have given his right hand in dowry for a wife who could neither cook, nor sew, nor raise children, a wife who committed adultery and passed wind in public, a wife who treated him like an animal — yes, he would take it and be fine with it because a disgraced man is still a man, and Ramzan wasn't a man, not really, yet the whole world expected him to be one; and the neigh-bours, dear God, *why haven't you married, a handsome man like you still living with your father* — and when his quiet demurrals spawned rumour — *he doesn't like women, that's why he's thirty-one years old and unmarried*, he couldn't decide if truth or rumour dishonoured him more, but ulti-mately, he decided it was better to allow the hearsay of homosexuality to flourish so long as his silence could cast doubt upon the whole matter, and yes, his silence engendered doubt, though mainly in himself, converting shame into rage and propelling it through his veins, his kidneys, his forearms, his little toes, and then returning to that second heart on which the names of those who slandered him were etched, and much later, he would recite those names over a satellite phone and those who had created those stories would fall victim to his own stories, *homosexuality* replaced with *rebel sympathies, Wahhabism, jihad*; but those stories were still unspoken, still unimaginable, and the purgatory of Dokka's wife, within which he was the unfortunate audience, remained interminable even after five hours of driving when he crested a hill and slammed on the brakes because right there, not two hundred metres away, was a platoon of Russian troops, and he viewed them as both conquerors and liber-ators, who might kill him but would free him at least from the perdition of Dokka's voice, and trembling with terror and gratitude he spoke the words that had been on his tongue for five hours. 'Stop talking, Dokka.'

A welcome quiet suffused the cabin, and Ramzan basked in it before fear retook him. There were two armoured personnel carriers, two UAZ jeeps, and a tank crowned with a machine-gun turret.

'Turn round!' Dokka shouted and shook Ramzan's arm by the sleeve of his jacket. 'What are you doing? Let's go!'

But he kept the ball of his foot pressed to the brake pedal. 'They have already seen us.'

It was true. The machine-gun turret had swivelled to face them and snow shot up behind the jeeps as they accelerated towards the crest.

'If we run, we're fucked. If we wait and are reasonable, we might survive. We're just sitting here. It's not yet a crime to be alive. You might even get a chance to finish telling me about your wife.'

The jeeps stopped twenty metres ahead and idled, while behind them the tank gradually ground up the incline. The soldiers who emerged were not the tattooed *kontraktniki*, like those Ramzan remembered from the *zachistka*; no, compared to those hulking Russian bears these were half-starved jackals. We may live to see the sunset, he thought.

Four soldiers bearing machine guns approached. He raised his open palms to the Feds. Dokka followed suit.

'You went to a filtration camp before. You survived. They didn't hurt you,' Dokka stammered, unable to convince even himself. Ramzan wanted to grab Dokka by his ears and shake that stupid self-deluded skull until its one grain of logic rang out. Leaning forward, he felt the empty space between his legs.

'Stop speaking, Dokka. Just be quiet.'

One of the soldiers approached the driver's door. He had

gone at least a week without shaving, but the growth couldn't conceal the concavity of his cheeks. All around the snow stretched indifferently.

'Water,' the soldier croaked. Misunderstanding the request, Ramzan held out his identification card.

'Water,' the soldier again said. 'We've been eating muddy snow for days. We need clean water. Can't you speak Russian?'

'I think we should give him water,' Dokka whispered, his opened hands still facing the windscreen. It was the first sensible thing Dokka had said that day.

'I have water at my feet,' he told the soldier. 'Don't shoot me.'

The soldier accepted the grease-smeared canteen, sighing as he brought the brim to his lips, and his relief became Ramzan's. The soldier didn't suspect that the water had spent the previous day circulating through the engine radiator.

Dokka's hands remained skyward when they were ordered out of the truck. Ramzan protested briefly and half-heartedly; he had, after all, given that first soldier a canteen of water, and was this how his hospitality was to be repaid? But he dropped the remonstration when that first soldier, his thirst now quenched, pressed the gun barrel to Ramzan's forehead. They lay face down in the snow with their wrists bound behind their backs in plastic zip-strips. To keep his head above the snow, Ramzan had to arch his back and puff out his chest and flail like a beached whale. From that uncomfortable vantage, he watched the soldiers unpack the sacks of rice and grain from the truck bed. A few more seconds and they would find the Makarov handguns, frag-mentation grenades, Semtex bricks and lead wires, and he would die here, flopping like a damned sea mammal, many kilometres from home. How he wished he had stitched his address into his inside trouser leg. He hadn't taken the precaution for fear that the security forces would implicate his father, but now, with snow melting through his jacket, he could think of no inhumanity grimmer than an unmarked grave. Perhaps he would be forced to lie upon Dokka to save ammunition. Such a death would insult the gunrunner. He would demand his own bullet. For the water canteen, they could at least do him that small honour. Beside him, Dokka had given up. The heat from his face had thawed a soup bowl in the snow. He wept into it.

'Don't worry,' Ramzan said. His tone surprised him. He could see the end and he was calm. 'Today, we'll find out whether the imams or commissars were right.'

'You're brave,' Dokka said. 'Here I am, crying. I dishonour you.'

How often is immense unhappiness mistaken for courage? He opened his mouth and filled it with snow. It melted as he listened to Dokka's sobs. The soldiers at least would remember which of the two had faced his bullet with clear eyes.

But the soldiers, in an act of unexpected compassion and restraint, decided not to summarily execute them. After finding the weapons, they pulled Ramzan to his feet, then Dokka. Shaking their heads at the mucus frozen to Dokka's lip, they turned to Ramzan, and spoke only to him. They were lost. Three nights earlier, the cold had killed their radio, and they had driven through blanketed fields in vain search for human habitation. They hadn't been tracking the red truck. It was an accident. As the gun barrels pointed them towards one of the UAZ jeeps, the commanding officer asked, 'Are you familiar with the Landfill?'

Ramzan nodded.

'Can you give us directions?'

'Directions?'

'I told you. We're lost.'

He could not believe it.

'If you take us there, you'll live. At least until we get there. That much, I guarantee. And likely after. I know a lieutenant there.'

'OK.' He didn't know what else to say. The commanding officer beamed gratefully. Afraid the man would kiss him, Ramzan made the first move to the jeep. His captors followed.

The soldiers led them down the hillside, tenderly, so they didn't lose their balance. The commanding officer opened the jeep door for Ramzan and cut the cable tie with the serrated edge of a hunting knife.

'Watch your head,' cautioned the commanding officer, who would never tell another soul of his military service. The woman he was to wed in three and a half years would know him as a hundred people – a husband, a father, a churchgoer, an primary-school teacher, a charity worker – and would never find a commanding officer in that population she so dearly loved.

Ramzan slid to the far side of the seat. Dokka sat beside him. A few uncomfortable minutes passed before the commanding officer reappeared in the passenger seat with a Marlboro Red, the rebel field commander's favourite brand, dangling from his lips. The officer and other soldiers watched him expectantly.

'What?' Ramzan asked.

'You haven't fastened your seat belt,' the commanding officer observed.

'My seat belt?' He glanced around. All the soldiers were wearing seat belts.

'We're not going anywhere until you buckle up,' the commanding officer said.

Ramzan nodded, yes, of course he was required to wear a seat belt, just as he was required to give directions to a torture camp, because stupidity was the single abiding law of the universe. He buckled up, and took a compass from his jacket pocket. 'Turn round,' he said. 'The Landfill is behind us.'

Within an hour Ramzan directed the jeep to the road that would take them to the Landfill. Ovals of melted snow appeared in the fields. Strangely curvaceous patches of damp dirt. The sun shone. At one point he yawned and felt the nudge of Dokka's elbow. The hollow-cheeked, grease-lipped soldier dozed beside him.

'I think Akhmed is sleeping with my wife,' Dokka said. Ramzan turned back to the window. Silvery branches darted past. The following summer would be beautiful. He had heard all he cared to hear about Dokka's wife.

Early December 2004. Two weeks before Dokka disappeared. In the cabin of the abandoned logging truck. The first conversation with the Cossack colonel.

'Ramzan Geshilov?'

'Reporting, sir.'

'Do you recognise my voice?'

'I don't, sir. Are you filling in for Captain Ivan Fyodorovich?'

'Is he the officer you report to?'

'Yes.'

'Yes, who?'

'Yes, sir.'

'I have fucked the wife of your superior officer eighty-seven times, and only the first three were before they married. Do you understand me?'

'Yes, sir.'

'I am told you are among our less incompetent assets in the Volchansk region. Is that true?'

'I don't know, sir.'

'At last, someone who tells the truth.'

'Yes, sir.'

'What's the weather like in Eldár Forest?'

'It is . . . it's sunny. And cold.'

'That's what the meteorological report states. I'm glad that the meteorologists are honest, at least for today.'

'Yes, sir.'

'Where are you this very moment?'

'The cabin of an abandoned logging truck. Three kilometres from the village proper. Sir.'

'Good. You are speaking to me rather than the cuckolded captain because a situation has arisen of the utmost importance. Since the captain can't solve the case of his missing wife, who disappears into my bed each Thursday, I wouldn't trust him with this. You see, the ballistics report has come back on a gun used in the assassination of an FSB colonel last year.'

'Last year?'

'Yes. A year to get a simple ballistics report. It's December 2004, and it's just come in. When I was last in Moscow I read that Chinese assembly plants can produce a new car in a few hours. And it takes a year for us to produce a ballistics report that connects the bullet in the head of an FSB colonel to the gun lying metres away.'

'Yes, sir.'

'The report has come back, and I want you to find where the gun came from.'

'Pardon me, sir?'

'Did you break wind?'

'No, sir.'

'Then don't waste a request for my pardon.'

'Yes, sir. It's just that I'm not sure how I'll find the origin of a gun fired a year ago.'

'It's one of those needle-in-a-haystack situations, is it?'

'With all respect, sir, it's a needle in a needle-stack.'

'On that account, you're in luck. It's one of your needles.'

'You must be mistaken. I haven't run so much as a tooth-pick in the past two years. Ask the captain, sir.'

'How about I ask his wife instead? No, I'm not concerned about what you claim not to be selling, but rather about what you've already sold. You see, the serial number on the Makarov pistol used to kill the colonel in December 2003 corresponds sequentially with the serial numbers of the Makarov pistols found in the back of your truck when our brave lads ambushed you and took you to the Landfill in January 2002.'

Silence.

'Are you still there?'

'Yes.'

'Who?'

'Sir.'

'This puts us in a rather difficult situation. In seeking information on the supplier of a gun used to assassinate an FSB colonel, we are immediately led to a person whom we pay to provide us with just that information.'

'I swear I had nothing to do with it, sir. Who was the assassin, sir?'

'A Black Widow. A *shahidka*. A separatist trained and sent by those animals in the mountains.'

'Was she taken alive . . . sir?'

'The *shahidka* was detained at a filtration point. Cleverly, she seduced the colonel, a man, I am told, so very well endowed that only the cavernous cunt of a Chechen has the latitude to accommodate him. No doubt hearing of the colonel's great girth, the *shahidka* used her powers of seduction. When they were alone, she shot him.'

'But, sir, why wasn't she checked for weapons?'

'If you still had a pair of stones between your legs, you would know that the average cunt of your womenfolk is capacious enough to conceal a rocket launcher. The colonel was a fool, no doubt, but nonetheless, he was still a colonel.'

'Yes, sir, but wouldn't it be more prudent to trace the *shahidka*, rather than the gun?'

'A gun can be identified more easily than a person. There is a lesson in that.'

'But the *shahidka* . . .'

'Irrelevant.'

'I'll do what I can, sir.'

'No, you will not do what you can do. You will do what you are told.'

'Yes, sir.'

'Numbers are the amoral language of absolute truth. These serial numbers do not lie. At some point you were in possession of that Makarov, and I will know the name and location of the next hands who held it. I was promoted to replace the departed colonel. I now hold his rank and command, and so, understandably, it is my chief priority to kill the architects of his assassination. Should I fall victim to a similar fate, and should the cuckolded captain be given my rank, I truly fear the fate of the Russian nation.'

'Yes, sir.'

'I see from your file that you have a father.'

'Yes, sir.'

'And he lives with you?'

'Yes, sir.'

'He turned seventy-nine this year?'

'Yes, sir.'

'He survived the Great Patriotic War?'

'Yes, sir.'

'And the deportations to Kazakhstan?'

'Yes, sir.'

'And eleven years there on the steppe?'

'Twelve, sir.'

'And you would like him to see his eightieth birthday?'

'Yes, sir.'

'Then give me names, Ramzan.'

'Yes, sir.'

'Or I'll sew your stones back on just to chop them off twice.'

The Landfill filtration camp was so named for having been built, or rather sunken, into the site of a partially constructed rubbish dump. Once, when Ramzan passed the site as a younger man, he watched a brontosaurial backhoe bite into the soil and scoop out a bathtub's worth of loose earth. But after the collapse, and the subsequent wars, plans to finish the landfill were postponed then abandoned completely. Only two of the eight proposed pits, each twenty metres deep, with the surface area of a football pitch, had been excavated. The concrete and plastic foundation, which would have trapped run-off effluvia, was never installed, and so rain and snow dissolved into a knee-deep sludge at the bottom of the two earthen pits. When Ramzan was taken there in the first war, he spent three days in Pit A before two guards lowered a sixty-rung ladder, doused his feet and legs in frigid water, and led him to the two-storey white building whose entrance still bore the sign REFUSE DISPOSAL ADMINISTRATION. Petitions calling to fill in the pits circulated after the first war. An unfortunate group of sixteen women widowed by the Landfill shovelled for a month, but failed to visibly alter the swampscape. Ultimately, the symbolic benefit of filling the two pits didn't hold up to the actual benefit of rebuilding roads, houses, schools, power plants, refineries and hospitals. No one imagined the pits might again be used. No one imagined there would be a second war.

But there was a second war, and now, in January 2003, having encountered the lost Federal patrol, Ramzan was imprisoned for the second time. He spent eleven days below ground, this time in Pit B, while Dokka was taken to Pit A. At the very least his ears would receive a welcome rest. He descended the now-rusty sixty-rung ladder and the guard shook him from it before he reached the final rungs. The sludge had frozen to a snowy dampness that only reached his ankles. The pit held two dozen others. Over the coming days, he would pray to the sky with them all, but only his conversations with the blue-eyed imam would remain etched in his memory. The guards lowered food and fresh water in tin pails attached to yellow cords that came irregularly, sometimes five in a day, sometimes one, sometimes in the middle of the night when the men would wake, gather and divide the provisions. The one thing the pit had no shortage of was space. Ramzan spent the daylight hours walking alongside its walls, wondering if somewhere the Feds had a modern prison, with electricity, bunks, cells and roofs, in which they housed not prisoners but banana peels, and potato skins, and broken shoelaces, and apple cores, and last year's calendars, and deflated tyres, and balled-up paper, and used tissues, and cigarette butts, and the last worthless slivers of bars of soap. Some compassionate guard, whose soul the imam would teach Ramzan to honour, had tossed in thin wooden planks, and a pavement the width of a balance beam stretched around the pit's perimeter. The names and villages of captives were carved into the clay walls. Men packed snow on the walls as far up as they could reach to moisten the clay, and after a few minutes scraped it off and identified themselves in block letters drawn by stick or finger. Information the Feds would torture them for was written here on the walls for all to see. It was well understood among the men that the Feds had as much sense as two bricks smashed together. It was also understood that pain, rather than information, was the true purpose of interrogation.

In the afternoon of the fourth day, Ramzan balanced on the slender pavement when the blue-eyed imam stopped him.

'Give me a boost,' the imam asked, nodding his bearded chin towards the wall where he had written half his name. At first, Ramzan refused. Since arriving he had done his best to keep his distance from the filthy, brutalised men, as though his refusal to acknowledge them were the tightrope he walked upon, saving him from falling into their ranks.

'Are you a general, hmm?' the imam asked. 'Or a Persian prince? Are your hands too delicate to help an imam old enough to be your uncle?'

'I'm not a Persian prince.'

'Then climb down from your throne and help me.'

The imam placed his muddy boot in the stirrup of Ramzan's woven fingers. He hoisted the imam, whose weight, held in Ramzan's straining hands, was greater than his size suggested. After an endless moment, the imam tapped him on the forehead with a muddy finger and Ramzan let the old man drop to the ground.

'Take a good look at it,' the imam said, pointing to his name and village. 'If it turns out you are a Persian prince, and they let you leave, you must remember me.'

'If they let me leave, I will forget everything here.'

'No,' the imam protested, wagging his muddy little finger at Ramzan. 'You must remember.'

'Why?'

'So that my nephews will know where to buy my corpse.' Ramzan nodded.

'I can afford it, you know,' the imam said, proudly. 'I still have my retirement account.'

When Ramzan turned, the imam asked, 'What did they get you for?'

'Smuggling weapons. You?'

'Height.'

'Height?'

'Well, the lack of height. The Feds came to my village for a counterterrorist operation. They were looking for some Wahhabi mastermind that was supposedly hiding there, but their only physical description of the man was that he had a beard and was less than two metres tall. They rounded up every short, bearded man, and many adolescents who didn't have beards but met the height description. On the reason-for-arrest line of my report, they wrote *too short*.' The imam shook his head and stared up at his name written in the clay wall, now beyond his reach. Ramzan was glad he'd stopped to lift the imam.

'It's funny,' the imam continued. 'My generation grew up in the Kazakh resettlement camps, and because protein was so scarce, it's not at all uncommon for men of my age to be short, but I've always been ashamed of it. My younger brother used to tell me that my shortness wouldn't kill me. He was only two centimetres taller than me, but I swear, he lived his entire life in those two centimetres, lording them over me, always asking if I needed help reaching the upper shelves. I wish he were still alive, just so the Feds could arrest him for being too short, too.'

'What can one do?' Ramzan said, shrugging.

'Pray,' the imam said.

The imam held court in the south-west corner of Pit B, perched on the seat of honour, an upturned water pail that had come loose from its cord. Each morning he led prayers and performed ablutions with snow that turned his hands a numb white. He insisted that God, in His mercy, would forgive their unclean state. He had memorised the entire Qur'an and lectured on the nature of evil, which, like a shadow, cannot exist independently of the good it silhouettes. Unlike the sheikh and mujahideen, he never tied politics to Qur'anic verse, and instead explained the righteousness of the faithful and the wisdom of the Prophet and the joyousness of a Paradise that is the summer to the winter of the world. Above all, he spoke of the end times and God's judgement.

But the interrogator would judge Ramzan before God would, and it was the interrogator's judgement that he feared. Each day he watched the ritual of men called forth. First the sixty-rung ladder was slid down the wall of the pit, and then the name of the summoned was magnified through a megaphone, so loud and static-laced it sounded like it truly came from the heavens. If the summoned hesitated, a warning shot was fired. The summoned climbed all sixty rungs to the sixty-first, street level, a place so distant the sky seemed closer. None of the summoned returned. An optimistic man might believe they had been found innocent, released, sent home to their families; but not even Dokka, in whatever comparable perdition he lived, would be capable of such optimism. As soon as the summoned reached the top of the ladder and stepped onto the snowy soil of the sixty-first rung, the imam began the funeral. The service was unlike any Ramzan had attended. No body. No shroud. No friend or neighbour who had known the summoned in any but this desperate condition. They were all dead, just a step or two behind the summoned, and they honoured him not as one who departs, but as one who has fully entered. The imam congregated the others around the damp plaque where the summoned had written his name and village. They read the name aloud, softly at first, then growing to a chant that rivalled the *zikr*, and made prayer from the name and sent it skyward. For twenty-four hours, or as close as they could calculate, the name and village of the summoned was left on the clay wall. At the twenty-fifth, the men gathered around the inscription. Each took a palmful of earth from the thawing ground and pressed it to the wall. Without the body, they could only bury the name, and when they could no longer read it, they knew the man was gone.

'According to *hadith*, he who nightly recites the sixty-seventh surah will be spared a torturous death,' the blue-eyed imam lectured one evening from the upturned bucket. 'You must all know that. You must all count on that. The surah describes the Merciful's creation of all seven heavens, each one above the other. The Throne of God sits atop the highest heaven, and lanterns adorn the lowest. The lanterns are our stars and comets, this firmament above our very heads.'

He glanced to the sky and lowered his face. He pulled a book of matches from his pocket and struck it. Soft yellow light gloved his hand. 'Take heart, my friends; we are already among the righteous. We are already with God.' He raised the match to his face, and his shadow was cast across the Landfill clay. 'Here is the lantern of our lowest heaven.'

From somewhere far above them, a name was called through the megaphone. The imam stepped down from the bucket and walked towards the ladder. 'With God,' he said, as he stepped onto that first and lowest rung.

Night fell. The moonlight covered Ramzan like a flimsy bed sheet. He lay on a strip of once-burgundy carpeting, which would capsize in the mud if he sat up, turned over, yawned or thought too hard. The stars shone much brighter here. The gauzy light of the Milky Way canopied Pit B, the nearest thing to a roof. Nothing in this or the next world was worse than physical pain. In the afterlife, as no more than a soul, he would be without a body to beat, skin to peel, blood to flow, eyes to gouge, fingernails to prise, lungs to drown, ventricles to stop, and so the retribution of God would always be gentler than the retribution of man. He held on to this one truth the next morning when his name was called through the megaphone. He held on to it as he climbed the ladder and saw, framed by the rungs, the names of those to follow. When ordered to disrobe, he complied. When one of the interrogating officers wanted a better view of the cratered skin that had been his scrotum, he complied. Those scars were seven years old. During his first detention in the Landfill, in 1995, in the first war, he had refused to inform. They had wrestled down his trousers, shown him the bolt cutters, and still he had said no. Screaming, thrashing, with his manhood half severed, he had said no. He had done that, and now he was ready to start saying yes.

He would have confessed everything, but they didn't ask, weren't interested, threatened to cut out his tongue and put pliers to his teeth if he spoke one more fucking word. Electric wires were wound around his fingers. A car battery was drained into his bones. God might have been watching, but it wasn't God's finger on the battery switch. The interrogating officers didn't speak. Instead he was an instrument they played, performing a duet, and in their own way they conversed through his sobs. They both wore very shiny shoes. That was all he would remember.

He passed out and was resuscitated by buckets of cold water so frequently that even the electricity in his veins couldn't warm him. The interrogating officers stepped out of the room to have a rest, and new officers entered. He had been in interrogation for three hours and they still hadn't asked him a single question. In a moment of calm, when the interrogators were asking each other about their weekends, he tried to find the beat of his heart among the burps and squelches, real and unreal, emanating from his blistered body. Before the second car battery was attached, the new interrogator guided Ramzan to the next room. He had trouble walking. He had forgotten torture could be so exhausting. The new interrogator, the one with less shiny shoes, held him upright, using his whole body as a crutch, and helped him walk. He carefully wiped Ramzan's forehead with a handkerchief before opening the door to the next room. A white wooden table scored with fingernail scratches stood in the centre of the room. In this realm of ceased expectation, the aquarium at the far end didn't surprise him. The blue-eyed imam was brought through another door. He didn't recognise Ramzan, or if he did, he refused to acknowledge the fact of his shame before a disciple. The imam was held down against the table. One of the guards pulled down his trousers and underwear. The interrogator with less shiny shoes, who had, moments earlier, so tenderly guided Ramzan down the corridor, went to the aquarium. He put on a pair of thick rubber gloves. He reached into the aquarium. The blue-eyed imam didn't know what was happening. From his vantage, he saw only the wall and the arms holding him. The imam couldn't see what Ramzan saw. He couldn't see the interrogator with less shiny shoes approach with the bucking, writhing black belt in his gloved hands, and the interrogator couldn't see the imam's face. The imam didn't understand what was happening, and neither did Ramzan. But when the interrogator with less shiny shoes pressed the eel, teeth first, between the imam's pale buttocks, it could be nothing else. The room went blurry, then black, and the imam's shriek followed Ramzan into unconsciousness. When he woke, he was back in the first interrogation room. The interrogator with less shiny shoes crouched behind him. His hands were wet. Ramzan promised everything, and the interrogator, like the parent of a child too old to believe in ghosts, watched him with disappointment, his clear eyes saddened by Ramzan's sincerity. The interrogator took off his jacket, rolled up his sleeves, laid the live wires on Ramzan's chest and mapped the border of their shared humanity. Ramzan offered his soul. He begged to be enslaved. The known universe contracted to the limits of the cement floor, and on it, the interrogator was both man and deity, prophet and god. By ten o'clock the interrogator with less shiny shoes asked his first question. By eleven the electrical wires were unwound from Ramzan's fingers. By noon he was allowed to dress. By one he was on the FSB payroll. He kept thanking the interrogator with less shiny shoes. Again and again and again, he thanked the man, and never before had he expressed such earnest gratitude. He would have followed the interrogator with less shiny shoes anywhere. It was God he found at the other end of the electrical wires. He was given a satellite phone and a three-hundred-page manual written in German, French, English and Japanese. He asked after Dokka, asked if he could buy back his friend's life. Yes, the interrogator with less shiny shoes told him, provided the village could raise a fifty-thousand-ruble ransom within a week; otherwise, the ransom would jump to seventy-five thousand for his corpse. Ramzan reached into one of the many pockets of the overcoat they returned to him, and timidly pulled out the plastic-wrapped notes. No one had thought to check his pockets. 'This is only half,' the interrogator with less shiny shoes told him. 'But I am, above all, a reasonable man.'

Ramzan waited for Dokka on the concrete stairs of the Refuse Disposal Administration. A hundred metres away, at the bottom of Pit B, his funeral was taking place. Perhaps one of the others sat on the imam's upturned pail, intoning the name of Ramzan Geshilov, the good and righteous man who had refused to inform and had died for it in the Landfill seven years earlier and only now was having his funeral.

The pebbles at his feet were round and pockmarked. His bare toes curled around them. There was no guilt, no shame, those would come later, but for now, just the blanketing white noise of relief, of this breath, of non-pain. He wore the rings of ten burn marks on his fingers. For the first time in his life he believed without reservation in the existence of a kind and generous God, as desert thirst teaches one to believe in rain. After an hour his red truck turned the corner, followed by a dust billow that swept past when the truck stopped. Dokka's gasps filled in the open passenger window. Leaving the engine idling, the interrogator with less shiny shoes climbed from the driver's side. He held up a red plastic bag, like a fish he had proudly caught. Ten fingers floated in the blood. 'Your friend gets these back when I get the other twenty-five thousand,' said the interrogator with less shiny shoes.

After Ramzan climbed into the driver's seat, after he bandaged Dokka's hands with bandannas and gaffer tape, he looked to the dash and saw that the interrogator – whose shoes, wet with blood, now shone in the afternoon sun – had left them with a full tank of petrol.

And, now, two years later, December 2004, two weeks before Dokka disappeared, when the dialling tone severed the

Cossack colonel's threat, and Ramzan packed away the satellite phone, and descended from the cabin of the abandoned logging truck, he did so with the same numbness that had allowed him to drive away from the Landfill two years earlier. Both times he heard Dokka's beseeching voice, and both times he did his best to ignore it. For the two weeks after the Cossack colonel's call, the two weeks in which his bowels clenched in a constipated fist, Dokka, not yet a ghost, haunted Ramzan. He ran through the twelve names he had already given the Feds, the twelve who had disappeared because he had become an informer two years earlier at the Landfill. What did a thirteenth matter? What did any one person matter when pounded against the anvil of history? He sat quietly and remembered Dokka as if he had already gone. Dokka always ended his questions with *or*, as if anticipating he would be denied: *Would you like to play chess, or...? Will the G-3 rations be handed out tomorrow, or...?* His generosity in opening his home to refugees, and his intransigence in demanding rent, even if payment was no more than a dull button, or a paper clip, or a piece of stationery for his daughter's souvenir collection. His brown eyes had twice grown dull: first after he lost his fingers, then after he lost his wife. His paddle hands. His slender toes taught the dexterity of a left hand. He could clasp a pencil between his first and second toe, and write in awkward letters so large only a sentence would fit on the page. His genius for chess.

The more Ramzan thought about it, the more awful it became. The Dokka unearthed in no more than a trowelful of memory was enough to break his heart. Dokka insisted on wearing button shirts, and how he dressed each morning, if the girl helped him, if he was too proud to ask his daughter for help, if he woke before dawn to begin the long arduous task of buttoning his shirt with his toes, Ramzan didn't know. On that frantic truck ride back from the Landfill, Dokka had thanked Ramzan for saving his life. Somehow they had survived and not even the agony of ten amputated fingers had been enough to make him forget his manners.

Two weeks after his first conversation with the Cossack colonel, he trekked back into the woods, back under the ice-encased branches, to the cabin of the corroded logging truck. He called the colonel and gave up Dokka, explaining that Dokka harboured refugees, and also likely rebel sympathisers, though he didn't add that most Chechens sympathised. He described, truthfully, how Dokka had asked for a weapon when they returned from the Landfill because he had feared he couldn't protect his family. He described, truthfully, how he had taught Havaa to shoot the Makarov pistol because Dokka no longer had the fingers to pull the trigger. It was the first unembellished account he had provided. The silver Makarov pistol was the sole piece of evidence, and though he gave extenuating circumstances, mitigating factors and reasonable doubt, the colonel wasn't interested in building a prosecution against Dokka. The colonel asked about Havaa, and Ramzan, with a tightening in his gut that promised no parole of his captive bowels, understood that when a man is implicated in the assassination of a colonel, his entire family must disappear, even if his entire family is an eight-year-old girl.

When it was done, and Ramzan emerged from the woods after speaking to the Cossack colonel for the second time, he forced himself to walk to Dokka's house. An ache radiated from his temples. He closed his eyes. What did you do with that gun, Dokka? You stupid man. I can't buy your life this time. With each step he discarded a piece of himself. Even as he gave up his neighbours, he cocooned himself in the rationale of exigency. Whether eating scavenged food or selling an old friend, they had all shamed themselves to survive. Greed didn't motivate his informing, at least not primarily; primarily, he informed by necessity, to survive, for his love and hate and above all awe of the power wielded by the interrogating officer with less shiny shoes. But by giving away Dokka and the girl, he had stepped into full accountability, and lost the shadows that had saved him.

A few seconds after the knock, the door opened by the ingenious foot-operated pulley system Dokka had designed from a timber saw band, a shopping-trolley wheel and a stirrup.

Dokka welcomed him, invited him in. Not a trace of suspicion. Dokka, he realised with painful clarity, was the only person, besides the Feds, who would speak to him. The only person who tolerated his voice, who would listen and respond, and it was at that moment, he would later realise, that the universe went silent. He could have pinned the gun on Akhmed, on anyone. Why, this one time, had he told the truth? Again Dokka invited him in. Only then, with Dokka's hospitality, friendship and conversation before him, did Ramzan understand why he had inflicted this visit upon himself.

'Oh, no,' Ramzan said, when Dokka beckoned to the kitchen table. 'I just stopped by to see if you needed any firewood.'

'You left a heap in the backyard just the other day.'

'Yes, I know, I just wanted to see if . . .' He bit his lip and glanced to the threshold, scuffed and worn by the feet of hundreds of passing refugees. It would record the footfall of those who would disappear Dokka and his daughter that night. He looked up into Dokka's brown eyes.

'Are you all right?' Dokka asked. 'You look ill.'

I'm sorry, Dokka. Look at you. I'm sorry.

'Ramzan?'

I came to say goodbye, he thought. 'I came to say hello,' he said.

Chapter 19

'SO THIS IS WHY THEY KEEP YOU AROUND?' Akhmed said to the one-armed guard, who just then, in the hospital car park, floundered under the weight of a heavy box. A blue throbbing vein surfaced on the guard's valiant left forearm. 'Do you moonlight as a professional mover?' Akhmed asked. He leaned against the jeep, casually smoking a cigarette. 'Half-off moving?'

'May I shoot him, Dr Sonja?' the one-armed guard asked, hopefully.

She smiled at these two buffoons – the one-armed guard threatened to kick Akhmed's arse with his *two* working legs – and they had to be buffoons, because every hospital employee with a kopek of common sense had left. 'I need his arms,' she called after the guard, who was chasing Akhmed across the car park. 'Don't shoot him until we get all the supplies inside.'

When they finished unloading, she went to the canteen cupboard. Behind the shoebox of loose cash, the clattering ID cards, the plastic bag of heroin stood the good stuff: cans of sweetened condensed milk. The sweet syrup gurgled from the cut triangle, a thick coating on her gums, and for a few succulent seconds her mind narrowed to the width of that sugary stream. 'Sweetened condensed milk will rot your mouth but preserve your soul,' advised her father's aunt Lena, who died in a Grozny nursing home at the age of one hundred and three, having outlived two husbands, six children, three grandchildren and thirty-two teeth. The maternity ward was empty, the trauma quiet, and Sonja closed her eyes, slipped into this unexpected peace as she would warm, cleansing water.

She climbed to the fourth floor. The swinging doors of the old maternity ward crooned as she entered. The droplet flame of her cigarette lighter guided her to an oil lamp and expanded to fill the glass chamber. When she lifted the lamp the light peeled back the shadows. In the years since their completion, Natasha's murals had faded and smudged as if a fog had fallen across the city. Even so, the degree of detail still amazed her. There, in the window that held half of City Park, a dog had been, for eight years now, relieving itself on a commissar's leg.

'You didn't show me this on the tour.'

He had changed into those ridiculous woman-sized scrubs and leaned against the door frame, trying and failing to act casual. Buffoons, imbeciles, orphans, lunatics and visionaries; family. 'I'm sorry,' she said. 'For earlier today.'

He shrugged; was there no end to the number of shrugging shoulders she was asked to decipher? 'What is this?' he asked, glancing to the walls.

'The old maternity ward.'

'On the fourth floor?'

'The genius of Soviet engineering,' she said, shaking her head. 'The hospital was designed in the early Brezhnev years entirely without the input of practising physicians. After the

Feds shot a rocket at the storage cupboard, we finally decided to move everything to the ground floor.'

The shadows slipped from his face as he stepped into the pool of lantern light.

'Did you draw these?' he asked, nodding to the nearest window mural.

'Natasha did.'

'What was she like?' he asked, tilting his face to her.

She had described Natasha to border guards, camp officials and aid workers. Hazel eyes, brown hair, one hundred and seventy centimetres in height, sixty kilograms in weight, no tattoos or piercings, no visible scars but cigarette burns clustered on her left shoulder; she incanted the litany, scribbled it on paperwork as an unconscious doodle, but how could an instrument as blunted as language express one as strange and fleeting as Natasha? Metaphors failed her; Natasha could not be summarised. What she possessed were losses: the loss of Natasha's laugh, the loss of Natasha's scorn, the loss of Natasha's begrudging love; and as a phantom limb can ache and tickle, her lost Natasha was still laughing, still scornful, still loving begrudgingly, burgeoning with enough life to make Sonja wonder if she, herself, was the one disappeared.

'Natasha was complex,' she said finally, which was as near to the truth as she could articulate.

'Is,' he corrected. 'She will come back. Like a George Bush.'

Smiling stupidly, she shrugged, at long last discovering the gesture's utility. Akhmed's cheeks bunched at the corners of his grin. His confidence was so big and brash she might believe it if she wasn't careful. It was that hope, lingering in the slimmest margins of possibility, that hurt her more than the loss; unlike Natasha, it never disappeared entirely.

'Talking about it doesn't do any good,' she said, glad, at least, that Natasha wasn't there to hear her admit it.

'Dokka was disappeared once, and he returned. Without his fingers, but still. I hope he does again.'

This is the hardest part, she could have told him, before time dulls the loss to a manageable ache. But he and the girl still joked with a levity Sonja couldn't have summoned a year after Natasha left, and that capacity for joy unsettled her.

'Would you love her,' she asked, unable to mask her unease, 'if you had children of your own?'

'It's hard to know,' he said. 'I've always loved her. But she is mine, now, more than anyone's. If I had a family, I might know better what to say. But she's mine. That I know.'

Once, after she had renounced her family in a childhood tantrum, her father had said, 'Your family isn't your choice.' Nearly thirty years later, while walking through City Park, she had seen two homeless men wedged into a single sleeping bag, their soot-stained arms wrapped around one another, and finally understood what her father had meant.

'It's funny,' he said, walking to the window. 'A friend of mine told me about this mural years ago.'

'Did he have a child delivered here?'

'I doubt it.' He stood in reverent concentration a hand's width from the plywood boards. 'He's nearly eighty.'

'She worked on them for such a long time. I'd never seen her devote so much of herself to anything. I was so proud of her. Deshi and Maali helped her.' Natasha had once described it as transcribing their memories, a turn of phrase so lovely Sonja was unwilling to share it with him.

'I'd forgotten completely, otherwise I would have asked to see them sooner. When Khassan told me about them, I was so moved that someone would go to the trouble. It seemed like such a big beautiful waste of time. You can imagine how much that would appeal to me. So I did something similar.'

Her heart rose a centimetre. Even disappeared, Natasha was still surprising her. 'Because of my sister's murals?'

'Yes, I suppose so. I told you about the wounded rebels that occupied the village? The Feds came next. Forty-one of my neighbours were disappeared. I remembered what Khassan had told me about the room with its view recreated on boarded windows, and I drew portraits of all forty-one on plywood boards and hung them throughout the village.'

'Everyone here is a fucking artist,' she said, shaking her head. 'If you people spent more time fighting and less time drawing, you might win a war now and then.'

'It was medical school that did it to me.' He leaned to her and dropped his voice to an exaggerated, conspiratorial whisper. 'I used to skip lectures and labs to sit in on art classes. That's why I'm a better drawer than physician.'

'I can't believe you told me that.'

'I'm trusting you with my darkest secret,' he said, so pleased with himself she couldn't avoid laughing with him.

'I could lose my job for knowing that and keeping you on. Criminal neglect.'

'Obviously you are a criminal, look at the company you keep. International smugglers and amateur artists.' His left arm had steadily edged towards hers. 'You could fire me.'

'It's too late for that,' she said, and focused on the women's scrubs cinched around his biceps, how ridiculous he looked. There had been fourteen since the lifts last ran: four Russians, six Chechens, two Ingush, one French physician, and a Finnish journalist, who she fucked before granting an interview. None knew her surname or patronymic; anonymity was the most comprehensive prophylactic. And the sex itself, infrequent and illicit and often awkwardly impersonal, fulfilled her more wholly than anything a husband could provide. As someone whose days were defined by the ten thousand ways a human can hurt, she needed, now and then, to remember that the nervous system didn't exist exclusively to feel pain.

'Even before those portraits, people from neighbouring farms and villages would come to my clinic, people who didn't have photographs of their lost ones. I'd draw them.' He said it as if it had happened centuries ago.

'Like a police sketch artist?'

'If I must be an -ist I'd prefer portraitist.'

And then it was so obvious.

'Draw her for me,' she asked. 'Now. Draw the face of the woman who told you my name.'

When he returned with a notebook and pencil, they sat at the worktop. He opened the notebook.

'I only barely remember her,' he said, in apology or indemnity, she couldn't tell.

She nodded at him to begin. If she opened her mouth, if she tapped that reservoir, nothing would stopper it. He folded the notebook at the spine and drew a line so soft it looked halfway erased. An oval. It could be anyone's head, even Natasha's. Next he drew two smaller ovals, right in the middle of her head, too long, until she imagined a fringe. The two eyes watched her from the page. When he began drawing the wrong nose, she squeezed his wrist.

'That's not . . .' She struggled to push words into the sentence. She would regret this. She knew she would. But she hadn't seen her sister's face in twelve months, two weeks and three days, and even more than Natasha's face, even more than her return, she wanted Natasha to end. 'Her nose was smaller,' she said.

For the next half-hour she gently corrected him whenever he strayed. He hadn't forgotten her face, she told herself; she was only helping him remember. And if she was deluding herself, so what? Weren't delusions better than desperation, false hopes better than none at all? As Natasha's calm, untroubled face emerged, Sonja's heart climbed her ribs. It drummed against each one, then rose to her neck, pressing against her throat. In a refugee camp or foreign country, somewhere far away, Natasha was safe. He drew a chin she would recognise in a crowd of thousands, then down to her perfect, unblemished neck. Not one cigarette burn; she hadn't told him to put them there. Something spectacular was happening in her chest. She hadn't expected this. On one sheet of paper in a notebook of two hundred and twenty, and with no more than a few millimetres of pencil lead, he returned Natasha to her and to the maternity ward.

'Please stop,' she said.

'I thought you wanted this?'

He reached for her shoulder and she turned away. 'I'll see you tomorrow,' he said after a moment.

'Take this with you.'

He lifted Natasha from the worktop and carried her from the maternity ward.

Chapter 20

SHE WAS SOLD TO A BROTHEL WITHIN BULLET range of Kosovo, and from there south through the breeze-block city of Tirana and across the Adriatic, where, rocking on the dull green water, she saw the face of the moon for the first time in five weeks. It, too, was cratered with cigarette burns. Her passport was her deed, her title and bill of sale, carried by whoever owned her today, travelling within reach of her hand but never in it. Through it all, she could count on a ritual as fixed in the day as sunrise and set. Every morning a shot of heroin inflated her head so it floated a metre above her neck until noon. By afternoon she's itching. By evening she'll do whatever they ask to get a shot that night. She's not the high-priced, high-class call girl she had imagined, borne by limousine to fancy hotels, where she knows the doormen by name and tips them generously when she saunters into the night a free woman. She couldn't buy a full bag of groceries with what the johns pay for thirty minutes. It feels like autumn, but maybe it's spring. She can't tell, fifteen storeys above the nearest leaf. She can't remember the year or the city, the taste of fresh air or the feel of her passport, her sister's voice or the love and desperation that compelled her to flee, but she stands by the window and remembers the view; in eight months, when it's all over and she's taking three-hour showers in a women's shelter, she will walk to the bathroom mirror and, angle by angle, she will draw it on the steamed glass. The men call her Natasha, but she doesn't know how they know her name. Finally Katya tells her that's what every girl from Eastern Europe is called, we're all Natashas to them. An average day consists of ten men, three cheeseburgers, eight glasses of tap water and two shots. A toothbrush, no toothpaste. A tube of mints, one after each man. The repatriated women are right: modern-day slavery, but there's nothing modern about it. Eight of you sleep on four bunk beds crammed into a bedroom. In the early morning, mid-afternoon, whenever the clouds part, when the heroin slithers into your blood and you forget your name, you stand at the window and thread the eternity of sky through needle-head retinas. Street after street the city goes on and every last building, right up to the horizon, stands. Sergey, the pimp, whose brother was sent back from Grozny in a zinc can, stopped smoking last week or last month and the spent pieces of his nicotine gum, spat out and dried on the floor, look like little grey brains. One Natasha died, seven Natashas left; a new Natasha walked in the room and asked if this was where the au pairs slept. You are all replaceable, all disposable. Sergey reads business books and listens to lectures on free-market capitalism and, sometimes, in the middle of it, you can hear the lectures through the wall, through the grunting flab atop you, and listening to *free trade* and *commodity economy* leaves you with a rich nostalgia for the relative generosity of totalitarianism. There is the night, the last night, the next night. The belt around your ankle, the two taps of the syringe, the blood into the barrel, the plunger pushing in. There is the woman named Anzhela but called Natasha. The woman named Nadya but called Natasha. The woman named Natasha, called Natasha.

Chapter 21

AT DAYBREAK KHASSAN LEFT FOR THE SERVICE
road half hoping to intercept Akhmed, but all he found was
a fresh set of footprints. Not knowing what else to do, he
walked back and forth, urging the dogs to do likewise, and
together they turned five kilometres of snow into a riddle no
one could solve. Khassan had taken off his gloves, periodically
oiling his fingers with butter, and for five kilometres lapping
tongues warmed his knuckles. The bald one, Kashtanka, shiv-
ered like a prenatal rat, and several times Khassan paused to
reattach the blanket tied by twine around the dog's pale torso.
In summer he bathed the dogs. If one fell sick he cared for
it. At the village edge, he knelt and they gathered to him,
leaping, licking his cheeks, leaning their paws on his back
and panting in his ears, diseased, unwashed, his, his, his. When
he stood, all six followed with Sharik at the rear. It wasn't
yet nine o'clock. The day stretched out and his path in it lay
as meandering and meaningless as the one he had left. Before
the bend in the road he saw Akhmed's house and across from
it the gap that had been Dokka's. If he had seen Akhmed
that morning, he would have had to ask permission to visit

Ula; if he had asked permission, he might have been denied. It was a better excuse than the frigid air to stay curled under the covers those extra minutes.

The dogs lounged in the snowy lawn to wait for him. He crept through the shadows of the living room, careful not to disturb the curtains, and into the bedroom where Ula slept fitfully. He hesitated to wake her, as if he were no more than her troubled dream and would dissolve if he touched her. Her hair clumped in greasy cords and she smelled of talcum powder. In the kitchen he filled a stew pot with clean water and set it beside the bed. He drew the covers to Ula's chin, so when she woke she wouldn't worry about her decency. Then, reluctantly, he rubbed her arm.

'Why are you here?' she asked without even the suggestion of surprise in her face.

'Do you remember me?' he asked, more urgently than he had intended.

She narrowed her eyes.

'I must have lived a thousand lives before this. I was a bird. I was an insect. I lived in the leaves. I don't know which life is the hallucination.'

'You're Ula,' he said. 'You're married to Akhmed.'

'Why are you here?' Again she asked the question; again he didn't answer.

Because his son was the reason she spent the day alone. Because keeping her comfortable, keeping her company, caring for her was the least he could do. Because he was lonely. Because he had forgotten a woman's companionship. Because the thought of talking himself senile to a pack of feral dogs didn't appeal to him this early in the day. He looked to the stew pot of water beside the bed. Because she forgot. Because she forgot everything he said. 'I'm here to wash your hair.'

She nodded and he peeled back the blanket, her skin whiter than a Russian's. Sometimes Akhmed carried her outside to the rocking chair and she would sit without rocking, swathed in blankets even in the sticky summer months. Khassan turned her so her hair hung off the side of the bed and into the water. The soap gave a fine lather, and he ran his fingers through the water, and broke the bubbles against her scalp, and washed away the grease and dead skin. After it was washed and rinsed, he wrapped her hair in a towel and propped her upright against the head-board.

'You look like a sheikh with that turban around your head,' he said.

'Why are you here?' she asked.

'I'm here to finish telling you a story.'

She smiled, pleased with his answer. 'You might have to repeat things. You may not know but my memory isn't what it once was.'

He began where he had stopped, on the steppe, where the next morning he and Mirza boarded the train from Kazakhstan to Chechnya. Eldár was a ghost town when the survivors among its former residents returned. Soviet soldiers tasked with building a new thoroughfare had uprooted all the tombstones from the village cemetery. Khassan entered the village on a street scrawled with epitaphs. Dust added an extra half-centimetre of height to the tabletop, the shelves and floor. The air was too thick to breathe, and so on his first night home, he slept outside. The next morning, under an awning of bulbous grey clouds, he buried the brown suitcase in the back garden.

He was thirty-one years old and enrolled in the history doctoral programme at Volchansk State University. On the day of Mirza's wedding, he barricaded himself in the university library. He had considered kidnapping her, as Chechen grooms had done since time immemorial when failing to receive the approval of a bride's parents. But he didn't want to earn a reputation as a bride kidnapper, particularly not among his professors, and besides, it was too late. That afternoon she would marry the botanist she'd been betrothed to since her ninth birthday, and if botany wasn't bad enough, the man also had a club foot and a collection of pressed flowers. All through the day Khassan read thick philosophical tomes, but not one explained the injustice of a world in which he would lose Mirza to a club-footed botanist with a passion for pressed flowers. The botanist was a decent man, but Khassan was in love, and thus capable of infinite hate.

About the time he began writing the book that would occupy his life, Khassan embarked on a smaller secondary project of historical reclamation. On notecards he recorded the recollections friends, neighbours and distant relations had of his family, and pinned them to the walls of what had been his sister's room. All were small and ordinary – his sister's hiccupping laugh, his father's wish for the smallest denominations of change so his pockets would jingle like a rich man's – but when he read them, alone in the house they once had shared, these unremarkable memories returned with an unforeseen force. When one wall was covered from floor to ceiling, he began populating the room with artefacts of Mirza, as though she too had receded into the past that had claimed his family. He followed her. When, at the bazaar, she purchased a ball of ruby-red yarn, he purchased the tangerine ball adjacent; when she wore a grey cardigan with silver buttons, he found that same grey cardigan, with brass buttons. While the club-footed botanist collected flowers, Khassan collected his wife. The notecard-papered room soon filled with the headscarves she'd never worn, the cigarettes she'd never smoked, and in the evenings he would flop into the teal-striped armchair, so similar to the navy-striped armchair in her living room, and would read while sipping from a teacup a centimetre narrower than hers, and for a few moments, if lucky, he would forget and she would be standing just out of sight, refilling the samovar, or perhaps knitting a pair of tangerine mittens, and his happiness became the one real artefact in the room.

So it went. Seven years passed before he spoke again to the real Mirza, on an autumn afternoon as uninspiring as every afternoon that autumn, when the blast of a Volchansk bus horn broke the silence. He had just left the library in a frantic search for matches when he heard the punched blare. He turned, and had the Prophet himself stood there, he would have been no more surprised. She wore the grey cardigan; the silver buttons really did look better than brass. The flailing ends of a ruby-red scarf tossed at her shoulders. The bus had braked less than a metre from where she stood; he could have bowed down and blackened his lips on that hallowed pavement. Their eyes met. She blushed; not with surprise or astonishment, but with the downcast embarrassment of one who has been caught.

He invited her to the university cafeteria. They picked awkwardly at a pastry plate, and she tried to convince him that she had come to the city for a dental appointment, and he gave assurances that he believed her. But her sheepishness dissolved as quickly as the spoonful of sugar in her second cup of tea. Her short, filed fingernails darted across the partition of silverware. They spoke for two hours, and when the cafeteria lady's disapproving glances lingered too long, Mirza asked for a tour of the library. She hurried from one stack to the next, wide-eyed and awed, and only later, when he'd checked out a dozen books for her, did he learn that this was her first time in a library. He carried them to his office, which did not, he could safely say, have the same impact. It was, quite literally, the broom cupboard. The brooms were gone – he'd thrown them out when he'd been assigned the office – but the cupboard was barely wide enough to accommodate the smallest university desk, which was wedged in so tightly tissue paper couldn't have slipped between it and the wall. Her days were empty, she confessed; would it be possible to come to the university a few days a week and read in his office? This Mirza was entirely different from the younger one who had smashed Stalin's plaster nose with the heel of her boot. Perhaps he had changed, too; but he loved her no less.

Twice a week they met at the corner, mindful of oncoming buses. He saw her in the grey cardigan with the silver buttons, the blue cardigan with the fake ivory buttons, the green cardigan with no buttons. They passed a cigarette back and forth, and when he felt the damp of her lips on the filter, the world became big and beautiful. His office could only accommodate one chair, so she would read her books there while he worked in the library. One afternoon he returned a half-hour earlier than usual and found her hunched over a huge stack of typewritten paper. From the flipped-over pages, he could see that she was at least two-thirds through *his* manuscript. A breeze would have broken him. 'This is wonderful,' she said, standing, as if baffled that he was capable of anything wonderful. His tilted gaze found her ankles. They were lovely ankles. She praised his book and he embraced her from gratitude rather than lust, but she didn't let go. Neither did he. She kissed his cheek, his earlobe. For months they'd run their fingers around the hem of their affection without once acknowledging the fabric. The circumference of the world tightened to what their arms encompassed. She sat on the desk, between the columns of read and unread manuscript, and pulled him towards her by his index fingers.

It was over in ninety seconds. He walked her to the *marshrutka* stop. When she boarded the shared taxi-bus, he followed. He sat beside her and angled his leg against hers, and they rode silently, two strangers with a secret held like a sheet of paper between their knees. She met him at the back of his house and at the door she stood red-cheeked and shivering, and he took her hands. She was his home. The only land that bound him. He led her to the notecard-papered room and didn't have to explain a thing. She saw the yarn and knew. She unwound the ruby scarf from her neck and added it to his collection. This time they undressed before making love. The birthmark he remembered so vividly was still there, a purple ink-spill across her kidney, the only part of her that hadn't aged. The affair lasted another eleven months, until she became pregnant. For several years she had tried with her husband, who had resorted to root-based aphrodisiacs brewed by an elderly widow — after the story spread, the widowed herbalist received enough business to become the wealthiest woman in the village, and soon received a number of marriage proposals herself — and whether the father was he or the root-remedied botanist, Khassan never knew. Akhmed was born on 1 July 1965; that was all that mattered. Mirza died when she was thirty-nine. Akhmed was seven. The cancer in her stomach was just eight months old. After she passed, Khassan and the botanist became friends. Both shared the same object of love and loss, and though they never discussed it, Khassan suspected the botanist knew. The botanist allowed him to be an uncle to Akhmed, a figure whom Akhmed could love without having to rely on, and in this way, regardless of true paternity, he was a better father to Akhmed than he ever was to Ramzan.

'Even you know that, Ula. You just have to look at how each turned out.'

When Khassan returned home, Ramzan was sitting at the table, though sitting generously described his posture, which slumped so low the chair back loomed over his head. The sharp reek of alcohol coated the air. Perhaps it had dissolved his son's spine.

Teetering against the table, Ramzan kept his voice steady; he still hadn't seen his father at the door. 'There's nothing to eat and I can't shit. I don't understand it, do you? How can I be constipated when you've given all the meat to those filthy dogs? The sleeping pills. Maybe it's that. Maybe it's the weather. Maybe December has frozen my bowels.' He spoke in the vacant monotone of a man who knew no one was listening, and it was awful for Khassan to hear his son's voice, whittled by loneliness, addressing an empty chair. A few years earlier, Khassan hadn't been able to get him to answer a yes-or-no question; now no question Ramzan posed and answered was so simple.

If not for Ula, Khassan would have shut the door and returned to his dogs. He would have followed them through the alleyways, through the refuse-strewn gutters, to the thin strips of twig shadow that made mazes on the forest floor, until their upturned snouts pointed to him, eager, hungry. If not for Ula, he would have ignored his son's voice in the morning and at midday and in the evening, when he said goodbye to his pack and returned home to prepare his insulin shot. The day would have silently joined the hundreds of others, if not for Ula. But he had spoken to Ula, and the relief of unburdening still lifted him, and today, he decided, would be the day he spoke to the one person who was waiting to hear from him.

'You can't shit?' he asked softly. He had forgotten the tone of chastisement. 'It could be the sleeping pills you take to fall asleep among ghosts. It could be Alman, or Musa, or Omar, or Aslan, or Apti, or Mansur, or Aslan the Hirsute, or Ruslan, or Amir, or Amir Number Two, or Isa, or Khalid, or even Dokka. Probably Dokka.' He layered his voice with all the animosity it could sustain. He had never spoken this way. For one year, eleven months and four days the pleas, admonitions and prayers he had wanted to utter never left his lungs. The weight of all he hadn't said hung like a dead organ in his chest. He could barely breathe. He, too, knew what it was to have waste you cannot dislodge.

Ramzan's face lit with surprise. 'I've been waiting to hear you say that,' he said. A beaming grin stripped the shadows from his features. Khassan's silence had been so long and lonesome that to Ramzan this voice of denouncement was both victory and absolution. The sound of his father's voice was all that mattered; its message was irrelevant. 'But you can't speak to me like that,' he added, clasping tightly to the thread and hoping argument would unspool more of his father's voice.

'You're telling me how to speak?' Khassan's temples throbbed. 'A son tells his father? A boy? A ...' He stopped before belittling Ramzan's manhood.

'You think you live ten centimetres off the ground, but who gets you the food you throw away to mutts?' Ramzan spoke with slow, savage joy, pinning each word to his father. 'In fifty kilometres I couldn't find enough aspirin to dull a hangover, but every other week I bring you insulin. You should be grateful. I allow you both to survive and to resent me for it.'

Khassan's breaths couldn't come fast enough. A dull, vice-like clarity crushed whatever fatherly affection survived the silence. For all the lies Ramzan lived by, he was still capable of speaking the truth, and it was for the truth, rather than the lies, that Khassan hated him. He had once held his hand over Ramzan's bassinet and the boy's fingers had wound around his like little vines. He had once lifted the boy and seen miracles in his deep, unblinking eyes. 'You are nothing to me,' he finally said.

But Ramzan, still grinning, still unaccountably joyous, said, 'Just like your book? Are you going to carry me to the woods and burn me?'

'I treasured that book more than anyone.'

'I know, more than my mother.'

'She knew exactly who I was when she accepted my proposal.'

'She thought you were Albert Einstein, that the honour of your genius would compensate for your neglect. You treat your dogs better.'

'That's not true,' Khassan said, uncertain how the conversation had turned against him.

'A genius, she thought. As if Albert Einstein would forget his wife's birthday.'

What had possessed him to speak? Two more silent years would hurt less than one more minute of this. He had expected Ramzan's vehemence, his blather, but hadn't expected his concision. Hadn't expected that the son who had destroyed his reputation, his name, his faith in human goodness, would find new ways to ruin him. More than his paternal failures, it was the grinning joy his son took in describing them that Khassan would remember. Eyes skewed with jubilation. Khassan recognised them as his own. It was the conversation he'd feared since Ramzan's birth. Since the woman who wasn't Mirza had said, in an exhausted ache, a word that should have wrapped them together: 'Ours.' Since he had held him, no more than a bald head and blankets, and wished the child in his arms were Akhmed. You poor thing. You never had a chance.

'I haven't been a good father, I know, I know, I know, I know, I know, I know, I know, I know, I know, I know,' and he kept repeating it, the needle stuck on this one proclamation he stated and restated so Ramzan wouldn't. 'But I never hurt you,' he said finally. 'I never laid a finger on either of you.'

'You were a mouth that only opened to eat. Just like now. And what's worse is you squandered what you had. You were physically capable of having a wife and son, but you didn't want us.'

'I'm sorry for what happened to you,' he said. Even in apology he couldn't name it. 2 March 1995, eight days after Ramzan's twenty-third birthday, he'd never forget the day. The transport truck didn't slow down when Ramzan was pushed from the back. The adult nappy they'd dressed him in was maroon. Finding his boy, right there, in the road, my God, his horror had left him speechless. Akhmed had treated Ramzan's wound and was the only other villager to know of it. For weeks Khassan had tended to his son, taking him meals in bed, reading him pulp fiction, coaxing the spark of life from his dull, brutalised eyes. Ramzan had never recovered, not fully, not physically, not existentially. The Landfill had snapped him as cleanly as a branch and all the tea and small talk in Chechnya wouldn't put his halves back together. He never spoke of what had happened there. His pride for what he had done and his disgrace for the consequence were so entwined that he couldn't even tell his father that he had been castrated for refusing to inform on his neighbours. 'I mourn the life you weren't able to experience,' Khassan said. 'For the father you might have become, for all our sakes.'

'And I mourn the father you might have been,' Ramzan said. The taunt peeled from his voice and behind it lay unvarnished, unfathomable need. Khassan's face felt so heavy. He had expected false accusations, dissemblance; he hadn't expected honesty. The floorboards ached as he turned to the door. In his head he heard the jingle from the television show that had followed the nightly news in the seventies, a stupidly cheerful song, sung by collective labourers, whose melody had once worked on his ears like a reverse alarm clock, a ringing that had let him know it was time to sleep, to rest, to dream; and though he hadn't thought of the song in years, it came to him now, every note, and he hummed it beneath his breath as he held the door frame, and wanted to die.

'You think I'm selfish, but I'm not,' Ramzan said, behind him, with unbearable sincerity. 'I meant what I said about the insulin. This will all be over, eventually. We just need to survive it. You can't survive without insulin. We both need food, right?'

'I'm seventy-nine years old. Seventy-nine. The rest of my life is not worth the rest of Havaa's or Dokka's or Akhmed's.'

'I'm not holding a gun to anyone's head.'

'Ramzan.' Khassan sighed. A wave of exhaustion seeped through him. 'You're putting the bullets in the chamber.'

'I'm just like you! You said you never laid a finger on my mother or me. I've never laid a finger on anyone either!'

'That's all?'

'That's all.'

'Just a name over the phone?'

'That's all!'

'Then another name, no? And another, and another, and another, and another, and another, and another, and another, and another, and another, and another, and then Dokka?' He found his own bewilderment reflected in Ramzan's eyes. His stupid, stupid child didn't understand what he was doing or why any more than Khassan did.

'It was for us. So that we'll survive together. You're the only person I have. You're my family.' It was the saddest, sweetest thing he'd ever heard. In another world he would have embraced Ramzan, kissed his forehead, held him so that his son's heart beat indistinguishably against his own.

He walked to the table, cupped Ramzan's shoulder. His grip was strong and consoling. He imagined Ibrahim on the mountaintop and the verses returned unbidden: *My son, I dreamt that I was sacrificing you.*

'You speak of family; then let Akhmed and Havaa be.'

'I know you want him for your son. I've known that my whole life.'

'And so what if he is, Ramzan?' Khassan asked, clutching Ramzan's shoulder. 'What then?'

Ramzan's face went flat, cold, depthless. 'None of us is bound to anyone by so trivial a distinction. Do you think paternity even matters? No, Father, no. We are the children of wolves. That's all, Father. He could be your son, your brother, your nephew, your neighbour, your friend, and I wouldn't save him.'

'And yet you save me. What a waste.'

Khassan walked to the door, opened it to the wind. He looked back. Ramzan watched him, as frozen and impenetrable as a winter pond. *You are mine. I recognise you. We twist our souls around each other's miseries. It is that which makes us family.*

Outside, his dogs were waiting for him.

Chapter 22

THE VILLAGE CHIMNEYS WERE SENDING UP smoke among the birch trunks when Akhmed heard a low whistle from the trees. Khassan, surrounded by his guard of feral dogs, stepped into the road with an orange hand cupping the torch. The dogs, watchful, ears erect, studied him warily.

'I didn't want Ramzan to see me waiting for you,' Khassan said. His fingers glowed.

'He was waiting for me last night, asking about Havaa.'

'I spoke with him today. For the first time in two years. My own son. I begged him.'

The statement knocked Akhmed a step back. Surprised, honoured, grateful that the man would break the silence for Havaa's sake, his sake, he set his palm on those radiant fingers and the road was dark again. 'It's all right.'

'I'm sorry, Akhmed, I'm—' A sob halved the old man's voice and Akhmed gripped his fingers. When his mother died, Khassan wept at the burial. When Akhmed's father died, Khassan provided the shroud. Akhmed had always remembered this, how Khassan had shared his mourning as if he were family. Dog paws pattered in the undergrowth.

'So they will come for me.' For years he'd lived with the fear of murder, torture or disappearance, as all men of his age did, and it was the senselessness that truly frightened him; that the monumental finality of death could come arbitrarily was more terrifying than the eternity to follow. But if his death severed the connection between city and village, it would be neither futile nor insignificant, and he would be more fortunate than many thousands of his countrymen.

'I don't know,' Khassan said. His hands shook under Akhmed's.

'And Ramzan doesn't know where I've been these past three days?'

'I don't think he wants to know. So long as the burden of disclosure is on you, some small corner of his conscience can stay clean.'

He imagined her right then, annoying Sonja, asking her to explain why faeces are brown, why ears bend, so young and silly and smart. She was a child without parents, and he was a man without children. Ten years earlier he couldn't have imagined claiming her, but the rules of that society had broken. There was no one left to say whom you could love.

'I won't say a word,' Akhmed whispered.

'I'm sorry.'

'Havaa is my only allegiance.' The moon outlined Khassan's face. Tears rimmed his eyelids, and his lips pressed into a tight frown, but he didn't appear contrite. If Akhmed hadn't known better, he would have thought it was an expression of overwhelming pride.

'Do you remember in the first war, Dokka carried a book with him everywhere?' Akhmed asked. 'Whenever the Feds passed, Dokka would open his book and start reading.'

Khassan gave a relieved grin. 'The Feds thought the rebels were illiterate, so by reading a book he proved he wasn't a rebel.'

'But it wasn't even a book, was it?'

'No, a journal. All the pages were blank. But they couldn't tell that.'

They laughed and the torch beam tore hoops in the shadows.

'And he wasn't shot,' Khassan mused.

'No, not then.'

Khassan pulled a Manila envelope from his overcoat and passed it to Akhmed. The exchange, Akhmed thought, was the nearest thing to a postal service in many years. 'I was hoping you could give this to Havaa. It's a letter, some memories of Dokka before he became a father. So she'll have something to look to when she's older.'

'I'm glad you're optimistic,' Akhmed said.

'What do I do? I know what honour requires, but *that*? To my own son? With my own hands? Am I expected to do *that*? Tell me what to do, Akhmed. You know that your name is the next he'll give the Feds. You tell me, what should a father do?' Khassan had leaned forward, his stale, quick breaths warming Akhmed's cheek, his hands reaching for Akhmed's shoulders. It was a peculiar sensation. They had never hugged before.

'I don't know,' Akhmed said. There was no right answer and he was too tired, too cold and too close to home to sift through all the wrong ones. 'I've never been a father. I don't know what you should do.'

'I'm not asking for your approval. I'm asking for your advice.'

Akhmed nodded. 'I'll think about it.'

Khassan stepped back and his face, paled in moonlight,

shifted violently. He opened his mouth, but for a moment only his eyes spoke. Akhmed would have filled the fragile space between them with gratitude. He would have thanked Khassan for the advice, the stories, the meals, the cigarettes, the silences, everything, even the interminable history lessons, they had shared over the years. He would have said that Khassan had been like a father to him, in the ten years since his own father had passed. He would have said it, but Khassan spoke first. 'I feel fortunate to know who you are, Akhmed. I've wanted to say that for a long time.'

Their eyes met and broke away. Such naked acknowledgement of their relationship embarrassed them both, and nodding, turning towards the village, Akhmed said nothing.

He entered the musty blindness of the living room and crept towards the bedroom's lantern light. 'It's me,' he said, in the doorway. 'How are you?'

Beneath the blankets, Ula turned and smiled lazily. 'Oh, just fine. Fine and fine. Your father came again. He told me a bedtime story.'

He prepared a dinner of lentils and canned apricots, pulled a chair beside the bed and ate with her. His poor Ula. She really was losing her mind. Her health had improved in recent months, but this insistence that she spent her days with his ten-years-deceased father dispelled hope for recovery. Just as well. Her mind was one less thing she had left to lose. In a cigar box beneath the bed he hid a hypodermic needle and a vial of heroin he had swiped from the hospital.

After cleaning the dishes, he found his copy of *Hadji Murád*, steadying the wobbling chest-of-drawers leg, and set it by the door. He secured the living-room blackout curtains before opening Khassan's envelope. Brass fasteners bound forty or fifty sheets. He parted the pages at random. *Your father loved your mother's nose. It was a big, ungainly thing, and he said it was still growing, and was slowly taking over her cheeks and forehead, so her entire face would soon submerge beneath her nose.* He couldn't start, not now, and slid the sheets back into the Manila envelope.

In bed he cupped Ula's bony hip. It wasn't the hip he'd held on their wedding night as he fumbled and grunted, so self-conscious about his performance he wasn't prepared for the embarrassment that accompanied the turn of her nose to the open window. But he loved it more, would miss it more. They used to argue about everything, quarrels that left them both hoarse the next morning, and they forgave each other in silence, with a cup of tea, a hand on the shoulder, unencumbered by the voices that divided them. He missed her scorn more than anything. How she looked at him as if he weren't there. How she knew what the whole village suspected: that he was an incompetent physician, a worse bookkeeper, a romantic, a man who was never happier than when sketching birds in the woods. How she knew that and still loved him. He ran his fingers through her hair. Days since he had last washed it, and still so clean. Praise Allah she is speaking to my father. If she is looking so far over the horizon, she won't see what's in front of her.

'Do you remember who I am?' he asked, but she had already fallen asleep.

'You know how those things were invented?' Sonja asked with a nod to the stethoscope the girl was using to listen to her own heartbeat. 'It was invented by a French physician who had a very fat patient. The patient was so fat that the French physician couldn't hear the heartbeat through his chest. So he invented a stethoscope.'

'That's weird,' the girl said, shifting the bell like an

indecisive chess piece. 'I've never seen a fat person before.'

'Never?'

'Never. But in my souvenirs I have the autograph of a man who used to be fat.'

The girl noted her heart rate on the chart Sonja had given her. Overcome by an inexplicable interest in medicine, the girl, draped in a lab coat that swished against the linoleum, had been following Sonja since dinner. It took the better part of an hour before Sonja realised the girl was imitating her. Her raw exasperation softened to a more delicate displeasure when the girl began scolding the air for carrying contagions. Poor child, she thought, let's hope she finds a better role model.

The girl held the stethoscope bell like a microphone and, while kicking a drooping tail of bed sheet, began interviewing Sonja. 'What's it like being a surgeon?' she asked.

'Wonderful. Next question.'

'Why don't you have kids?'

'They ask too many questions.'

'Who did you bribe to get into medical school?'

'Surprisingly, no one at all.'

'And are you the only woman surgeon in the world?'

'It feels like it.'

'What's your favourite disease?'

'Chlamydia.'

'If they let you become a surgeon instead of a wife, would they let me become an arborist instead of a wife?'

'Who's "they"?'

'You know.'

'Tell me.'

The girl's face hollowed with resignation; it had been a long time, but Sonja remembered what it was to have that face, what it was to feel you were no brighter than the dumbest man, no stronger than the weakest boy, and with those ideas crowding your head no wonder subordination was the only inevitable outcome. She sat on the hospital bed beside the girl, remembering what it was like to have that face, and pitying it. 'Listen, Havaa,' she said, summoning as much generosity as she could muster at this hour of night, 'you can be exactly the person you want to be, OK? It may not seem that way, but things change when you get a little older. If you work hard, and give up certain things, and yes, resort to bribery now and then, you'll be an arborist, or a sea anemonist, or anything else you want.'

And they kept talking, passing the stethoscope bell back and forth.

'Do you have any questions for me?' the girl asked at the end of the interview.

Since Akhmed had left that evening, Sonja had held the question as she would a long-awaited letter, terrified of what the envelope contained. 'Did a Russian woman ever stay at your house?'

'Which one? Lots of people stayed with us.'

'Her name was Natasha.'

'Probably thirty Natashas at least.'

'She looked like me.'

Havaa gave her an appraising look. 'Then no.'

'Like me only beautiful.'

The girl tilted her head. 'I can't imagine that.'

And it struck her. Why hadn't she thought of it sooner? Akhmed's sketch. She was upright and out of the room before Havaa could ask where she was going. Why had she asked him to take the portrait? Where would he have put it? She climbed to the fourth floor and worked her way back to her room, checking the new and old maternity wards, the land-mine man's room, the empty administrative offices, the waiting room. While searching, her mind flashed to the day she had purchased the Buckingham Palace guard nutcracker. True to form it had endured flights across Europe, every bump of the Samsonite and even the shame of Alu's name, without once breaking composure.

She had found the nutcracker in a corner shop sticky with the residue of a spilled fizzy drink, where she stopped for cough drops before attending a lecture. It was four weeks to Christmas. The first war wouldn't officially begin for twelve more days. She had bought it without once thinking of Natasha, on a whim, because Buckingham Palace was what foreigners thought of when they thought of London and she, Sonja with a *j*, was nothing if not foreign. Grey clouds lined the horizon as she climbed the escalator at Holborn and crossed Lincoln's Inn Fields to the Royal College of Surgeons. There, at a neurosurgery lecture, she transcribed the snaking syntax of British academia in a bright pink notebook she had found in a fifty-pence bin. Attached to the Royal College was a museum dedicated to the history of anatomy and pathology. After thanking the lecturer, and pausing in the atrium for a cigarette and cough drop, she strolled through the museum's curious exhibitions. There was a display detailing the history of non-Egyptian mummification. An alcove devoted to the tibia. One room exhibited the 1,474 skulls collected by nineteenth-century physician Joseph Barnard Davis. A fractured skull of a Roman woman found at Pompeii. The skulls of nine Chinese pirates hanged in Ningpo. Congolese from Leopold's rubber plantations. But the skull that haunted her was that of a Bengali cannibal. Fully intact, the mandible still locked against the temporal, the twenty-two bones that constitute a human skull all accounted for. The eight bones forming the neurocranial brain case bathed in halogenated light. From the size of the plates, the prominence of the supraorbital ridge and temporal lines, as well as the overall size and solidity of the skull, she knew it belonged to a man. The skull appeared no different from those of the Chinese pirates, the Congolese plantation workers. She read the placard written a century and a half earlier by a Victorian phrenologist. *There are no character-istics to distinguish the cranium of a cannibal from that of an ordinary man.*

That morbid association between the cannibal and the nutcracker, one which she never mentioned to Natasha, was all she thought of while searching for the portrait. She finally found the notebook on the canteen worktop, beneath a stack of folded linen. From the last page Natasha observed her calmly, through eyes unclouded by judgement or resentment, her hair held back with a headband she had never owned, her ears heavy with earrings that didn't exist. Clearly Akhmed hadn't met her.

Her footsteps, slowing to a processional as she neared her room, tapped like the last drops falling from a stopped tap. She wanted to know and didn't want to know; the two were always there, always tearing at her, a tug-of-war in which she was the rope. But that was OK, she told herself. The truth was one more rumour passed along the refugee lines, another hallucination she could freely disbelieve. When she entered the room the girl was already asleep. She slid the portrait into one of the drawers, thankful to postpone the answer for one more night.

Chapter 23

THE SECOND WAR, WHEN IT CAME TO VOLCHANSK, came without bomb blasts or mortar rounds, tracer bullets or tank treads. It came through the bazaar at first, a few more kopeks per gram of cardamom, a few more rubles per carrot, the deprivation subtle enough to blame on currency inflation, or global markets, or natural disasters. Then the electricity went. But the municipal power lines, restrung after the first war, never had carried a current for more than two hours at a stretch anyway, as likely to come at daybreak as midnight, fifteen or twenty minutes for Natasha to charge her batteries, pull news from the airwaves, hop in the shower and blow-dry her hair before the lights flickered and the city collapsed back into darkness. The tap water went next. With the remaining civilians she drew buckets from unboarded wells and strained the water through pillowcases before boiling it. Then food shortages. No milk, then no plums, then no cabbages, then no cornmeal. Even the feral animals quietened, the dogs stopped howling, the songbirds stopped singing. And though Federal forces invaded Chechnya in August 1999, the second war didn't begin for Natasha

317

until the afternoon in 2001 when it marched through the doors of Hospital No. 6.

The skies of the maternity ward mural were as placid as on the day she had drawn them when she mistook the first crack for thunder. Gunshots followed as quickly as her footsteps as she ran downstairs. In trauma, Sonja and the nurses huddled by the aluminium filing cabinets.

'We could evacuate them to a village,' Sonja suggested. 'We have a truck.'

'No,' Deshi said. 'We keep them here. This is a hospital. They belong here.'

Maali assented. 'Let's use them as human shields.'

Natasha tried to wedge herself into the conversation, but as usual the triangle wouldn't widen into a square. She took a deep breath and turned. This isn't about you, she told herself. Your reaction is the only thing you can control. Who would have thought those books Sonja had brought with her the day she found ice were worth reading? In the five years she had worked here her emotional spectrum expanded beyond the monochromatic depression that had tinted her early days of recovery. *Recovery.* What a strange, wondrous word. None better defined her gradual reintegration into humanity. Nearly nine months of confinement, forced prostitution, beatings and heroin addiction, but she had come back. No one was more surprised than she herself, and no one was happier than Sonja. When Natasha was a teenager she once fell asleep on the roof and woke the colour of borscht. The following week all the popular girls at school came in sunburned, and a week later the girls that wanted to be popular, until the principal, in an impromptu assembly, explained that girls had been known to roast alive while sunbathing. The memory was still there, tucked away in folds of time, and she found it again, with a smile, on the afternoons she climbed to the hospital roof to lie in the sun. Entire hours passed without her once thinking of Italy.

The nurses didn't want to hear from her, but the patients did. An elderly woman, Xenia, patient number 29395, repeatedly asked 'What is happening?' more confused and hesitant with each reiteration, as her neighbour, her first cousin, begged her to shut up because her insufferable voice would kill him faster than any bullet or bomb. When the Whites had swept through Volchansk eighty-one years earlier, Xenia had asked her cousin the same question and her cousin had answered. Xenia had been six, her cousin seven. Her voice had been lovely then.

'We're working it out,' Natasha said. 'Don't worry. Would you like some ice?'

Xenia gave her cousin a smug smile and nodded.

'Bring me the tongue depressor!' the cousin shouted after Natasha.

Two days earlier, when Xenia had arrived with pneumonia, Sonja had treated her lungs with the respect a plumber shows to blocked septic pipes. Her sister's work was undeniably good, but its execution bothered Natasha. To work in these circumstances a surgeon must reduce each patient to her body, but this was an attitude shared by the traffickers, pimps and johns populating Natasha's private perdition. So while Sonja examined a cracked pelvis without once meeting the patient's eye, or addressed the patient by placard number rather than by name, Natasha sequestered herself in the fourth-floor maternity ward, where whole days passed without their paths crossing, where the wails of newborns reminded her that life is louder than its pulse. While Sonja debated the merits of evacuation, Natasha fed Xenia crushed ice with a plastic spoon and told her exactly what was happening.

Boot fall, echoing down the corridor, ended the debate. The security guard ran through the double doors, his arms pumping, his shirt tail flapping behind him. 'They're here,' he called. He ran right past Sonja and out the back door, announcing his immediate resignation in a breathless shout.

'Who?' Sonja called after him. 'Feds or rebels?' No answer. Xenia held an ice cube in her mouth, afraid to break it. No one spoke. The shuffle of military boots paused at the closed double doors. The air was stretched so taut Natasha could have walked across it. A sharp kick, initially mistaken for a gunshot, jolted them all and flung open the double doors. Four bearded men entered with machine guns raised.

'I retired seven years ago,' Deshi said to no one in particular.

'We hereby liberate this hospital for patriotic use for the glorious campaign for national independence,' the shortest rebel declared. Dirt powdered his cheeks. Blood stained his shirt and trousers. He glared at the room, daring them to blink. 'Who's in charge?'

Across the room, with an exasperated roll of her eyes, Sonja raised her hand.

'I am the field commander of the fourth brigade of the National Military of the Chechen Republic of Ichkeria,' the shortest rebel said. He lowered his gun and took small, plodding steps to Sonja. 'There are forty of us. Most need medical attention. Everyone needs food and water.'

'We could amputate all their legs,' Maali suggested, but the limping entrance of thirty-six more rebels made permission a formality. Sonja agreed to treat the wounded provided they removed their boots. They corralled the rebels in one of the ghost wards, sharing an unspoken consensus that the quicker the work was done, the better for all involved. The rebels asked for treatment by ascending order of rank, rather than by triage. The lower ranks were first into battle, the commander explained in a clipped northern accent, and thus had suffered the longest. Natasha's throat tightened as she cut through the trouser leg of a curly-haired private. Nothing but pale down on his cheeks and pink clouds in his eyes. She hadn't touched a man's trousers in five and a quarter years.

'What are you doing?' he asked, supine on the hospital bed.

'Giving you shorts. You have lovely legs.'

'Where are my legs?'

'Still here. Don't worry.'

She tried to be gentle, but shrapnel had cratered his left calf. 'Hold on,' she said. 'Just hold on.' Her sweat-slickened fringe stuck to her forehead. She wanted to ask his name, but what if he died and she was left here with his name? The name Natasha wouldn't learn was Said. He came from a Grozny suburb, where his mother, a veterinary assistant, brought home the litters abandoned on the clinic doorstep. The war had already taken his mother, but he would live to return home to her cats, which had multiplied to the population of a village during the war years, feasting, as they did, on the burgeoning estate of rats and mice. Working odd jobs and sacrificing the comforts of wife and family, he would spend his life caring for the descendants of his mother's cats. Eight hundred and eighty-two, all named for his mother, though he would never know that exact figure. In sixty-six years, on his deathbed, he would remember that distant afternoon, when the fingers of a beautiful nurse had mined metal from his legs. He would remember it as the moment of greatest intimacy he ever had had with a woman. Then he would remember his cats.

Natasha called to Sonja, asking for pain relief. The young

man was incoherent, addressing his mother in a jar of cotton swabs. Across the room, the surgical saw paused, but Sonja didn't look up from the half-severed arm. 'You'll have to get it yourself,' she said calmly. Given her history with the drug, Natasha never prepared or administered the heroin. Dreams of bent spoon handles persisted, and five years clean she was still afraid a cigarette lighter could reheat her cravings. But she peeled off the latex gloves and jogged to the canteen. Now wasn't the time for caution, not with that boy on her hospital bed. In the cupboard, behind an armoury of evaporated milk, she found it. It compacted in her grip, filling the corners of the plastic bag. Alu's brother had claimed there wasn't enough talc in the bag to powder a baby's bottom. The Italian junk Sergey had shot into her had contained enough to service a nursery, and even that had laid electric lines where her veins had been. But this? Ninety-eight per cent pure? She spat in the sink; she was salivating. You *can* control your reactions. You *can* control your reactions, she repeated. It took two minutes to cook. She only had to take one syringe to the trauma ward, but for the twenty-metre walk, when she was alone with it, she felt vastly outnumbered.

When it came time to treat the commanding officers, the last packets of surgical thread had already disappeared into the limbs of their subordinates. The field commander, the last to receive medical attention, lay on Sonja's cot. The blood of his command soaked the sheets, and when his bare shoulders touched it, he sighed. Between his beard and his eyes, a slim band of soil-coloured skin suggested many months of sunshine and malnutrition. Natasha watched while her sister treated him. A long, semicircular gash split his left pectoral. 'My chest is grinning at me,' he observed.

Sonja flooded the wound with saline and iodine. With

forceps she pinched through the gash for shrapnel fragments. It had begun to clot, but wouldn't heal without stitches. The rebels looked on with reverent interest.

'We have a problem,' Sonja said. The commander nodded to the ceiling. 'We need to get you stitched up, but we're out of surgical thread. We simply don't have the supplies on hand to treat so many field injuries.'

'He can have mine,' murmured a thin man, whose beard was half shaven to accommodate thirteen stitches on his left cheek. A chorus of offers followed. Even those without a single stitch vociferously pledged their surgical thread.

'It isn't sanitary,' Sonja said with a finality that ended debate. None appeared too disappointed that his offer was declined. 'Don't you have field medical kits? Anything we can sterilise and sew into you?'

A junior officer appeared with a small green bag. Natasha sifted through it while Sonja held a compress to the wound. She pulled out a pink toothbrush with a fan of grey bristles, a small bottle of non-alcoholic mouthwash, a tube of fluoride whitening paste, five tubes of toothpaste, on which the five daily prayers were written in black marker, and three rolls of unwaxed dental floss.

'The floss,' Sonja said. 'It might work.'

The field commander grimaced as the alcohol-wetted floss followed the needle through his skin. He refused the offer of pain relief. Natasha admired his abstinence.

'Have dentists begun enlisting?' she asked as Sonja slipped the needle in a fifth time. If he refused anaesthetic, she could at least offer the distraction of conversation.

'No, it was a captain's private supply.'

'Did he have fine teeth?'

'Yes,' the field commander said. His open mouth revealed a more relaxed philosophy towards dental hygiene. 'They were beautiful, beautiful things. He brushed five times a day, always before prayer, as if performing an ablution on his mouth.'

'Was he conscious of his health in general?'

'Not really. He smoked no fewer than two packs a day.'

'He sounds like a strange man.'

'You get that way. In the first war I fought with a man who went through a roll of antacids every day.'

'That can cause an electrolyte disturbance: hypercalcaemia. Stones, bones, moans, groans, thrones and psychiatric overtones. That's the mnemonic,' Natasha said, and repeated *psychiatric overtones* to herself. She wondered if Maali had a taste for antacids.

'I doubt it matters. He's very dead now. Besides, we ate nothing but buckwheat kasha. No, he took antacids as a calcium supplement. He was terrified of osteoporosis.'

She nearly laughed. 'How old was he?'

'Twenty-two.'

'You are all insane.'

The field commander winced as Sonja pulled the stitches tight. 'It just becomes easy to convince yourself that caring for a small part of your body will act to protect the rest. As though Allah wouldn't be cruel enough to steal the life from a man with perfect teeth.'

'Did it work?'

'We left his mouth open when we buried him so that in Paradise he can flaunt his teeth to the angels.'

The rebels spent the night in the ghost ward. None snored; even in sleep they were wary. In the morning they pointed the hospital beds of their wounded comrades towards Mecca. Natasha ladled a dense pulp of oats and powdered milk into their bowls. With Sonja and the nurses, she checked the bandaged burns, stitched lacerations, the broken bones splinted between sterilised wooden strips. Only the rebel with the amputated arm would be left behind. The field commander prayed for him, then rooted through the man's rucksack for anything that might connect him with the insurgency.

'You're a civilian now,' the field commander said. 'Enjoy the peace you have fought for. We'll take your arm for burial, but must leave you here. If you want to stay, the lady doctor said the position of security guard has recently opened.'

Complying with his insistence to be treated last, Natasha served him the final bowl of oats from the canteen. The surface had cooled to a carapace the field commander tapped twice with his spoon before breaking.

'Where are you going next?'

'South,' the field commander said. 'To the mountains.'

'Try to find a doctor or veterinarian before then. If this gets infected, the Feds will be your smallest problem.'

'In our condition we probably won't make it further than Eldár today.'

Only two of the field commander's shirt buttons matched the brown fabric, whose original colour would be anyone's guess. Natasha pulled the shirt past his shoulder and covered the stitches with a fresh bandage. The dental floss had worked. 'I was in the mountains once,' she said. 'I climbed right across the border.'

'In winter?'

'Spring.'

'The winter will be difficult. We need supply lines. Good middlemen. Maybe we'll find someone in Eldár. You're not looking for a new profession, are you?'

As his contribution to the hospital, the field commander left the bag of toothpaste. He stood stiffly by the door as his command shuffled out. Alone, he turned to the sisters.

'Thank you,' he said, bowing slightly. 'You are kind, decent, and if I can risk impertinence, quite attractive. There must be some Chechen in you.'

'I have a favour to ask,' Sonja said. 'Would you write us a letter of safe passage, so we can, should we need to, travel through rebel land?'

The field commander had two sisters of his own, older by one and three years, who teased and chided and always took care of him. He kept their names written on the sheet of paper stitched in his trouser seam. He trusted them with the name of his first crush and would trust them with his eternity. He smiled and searched for a pen.

When the field commander departed, and the double doors swung closed, Natasha returned to the maternity ward almost believing the war had left with him. Six days later the Feds would enter the city. They would launch a single mortar round at the hospital in retaliation for sheltering rebels. That round would hit the fourth-floor storage room. Maali would be searching for clean sheets. She would land atop the rubble, four floors below, her pulse slowing in her wrist. A syringe would be prepared and half injected, but death would relieve Maali's pain before the drug took effect, and the senseless, screaming world would go quiet when Natasha slipped that same syringe between her toes, and with a push of the plunger, sent Maali's blood into her own.

The Fourth
and Fifth Days

Chapter 24

1994 1995 1996 1997 1998 1999 2000 2001 2002 2003 **2004**

HAD HE SLEPT ON THE DIVAN, HE WOULD HAVE seen the letter to Havaa. Had the side lamp still held even a spark of electricity, he would have seen the letter to Havaa. Had he risen an hour later, when dawn threw its bright beams across the floor, he would have seen the letter to Havaa. But he hadn't seen it, and now Havaa was galloping across the waiting room, her face a flower head, a moon, a cannonball, and then it was there, punching into his gut, knocking the breath from his lungs, and only then, with her arms belted around his waist, did he remember the letter from Khassan which he had forgotten to bring.

'You're here,' she proclaimed to his hip bone.

'Where else would I be?' He didn't fully appreciate what the girl knew, that *here* was a special, unlikely place. She thought he could have disappeared by now, too. That he could be with her father, wherever that was, and whatever that meant. But he was here. The sharp sting of bleach preceded Sonja's footsteps and they both looked to the door before she appeared. Her bright white scrubs could belong to a doctor in Moscow or London or Berlin. Should he ever disturb a sleeping landmine, or cross the path of a bullet, he would want to be treated by a doctor wearing those scrubs.

The previous night, as he had sketched the portrait of her sister, he had fought the urge to lean in so his left knee would touch her right. Two years had passed since he last touched a knee like that. And before that? When had he touched Ula's knees with anything like desire? Caring had refined his passion, once as raw and combustible as crude oil, into a dimmer, longer-burning love.

'So this is the Tolstoy book?' She nodded to the chair where *Hadji Murád* lay. That, he hadn't forgotten.

'Yes, the one he wrote about Chechnya.'

Pulling back a stray lock of hair, she drew a question mark around her ear. He handed her the book. She flipped to the last page.

'What are you doing? Don't read the last page.'

'I always read the last page first,' she said, without looking up.

'That ruins everything. The whole book is working towards the last page.'

Her lips pursed to a pebble. The paper cover bent in her grip, as if she were steadying her hands. The amphetamines? But she spoke in a flat, uninspired tone. 'If it's not an ending I think I'll like, then I won't read the book.' She handed it back to him.

'Are you serious?'

'He gets decapitated on the last page. That's not an ending I want to read.'

She was harder to pin down than the last pickle in the jar. Here he had thought he would impress her, thought they would have conversations about the book's images and themes, a literary salon in a city without electricity.

'But it's the great book. It's a century and a half old and still the best book about the first and second wars.'

'Why would I want to read what I'm living?'

'You prefer escape?'

'You've been here four days,' she said. 'Keep coming back, and we'll see if you still think books are worth arguing over.'

Akhmed, Deshi and Havaa went to the weekly aid distribution point, so shortly after eight, when a man was carried in with an exhaust pipe lodged in his chest, Sonja received him alone. The man, an army contractor, had been plagued by asthma for all of his twenty-one years. After living his life as a drowning man, his final breath, nineteen seconds after the car bomb detonated, entered him effortlessly, the easiest inhalation of his life, through the metal trachea jutting from his chest, and into his collapsed lung.

But Sonja only knew him as a corpse. The handful of amphetamines that had propelled her through a sleepless night lingered in her veins. She wheeled him into the trauma ward on a hospital bed, and sat beside him as moths fluttered overhead. His head lolled to the side and his eyelids snapped open. She began speaking to the corpse – who was, in all respects, a wonderful listener – and became so engrossed in the hallucination she lost track of the real world behind her where Akhmed's footsteps sounded in the corridor.

'Honour the dead?' Sonja was saying, her face level with that of the corpse. Akhmed watched from the doorway. 'Yes, but only if the dead are honourable. No, of course I'm not casting aspersions. It's OK if you feel rotten. You just died. Don't be too hard on yourself. Now, I must ask if you can see my sister down there. Yes, I know it's crowded, but please have a look. I can wait. And while you're at it, would you save me a chair? Oh, I should have known it would be standing room only.' Akhmed couldn't see her face, but her exhausted voice was enough to make him ache. 'You say you've had trouble breathing?' she said, speaking into the exhaust pipe as if into a microphone. 'It appears you have a bronchial growth.' When she took the man's face in her hands, Akhmed stepped into the room to save her from whatever was happening inside her head. 'There are no characteristics to distinguish the cranium of a cannibal from that of an ordinary man,' she told the corpse. 'But I can tell we would have had a grand time, you and I.'

Two hands, on her shoulders, pulled her gently from the corpse before it could answer, before it could tell her if Natasha was down there with him.

'Not you, too,' Akhmed said, wearily. His skin was a degree or two warmer than the corpse's. His navy *pes*, a size too small, still roosted on the back of his head. 'Someone here has to stay sane.'

The big oaf led her to the office that was her bedroom. He was like a pool of water she'd fallen into; she hit, hit, hit and he was still there, around her. She'd been awake for ever. The flap of moths was overwhelming. In the office, he pushed her into the overstuffed executive chair. 'You need to rest,' Akhmed said, in a tone of authority obviously an imitation of her own.

'And who do you think you are to order me around?' she asked. Already she missed the corpse. He was a much better conversationalist.

'I think I'm someone who slept last night.' He scanned the bookcase, selected the thickest book from the bottom shelf, and dropped it on the desk. 'A medical dictionary. If you won't read Tolstoy, read this. It will put you to sleep in no time.'

When the door closed behind him, she scrutinised the dictionary, wary of subterfuge. She hadn't opened the book in years. A surgeon of her skill had no need. Slowly, fearing further hallucinations hid between the covers, she opened the book. It was just as dull as she remembered.

But she was already in, and the crowded little script calmed her. The definitions had the stately reassurance of orthodoxy, reminding her of the pre-war years, when she had relied on the reference book to complete her weekly assignments, when she had sat at her desk, her ears plugged with cotton balls, as that awful thudding Natasha called music had pounded from the next room, when she still believed the meaning of a thing was limited to a few tersely worded clauses, but nothing, she now knew, could be defined in exclusion, and every insect, pencil and grass blade was a dictionary in itself, requiring the definitions of all other things to fulfil its own.

Her fingers shadowed the thin pages and the words appeared written on her skin: the average weight of a hand, interpretations of a knuckle. A shawl of post-high drowsiness wrapped itself around her. She hated to admit it, but Akhmed had been right. Then, halfway through the book, at the bottom of the 1,322nd page, circled in red ink:

Life: a constellation of vital phenomena – organisation, irri-tability, movement, growth, reproduction, adaptation.

The breaking sky could release no more striking a pronouncement. She repeated it to the unmade bed, to Havaa's still-packed suitcase, to the desk of the former geri-atrics director. Not once had she ever marked a dictionary, but here this was, encircled by the same red pen she'd kept on her bedside table. She stumbled into the corridor, reached out but couldn't find a wall. Her legs felt as stiff as they had been on the day she had tried to make her own trousers, but when she lost her balance, when she fell forward, Natasha wasn't there to catch her.

When she woke on the floor, the insides of her cheeks felt like the insides of lemon rinds. She rubbed her temples and checked the unlit overhead lights, but, thankfully, the ceiling was still. In the storage room she pulled a pack of Marlboros from the fresh carton. The crinkle of the plastic wrapper followed her down the corridor. At the door the one-armed guard declined her offer of a cigarette. Shards gleamed in his ashtray. His name was Mohmad. He didn't particularly enjoy this job, but he knew enough to know that any man was fortunate to have work these days, particularly amputees. In Ingushetia he had an eleven-year-old daughter he didn't know about, who was waiting for him to call. In two and a half years he would hear her voice for the first time.

She smoked three cigarettes before Akhmed appeared behind her, warming his hands around a mug of steaming water. 'Marlboro?' she offered. He lit the cigarette from her ember.

'You look much better,' he said. The corners of his lips inched towards a grin.

'Shut up.'

'Nothing like a little beauty sleep.'

'I'll set your scrubs on fire if you say another word.'

The incipient smile sagged into an expression of surrender. 'They came back for him,' he said. 'Whoever dropped him off.'

'Bringing a dead man to a hospital. Do they think we're magicians?'

'Medical miracles are the only miracles most of us will ever see.'

He had her on that one. 'You're a believer,' she said. That explained his incompetence as well as anything.

'I believe in some things.'

'In God.'

He shook his head.

'But I've seen you pray at noon.'

'That's like asking if I believe in gravity,' he said. 'It doesn't require belief.'

'I've always thought Marx's view on religion was the one thing he got right. Faith is a crutch.'

'If you step on a landmine,' Akhmed said, 'the crutch becomes the leg.'

Westminster Abbey was the only steeple she'd ever stood beneath, a tourist guidebook, rather than a prayer book, in hand. God, like everything kind and good, lived in London. She dropped her gaze to her hands and picked at the white calluses that scalloped her palm.

'My goodness. These belong to a lumberjack,' he said, lifting her hands, examining them with a mixture of awe and pity. 'Woodsman hands.'

'I hate my hands.' Aloud it sounded as small and petty as it had in her head, but they were horrid things, these hands, a crime for which she felt the immediate relief of confession. 'How could such things grow from a woman's wrist?'

'You've chosen the wrong profession. If not a lumberjack, you would have made a marvellous strangler.' With the unexpected sensitivity of a surgeon, his fingers drifted up her forearm.

'I keep thinking in Latin,' she said. He paused on her ulna. 'The names of bones.'

'Latin is a problem with which I have no experience.' He squeezed her bicep. 'You should think about anatomy like I

335

do. This is your arm. It's only your arm. This is your shoulder, nothing less than your shoulder. Your neck is only your neck.' His finger rose to a chin that was simply her chin, cheeks that were her cheeks, a nose that belonged to no one else. 'And lips,' he said, leaning to her. 'Our lips.'

A moment and she pulled away, frowning back at the hospital and smoothing out her scrubs. Of the varying shapes of love, grief, anger and terror that had inhabited these scrubs, optimistic anticipation was a new one. She looked to his big, stupid face, blushed, and turned away. What would Deshi say if she saw her like this? The shock might very well make her act on her ten-year-long threat to retire.

'I'm going to the fourth floor,' she said, finally. 'You could meet me there in a half-hour.'

'Even though I'm not a very good doctor.'

'Even though you are criminally incompetent.'

He opened his hands. Not one callus.

'Don't make fun of my lumberjack hands.'

'I'm not,' he said.

'You are,' she said.

He squinted across the car park to the armoured truck, thinking of the previous day, perhaps, how she had ambushed him in Grozny, how repellant a woman she was for putting a gun to his head one day and her lips to his the next. When he asked for the keys to the truck, claiming he had forgotten his scarf in the passenger seat, she felt too relieved to dwell on the fact that he hadn't worn a scarf the day before.

Their footsteps from the previous evening were still evident in the dust of the fourth-floor maternity ward. Natasha's murals seemed to study her, as if she were their creation. Unsettled at the thought of standing alone among these ghosts, she went to the corridor and opened the storage-room door for fresh air. The smashed city stretched to the frozen river. International law prohibited the targeting of medical facilities, which explained why, in a city where eighty per cent of free-standing structures had been flattened, the hospital still stood. The shell that had crashed into this very room had been an act of reprisal rather than war. Natasha had collapsed with the walls, fallen with Maali, kept aloft by momentary updraughts, then plunged ever downward, until the earth had yawned open and she had entered it. Sonja knew the two had been co-conspirators and confederates, sisters to ambitious, demanding women. She knew Natasha hadn't been right after Maali's tumble. She didn't know that Maali, eighteen minutes Deshi's junior, had lived her sixty-seven years in those eighteen minutes, finding room there for every dream, fear and exasperation, setting her watch eighteen minutes ahead so she could pretend she had Deshi's experience, always wondering what her life would have been like if she were just eighteen minutes older. Natasha had loved Maali for this as much as for her demented enthusiasm for amputation, but Sonja didn't know it. In four months, when cleaning out a filing cabinet, she would find municipal buildings drawn on the back of payroll forms. Long, uneven lines of Maali's penmanship disfigured Natasha's sketches, her critiques sometimes playful, sometimes damning, but always invested, and in those sketches, framed and hanging in the waiting room, as they would be within an afternoon, Sonja would see what the two younger sisters meant to each other.

The stairwell door slammed shut. They walked to each other until their silhouettes converged. In the darkness she found his eyebrows with her thumbs. They went to the third maternity bed, and she sat on the edge, and he stood between her legs. Her thighs clasped his hip bones. From the far side of the room the lantern dimly bathed them.

'I think there is a bee on my behind,' she said.

'You're still hallucinating,' he said.

'You should slap it away, just in case,' she said.

She reached under his shirt, spread her hand across his abdomen, and tried not to think of which organ lay beneath which finger. 'This is your stomach,' she said, mimicking his tenor. 'Not your brother's stomach, not Stalin's stomach, but your stomach.'

'You make me sound like a serious man.'

'You certainly aren't that.'

They undressed by degree, a button here, a shirtsleeve there, making a show of their shortcomings, their bodies androgynous with deprivation. It was remarkable to trust someone enough to be silly like this. She lay back. It was dark. Her lips found his.

'Goodnight to you and your ugly nose,' Deshi told Akhmed as he was leaving. A buoyant confidence swelled in him and as he stepped into the navy twilight and trekked towards the village he finally felt part of the top ten percentile. Never had he been so honoured by being addressed in the second person.

But the radio antenna listing from the bonnet of Ramzan's truck, parked before his house, punctured the sweet feeling inside him. Akhmed smiled sadly and trudged forward, balling his fists in his coat sleeves. The coat was fifty-eight years old, canvas military grade, about the only thing the Red Army had ever done right. It kept him as warm as it had kept his father and his father's father and the idea of three generations sheltered by the same stiff, unyielding fabric gave him greater comfort than the coat itself ever could.

Again Ramzan questioned him, and again he claimed ignorance.

'You disappoint me, my friend,' Ramzan said. Ramzan's coat was six months old. It would never warm another set of shoulders. 'You're a doctor. Think logically. Think about your wife. Think about yourself. Think about your silence. It's reckless.'

'I owe Dokka my silence more than I owe you anything,' Akhmed said.

'Owe? We're beyond obligation,' Ramzan said. 'We wear clothes, and speak, and create civilisations, and believe we are more than wolves. But inside us there is a word we cannot pronounce and that is who we are. I know you think you are being noble, that this is some terrific act of sacrifice. You probably believe that because you fucked Dokka's wife two years ago, you owe it to him to save his child. But let me be clear, Akhmed. You don't. She is not yours.' Ramzan's voice cracked, and he steadied himself with two deep breaths. It wasn't an act. 'I know you think I'm a traitor and a coward, Akhmed. And you're right. But that doesn't make me wrong. I'm telling you this because we were friends. You don't owe this to Dokka.'

Akhmed hadn't lusted for Esiila before the wars, hadn't thought of her as more than the wife of his closest friend. She could have been anyone. He had just wanted to hear his name breathed in his ear, a body warm and damp beneath him, whole and alive and a world away from pain. Was it such a sin? No, of course not. But Dokka. There was Dokka. Now he stood up for them, as if he were a hero rather than a hypocrite, as if he hadn't betrayed, dishonoured and broken the family whose last living member he now offered his life to save. Ramzan stood across from him, but he knew that in their hearts, they stood on the same side.

Pale moonlight fell across his snowy boot tracks, and Akhmed suddenly saw the fragility of the plan he'd designed over the past day. The girl would be safe, he had assumed, if he severed the link between the village and the city, and the link was him. But this meant trusting that Sonja would care for the girl. It meant trusting an erratic, overextended surgeon, who had put a gun to his back a day earlier, with the girl's life. It meant pushing through his endless doubts and trusting, however misguidedly, the decency he believed was buried inside Sonja.

'Why do they want the girl, Ramzan? You still haven't tried to explain.'

'Revenge,' Ramzan said flatly. 'Dokka fucked up.'

'But what did he do?'

'Akhmed. So many questions. If you had learned to keep your mouth shut, your eyes on your feet, you would have had a happier life.'

'They already have Dokka, Ramzan. Why do they need the girl?'

Ramzan shook his head. 'Because the life of a Russian colonel doesn't equal the life of a Chechen arborist.'

'You can't mean that—'

'A few days after we returned from the Landfill, Dokka asked me for a pistol. He wanted to be able to protect his family, so I gave him one of the Makarovs I'd kept from our final fucked-up gun run. That same Makarov was later used to assassinate a colonel.'

'But Dokka couldn't have been an insurgent. He couldn't hold a gun in his hand, much less fire it!'

'That doesn't matter when the serial number on the pistol used to kill a colonel sequentially matches the serial numbers of the guns those lost soldiers took off us before they left us at the Landfill. The Feds made the connection. I couldn't give Dokka up, because they already had him.'

'But why do they want the girl?'

Ramzan gave him a sad smile. 'You know the saying, *As the son inherits from the father, so the father inherits from the son*? The Feds have made it official policy. There is a campaign to disappear not only suspected insurgents but their relatives as well. The idea being that you are less likely to go into the woods with the rebels if you know that your house will burn and your family will disappear. Rebel recruitment has plummeted in recent months. It's part of the new hearts-and-minds strategy. It's how they will win the war on terror. They will kill Havaa and call it peace.'

Akhmed's head hummed with the shock of how not shocked he was. What Ramzan said made sense to him. He understood why the Feds would want to kill a child. Accompanying that understanding was a second, equally shameful recognition: this incomprehensible war would take from him even the humanity to find it incomprehensible.

'Why are you telling me this?'

'Because I'm trying to save you.'

When Ramzan returned from the Landfill the first time, with that wound between his legs, Akhmed had saved him. They never said it, Ramzan never thanked him for it, but they both knew that the week he spent treating the infection was just that. If a stranger were to put his ear in the space between them, he would hear the dull roar of that knowledge.

'Isn't it too late for that?' Akhmed asked.

'No, not yet.'

'Yes, it is.'

'If you give up like this you really will be the stupidest doctor in Chechnya.'

Akhmed allowed himself a smile. This was the Ramzan

he remembered. 'That honour has been mine for some time.'

'You probably think you are a hero or a martyr, don't you?' Ramzan asked. 'You probably think you are a saint for refusing the Feds. I know, Akhmed, I know what you're thinking. You're thinking that by refusing me you're refusing them. But let me tell you, my friend, I am nothing. I am no one. I am so much easier to refuse than those to come. You're thinking that you will be as silent to them as you are to me. But you won't, Akhmed. You just won't. You might believe that you will be brave, that you will hew to your convictions, but you have never been to the Landfill. They won't ask you where the girl is. They will make you bring her to them, and you will watch yourself do it. Look at me, Akhmed. Once I was like you, and soon you will be like me. They are in the business of changing lives, Akhmed, and they are the very best.'

This was his greatest fear. Could he stay silent? Could he withstand what awaited him? He told himself that his love for the girl would fortify him against any torture, but this, like so much of what he told himself, was a lie. After all, he was squeamish at the sight of blood; what would he say when lying in a puddle of his own? But he saw no other way. He would pray for the strength to stay silent, for a quick heart attack, and leave the rest to God.

'You remember in '95, my first trip to the Landfill?' asked Ramzan. 'It was my twenty-third birthday and I had the bad luck of bicycling to the city on the day of a rebel ambush. That's the only reason they took me. I was a young Chechen man on the day rebels decided to attack the Feds outside of Gudermes, so they took me to the Landfill and you know what they did. You stitched me back together. For so long I worried you or my father would ask why it happened, and I was always afraid of it, afraid of the asking and how I would answer. But neither of you ever did. You're both too polite. But don't you want to know what happened? You're always asking *why*, Akhmed, so let me tell you. It happened because they asked me to inform on my friends and neighbours, Akhmed. When they threatened to beat me, I said nothing. When they threatened to electrocute me, I said nothing. When they threatened to castrate me, I said nothing. I said nothing, Akhmed. Whatever you think of me, you remember that once I said nothing when a wiser man would have sung. And the interrogators, they couldn't believe it. They called in others to examine me. I was there on the floor, and above their faces were dark ovals silhouetted by the ceiling lights. They had beaten me hard and I couldn't hear right, but I kept saying no, with every breath I had. The only reason they let me go, the only reason they didn't shoot me right there was out of perverse respect, some sort of professional courtesy. But I wish they had shot me, Akhmed, because the good part of me died there, and all this, everything since, has been an afterlife I'm trying to escape.'

Akhmed had never been in a fight before, but right then he had to concentrate on controlling his hands. On their own they would have strangled Ramzan to keep him from saying one more word. Whether this was confession or ruse, Akhmed couldn't say, but the anguish was there for him to see in Ramzan's face. 'Why did you start saying yes?'

Ramzan trembled beneath his folded arms. 'A second war. A second trip to that place. I knew what was coming. I knew it never stops. They put a shame inside you that goes on like a bridge with no end, the humiliation, the fucking humili-ation of knowing that you are not a human being but a bundle of screaming nerve endings, that the torture goes on even when the physical hurt quietens. People treated me differently when I came back the first time. They gossiped, told rumours about me because I still lived with my father, couldn't marry, and then I was a fucking joke to those for whom I'd sacrificed a wife, children, family, a life. When the Feds took Dokka and me to the Landfill, when I said yes, when I told them what they wanted, when I agreed to inform on anyone, I wished I had done it in '95, in the first war, *that* is my biggest regret. If I had said yes from the beginning, I would still be a man. I'm not asking for your friendship or forgiveness, Akhmed, just tell me you understand. Please give that much to me.'

Ramzan stepped forward to embrace Akhmed, and in the moment before he came to his senses, before he planted his hands on Ramzan's chest and gave him a sharp shove to the ground, Akhmed wanted to take Ramzan in his arms, as a patient, as an old friend, and fix all that had gone wrong in him.

'I don't,' he said as he pushed Ramzan. Ramzan tumbled and the next moment Akhmed knelt over him, fist raised, ready to beat Ramzan as the interrogators had beaten him, for what he had done to Dokka, to Havaa, to the entire village, to himself. Ramzan covered his face with his hands and tried to crawl away on his elbows. 'Don't hurt me, don't do it, don't hurt me, mercy, have mercy,' he pleaded, eyes closed, collapsing into a foetal position, weeping into the brown snow. Akhmed stood, disgusted with himself, with the man at his feet, with the war that had reduced them to this. 'I don't understand,' he said, but Ramzan could hear nothing above his own calls for mercy.

After checking on Ula, he drew closed the blackout curtains and lit the living-room oil lamp. Khassan's letter lay on the divan, where he had left it the previous evening. How could he have forgotten it? He really was an idiot. Through the closed door he could still hear Ramzan's faint crying. The previous night Khassan had asked his advice, and he thought he had understood what was the right and honourable answer, but no longer. Crammed in his jacket pocket were the two letters of safe passage he had taken from the glovebox of Sonja's truck that afternoon on the pretext of searching for a non-existent scarf. The glovebox held dozens of letters of safe passage and he hoped she wouldn't miss or need these two. He slipped them into the larger Manila envelope that had held Khassan's letter, added a one-word note to Khassan, then sealed and addressed it: *For K, 56 Eldár Forest Service Road.*

Back in the bedroom, he undressed Ula. He carried her to the bathroom and the water rose, so slightly, when he set her in the tub. She had never learned to swim. As a girl she would scoop carrots from her mother's stew and feed them to the rabbit that lived in the back garden; her mother trapped the rabbit one autumn afternoon and made stew from it, and for all their time together, Ula refused to explain to Akhmed her aversion to carrots. He washed her neck and shoulders. He lifted her elbow and scrubbed the divot of soft underarm hair. Her mother had spoken of lust as if it were a loaded firearm, and when, one summer, the big-eared boy who lived across the village transformed into something right-sized and beautiful, she concealed her affection, holstered it to her chest, because she knew the shame of it could kill her mother. He washed her elbows and wrists. With a toothbrush he scoured the rims of her fingernails. He washed her nape and her back and slalomed his fingers down her spine. Her older brother was born touched, kept in a room with the curtains always drawn shut, this wailing, incomprehensible heart beating against the walls of the family house. For nearly as long as she had feared him, she had been ashamed of her fear, and wanted to reach through his madness to the part of him that could, at times, be so gentle, and embrace it. He washed her chest, the skin that had been breasts. He washed her hips, her stomach, swirling soap into her navel. She had been so afraid of Akhmed when she met him for the first time, on a June morning, on her front steps, the branches clutched by blackbirds. In the eight years since their betrothal he had become a local celebrity. He could have any girl. He could have anyone. Her mother invited him in without fear of embarrassment because a cousin had taken her older brother for the day. He washed her pubis, vagina and anus. He washed her thighs. He washed her knees. He washed her calves. For as far back as anyone could remember, she had wanted to be a mother. He washed the tops of her feet, her soles, all ten toes and the gaps between. She would have had eight girls, treated them like the very reason her lungs drew breath, whether they were normal or touched, whether they ate carrots or not, she would have loved them, and given herself to them; she would have given each a pet rabbit; a mother, she would have been a mother if her body and Akhmed's had only worked the way they were supposed to work. When he finished, they were both clean.

He wrapped a towel around her shoulders and with long, vigorous caresses, rubbed her dry. He couldn't stop worrying that she might catch a cold. Four hours earlier, he had come inside Sonja, and now he was brushing his wife's hair. Nagging doubt was the nearest he came to guilt. He looked into the eyes of the wife that had become his ward. A smile was buried in his beard. He had never loved her more.

He helped her into a nightgown, pulled the covers to her chin, and lay beside her. 'Any visitors today?' he asked.

'No,' she said. 'I was waiting for your father, but he never came.'

So much of his marriage was a disappointment – childlessness, ailing health – but they were blessings, now, in the end, when he had to let go. Yet he'd grown to depend on the act of longing. He performed his nightly ablutions and prayed, but the ritual was empty, mechanised, and he recited the words as he would a recipe. The pearl of faith had dissolved, and at its core was a sand grain of doubt, and he held on to it, knowing that doubt, like longing, could sustain him.

Later that night the wind carried the low rumble of approaching trucks. He was fully dressed, wearing thick wool socks and his fifty-eight-year-old coat, because wherever they took him would be cold. By the time the trucks pulled up to his house, he'd already loaded the syringe with enough heroin to stop the heart of a healthy man. Her long, slow breaths filled the room. He took the time to disinfect her skin. Outside, truck doors slammed shut. Praise Allah for her hallucinations. Without them he wouldn't have the strength to push the plunger and for ever numb that precious vein. But she was convinced that his ten-years-dead father had visited her this week, so even when her eyelids flashed open, and a bleary, misapprehending plea poured forth, he looked away, because a woman who spoke with ghosts was nearly one herself and would forgive him for taking her the rest of the way.

Her breaths slowed. Her eyes drifted to the left, to what-ever came next. He held her hand. It stayed warm. Once, three months after their wedding, he had held that hand through two kilometres of sun showers that had left them drenched and shining and purified to each other. He closed her eyes. He put a small bandage on the pulseless vein. This was it. God could ask no more of him. The fists of the security forces pounded at the front door. The Manila envelope containing the two letters of safe passage lay on the floor, beside the bound pages of Khassan's letter to Havaa. Would she ever read it? Would she ever know her father made furniture from his book boxes? The pounding grew to splintering. The underside of a corpse was the only place the security forces wouldn't look, and he slid the Manila envelope and Khassan's letter beneath Ula's body. He kissed her forehead. She was gone and he still couldn't say goodbye. 'We will never be dry,' Ula had said. The sky was pouring. She was there.

When the men broke through the door, he was on his knees. He prayed for his wife, that in Paradise Allah would give her a body that worked. He prayed for Sonja, that she would find companionship. He prayed for Havaa, that she would live to die a natural death. He prayed for Khassan, and for Dokka. But when the men started beating him, when they taped his mouth and threw him in the back of the truck, he prayed only for himself.

Chapter 25

THE TUESDAY NATASHA DEPARTED HAD BEEN THE third warmest December day in living memory. Sonja's coat still hung on the coat stand, where she had left it earlier that morning, after raising the window sash to test the air. The illness Natasha had claimed, when Sonja tapped on her door with fingers still warm from their reach into sunshine, was, in fact, withdrawal. Ever since Maali had fallen with the fourth-floor storage room, Natasha had numbed herself with pinches of heroin. Not counting the first dose, stolen from the syringe intended for Maali's forearm, she only snorted the powder. No more than once or twice a month for the first year, infrequent enough for her to believe, with some justification, that she was in charge of the heroin rather than the other way round. But then there was the time she delivered three stillborns in one week, the time the winter freeze slid right into the third week of May, the time an ache crept its way into her left ankle and stayed for months, the time she woke feeling as rotten as sunken squash and twice as ugly. The world must have grown crueller, because soon she was finding reasons to snort on a daily basis. Maali's fall, Sonja believed, was the cause of her malaise, as if Natasha had been tethered to the nurse, as if her regression could be so neatly explained. Even as Natasha broke her standards faster than she could lower them, one was immutable: she would never use a needle again. So late the previous night, when she had found herself planting a syringe in that familiar place between her toes, she had promised herself she would leave the next day. To her great surprise, she woke in the morning. To her greater surprise, she kept her promise.

She made her bed, cleaned her room as best she could, and packed what she needed in Sonja's black Samsonite. Before leaving she sat at the kitchen table her father had built for them himself from ash wood. It was a rickety thing, with nails that kept falling out and books of matches under two of the table legs, a table the poorhouse would refuse, but one she had eaten from her entire life because spilled tea and tetanus wouldn't kill anyone as fast as a pride-wounded father. She tried to draft a note to Sonja but all alphabets failed her. What could she say? Wouldn't any excuse read like an insult to the sister that had, she could now acknowledge, given up a decent life in London for her? No, better to say nothing for now. She would get word to Sonja from the camps, when she had gone too far to turn back. Had she known the heartache her wordless departure was to cause, she would have written down the sentence pounding in her head: *Thank you, Sonja.*

She marched down the service road away from the city, towards the border, on the trodden path of some fifty thousand previous refugees. Where would she go from the camps? Turkey, Armenia or Azerbaijan most likely, but she would rather go to China or Hawaii, a country where no one could speak Chechen or Russian. She wanted to hold foreign syllables like mints on her tongue until they dissolved into fluency.

The wet leaves paving the service road caught in the suitcase's wheels. Such a warm day, but she was cold. By sunset she had walked only the eleven kilometres to Eldár.

The last time she passed through Eldár had been in the bed of a canvas-canopied truck with five women. She hadn't known its name then. The service road widened into the trunk of the village road, from which unnamed side streets branched into the shadows. Even if the overhanging electrical lines carried a current, no street lamps stood to light those crevices. She came to a porch where two women knitted and gossiped in the warm air and she asked for a room. They nodded down the road.

A third of the houses were ruined by fire or explosions, or even by the former occupants themselves, who, like farmers sowing their fields with salt, believed destruction to be the final act of ownership. Portraits hung eerily from electrical poles and doors, their faces staring blankly at her. She asked an elderly man for a room and he directed her further down the road to a house with a green door where a man named Dokka kept beds for refugees travelling towards the border.

The man named Dokka opened the front door with his foot. He regarded her suspiciously, and she worried her skin, paler since September, revealed her ethnicity. But then his hesitation burst into a firework of recognition. 'Natasha!' he exclaimed, opening his arms in welcome. Attached to them were two hideous, fingerless hands. She stepped back. He knew her name, but they had never met. Those things at the ends of his wrists wouldn't have slipped her mind.

He asked if she remembered him.

'I'm sorry. How would I?'

He laughed, loud and brightly, while she stared at his hands. Those, at the very least, were no laughing matter. 'I met you seven years ago in the maternity ward of Hospital No. 6. I'll never forget you, not for the rest of my life. I am Dokka. You delivered my daughter, Havaa.'

She repeated the name, but couldn't match it to the several hundred newborns in her memory. Behind him stood a little girl with almond-brown hair, green eyes and ten fingers, all there. Natasha began to ask about the refugee beds, but Dokka cut her off. 'Come inside. You can stay as long as you'd like.'

The rooms themselves appeared amputated at waist height; nothing stood out of a child's reach. Dokka, politely declining her offers of assistance, used his hands like forceps as he bustled around the kitchen. He pinched a matchstick between his teeth, struck it against the wall, and spat it into the open stove. Over four years he had brewed tea for perhaps two thousand refugees, but there had been no pot he wanted to taste finer than this one. Again she offered help, but he had brewed tea for two thousand without faltering, and only needed her help drinking it.

'You're going to the refugee camps?' he asked. She nodded. She'd heard stories of overcrowded camps, where a single tap left running would supply water for three thousand souls, but the blessing of rumour was its boundlessness, and she could disbelieve what she wanted. Despite all that had happened, Sonja's description of London lured her. She wanted to live there.

'You shouldn't be travelling alone. There are soldiers and bandits, often the same people. You should travel in a group with at least one man.'

She couldn't help smiling. 'I've done that before. It didn't work out.'

'And you're ethnic Russian? No, no, no.' After a moment Dokka gave a knowing nod to the empty seat beside Natasha. 'Before you leave, we will think of something.'

When the girl returned a half-hour later with a treasure trove of pine cones, bird feathers and dried leaves divided by colour, her father, in a tone of familiar exasperation, asked her to remove her muddy boots. She carefully placed her findings on the kitchen table and followed them into the bedroom. She still hadn't said a word to Natasha. Standing before the open cupboard, Dokka explained that his wife had died that spring. He missed her greatly, not least because her passing had left the household with only one pair of functioning hands, still too small and weak to chop firewood, but he had a cupboard full of her clothes, which the moths would feast upon before Havaa could grow into them, so she should, he said while walking out, in short, have at it. As she undressed she turned to hide her burn scars, but the girl had seen worse and studied her without judgement or disgust. Without a mirror, she had to ask the girl's opinion of each dress. The girl shook her head no, no, no. She had seen her mother in this dress and that dress, each one of which pained her to see worn by a stranger, and she nodded yes only when Natasha put on a maternity dress, the only one in the cupboard she hadn't seen her mother wear.

After dinner, Dokka gave her a clean bed sheet and showed her to the room that had been his daughter's. In the world beyond were two thousand and eighteen souls who had slept in that room, and remembered that room, and would harbour it in their thoughts for no fewer than ninety-nine years, when a little girl that Havaa had once watched sleep, the last living of the two thousand, closed her eyes for the last time.

Havaa lay on the bottom bunk of the bed beside Natasha's, and, propped on her elbows, peering into Natasha's upside-down eyes, asked to see Natasha's hands. 'You still have yours,' she said, bending Natasha's fingers.

'I intend to keep them.'

'My mother kept hers and she still died.'

'They usually don't play much of a role in that.'

The girl wasn't so certain. 'My father said your hands were the first to hold me.' She had stopped flexing Natasha's fingers and was now holding them, squeezing them, firm.

'I helped your mother give birth. I made sure she was clean and comfortable. When you popped out, I made sure you were, too.'

'I saw baby rabbits once,' the girl said proudly. 'Did I look like that?'

'No, not at all. You were beautiful.'

A grimace crowded the girl's face. 'I wanted to look weird.'

'You did look weird,' Natasha said, a beat too quickly.

'I don't believe you.'

'Your legs were growing out of your shoulders, arms came out of your knees, and you were breathing out of your bottom. I had to fix everything. I missed lunch that day because of you.'

The girl beamed above her. 'Are you going to help children in the camps?'

'It's been a long day. Let's talk about that tomorrow.'

The girl snuffed out the lamp and thin, tapering smoke unwound from the wick, drifting into Natasha's yawn. She could count the bed slats through the limp mattress. The heavy blankets, grey, coarse enough to clean a frying pan, smelled of every body they had ever warmed. Where was her sister right now? And was she asking the same question? There would be time for guilt, for second guesses, for turning back, but this was the time for rest, and as she slipped into sleep, a sleep so deeply peaceful not even the long fingers of dreams would reach her, she heard the girl say, 'I'm glad you have yours. Otherwise I would have fallen.'

At breakfast Dokka urged her to stay for another night

or two. Another group of refugees might pass through, one she might join. It was wisdom a child might summon, but coming from him, from his kindness and hospitality, she decided to stay, even though she was only a dozen kilometres from home. The girl hid her smile behind a spoonful of kasha. Havaa wanted to show her the forest, and after washing their dishes they returned to the bedroom to dress.

'Do you want to see my souvenir collection before we go?' Havaa asked. 'I have a collection of all the people who've stayed here.'

She opened the drawer before Natasha could suggest they see it when not dressed in enough layers to roast themselves alive. There was a pressed flower head, plucked from Ukrainian soil twenty-two years earlier, the only entry in an otherwise empty journal. Three brass buttons that had fastened the blazer of a thrice bankrupted businessman, who, in Hoboken, New Jersey, had already put in the paper-work to open the collection agency that would make him a millionaire in eight years' time. A key ring with two keys that opened the front door to a house that no longer existed.

'You have to give me something before you go,' the girl said.

'I'll give you the teeth from my mouth if we can just go outside now. There is a wetland forming in my underwear. I can feel tadpoles.'

Taking her by the hand, the girl led Natasha through the undergrowth until the forest forgot the service road and the birch trunks blocked out the village chimneys. The loose soil felt odd under her boots. When was the last time she'd lost the texture of asphalt, concrete or linoleum beneath her toes? When she hiked over the border with five woman whose names she still didn't know. This was nicer.

In piles of wet, rotting leaves they found maggots and

larvae and crustaceous creatures, which they both agreed were better suited to oceanic depths. They found a mountain range of deer dung scaled and mined by a brigade of red ants. The sun was burning a hole in the middle of the sky, and Natasha was wondering if Dokka's hands were capable of making *siskal* for lunch, when the girl stopped suddenly. 'What's wrong?' Natasha asked.

The girl nodded to a parting, twenty metres away, where two lengths of aquamarine lay like misplaced strips of sky. As they edged forward, Natasha saw the aquamarine didn't belong to the sky, but rather to the legs of straw-stuffed blue trousers.

'A scarecrow?' Natasha asked. A faded Red Army-issue shirt languished above the trousers. Nine soldiers had lived and died in that shirt. The scarecrow, drunk, judging from its borrowed birch-trunk backbone, had been decapitated. Nailed to the tree, where the head should have been, was a moss-devoured board.

'No,' the girl said. 'It's Akim.'

'Who's Akim?'

Too young to explain in words, the girl's face was old enough to show the loss that was that name. Natasha, not understanding what this meant, was briefly annoyed, believing it profligate to expend pity on a scarecrow when there were more deserving life forms, but of all people, who was she to judge how a girl disburses her empathy? She wrapped her arm around Havaa. The whole of the girl's bony shoulder fitted in the cup of her palm, and the girl reached up and held on to her fingers. If Akim could have seen the two of them, he would have taunted them for weeks.

After dinner that evening they were joined by a man, tall, slender and bearded, in whose presence Dokka grew aloof. His name was Akhmed. He asked about the hospital, showing particular interest in the hiring process. The hospital hadn't adhered to those formalities since before she arrived — she had never even taken a first-aid course, she confided — and if he still wanted to work there Sofia Andreyevna Rabina would surely hire him. The brilliance building behind his eyes faded when she added that no hospital employee had received a salary in many years. And then he asked a peculiar question: had she ever used dental floss for stitches? Natasha was questioning his sanity when he described a rebel field commander who, two years earlier, had arrived in the village with his chest held together by dental floss. That would be Sonja, Natasha said, she could stitch a lion to the back of a wildebeest. He had never seen finer stitching of any other material, much less dental floss, and could vividly recall the twenty-three stitches curving along the crescent wound, which the commander had called the grin on his chest, and the memory had haunted him, reminding him of the unexpected wonders a capable mind might conceive. Natasha wholeheartedly agreed, and encouraged his misconception that Sonja worked miracles, not from malice, but from a budding pride that stretched all eleven kilometres home.

Dokka didn't say a word to Akhmed, not even in greeting or farewell, and when the man left, Natasha asked if he had come invited.

'He comes once a week,' Dokka explained. 'Usually when travellers are staying. He likes talking to people, getting news from the outside. And he helps with the tasks Havaa's hands are too small to perform. Chopping firewood and the like.'

'But you don't care for him?'

Dokka gave a sad smile. 'He was my closest friend once. It pains me that I can't decline his assistance.'

In the bedroom, Natasha undressed under the girl's inquisitive stare. 'Did they take you to the Landfill, too?'

'No,' Natasha said.

'Then why are there marks on your shoulders?'

Instinctively she reached back and covered the knotted scars. Some three dozen stippled her left shoulder and neck, and had Sergey not switched to nicotine gum, there would have been some three dozen more. 'It's nothing,' she said, quick to throw on a nightdress. 'I fell asleep in the sun once. I couldn't sleep on my back for months after. Just a reminder of my foolish younger self.' After she brushed her teeth, she asked, 'Did the scarecrow walk into the woods by itself?'

'I helped him,' the girl boasted.

'He must have been heavy.'

'It took me three days. I dragged him along the road and hid him each night so no one would take him.'

'Why?' Natasha asked.

'For Akim.'

'You mentioned him earlier. Who is he?'

'No one really.'

'Is he like an imaginary friend? My sister and I, when we were children, we pretended we had an imaginary sister.'

'No!' the girl said, horrified by the suggestion. 'Akim's not imaginary.'

'I'm sorry, I was just asking.'

'You're mean.' Natasha felt like she had stepped into a foreign country whose customs and manners she didn't comprehend, where her gestures of concern were taken as affronts. The Samsonite was still unzipped from when she had retrieved her wool sleeping socks, and through the opening she saw the black fake fur hat of the Buckingham Palace guard nutcracker. Without pausing to consider the thousands of kilometres the souvenir had already travelled,

358

or that she might need this totem to draw strength in the uncertain days, she pulled the toy from the suitcase and presented it to the girl in appeasement.

'Here,' she said. 'A souvenir.'

The nutcracker was as wide as the girl's hand and twice as long. As she studied it, her curiosity consumed her anger. 'Who is this?' she asked.

What was the name they had given this little wooden man that never laughed? She lay back, more afraid of losing the name than the nutcracker itself, but there it was, years since she last spoke it and it was right there.

'Alu,' she said.

Five nights and the refugees Dokka promised still hadn't come; on the morning of the sixth day, she announced she was leaving. After breakfast Dokka asked her to join him in the bedroom. Six ribbons looped around the six drawer knobs, and Dokka fitted his wrist into the first, opening a drawer that contained jewellery, foreign coins, wristwatches and wallets, a more extravagant version of his daughter's collection. 'Right there,' he said. 'You see the red bandanna? Take it.'

The bandanna wrapped around an L-shaped object. Its weight substantiated her fear the moment she lifted it.

'It's a Makarov semi-automatic pistol,' he said. 'You simply unlatch the safety, point at the target and shoot.'

But for the beige handgrip, the gun was silver; a passing cloud dulled its lustre. She had seen guns on television and at the bazaar, in the hands of rebels, soldiers and gangsters, pointed at her in City Park and the Breaking Grounds, but she had never stood on this side of the barrel before.

'I'm just as likely to shoot off my own head as anyone I aim at,' Natasha said. She didn't want the gun and told him as much, but he insisted, saying Comrade Makarov would keep her safe on those dangerous roads. 'Do you arm all your guests?' she asked with a smile.

'You're our first.'

'Why?'

'After I lost my fingers, I thought Havaa should learn to shoot. But when I think about her shooting at the Feds, and what would come after that . . . She knows to run. It's better if we don't have the gun.'

'But why give it to me?'

'Because I want to protect the person who gave me Havaa.' She could think of no refutation. He insisted she keep it on her person, and it pressed against her left breast as she hugged Havaa goodbye. The girl clung to Natasha's fingers, and Natasha shook them both away, with gratitude, and hurried into the cool daylight before their affirmations of goodwill crippled her. Her boot heels bit into her ankles but she wouldn't stop to slip on extra socks before she had travelled far enough from Dokka's house to preclude the possibility of returning. The wood, brick and breeze-block dwellings grew smaller as she reached the village's southern end. A stubble of dead grass filled the ungrazed fields. The forest closed round the road. Hanging from a tree was a final portrait, a woman with long, dark hair and an aquiline nose, whom Natasha recognised but couldn't identify. Of all the village portraits, this was the most detailed and closely observed. In the centre of the otherwise serene portrait, the woman's lips opened, just a centimetre, revealing no more than a sliver of her tongue, the forty-second portrait, if Natasha were to count, the only one whose subject opened her mouth in speech or sigh, a word spoken and heard for eternity, or an expression of longing, though whether it belonged to the woman or the artist, Natasha couldn't say.

She stared at the portrait for several minutes before understanding, belatedly, why the woman looked so familiar. Perhaps those chestnut-sized eyes recognised her. Natasha was, after all, wearing the woman's maternity dress.

She made it twenty kilometres by the time the sun set. She had hoped to come to a village where she might enjoy a morsel of Dokka's hospitality, but the scavenged remains of logging encampments were the only signs of prior habitation. All else was woodland. She went deep enough into the trees that not even the glimmer of a campfire could be seen from the road. Recalling the lessons of the City Park Prophet, she built a fire from dried branches and dead leaves. Dokka had given her a G-4 humanitarian aid ration: three cans of evaporated milk and one tin of processed meat. The Feds who doled out the G-series aid claimed it was enough food to support a man of average height and build for three days, thus corroborating her long-held suspicion that everyone in Russia was either a midget or a fucking idiot. She cut the evaporated milk with canteen water, shaking the concoction until it came out in glossy, fire-soaked dribbles that beaded the canteen lip like golden roe. When it came time to sleep, she extinguished the flames and, as the City Park Prophet had taught her, spread her sleeping bag across the charred ground so it would pleasantly toast her backside as she drifted away.

The next day she hiked ten or twenty or forty kilometres. The following day, maybe more, maybe less. A thousand times she considered turning back but the huff of every cloud in Chechnya was no bleaker than another afternoon in the hospital corridor, fighting the ten steps to the canteen cupboard. And my God, the Samsonite suitcase, why had she thought this was a good idea? Gravel and dirt caught in the wheels as it slowed from a rolling suitcase to a dragging suitcase to an anvil with a retractable handle. What sort of lunatic shows up to a refugee camp with a Samsonite? She packed so much emotional energy into that suitcase she had none left to consider what she had done to Sonja.

Each day the mountains grew taller. Filtration points and checkpoints abounded, most manned by young soldiers too timid to investigate movement in the woods. But on the evening of the fourth day, carrying on her shoulders all twenty-eight weary kilometres, Natasha came to a filtration point larger and better lit than the others. The chain-link fence, crowned with razor wire and stretching along the pasture and into the woods, prevented the usual circum-navigation. Had she arrived at the checkpoint when the sun warmed her bones, she might have turned back and taken the connecting road she had passed two hours earlier. Had it been summer, and the ground hadn't needed to be warmed and dried by fire, she might have bedded in the woods and waited for the morning to illuminate her options. But it was neither earlier that day nor earlier that year. It was night; it was cold; her bones hated her; she just wanted to get to the other side, warm the ground, and sleep and sleep and sleep. Besides, she was a refugee destined for a refugee camp, and in her exhaustion she believed the soldiers would honour the international law guaranteeing her safe passage.

A halo of floodlight surrounded her; whether it guided or followed her, she couldn't say. A megaphone demanded she keep her hands in plain sight. Fatigue and haste had clouded her judgement, and only now, as she walked in that brilliant circle with one arm raised, the other pulling the suitcase, did she begin to worry. She'd imagined that home-sick boys a year out of school would man the filtration point as they had the others. But when she saw the prison tattoos on their hands, when the bespectacled official frowned at the fifty-ruble note she presented in lieu of a passport, she saw her mistake beyond all doubt. These were *kontraktniki*, and this was the front line rather than a checkpoint. The Makarov weighed more every second it went undiscovered. The men found her sanitary towels suspicious enough to inspect, yet hadn't searched her. They gathered around her portable alarm clock like uncomprehending tribesmen. All the while the gun grew heavier on her breast.

She drew her mind to the Rome women's clinic, which, despite every aspersion she had cast at it, was in memory another term for rescue. Her blood had been drawn and filtered through a vending machine that flickered with red and yellow numbers. She had tested positive for a half-dozen sexually transmitted diseases, all of which sounded like geometry terms. In group, listening to the confessions of women who missed their pimps, who were terrified of what their families would say, who didn't sleep for fear of waking up in the brothel, she had nodded in recognition. Strangers from Poland and Turkey and Siberia had spoken with her breath. Her hope of rescue had taken so long to die. It had survived the Breaking Grounds, Kosovo, the beatings, rapes and heroin. It had survived longer than denial and indignation, longer than three of her teeth. It had survived until the day a john's wallet had fallen from his trousers, opening on the floor. The transparent plastic sleeve had held a portrait of a boy and girl dressed in matching sweaters and smiling uncomfortably. She had begged him, a father, a family man, to rescue her. But he had just looked at her as if she'd asked him to staple feathers to her arms. When her turn had come, she told the other women and they had looked at her and nodded.

But rescue was another country, and she didn't know if she would make it there. The soldiers kept unpacking and unfolding, unravelling and unwrapping, while on her chest the Makarov grew to a Kalashnikov, then a Katyusha rocket launcher. The soldiers were ripping the wheels from her suitcase and still hadn't touched her. As she tightened her headscarf, she finally understood. The soldiers thought she was a traditional Chechen woman.

An older officer, fragranced with enough aftershave to inebriate lesser men, emerged from the camouflaged outhouse that constituted the checkpoint office. Golden stars glimmered from his epaulettes. A double-headed-eagle perched on his tie clip. His hair parted above his left ear and was plastered across his balding crown. Nothing escaped his wide blue eyes. The soldiers addressed him as colonel.

'I apologise for the inconvenience,' he said, in round-bodied Russian. 'You will be on your way shortly.'

He spoke a hushed order to the soldiers. She had no reason to doubt him when the soldiers obligingly began to fold her clothes and tie her suitcase back together with twine.

'This way,' the colonel said. Guiding her by the arm as a gentleman might, he walked her towards the forest. 'You need to sign a few pieces of paperwork before we can let you through. Unfortunately, it's located at an outpost a half-kilometre west of us.'

She didn't know at which step the truth crystallised in her mind, whether it was the fifth step or the sixth, the eighth or eighteenth, but long before they reached the woods she knew what this man would do to her. The colonel, a man who blamed the wars on the fact that his first wife once lived here, still hadn't decided.

The whole way the colonel spoke in the honeyed, empathetic tone of one every bit as frustrated by bureaucracy as she was, who would, of course, let so sweet a refugee pass through unhindered were such a decision his to make. He didn't slur his words. His arm held her so gently she wanted to believe they really were walking towards an outpost in the middle of a forest filled with paperwork. Every so often, he smacked his bubblegum.

When they reached the edge of the woods, he told her to stop. The light of the filtration point shone in his eyes, but they were beyond even that questionable society. He untied her headscarf and slithered his fingers through her hair. His first wife had been the first of five. Each one met the others after her divorce and with each other they pieced their lives together. His five wives would be bridesmaids at each other's second weddings. Their children by second husbands would be christened together, and much later, two of their thirty-nine grandchildren would join in a marriage that would not end in divorce. The friendship of his ex-wives was the one decent thing the colonel had created in his forty-seven years.

'Take off your clothes,' the colonel instructed wearily, as if this were one more duty the bureaucrats asked of him.

'No,' she said. She had never denied a man like that. Her mouth had gone dry and her whole body hummed as she said it again. 'No.'

'Take them off,' the colonel repeated.

'No.'

The back of his hand crossed her cheek with a violent crack. He massaged his knuckles. Had he been angry or lustful, she might have surrendered, but his face revealed no emotion, nothing to suggest either of them was human. In four brothels she had met every shape of desperation God had given testicles, and the only men she couldn't forget were those who needed to impart pain rather than receive pleasure. The colonel's backhand burned against her cheek. Beneath that cemented hair, the colonel was every man in the Mediterranean she still remembered.

'OK,' she said. 'I will.' Even her surrender didn't stoke a flicker in his eyes. She reached for her coat buttons. A marching band had taken residence in her chest. Her veins vibrated. She unbuttoned her overcoat but would not then, or ever, shrug it off. It took all her strength to lift the Makarov from her inner coat pocket. Her palm held the burden of battalions, the mass of a hundred thousand lost limbs, and her hand didn't tremble. She unlatched the safety and aimed the pistol at the bridge of his nose. Judging from the colonel's expression, she might have been aiming a pastry. He smiled. Had she not walked through all of Hell's flames, she might have believed she could forfeit her dignity. But she knew better, and then he knew she knew better, and her glare crushed the air between them and in it was, for him, finally, the understanding that he would never return from here.

'I—' he began, and she squeezed the trigger without hesitating. More than anger or fear or hate, she felt a deep disappointment in the colonel for speaking. He should have known words wouldn't lead them from the woods. She was a poor shot. Though she aimed at the man's forehead, the bullet raked the left side of his skull. His ear yanked off as if held by wet clay. Mucus ran from his nose and melted into sweat, blood, tears and whatever else pasted the moonlight to his skin. He shrieked, and she smiled at the great bellows he had hidden in his chest. His pain broke the register of adult expression, exiting his lips in the high-pitched and familiar wail of an infant. She knelt beside him. She leaned to his face. His screams rose in bursts of hot steam from his lips. So this is what it's like. This is just how much you can make a person feel. She didn't know she was the deepest wish come true of five women a half-continent away. She pressed the pistol to his temple and stared into the wide wound of his eyes with the righteousness of one rendering a service to a stranger. She was patient. He stared at her and she waited until the terror of what was to come dissolved the stones of his eyes. Blood gurgled from the opening that had been his ear, but his hair, parted just above it, was unmoved.

'You'll have to walk into the forest alone,' she said. He thrashed his arms before three squeezes of the trigger for ever stilled them. A silence followed. She closed her eyes. Her hands finally began to tremble.

Then sprinting footsteps, shouts of *colonel*, parabolas of torchlight scanning the ground. The bare branches gestured welcomingly. She could flee, but how long would she last? A few hours? A day or two at most until tracking dogs pulled her scent by the lungful from the Samsonite and found her? No, she was done hiding, done bargaining. She had known that from the moment she reached for the pistol. To live with dignity meant a premature death. One of the roving circles of torchlight caught the fingers of the colonel's outstretched arm. A few minutes later another torch fell upon them, and this time Natasha and the colonel were not overlooked. The shouts of *shahidka, shahidka* made her smile. She stood firm, steadying herself against an oak tree, and managed to fire twice more before a machine-gun round opened her stomach and dropped her to her knees. It was supposed to hurt, but this much? The first-time mothers said it hurt more than they had ever imagined. And was it worth it? she would ask. Oh yes, they would say. Oh yes. The torchlight fell upon her again. The second bullet put a hole in her chest, and she felt her breath leave, but neither the third, nor fourth, nor fifth, nor sixth, nor seventh, nor eighth, nor ninth, nor tenth, nor eleventh, nor twelfth, nor thirteenth, nor fourteenth, nor fifteenth, nor sixteenth, nor seventeenth was seen, or felt, or heard.

Chapter 26

THE HOUR HAND REACHED EIGHT, EIGHT AND A half, nine, nine and a half hours in the morning, and still no sign of Akhmed. The girl asked for him as soon as she woke, but Sonja had sidestepped his name as if it were a puddle on the road, and they hadn't spoken of him since. 'Talking accomplishes nothing,' Natasha had said, and for once, in her heart, Sonja knew her sister had been right. It was the fifth day after Dokka had disappeared.

When the hour hand reached eleven, Sonja went to the canteen for a glass of ice to calm her nerves, and found a slip of white paper on the counter. *If you find my body*, it said, *return it for burial.* She crushed the note into her pocket but then took another look. The full address was *38 Eldár Forest Service Road.* Akhmed's village. Was this what he had kept stitched in his trousers? Sixteen hours earlier they had lain on the narrow maternity ward bed and held each other so neither would roll off. When he stood and hitched up his trousers, she had noted a small tear near the knee, which he had blamed on a stray line of razor wire, even though she didn't ask. She ironed out the wrinkled slip of paper

368

with her thumb. It was the penultimate message she would receive from him. In a shoebox in the canteen cupboard, atop six dozen others, his ID card was to be the final message, though she wouldn't find that for another five days.

With the note now folded in her jacket pocket, she drove to Eldár. Bereft of leaves, the trees looked skeletal. This was the road Akhmed marched down to and from the hospital. The one he *marches* down, she corrected, careful to keep him alive while she still could. Clouds veined the sky. Grain stalks swayed with what little breeze there was. The forest had overtaken much of the farmland, but as the road curved through a field, she came upon the frozen carcass of what had been a wolf.

Eldár was no more than a saucer beside Volchansk, the type of village one would only stumble upon when lost. Save for the street portraits, its name was all that distinguished it from a thousand other ruined villages. She tracked the addresses, no small feat when so few doorways stood, and parked in front of number 38. Across from Akhmed's house, frozen ash stretched beyond the charred foundations of a house, across the field, and into the woods. It had been Havaa's home, and the realisation pulled a wire of grief straight through her stomach. Havaa and Akhmed had only become real when they were plucked from nowhere and deposited in her life. She knew what had happened to Havaa's father and her home, but here the girl materialised in her mind as she hadn't before. She turned her back on the ruin.

The door to number 38 hung from its top hinge. As she entered her stomach clenched, as it did each time she stepped into the operating theatre knowing she couldn't save the life before her.

For her first nine years, she had travelled to her maternal grandmother's flat in Grozny for Christmas and New Year.

Her grandmother had moved from Moscow to Grozny in the late forties, among the ethnic Russians sent to repopulate the republic after the deportation, and had taken with her the goose-down mattress she had inherited from her parents. The grandmother's parents, Sonja's great-grandparents, had hidden the goose-down mattress in a haystack for three years following the Revolution, when the price of owning such an extravagance had been nine grams of lead. The grandmother's parents had lost to the state nearly everything of lesser value than their lives: the farmland, the farmhouse, nearly all their clothing and furniture, even the donkey they had named Vladimir Ilyich. Through it all the goose-down mattress lay beneath the haystack that neither the commissars nor the Cheka agents had thought to disturb. When they moved to Moscow, they prized their rescued mattress as a happy memory of what life had been like before a band of angry men overly fond of facial hair had deigned to liberate them. Even in the Great Purge, when they hid the goose-down mattress beneath their bed and slept instead on a thin mat of straw, they pulled it out on birthdays and anniversaries to remember the way life once had been. Sonja's grandmother was conceived on that mattress, birthed on that mattress, and sixty-four years later she died on that mattress. For its long life, a life that outlasted the Soviet Union, the mattress retained the damp reek of haystack. It marked Sonja's first nine Decembers, and now, in her thirty-fifth, she pushed open the rickety door of Akhmed's house and found the scent of her grandmother's mattress inside.

The living room had been violently shaken. A fallen bookcase leaned against the divan. On the floor were twelve kopek-sized circles connected by slender shafts of light to twelve bullet holes in the ceiling. She called his name, but the house wouldn't respond with even an echo. A trail of glass led to the kitchen where the kettle and two cans of evaporated milk were the only intact containers. In the bedroom, a body rested beneath the sheets. A hypodermic needle lay on the floor beside the bed. Akhmed's wife, Sonja realised. She slowly peeled back the sheet. Out of habit, she felt for a pulse. The woman's hair smelled of pears. Her hands were smooth, uncalloused, beautiful. Pressing her fingertips to the woman's forehead, she found herself for the first time in many years standing before a corpse without guilt, a mourner rather than a failed surgeon.

She didn't know the woman's favourite colour, or her favourite food, or whether she had, as a child, preferred her father's company to that of her mother; she didn't know the sound of the woman's voice, whether it was as small as her body suggested, or much larger, growing as her flesh shrank. She didn't even know the woman's name. But she knew this woman had a husband, and he had been a decent man, yes, *had been*. Akhmed died the moment she saw his wife in bed. He wouldn't return. Whoever came upon this house next would find fallout, chaos, and would not see the way Akhmed had lived; a stranger, a refugee, would discover this place and never the man and woman it had belonged to.

She found a broom and dustpan in the kitchen cupboard and swept up the broken dishes and jars and teacups. She righted the living-room bookcases and, unsure of how Akhmed had ordered the books, she arranged them alphabetically. She wiped up the plaster shaken loose by gunfire and nailed a wooden board over the bullet holes. She scrubbed the black grime from the basin with steel wool. For more than two hours she tidied the house. The rooms contained so little they were quickly restored, and by early afternoon she had no choice but to face the bedroom. Dust blanketed the chest of drawers, carpeted the floor, filled the frame of their wedding photograph. She pulled a fistful of white athletic socks from the drawer. 'Do you mind if I borrow these?' she asked, and took the silence as permission. She cleaned the chest of drawers, floor, windowsill and panes. The edge of the bed, rim of the lamp and the books stacked on the bedside table. *Hadji Murád* was among them and she set it aside knowing this once she'd break her long-standing policy against sad endings. In one of the chest drawers she found several dozen charcoal-drawn portraits of the woman now lying dead in the bed. In the drawings her cheeks were fuller, her eyes open and clear. In every one she smiled.

When she finished dusting, she turned her attention to the bed. 'Several hours after death the sphincter and bladder muscles relax,' she said softly. 'It isn't right to spend an eternity in soiled underwear. I'll clean you, OK?' She pulled back the covers and stripped off the nightdress. Wearing the socks like gloves she washed the woman's thighs and buttocks, and then dressed her in a light brown skirt, a garden-hose-green sweater and a burgundy headscarf. She looked like a bouquet of roses. Akhmed had told her that his wife hadn't walked in more than two years, so after pulling on the last pair of clean socks, she wedged the woman's feet into a pair of tennis shoes. 'Now you can walk wherever you want.'

After cleaning and dressing the woman, she returned to the Manila envelope and collection of pages she'd found hidden beneath her body. The Manila envelope was addressed: *For K, 56 Eldár Forest Service Road*. This K, whoever he was, lived only a handful of houses away. She set it aside and picked up the fastened pages. They appeared to form a letter or journal entry. The first sentence read: *This is about your father.* She flipped to the last page to read the last sentence, as was her custom, then moved up to the last paragraph, and then the last page:

There is little ink left in the pen, even less energy in my hand, and the time has come. This story ends where you begin. You were born in a hospital. I drove your mother and father in the truck I purchased my son for his sixteenth birthday. Your mother's face was as red as the paint. Your father kept telling me to drive faster. The maternity ward was on the fourth floor of the hospital. Your father and I helped your mother climb the stairs. When her feet failed, we carried her. She was worried her hips would crush you. Even before you were born, she worried for you. It was amazing to see her love you before you even met. Perhaps our deepest love is already inscribed within us, so its object doesn't create a new word but instead allows us to read the one written. For their entire lives, even before they met, your mother and father held their love for you inside their hearts like an acorn holds an oak tree. You were their rain and sun, their morning and night.

In the maternity ward the nurse put your mother in a bed and I held her left hand and your father held her right. Custom says that a man shouldn't be present at a birth, but we didn't listen, we were there. On the boarded windows were drawings of a city that no longer existed. You were born within the memory of a kinder past. Your mother's screams opened her jaw so wide you could have come from her mouth. Never have I seen your father so afraid. Then, you arrived. We were all there, waiting for you. The nurse held you in her hands. You didn't breathe. We held our breaths waiting for you to find yours. And when your mouth opened, and your lungs burst, we knew they would never be empty. And your father, I have never seen a man more joyful.

The nurse who delivered you was named Natasha. All these years later I remember her name because she had remembered mine. She had read my book, Origins of Chechen Civilisation, *one of the four score who ever had. Hers were the first hands to hold you. When you were suffocating, she taught you to breathe.*

Your mother's were the second hands. She looked at you as if she had been born to you. She passed you to your father. The corners of his eyes crinkled. His heart had been the acorn. Now it was the oak tree.

Those are the first three pairs of hands that held you. How I hope you will live long enough that I will never know the final three.

'What is her name?' the nurse asked, as your father held you to his chest.

'Havaa.' He spoke your name like the rhythm of a pulse.

When they took him, he held your name right there in his chest, and you were with him, even if you don't know it. When he reached the end, he did not die. He called your name and began to live in you.

She set down the letter. If her pounding heart spoke a name, it was one she didn't recognise. Her sister had delivered hundreds of newborns in the seven years she had worked in the maternity ward, hundreds of Havaas, and they were her patients, not her children, neither more nor less loved than the other lives begun and ended, saved and lost, revived and mourned within the grey granite walls of Hospital No. 6. But Sonja couldn't name those countless others, had not shared with them a mattress or a room or an energy bar, would not recognise their faces on the street or in the bazaar or at the cemetery, did not wish for them what she wished for Havaa, a need, newly made, to save this one life her sister had brought into the world.

Before leaving she surveyed the rooms a final time. Akhmed's wife lay peacefully, her hands at her sides, her bright white tennis shoes ready to take her anywhere. Sonja propped the front door as best she could and wondered who would enter next. The vacant house would become a haven for refugees who had heard of a hostel on Eldár Forest Service Road. It would never again be as clean as it was the afternoon Sonja left, as one might expect, as some three thousand souls were yet to shelter there.

She drove to the address marked on the Manila envelope. A red pickup truck parked in front of the house was better kept than any others on the street. Green antifreeze beads lazed in the sludge of the half-shovelled walk. She knocked on the door. A minute passed before an elderly man opened the door and gaped at her, his unhinged eyes filled with such bewilderment she wondered if he saw her as a ghost.

'I'm sorry to bother you. I'm Akhmed's . . .' What? Employer? Supervisor? Colleague? Lover? Five-day acquaintance? She held out the Manila envelope. 'I'm his friend. Are you K?'

'Khassan,' the old man mumbled. He reached for the envelope as if it weren't there, as if his hand would pass through the paper, through her, into eternity. 'Where did you . . .'

'In his house. I found it there. He was taken last night.'

'I know. And Ula?'

'Ula?'

'His wife,' the old man said.

'She's there, but she's gone too.'

The old man nodded, barely there. He squeezed the

Manila envelope and traced the address with his index finger.

'Are you OK?' she asked. He looked like he might fall over.

'Thank you for bringing me this,' he mumbled.

She was halfway to her truck when she heard the Manila envelope tear behind her. Her truck was right there, next to the red pickup, and she just wanted to leave. That Manila envelope contained a final message, but it wasn't hers, and she didn't want to know what it said. She slid the letter to Havaa in the glovebox, between the letters of safe passage, without noticing that two were missing. Driving away, she fitted her lips around the round, sonorous name. *Ula. U-la.* The name made her lips pucker, waiting to be kissed by the reply. Had she known the name earlier, she would have dressed the wife in a gown and shawl, rather than a skirt and a sweater, so she would, for all time, look as elegant as she sounded.

Chapter 27

BENEATH THE STARS, WITHOUT THE INTERFER-
ence of cloud or wind or leaf cover, the low rumble of diesel
engines murmured through the open window where Khassan
waited and listened. When the bedside-table clock read 12.15
a.m., the splayed headlights of three trucks parted the darkness. A minute later, in front of Akhmed's house, the trucks
were parked, engines idling, passengers disembarking, men
from the security forces, whom Khassan, with his head
craned out the open window, saw only as black silhouettes
lit up by the headlights before returning to shadow. It was
12.16. Entire years had passed when he was rich enough in
time to disregard the loose change of a minute, but now he
obsessed over each one, this minute, the next minute, the
one following, all of which were different terms for the
same illusion. At 12.17 the knocking began. Khassan couldn't
see the masked security forces first pound then kick at
Akhmed's door, and at this distance the thuds might be
mistaken for a less violent act, an insomniac carpenter, a
couple keeping themselves warm in bed, but a minute later
came the unmistakable splintering of wood, twisting of door

377

hinges. Khassan gripped the sill. He could see nothing but the pale flood of headlights. *You are a coward,* Mirza had said a half-century earlier, and he heard her as if she stood just behind him. *You are a coward.* But what could he do? Run out? Reason with the masked men now entering Akhmed's house? At best, they would arrest and take him wherever they were taking Akhmed. At worst, both would be shot for his intervention. And Havaa, what would happen to her? His face broke out in a cold sweat and his hands tightened their grip against the sill. He tried moving his feet towards the doorway, but they weren't listening. Not once in his seventy-nine years had he felt more useless, more powerless, more afraid. *You are a coward,* Mirza said in his ear, but she didn't know what they do to people in the Landfill. At 12.21 came a burst of twelve gunshots, enough to kill twelve Akhmeds, but no shadows crossed that wide wound of headlight. Unable to see, unable to move, he tuned his ear to the frequency of Akhmed's broken bones, his bruised flesh, his gouged eyes, his ruptured organs, his snapped fingers, his busted cheeks, his smashed temple, his collapsed skull, his sobs, his surrender, his defeat, his gasps, his pleas, his promises, his prayers, his final breaths, his last memories, of his mother's embrace or Ula's thigh or a dog's bark or a bullet rushing through a pink brainy cloud, whatever Akhmed might hold to as the whispers cease and the silent ascension begins. Akhmed's pain would be the only sound loud enough to break through Mirza's flat incantation, *you are a coward a coward a coward,* but Akhmed made no shout, no plea, no call for mercy that Khassan could hear. The only sound to escape the house was the clatter of dishes, the white plates with chipped edges, the small saucers Akhmed used to use to fool his stomach, the teal blue teacup, the one with the crimson rim from which Khassan had sipped the fancy Indian tea someone's in-law had given one of them, and how could a teacup shatter when padded in so many layers of memory, how could this be happening again, how could Khassan stand at this same open window where four nights earlier he had listened to the same smashing dishware, had stared into the same unblinking headlights, had felt the same disgrace rip through him when Dokka was disappeared? At 12.27, shadows lumbered into the stream of headlights and among those shadows was a flailing form, so faint a contortion no one save Khassan would recognise it as Akhmed. A moment and the shadow vanished back into blessed darkness, and the truck doors snapped closed, and Mirza's accusation clamped him to the windowsill, and the headlights pulled the trucks back to the underworld they had emerged from. As the last truck passed Khassan's open window, Akhmed's muffled cry finally reached him.

The sun had risen by the time his mind slowed enough to slip away. He dozed, but didn't rest. In his dreams he wandered through grass frozen into fields of stiff white ribbon. He had hated Kazakhstan so much. He'd never imagined he might look back on exile as his happiest years.

At ten he woke and for three hours stared at the ceiling as he marshalled the courage to stand. The house was silent. He slid through Ramzan's half-opened door, as he had dozens of times before when he had something to tell his son. Ramzan lay on the bed, mouth agape. Khassan crept to the chest of drawers, where he withdrew the *kinzhal* from the top drawer. He had received it from his father, and his father had received it from his father's father, and so it went, a century and a half of fathers and sons. It was the oldest thing he had ever owned not counting the trees at the back. Near the handle the blade went brown with the blood of an imperial conscript, or perhaps it was just rust. His father had taught him to thrust it forward, turning the blade before ripping it out, in case Tsar Alexander II might rise from the dead to pillage Eldár.

The edge followed the grooves in his palm, his life line, his love line. He carried it to the bed and wrapped the blade in the blanket so it wouldn't wake Ramzan prematurely. He took a breath and the air filled him completely. The previous night was a place he wouldn't return from. After the head-lights had faded, he had crossed and uncrossed his fingers, picked up and set down the water glass, and amid these trivial gestures, he had died. 'You are nothing without love and pride and family,' he had once told Akhmed. The first two had disappeared the previous night in the back of a truck; he was on his way, fingering the blade that would soon cut through the third.

'Did I ever tell you the story of the cobbler's drunken son?' he softly asked. Ramzan heard nothing. 'When I was a child, our village was plagued by a cobbler's son, an eighteen-year-old who inflicted more property damage than could be expected from a man who couldn't make his two feet move in the same direction. The cobbler was respected throughout the village until his son discovered the effects of fermented beet *samogon*. The alcohol made pariahs of them both, proving right the aphorist who first stated that as the son inherits from the father, so the father inherits from the son. For years the cobbler appealed to the imam, apologised to the fathers of the women his son dishonoured, and paid for, replaced or returned the stolen goods. He offered to mend the shoes of any soul his son had wronged. So it was. But there came a point when the son's capacity for ruin outpaced the cobbler's capacity for restitution. He was in debt. Half the village walked on shoes paid for by his son's drinking. One day the son vanished. No mention of him, no funeral, no gossip of work on a distant collective farm; he just disappeared. A month later my grandfather visited the cobbler with the village elders. They took him honey and raisins and welcomed him back. I, still a boy, was told to honour and respect the cobbler, as all the villagers were, because he had put the good of our small society, our *teip*, above his own. His son's name became a blasphemous word, erased from the collective memory, stricken from even the whispers of women. The story, when told, always ended at this pinnacle of honour and sacrifice. It never went on to tell how the cobbler, who didn't mend another boot in his life, lived to the age of ninety-nine as a hermit, drinking himself senseless every day and night, alone but for the ghost of his son, whom he pleaded with in unbearable calls that I could hear from the far side of the village.

'They never tell you about that part, about how long you might live with it,' Khassan continued. He held Ramzan's limp fingers. Thirty-two and three-quarter years had passed since he had first felt those fingers and they had astonished him, delicate as sparrow feet and holding on to his thumb as if he were the sturdiest branch in the forest. 'They never tell you about that part.'

For two long years he had hated himself for imagining this moment. Disappearance by disappearance he had tallied the lives his son had extinguished – and if Ramzan hadn't snuffed them, he'd held them to the wind – Alman, Musa, Omar, Aslan, Apti, Mansur, Aslan the Hirsute, Ruslan, Amir, Amir Number Two, Isa, Khalid and Dokka, postponing this inevitability until the next day, the next disappearance, until he watched Akhmed's beaten shadow eclipse the flood of headlights, and knew the next day would be the last. Twenty-one years and five months earlier, Ramzan had bounded from this bed and out that door to the kitchen, shirtless and wide-eyed with awe; he had pointed to a single hair sprouting from his underarm, as thrilled as if he'd found a diamond there. 'You were right about the trumpet blast,' Khassan said. The regret was already there, a blank wall he'd spend the rest of his life staring at. 'These are the end times. There can be nothing after this.' Now that it had arrived, all his talk of mountain-top sacrifices seemed the absurd, grandiose fantasies of a confused old man. There was no voice in the sky.

Ramzan's chest rose and fell, oblivious to the decision already made by the hand holding his. Khassan had held that chest when it was no wider than a chicken's, had held it to his own and felt something so tender and precious pass between them that he would have done anything for this boy. But this? Had the bottle of sleeping pills not sat open on the bedside table, he would have acted sooner. But from the many times he had perched on the mattress, he knew the pills would keep Ramzan comatose until evening. He could wait. Now that he had, in his heart, stepped over the edge, it didn't matter how long he fell before hitting the ground. 'I want to tell you something,' he said. 'But I don't know what. I don't know.' Pride wouldn't allow apology, not even now. 'You are my son. You are mine,' he whispered, as a spell, as a gift, a last lullaby, a branding. Ramzan's head turned, so slightly, into the pillow, and it nearly broke Khassan to see this shimmer of life. Sleep, just a while longer, that's it, where else can you go where you neither suffer nor cause suffering? Khassan lay on the bed and breathed with his son. He followed Ramzan's lead. Together they drew from and gave to the communal air, his open hand on Ramzan's chest, rising and falling in this silence they made.

Three knocks broke it. Khassan sat up and carried the cavern in his chest to the front door. No one in the village, not even Akhmed, had visited the house since Ramzan's collusion became known. Were his former friends standing on the other side with honey and raisins to welcome him back into society? You are too soon, he wanted to cry. I haven't done it yet. I'm still climbing to the summit. He blotted his forehead with a purple handkerchief before opening the door.

On the other side stood a woman foregrounded against the teal sky. She wore a padded grey coat over scrubs. 'I'm sorry to bother you. I'm Akhmed's . . . I'm his friend. Are you K?' She passed him the Manila envelope he had given Akhmed two days earlier. His pulse quivered as he accepted it; if it still contained his letter to Havaa he would give up. But his address was written on the Manila envelope by Akhmed's hand. The contained correspondence was thinner than his. 'In his house,' she said in explanation. 'I found it there. He was taken last night.'

That shadow floundering through light to the dark bank on the other side. The dementia that was to consume his memory in nine years would leave him that. When all else had faded, those headlights would still shine; they would be the light at the end. He could hardly speak, think, act, breathe. What was happening? What was this? He discovered Ula's name between his lips. The woman dropped her eyes and shook her head, respectful but firm, perhaps accustomed to delivering bad news. As soon as she turned to the road, he tore open the Manila envelope. It held two letters. One was written by an FSB colonel, the other by a rebel field commander. Each letter gave orders for the unhindered passage of its unnamed bearer. A third message lay at the bottom of the Manila envelope, written on a scrap of paper so slight he nearly missed it. *Mercy*, the note read. *Mercy.*

The dogs, dozing beside the house, stretched their legs

on the ground and lumbered after him, Sharik last, as he hurried to Akhmed's house. He held the Manila envelope against his chest, blocking it from the wind.

The front door was propped against the door frame. He passed over a clean living-room floor, an inexplicably alphabetised bookcase, and the dogs followed, Sharik last, because the front door wouldn't close, and what did it matter, they were cleaner than the last beasts to enter.

Ula lay fully clothed on the unmade bed. After the past hour watching the rise and fall of his son's chest, he knew immediately that she was gone. White tennis shoes jutted from the end of her baggy brown skirt, as if in death she would be reborn in good health, given a newly wired nervous system, allowed in her private paradise an afterlife of marathons. He closed the bedroom door, afraid the dogs might nibble at the body. Claw patter trembled through the thin walls. If he had to come back, he would be a dog.

For a moment he stood by the door, surprised by the scent of soap. Then one foot forward. Then the other. He folded her hands together and placed them on her stomach. The room was clean, as was the body, and though he could explain neither, he wasn't surprised. A burgundy headscarf framed her face. Cupping her skull like a fragile bowl into which he had poured his most valuable possessions, placing his thumbs on her lids, he opened her to the dead afternoon light. She stared straight through him, to the unfolding infinities that bookended her thirty-five years, through him to the place where they would soon meet, when the trumpeter's breath failed, when he would descend the notes of the final melody to the silence where Mirza waited.

He could have wrapped her in a white elasticated bed sheet, the nearest to a burial *kafan* in the depleted cupboards. The body was usually washed in scented water, but a martyr was buried unwashed, in the clothes she died in. He could have enshrouded her. She weighed so little. Even a man of his age could have carried her outside. In the backyard he might have set her on a cushion of snow. The ground was frozen. He could have plunged the spade head but the ground would hold. He knew no burial prayers, but he could have stood quietly and let canine panting mark the minute. He had spent his entire life burying, and unearthing, and reburying the dead, and he could have done it once more. The spade would have scraped through the frost. A shovelful of snow scattering on her torso. Three thousand years before a Russian empire existed, native tribes buried their dead in kurgans that grew so large they became part of the land, surviving the construction and collapse of subsequent civilisations. He would have thought of this as he entombed her. He would have shovelled until he couldn't lift the spade, until the tomb reached his chest, until it compacted into a monument that would last until the spring thaw. But he didn't have the energy to do more than close her eyelids, fluff the pillow beneath her head and point her towards Mecca.

At home he picked three sets of clothes. Extra layers, heavy on wool; no longer could he rely on the comforts his son provided. He searched his cupboard for something to pack his clothes in but only found a laundry bag. He'd never thought to replace the brown suitcase after he buried it, never thought he would leave Chechnya again. At the centre of his small bundle of clothes was the ruby-red scarf Mirza had unwound from her neck and placed in his hands, one afternoon, long ago. In the kitchen he packed alcohol swabs and syringes and insulin vials and all the food he could find in withered plastic shopping bags. On the kitchen table Ramzan's keys radiated from their ring and he placed them in his pocket. He didn't know where he would go. He had journeyed through Poland, Czechoslovakia and Germany. He had, once, taken a victorious shit on a Reichstag commode. And from there to the Kazakh steppe, where, to the horizon, nothing sounded louder than the wind. He had travelled a quarter of the way around the globe without taking one step voluntarily. This was his home. For every barrack floor, muddy trench, outpost tarpaulin, bunker cot and fallow field he had ever slept on, the memory of home was his only rest. Returning in 1956 he had vowed to never leave. Better to die here, he imagined, than endure another exile.

He crossed the hall to Ramzan's room. Neither his *kinzhal* nor his boy had moved. If he could reach back he would hold his son, love his son, and untangle the knot his soul had become. He would find the ends. 'Why are you my father?' the boy had asked one August afternoon, twenty seconds after asking, 'Why is the sky blue?' and forty seconds before he asked, 'Why do people get old?' They were sitting outside. Khassan had been teaching his son to eat shelled sunflower seeds and he held his breath long enough for the question to pass. 'Why are you my father?' the boy asked again. It was two years before he stopped asking for a bike, five and a quarter before he stopped asking his father for anything. Khassan had never found an answer. If he could go back he would make one.

He closed Ramzan's door behind him. The time for answering had ended and the peace of the afternoon articulated all he wanted for his son. The shopping bags, laundry bag and two letters of safe passage waited at the front door, and as he reached for them, a question hit him like the face of a wall. Who was that woman and why had she come to deliver Akhmed's answer? Had she known she would deliver him from his son? It didn't matter. He would forever remember her as an angel dressed in an overcoat and scrubs, sent to stay his hand.

He locked the door behind him and crossed the packed snow to the red pickup. The dogs followed him, sniffing at the plastic bag of insulin, syringes and chicken thighs. He set the bags on the passenger seat and turned to the dogs, six in all, lean-boned and matted and blind and bald.

'I'm leaving,' he said. His voice cracked with sorrow as the dogs tilted their snouts to him. Killing his son had seemed less reprehensible than abandoning these dogs. 'I don't know where I'm going. I don't know what will happen.'

Tears fell down his cheeks. Two of the dogs ran after a hallucinated mouse, while the rest stared up at their broken benefactor with the same incomprehension that had made a home between his ears. 'I can't promise anything, but I will try to take care of you. If you want to come, I will take you.'

He climbed into the truck, set the two letters of safe passage in the glovebox and started the engine. He eased the brake and let the truck roll at a walking pace, waiting to see what would happen. In the rearview the dogs licked each other, tumbled on the ground and went on in a world without him. Gravel shot back when he pushed the accelerator and the ears of the bald dog perked, and when she turned the other dogs noticed, and their snouts swivelled towards the truck as they galloped as one animal, a twenty-four-legged, twelve-eared beast, racing to reclaim their seventh head. He unlatched the back and one by one they jumped into the bed of the pickup truck, Sharik last.

Passing beneath the portraits of the disappeared he saw them as if for the first time. No one else would remember the artist's face, but he would. When he reached the end of the street, he kept driving. When he reached the end of the village, he kept driving. Wind tossed the dogs' tongues and they shook their heads wonderfully. The serrated ridge of mountains cut into the horizon and he drove towards it. The passing refugees had speculated wildly, believing any rumour large enough to hope on. He didn't know what lay on the other side. He didn't know that the disease that would in nine years erase every memory but the headlights was already brewing among his neurons. He didn't know that his son would live alone in the village for three grief-stricken years, wondering and waiting for his return before moving to a mountain hamlet, where he would keep wondering what had happened to his father, without ever finding out, for another fifty-seven years. Khassan didn't know and he drove. He was seventy-nine years old. He was beginning a new life.

Chapter 28

'IF YOU COULD GO BACK, WOULD YOU LEAVE London?' Natasha had asked the question on a cool Tuesday morning in March 1998. They were on good terms that month, sharing the last drags of a cigarette in the hospital car park as loose debris rustled under what seemed too pleasant a shade of sky. 'If you could go back, would you leave London?' Of the thousands of times she had considered and still would consider the question, that had been the only time it had been posed as if an answer lived on the other side of it. 'If you could go back...' There was a time when she had indulged in the hypothetical for hours a day, plotting the map that had led her here. But no life is a line, and hers was an uneven orbit around a dark star, a moth circling a dead bulb, searching for the light it once held.

The visit to Akhmed's had taken longer than she anticipated, and as she parked the truck and crossed the car park, the premonition of impending disaster pressed on her. But Deshi's heavy, dozing breaths were the only sound in the waiting room. Sonja jiggled her chair. The knitting needles began working in her hands before Deshi opened her eyes.

'Anything?' Sonja asked.

'No, slow week. The landmine's brother took him away, our only visitor.'

'That's it? Nothing else?' She held the edge of the check-in counter, where a pen, long dry, remained tethered by a thin metal chain. How could it be that today, of all days, the emergencies of God and of man rested?

'Nothing else,' Deshi said, without lifting her gaze from the needle tips. 'Not a single patient in the hospital.'

'We could shut it down.'

Deshi smiled; not a day passed that she didn't regret asking Maali to fetch clean linen; not a day passed that she didn't hold Maali amid the rubble of the falling fourth floor, holding her as she had when Maali fell from a climbing frame, four years before the deportations, when Maali was crying and Deshi was the only one who knew how to comfort her. 'Where would she go?' Deshi asked.

'Holiday.'

'All that education and she finally says something smart.'

'I can't remember the last time the hospital was empty.'

'No, I can't either.'

'It won't last.'

Deshi shook her head. 'Why spoil such a lovely afternoon with talk like that?'

'I'm just being realistic.'

'I bet she'd be realistic on a summer day, too,' Deshi said.

'I thought you were done gambling?'

'I would have liked to play cards with Akhmed. I'd have won the trousers from his legs.'

Harbouring the small joy of that achievement, Sonja smiled. 'I'd have liked to see that.'

'I don't suppose we'll be seeing him again, will we?'

'No, I don't think so.'

'A shame,' Deshi said. That simple epitaph was the last they would ever say of Akhmed. A finger materialised from the tips of Deshi's needles. 'Who are you knitting that for?' Sonja asked.

'Our young friend. She's had her hands balled in her sleeves all week.'

The girl. Sonja hadn't considered what Akhmed's disappearance meant for the girl, who had, in less than a week, lost everything she had known. The day had spared legs from landmines and hearts from cardiac arrest, but it hadn't spared her. 'Where is she?'

'I retired ten years ago,' Deshi said. Another ten would pass before she acted on it. Three after that she would die of throat cancer, but not before falling in love with her oncologist. 'Go and find her yourself.'

Eventually Sonja found the girl on the fourth floor, crosslegged within the doorway that framed the charred canvas of the city. Sonja sat beside her. 'I'm sorry.'

'Will he come back?'

'I don't know,' Sonja said, and immediately regretted it, knowing how much false hope one can cultivate in the soil of those three words. 'Probably not.'

The girl nodded to the city.

'It's hard, Havaa, I know. The same thing happened to my sister.' But that was a lie, wasn't it? She spoke of Natasha as if her sister was one of the disappeared. She wanted a share of the national suffering, to blame the Feds for the fact that her sister didn't love her enough to say goodbye. There was, at the centre, an unnameable darkness around which she circled but couldn't touch. 'I don't know where she is. I don't know if she's alive or dead. I know nothing.'

'How do you find them?' the girl asked. She lifted her gaze to Sonja as if teetering on the precipice.

'I don't know, Havaa. I'm sorry. I don't. Maybe we try to

find them in other people. In kindness and generosity; those things don't disappear.'

The girl gave a deep, mucus-rattled snort. The answer wasn't the one she wanted, but Sonja had learned to be realistic when discussing death. Even if the answer put no distance between the girl and the hole the war opened within her, it was, Sonja hoped, enough to keep her holding on.

Havaa reached for her hand, and without thinking, Sonja felt for her pulse. Her radial artery rose and fell against Sonja's finger as a gentle reminder. She pressed her palm to Havaa's forehead.

'Am I sick?' the girl asked.

'No, you are in perfect health.' And as she said the words, they seemed like a small miracle. She held Havaa's wrist, bending the joint back and forth. Through faded blue sweatpants, she felt the shape of Havaa's calves and knees. These legs would stand and walk and run. These arms would lift and embrace and let go. This person would grow and adapt and live; Sonja would make sure of it. 'Your family isn't your choice,' her father had said, to quell a tantrum, many years earlier, and without wanting to, she kept discovering what he had meant.

'What are you doing?' Havaa asked.

Spools of raw gratitude unravelled in Sonja. She was an idiot to be so impressed by legs that walked, wrists that bent, hands that held. Instead of explaining, she focused on the sensation of good fortune, of undeniable blessing, so she could later return to this memory to marvel at the girl's body, how remarkable it is, this human matter.

'I have no idea what I'm doing,' she said, and helped the girl to her feet. 'You kept your suitcase packed just in case you had to leave again, right?'

Havaa nodded.

* * *

A half-hour later they left the hospital. Block after block passed unchanged but for the location of craters, the dispersion of brick. A one-way sign pointed to the sky. Three emaciated black dogs watched them from across the canyon of a grocery basement, but thankfully didn't follow. All through it Sonja's head hummed. She held the girl's suitcase in one hand, and her hand in the other. She tried to remember the name of the street she had lived on.

This is what there is. Scorch marks fanning like massive seashells across the ground. Clouds gathering at the horizon. The unevenness of earth. The small heat she holds in her hand. A hand that is her hand holding a hand that is the girl's hand. This is it.

Somehow her feet recalled what she had forgotten. They led her. Her apartment block hadn't fallen. Blast tremors had opened the windows, but the building stood. They climbed the stairs.

'A nice woman lives here,' she said as they passed Laina's flat. 'Maybe you could spend time with her while I'm at the hospital.'

The girl nodded. They stood at the front door. 'I haven't been here in many months,' she said. She unlocked the door. Dust covered everything but the ceiling. She would deal with it tomorrow, or the day after that; she had cleaned enough for one day. The entrance bore no sign of break-in. The looters had long since emigrated. She lit a candle.

For dinner Havaa skinned and cut the sprouts from two potatoes, while Sonja found a car battery with enough juice to put a pot of water and rice to boil on the hotplate. When they ate, Sonja described the chopsticks people in Asia use to eat rice. The girl attempted it with two pencils, and after five minutes of failure, declared Asia an invention of Sonja's imagination. When they finished, Sonja led her to Natasha's room. Out of habit she knocked before opening the door. The bed was still made. The desk chair sat at an angle, as though its owner would return any moment to write a note, a letter, an explanation or an apology.

'This is where you'll sleep,' Sonja said. She set the suitcase on the edge of the bed and cleared the lower drawer of Natasha's jeans and sweaters. Natasha had taken the burgundy cardigan Sonja had given her for her eighteenth birthday, the one she hated and never wore, and wherever she was, Sonja hoped the temperature dipped enough for her to try it on. 'You can put your things here.'

'Am I going to live here?'

Sonja hadn't thought that far ahead. 'Do you want to?'

The girl surveyed the room, inspected the cupboard, checked under the bed. 'I get the whole room?'

'The whole room.'

'And I don't have to share it?

'It's all yours.'

The girl slowly nodded and leaned into Sonja, listening to the gurgle of her organs, these marvellous things we ignore, forget and take for granted. 'Come on,' Sonja said. 'You should unpack before either of us changes our minds.'

Havaa unlatched her suitcase and pulled out balled grey socks, a sweater, a skirt, two headscarves, white underwear patterned with little pink bows. Then came the strange and wonderful artefacts. A marriage licence from 1942, given by a couple who had been married for sixty-one years and no longer needed the document. A photograph of a slender man wearing a pea jacket that now hung in a cupboard in Saudi Arabia. The eighty-first draft of a love letter. The uncancelled stamp that would have sent the unwritten eighty-second draft. A prayer book opened by two hundred and six yearning hands.

'What is all this?' Sonja asked. In three weeks, when she would help Havaa build a case to display these treasures, Sonja would use her surgical saw, for the first time, to create something.

'My souvenirs,' Havaa replied. She spaced them across the drawer with greater reverence than she'd shown her clothes. 'From the refugees that stayed at our house.'

There was a silver ring that had made a thirty-eight-year-old mother of two feel like the most glamorous woman in Grozny. An address book that an unfaithful husband had given Havaa so his wife's ghost wouldn't find it among his possessions. A dried seahorse that a father gave his six-year-old daughter in lieu of a pony. A Taj Mahal key chain that a refugee in southern Russia regretted giving away. A tie clip that a cosmonaut carried to space and back. And a Buckingham Palace guard nutcracker.

'What's that?' Sonja barely got it out.

'That's Alu,' the girl said. In three weeks and one day, with her palm aching wonderfully from sawing through wood, Sonja would tell her about Buckingham Palace. 'He's an idiot.'

'Who gave you Alu?'

'One of the women who stayed at our house.'

'One of the refugees?' Sonja asked. In eight months, she would begin telling the girl about Natasha, and it would take her the rest of their time to finish the story.

'I introduced her to Akim,' the girl said. 'She was nice.'

'What was her name?'

'I can't remember. Lots of people stayed at our house.'

'But you remember Alu's name.' In eight and a half years, she would have already taught the girl every lesson she had scribbled in her secondary-school notebooks. In ten and three-quarter years, the girl, then a first-year biology student at the newly constructed Volchansk State University, would begin teaching her.

'Alu didn't leave.'

'But what did she look like?'

'She had all her fingers.'

'What else? What else?' In twelve and a third years, the girl, now a woman, would accompany Sonja on a five-day holiday to London. When the night porter asked, 'Would your daughter care for a herbal tea?' it wouldn't cross Sonja's mind to correct him; it wouldn't have crossed her mind for some time. At the end of five days, they would leave London. Sonja would never see the city again. Havaa would.

'She was very pretty. I was nervous she wouldn't think I was pretty.'

'Was she happy?'

'I don't know.'

'Where was she going?' When the girl, she would forever be the girl to Sonja, went to Lake Baikal for two years to write her dissertation on the effects of climate change on freshwater microorganisms, Sonja would briefly consider sleeping at the hospital. But the world had long since stopped shaking, and no one would tolerate such eccentricity, not even from the distinguished head of surgery.

'Probably to a refugee camp.'

'But where, which camp?'

'I don't know.'

'Think hard. Where?' In twenty years Sonja would find Natasha's name beside her own, in the final sentence of the acknowledgements of Havaa's dissertation. The dissertation would be published to some acclaim, and on dusty university bookshelves in a half-dozen countries, the two sisters would share an afterlife in that final sentence, one comma away from Akhmed and Dokka.

'I don't know.'

'Was she alone?'

'Yes, she was alone.' In twenty-eight years and seven months, at a limnology conference in Cologne, the girl would meet the man she was to marry nine years later. At the age of forty-six she would have her one and only child in the same maternity ward she was born in, a boy to carry her father's name; hers would be the second hands to hold him. At the age of sixty-eight she would hold her first grandson, also to carry her father's name; hers would be the third hands.

'And she left your house?'

'I said goodbye and she left.'

'What direction, then? What direction did she go?'

'Down the road. There's only one direction you can go.' The girl would outlive her husband, her son, one grandson and every soul she had met before the age of eleven. She would outlive twenty-three of her teeth, three of her toes, one of her kidneys and all the brown of her hair.

'Then where is she?'

'I don't know.'

'But you saw her.'

She would die at the age of one hundred and three, in the geriatrics ward of Hospital No. 6, in a room that had been the director's office, then Sonja's bedroom, and finally a regular hospital room, a room Havaa would remember as many thousands of refugees remembered her own childhood bedroom, a room that had been there when it was needed.

'Where is she? Please, Havaa. Please.'

The girl wrapped her fingers around Sonja's. She looked up. Her eyes were green. 'We don't know where she went,' she said.

They never would.

Chapter 29

THE MEN IN PIT B WOULD REMEMBER HIM AS A quiet man, if they remembered him at all. They would remember how he fastened his shirt buttons with his toes, how he had learned to live without his fingers. He was anxious, hungry and scared, but they all were. At night they slept in the brown snow on sheets of carpet, slabs of plywood, whatever they could find. Though they all had nightmares, some would remember how the fingerless man kept repeating *is she... is she... is she... is she... is she...* before another man shook him awake.

Four nights after the fingerless man arrived, another man climbed down from the sixty-first rung. He curled near the side of the wall and slept. In the morning, the new arrival scanned the prisoners. His eyes found those of the fingerless man through the small crowd. It was clear that they had known each other from their past lives on the sixty-first rung, but whether they were brothers, or friends, or rivals, or enemies none could say. The men, those who had been there for months, had seen how the Landfill could twist one's sense of honour and obligation,

398

how in this underworld even a hated face was a welcomed one.

The new arrival examined their wounds, and though he didn't do a very good job, they called him the doctor. He was quiet. By night he neither screamed nor snored, and by day he rarely answered questions with more than a nod or shake of his head. When they commented on his reticence, he said he was practising for his interrogation. The men, those who would leave without their fingers, their mental health and parts of their souls, but would leave, might remember the carving of epitaphs on the clay wall. Though surprisingly self-sufficient, the fingerless man was unable to write his name. The doctor helped. The two epitaphs were carved so close together they looked like one.

A few days later, the fingerless man and the doctor were summoned to the sixty-first rung. The fingerless man had difficulty climbing. The doctor helped. For the following day and night, the men at the bottom of Pit B, those who would survive and those who would not, prayed at the epitaph of the fingerless man and the doctor. Twenty-four hours after the two ascended to the sixty-first rung, the men of Pit B, those who would break and those who would not, each packed a fistful of clay into the wall. Their palms were wet and cold, and they were solemn. When the names of the two men were buried, everyone knew they were finally gone.

But if they were to remember anything of the fingerless man and the doctor, they would remember the initial conversation, when no one was sure what the two meant to each other. The doctor had approached the fingerless man. For a moment they stood apart, each uncertain of the other. Then the fingerless man opened his arms, and the doctor stepped into them, and the two men swayed as they held each other, revolving in a private *zikr* that they alone understood. No one knew what to make of these two men who had found each other in the mud of the Landfill and begun dancing. No one had ever seen anything like it. The doctor whispered, wary of the other men, and no one could say what passed between the two as they turned together, whether a confession, or a story, or an apology. Someone claimed to have heard the doctor repeat *she is safe*, three times, but the man who heard this received regular visits from his deceased in-laws, and no longer trusted his senses. What all heard, what all remembered, was the fingerless man leaning back in the doctor's arms, lifting his face, and laughing, a sound none had heard in many days, his cheeks wet as he roared a name – *Havaa, Havaa, Havaa* – and those who witnessed would remember how here, in Pit B, a man who had lost his freedom and his fingers, and would soon lose his life, had found in that name an immense, spinning joy.

Author's Note

In writing this novel I drew from the following sources, all of which I would urge anyone interested in Chechnya or modern Russia to read.

To get a glimpse into the day-to-day life of a wartime Chechen surgeon, I relied on Khassan Baiev's magnificent memoir, *The Oath: A Surgeon Under Fire*. Anna Politkovskaya's haunting, harrowing *A Small Corner of Hell: Dispatches from Chechnya* was always in arm's reach, and I have included several of her anecdotes in altered forms. Baiev and Politkovskaya are two of the few heroes of the Chechen conflict, and their writing is essential and courageous testimony.

For descriptions of and insights into wartime Grozny, the deportations and the Caucasian petroleum industry, I turned to *The Angel of Grozny: Orphans of a Forgotten War* by Åsne Seierstad and *Allah's Mountains: The Battle for Chechnya* by Sebastian Smith. In chapter 12, a number of the descriptions of Chechnya between the collapse of the Soviet Union and the First Chechen War are drawn from Smith's journalism; additionally, Sonja's attempt to recreate for Akhmed the ruined Grozny square is based on Smith's account of a Chechen woman doing the same for him. Both Smith and Seierstad have spent extensive time reporting from Chechnya, and together their books form a panorama of the past two decades in the Northern Caucasus.

In writing of the *zachistka* I drew from Andrew Meier's description of the Aldy *zachistka* in his vast and powerful *Black Earth: A Journey Through Russia After the Fall*. While researching his book, Meier travelled from Chechnya to the Arctic, from the Pacific Ocean to the Gulf of Finland, and has created the most encompassing single-volume account of post-Soviet Russia that I've yet read.

For Natasha's journey through the Breaking Grounds and into Western Europe, I turned to *The Natashas: Inside the New Global Sex Trade* by Victor Malarek and *Sex Trafficking: The Global Market in Women and Children* by Kathryn Farr. *One Soldier's War* by Arkady Babchenko, *Towers of Stone: The Battle of Wills in Chechnya* by Wojciech Jagielski, *The Chechens: A Handbook* by Amjad Jaimoukha and *I Am a Chechen!* by German Sadulaev provided valuable historical and cultural context. Joseph Barnard Davis and his 1,474 skulls come from *Human Remains: Dissection and Its Histories* by Helen MacDonald. I owe debts of influence and inspiration to the body of fiction dealing with political disappearances, particularly Daniel Alarcón's *Lost City Radio* and Michael Ondaatje's *Anil's Ghost* — both novels include scenes of artists summoning images of the missing, which inspired Akhmed's portraits. Sonja's scene with Ula owes a debt to 'Old Boys, Old Girls' by Edward P. Jones. The axis on which this novel rests is formed from two narratives shared by Islamic and Christian traditions — that of a parent asked to sacrifice a child, and that of an orphan delivered into the family responsible for her orphanhood — and in thinking of these, I'm grateful for N. J. Dawood's elegant translation of the Qur'an and *The New Oxford*

Annotated Bible. Finally, *Hadji Murád,* the last and among the most powerful of Tolstoy's novels, appears in a beautiful translation by Richard Pevear and Larissa Volokhonsky in *The Death of Ivan Ilyich and Other Stories.*

Acknowledgements

My gratitude to the Stanford Creative Writing Program, the Iowa Writers' Workshop, the Truman Capote Literary Trust and the Patricia Rowe Willrich Fellowship for supporting this novel, and to the Bread Loaf Writers' Conference and the Sun Valley Writers' Conference for their votes of confidence.

This book couldn't have found a more phenomenal editor and advocate than Lindsay Sagnette. My thanks to her, Becky Hardie in the UK, Anne Collins in Canada, Molly Stern, Christine Kopprasch, Rachel Rokicki and everyone else at Crown. I'm grateful to Tom Jenks, Carol Edgarian and Josh Clark at *Narrative* magazine, where Sonja, Akhmed and Havaa first appeared, and to Olga Zilberbourg, for fielding my many Russian-related questions. And a big thanks to Austin Ratner and Christina Minami, brilliant novelists and physicians both, for pointing out my many medical inaccuracies.

Chechnya has been utterly transformed in the past decade, in large part due to the efforts of a younger generation determined to rebuild the republic. My thanks to those whose help and hospitality made my travels in Chechnya possible. All these pages aren't enough to convey my appreciation and respect.

At Stanford, I'm grateful for the support and feedback of Eavan Boland, Adam Johnson, Elizabeth Tallent, Tobias Wolff, and the Stegner Workshop that graciously read long pieces of this novel: Josh Foster, Helen Hooper, David Kim, Dana Kletter, Justin Perry, Shannon Pufahl, Nina Schloesser, Justin Torres, Juliana Xuan Wang. And at Iowa: Erika Jo Brown, Scott Butterfield, Ethan Canin, Andres Carlstein, Lan Samantha Chang, Patrick Haas, Michelle Huneven, Allan Gurganus, Alexander Maksik and Elizabeth McCracken. Jay Muranaka for his friendship. Christina Ablaza, Connie Brothers, Krystal Griffiths, Deb West and Jan Zenisek for having the answer to just about everything.

To my family, my friends from DC, and people who still know me as Hal: thank you.

Peter Orner, my thesis adviser, was the third person to read this novel.

Janet Silver, whose insight and generosity is felt on every page, was the second person.

M. was first.

Anthony Marra was born in Washington, D.C. During his university years he spent the summer working as a night porter and doorman at a five-star hotel in Edinburgh, and from there moved eastwards, studying first in Prague and then in St. Petersburg. He was one of the first foreign tourists to visit the post-war republic of Chechnya, and was interviewed on three Chechen television programmes as a result.

He has an MFA from the Iowa Writers' Workshop and is currently a Wallace Stegner Fellow at Stanford University. In October 2012, he received the Whiting Writers' Award, presented annually to emerging writers of exceptional talent, whose previous recipients include Jonathan Franzen, Tony Kushner, David Foster Wallace, Jeffrey Eugenides and Michael Cunningham.

Read On For

A Reader's Guide

A Conversation with Anthony Marra

Recommended Reading:
Far-Flung Fiction

A Reader's Guide

Garnering rave reviews, *A Constellation of Vital Phenomena* is an unforgettable debut novel that deftly explores the human cost of war — and the healing power of hope. In this haunting masterwork, award-winning author Anthony Marra transports us to a snow-covered village in Chechnya. It is 2004, and an eight-year-old girl has just watched Russian soldiers abduct her father and set fire to her house in the middle of the night. Accused of aiding Chechen rebels, her father has suffered the brutality of the Feds before. Fearing the worst, their lifelong neighbour Akhmed rescues the girl and seeks refuge at the bombed-out hospital run by Sonja, a brilliant but tough-as-nails female surgeon. Resistant at first, the doctor soon discovers that her new visitors may hold the key to finding her missing sister. Over the course of five extraordinary days, their worlds will unravel in unimaginable ways, culminating in a breathtaking, ultimately affirming turn of fate.

This guide is designed to enrich your discussion of *A Constellation of Vital Phenomena*. We hope that the following questions will enhance your reading group's discussion of this stirring meditation on loss and redemption.

Questions and Topics for Discussion

1. Before reading *A Constellation of Vital Phenomena*, how much did you know about Chechnya? Which of the novel's cultural details surprised you the most? What can fiction reveal about history that a memoir or history book cannot?

2. How did your image of Akhmed shift throughout the chapters? Despite his many weaknesses, how does he become a source of strength for the loved ones in his life? How does his art restore the humanity around him?

3. Why is Sonja able to remain clear-eyed and resilient? What does she teach Havaa about being a woman, and about the limits of being a healer?

4. Discuss the betrayals that drive the storyline. Would you become an informant if your life depended on it? Can suspicion and corruption ever rise to a level that makes loyalty impossible?

5. What is Dokka's greatest vulnerability? What do his daughter's memories of him say about his hopes and fears?

6. Discuss the title (in chapter 24, Sonja stumbles across it in a Russian medical dictionary's definition of life). What is phenomenal about the life force and the body's intricate capabilities?

7. What is Khassan's key to survival? Is his image of homeland and heritage accurate?

8. What is the effect of the timeline, encompassing five days

in 2004 and flashbacks from a decade earlier? How does this approach echo the reality of memory and longing?

9. What does it mean for Sonja and Natasha to be ethnically Russian? When is this an advantage, and when is it a disadvantage? How are cultural identities shaped in the midst of political, military, economic, and religious power struggles?

10. What accounts for the very different fates of Natasha and Sonja? Is Natasha's beauty an asset or a liability?

11. How is the concept of family – from the sisters' relationship to Akhmed's marriage to Ula – transformed in a land of warlords?

12. In his review for the *Washington Post*, Ron Charles describes the novel as 'a flash in the heavens that makes you look up and believe in miracles.' Discuss the book's closing lines in that context. What does *A Constellation of Vital Phenomena* ultimately say about anguish and joy?

A Conversation with
Anthony Marra

Q. Why write about Chechnya?

A. I first became interested in the region as a college student
in St. Petersburg. I arrived in Petersburg shortly after the
journalist Anna Politkovskaya was assassinated, presumably
for the reporting she did from Chechnya. I realised that
Chechnya was a place I didn't know how to spell and couldn't
find on a map, but the ramifications of the wars there had
reached as far north as Petersburg, where on a daily basis
I saw Russian veterans soliciting for alms in the Metro
stations. I began reading non-fiction accounts of Chechnya
and quickly became fascinated. Its history and culture has
inspired writers like Tolstoy, Lermontov, and Pushkin. The
accounts I read of ordinary people in remarkable situations
were the kinds of stories that I felt needed to be brought
to life through fiction.

But to answer the question of why set a novel in Chechnya,
my answer would be that it is a setting that magnifies and
dramatises the moral conflicts of characters in extraordinary
ways. This cast of characters wants what we all want – to

live peacefully and provide for our loved ones – but their circumstances require them to make decisions the reader will hopefully never have to make, but nonetheless, understand.

Q. Readers and reviewers have commented on the beauty of the language in this novel. Can you talk a little about how you wrote it?

A. I ended up writing four first-to-last word drafts. Each time I finished a new draft, I'd print it out, set it in front of my keyboard, and re-type the entire novel. Because re-typing mimics the original act of creation, it taps into whatever creative well the sentences first rose from. The novel changed from draft to draft, then, from within, organically, rather than from changes that were superimposed on it. There's a scene early on when Khassan despairs as he realises that he must again re-type his 3,000-plus page history. Thankfully, *Constellation* isn't nearly that long, but I still knew exactly how he felt.

I also kept a daily word count record. My goal was to hit a thousand words every day. The days when I recorded zero words felt like wasted days. I grew up going to church and Sunday School each week, and at long last, I was able to put that Catholic guilt to good use.

Q. The novel has some dark moments, but at the same time, it's filled with moments of humour and hope. How, and why, did you blend instances of death and loss with levity?

A. I once heard Allan Gurganus say that writers should strive to make readers laugh and cry on every page. It's a tall order, but I absolutely agree with the reasoning. Novels need the high as well as the low notes in order to be true to the emotional reality of life. When I traveled to Chechnya, I was repeatedly surprised by the jokes I heard people cracking. It was a brand of dark, fatalistic humour imprinted with the absurdity that has become normalised there over the past two decades.

A book I thought of while writing *Constellation* was *City of Thieves* by David Benioff. Benioff's novel pays tribute to the immense suffering caused by the Siege of Leningrad, but it's filled to the brim with life, love, humour, even joy, all of which only enhance and make more real the underlying historical tragedy. Hopefully, *Constellation* works in a similar fashion.

Q. Your writing style is unusual in that you move back and forth between the present and the past. Was that a conscious choice?

A. War breaks cities, buildings, and families, but also time and the way stories are constructed. To tell this story in a straightforward, linear fashion would fall short of capturing the absurd, recursive manner in which its characters assemble their chaotic narrative. All the characters in *Constellation* are trying to piece back together their fragmented lives, and I wanted to embody that in the novel's structure. As each character attempts to rescue what has been lost, the novel mends their individual stories into a communal whole.

Q. What has been the greatest influence on your writing?

A. My mom has six siblings and my dad has four sisters and between them all there are more cousins than I count, which means that family events have always been filled with voices, stories, and laughter. From an early age I learned from them that stories are how we understand one another, how we preserve the past, and how we make meaning from the chaos of our lives.

Recommended Reading:
Far-Flung Fiction

State of Wonder by Ann Patchett (Brazil)
A perfectly constructed and beautifully told story of ambition and loss in the Amazon.

The God of Small Things by Arundhati Roy (India)
Roy invents a peculiar and dazzling poetry to tell a story of twins in southern India.

The Orphan Master's Son by Adam Johnson (North Korea)
In a feat of imagination, research, and empathy, Adam Johnson takes the reader into the dark heart of the North Korean ruling class.

We Need New Names by NoViolet Bulawayo (Zimbabwe)
Bulawayo tells the story of a Zimbabwean childhood in language that sizzles with energy.

Brief Encounters with Che Guevara by Ben Fountain (Haiti, Columbia, Myanmar, Sierra Leon)
A collection of short stories, each of which packs the punch

of a 400-page novel. By turns comic and tragic, these stories are every bit as wonderful as Fountain's brilliant novel *Billy Lynn's Long Halftime Walk*.

The Vagrants by Yiyun Li (China)
Li presents a bleak portrait of life in provincial China through a wide range of characters.

The Feast of the Goat by Mario Vargas Llosa (Dominican Republic)
A harrowing and meticulously orchestrated look at the assassination of Dominican dictator Rafael Trujillo and its aftermath.

The Sound of the Mountain by Yasunari Kawabata (Japan)
In spare, evocative language, Kawabata captures the rhythms of family life in postwar Tokyo.

To the End of the Land by David Grossman (Israel)
A mother begins walking when her son goes to war, resulting in a novel that is glacier-like in size, pace, and ultimate power.

I Served the King of England by Bohumil Hrabal (Czechoslovakia)
Hrabal, an unjustly under-read novelist, takes the reader on a trip through twentieth-century Czech history with the often hilarious story of a hotel waiter.

Save the Sharks!

Sharks come in all sizes.

The biggest shark, the whale shark, can be up to 60 feet long. The smallest, the dwarf lantern shark, can be six inches long.

Sharks don't have bones!

They have cartilage instead. Your nose is made of cartilage! Cartilage is light, so sharks float easily.

Sharks eat everything.

Sharks eat octopuses, plankton, shellfish, fish, crabs, seals, and turtles. Many sharks are at the top of the food chain. Scientists have discovered strange things in the stomachs of sharks, including bottles, cameras, trash, tires, and hooks!

Sharks lose their teeth and grow new ones.

A single shark can shed thousands of teeth in its lifetime. The next time you go to the beach, try hunting for shark teeth in the sand. Hint: They are usually black, brown, or gray!

Did you know that sharks live all over the world?

They live in shallow water and in very deep water, too.

Sharks are as old as the dinosaurs.

Prehistoric shark fossils believed to be 455 million years old were discovered in Colorado.